A Vengeful Wind

A Novel of Viking Age Ireland

Book Eight of The Norsemen Saga

James L. Nelson

Fore Topsail Press
64 Ash Point Road
Harpswell, Maine, 04079

ISBN- 13: 978-0692169216
ISBN-10: 0692169210

To George Jepson, the Rick Blaine of maritime literature, with thanks for all you have done for me, all you have done for all of us, all these years.

PLATE 1

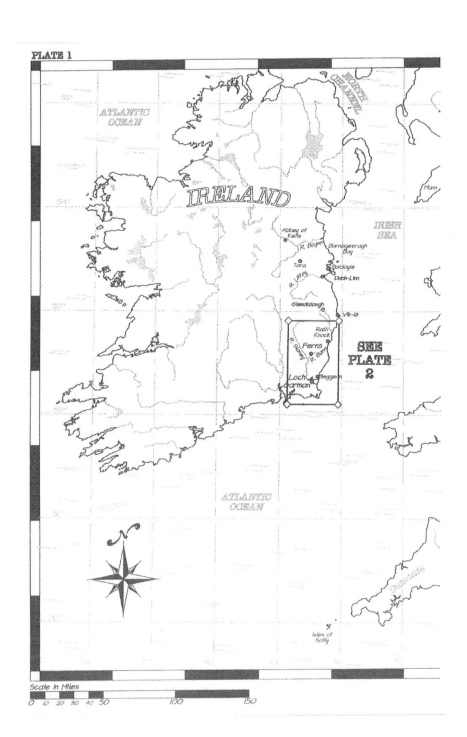

ATLANTIC
OCEAN

NORTH
CHANNEL

IRELAND

IRISH
SEA

Mann

Abbey of
Kells
R. Boyne
Bornageeragh
Bay
Tara
Baldoyle
R. Liffey
Dubh-Lim

Glendalough

Vík-ló

Rath
Knock
Ferns
R. Slaney
R. Bann

SEE
PLATE
2

Loch
Garman
Beggerin

ATLANTIC
OCEAN

N

Isles of
Scilly

Scale in Miles

0 10 20 30 40 50   100   150

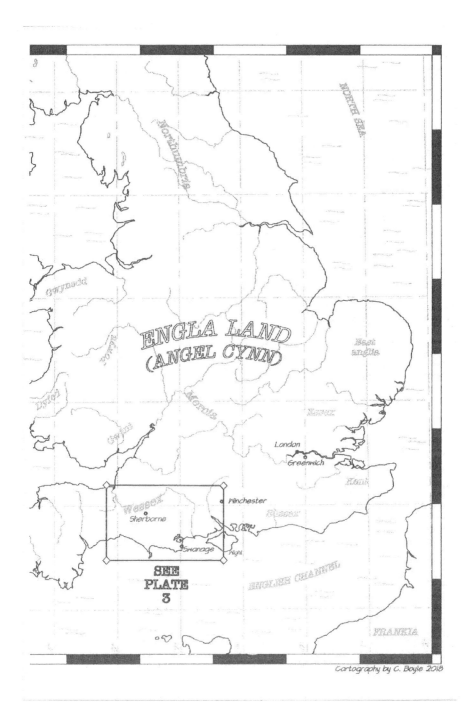

PLATE 2

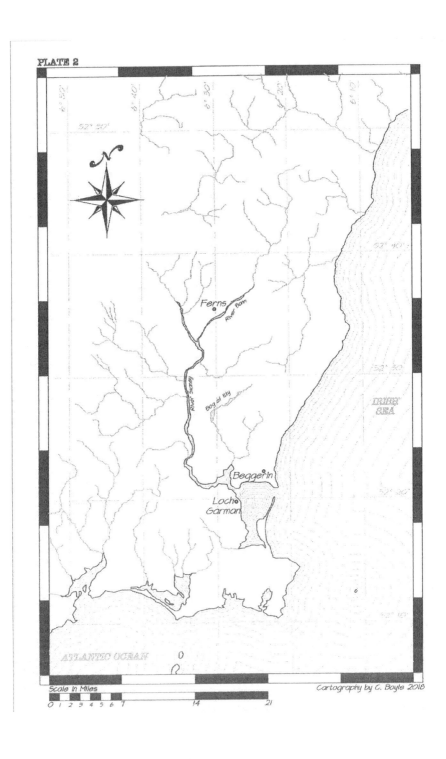

52° 50'

Ferns

River Bann

River Slaney

Bog of Illy

Beggerin

Loch
Garman

IRISH
SEA

ATLANTIC OCEAN

Scale in Miles

0 1 2 3 4 5 6 7   14   21

Cartography by C. Boyle 2018

PLATE 3

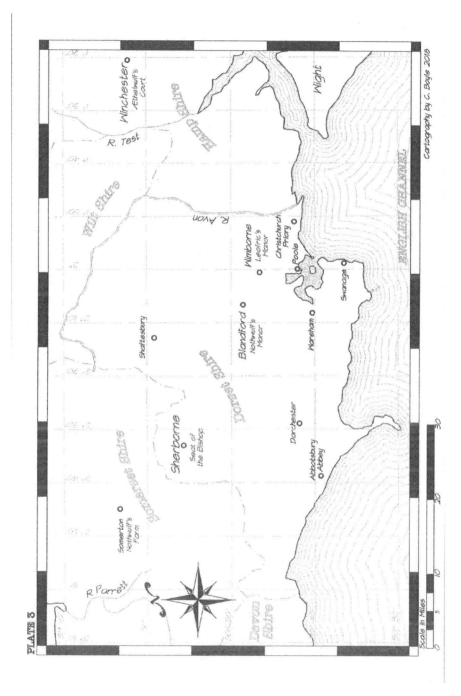

The Viking Longship

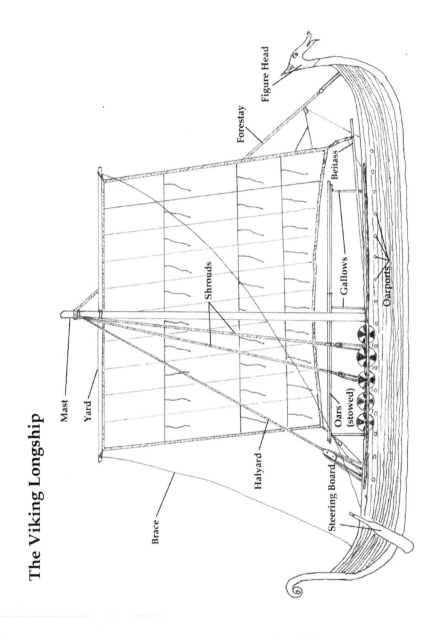

Figure Head

Forestay

Beitass

Gallows

Oarports

Shrouds

Mast

Yard

Oars (stowed)

Halyard

Steering Board

Brace

For terminology, see Glossary, page 333

Prologue

The Saga of Thorgrim Night Wolf

There was a man named Thorgrim who was called Night Wolf and he lived in Vik in the country of Norway. As a young man he had been a warrior in the service of a wealthy jarl named Ornolf the Restless and had spent many summers raiding to the westward. Thorgrim was of great service to Ornolf, who favored him above all his men. Ornolf grew even richer from the plunder, and Thorgrim also became a wealthy man. Ornolf gave Thorgrim the hand of his daughter in marriage, and they were happy and prosperous on their farm. They had two sons, one named Odd and one named Harald, and two daughters named Hild and Hallbera.

Many years passed and Thorgrim's son Odd grew to be a man and married and had a farm of his own. Harald was nearing manhood when his mother, Thorgrim's wife, whom everyone loved very much, died giving birth to their daughter Hallbera. Thorgrim Night Wolf was grief-stricken at her death, and when Ornolf the Restless asked him to once again go raiding to the west, he agreed, and he brought Harald with him. Harald, like most young men, was eager to prove himself in battle, and Thorgrim felt it was time he should do so. Harald was fifteen years of age when he sailed with his father.

Ornolf the Restless took his ship, which was called *Red Dragon*, across the seas to Ireland, where he meant to spend the summer raiding and then return with the plunder to Norway when the season was done. But the gods did not intend for them to return so easily, and one obstacle after another was put before them.

Among the riches they plundered, Ornolf and Thorgrim took a crown that was much prized by the people of Ireland, and the men of the *Red Dragon* suffered many trials because of it. Thorgrim was greatly wounded, such that he could not sail at the end of the season, and he and the others spent the winter in the longphort of Dubh-linn.

The next summer they tried once again to return to their native country, but the gods sent a wicked storm from the east and their ship was driven back to shore. They found refuge in the longphort of Vík-ló, which was then ruled by a lord who was called Grimarr Giant. Now, it happened that Thorgrim and his men had killed Grimarr's sons in Dubh-linn, though they had not known who the men were. When Grimarr discovered this, he vowed revenge and once again Thorgrim and his men were made to fight lest they be cut down. In this business Ornolf the Restless was killed, though he made a good death. Grimarr Giant was also killed and Thorgrim Night Wolf became the lord of Vík-ló.

Once again, the season for ocean crossings ended and Thorgrim and his men were made to overwinter in the longphort. They spent their time well, repairing the walls, cutting timber, and trading with the Irish who lived nearby and who did not fear to approach the home of the Northmen. They also built two ships, fine vessels with room for more than thirty oars in each. Thorgrim named one *Blood Hawk* and the other, which he had built for himself, he called *Sea Hammer*, so that the god Thor might look on it with favor.

It rained very much, as it was wont to do in that country, and despite their labors the Northmen grew restless during their time at Vík-ló. When at last the rains grew less and the season to go a'viking was on them once again, Thorgrim and his men set out to raid a great monastery called Glendalough. But they met with many betrayals during that time, and many were killed, and it was only through great courage and cunning that Thorgrim and the others who lived were able to return once more to Vík-ló.

During this time Harald was always at Thorgrim's side, and he grew quickly from a boy to a man, both in his size and in his skills as a warrior and a leader of men, like his father. Harald was of no great height, but he was very strong and broad of arm and shoulder and soon he was known as Harald Broadarm.

After Thorgrim and the others were betrayed at Glendalough, they tried once again to sail for Norway, this time hoping to raid along the coast of Ireland and increase the wealth they had already gained, which was considerable. At this time they fell in with a Frisian named Brunhard, who commanded three ships. These ships Thorgrim tried to capture, but Brunhard was a clever shipmaster and he led Thorgrim on a great chase until at last a storm wrecked their ships at a place that the Irish called Loch Garman.

Thorgrim now had four ships, but they were much in need of repair before they could sail to the east, so Thorgrim and his men built a longphort where they could do that work. They were skilled shipwrights, and could work with wood and iron, but they could not make sails because they did not have looms or the skills to make cloth. So instead of raiding the monastery nearby, which was called Ferns, they bargained with the people there, offering silver in exchange for cloth. This, too, led to many troubles, but in the end the cloth was promised to Thorgrim and the others and work on the ships began.

Having many men of great skill, it was not long before the ships were ready for a sea voyage to the east. Thorgrim, however, was no longer certain that such a voyage was the proper thing for him and his men.

For more than two years the gods had prevented them from leaving Ireland, and Thorgrim was coming to believe that they never would. Though he mostly despised Ireland, where the rain was a constant plague, still he could see it was good land for farming, and though it was wet, it was not at all as cold as his own country. An Irishwoman named Failend had joined the company of the Northmen, and she acted the part of Thorgrim's wife. He was well pleased with her, and she made it more bearable for Thorgrim to remain in that country.

During the winter at Vík-ló, Thorgrim and his men had turned that place into a proper longphort, one that could well serve as a home to them, and a good one, and Thorgrim did not doubt he could become lord of it once again.

All these thoughts were in Thorgrim's mind, and soon he resolved that he would no longer try to leave Ireland, but set himself up once again as the lord of Vík-ló. These thoughts he kept to himself, however, not even telling Harald, for he feared that voicing them would bring bad luck to his plans. But he kept them in his heart and each thing he did he did with the idea that he and his men would return to Vík-ló and there make their homes.

Here is what happened.

Chapter One

Listen! The choicest of visions I wish to tell,
which came as a dream in middle-night…

The Dream of the Rood,
8th Century Anglo-Saxon Poem

Summertime had come at last to Dorsetshire. It had come slowly, grudgingly, as if the springtime were too great a burden to push aside. But finally the rains began to fall warmer and less frequently, the leaves emerged, warily, and finding the weather agreeable had burst forth at last. The seas had stopped their vicious pounding of the long sand beaches and the steep shores of that inhospitable coastline. The shire seemed to be turning its face to the warming sun, like all of those shires that made up the kingdom of Wessex, like all of those kingdoms that made up the land called Angel-cynn.

Along the edge of the sea which formed Dorsetshire's southern border the air was filled with the smell of ocean brine and wrack pushed up on the sand and drying black in the sun. Those villages, such as Wareham and Swanage, huddled on the edge of the land, were filled with the pungent odor of the fishermen's catch, tossed to shore from the wide, heavy boats from which the men cast their nets.

The villages themselves seemed to live between the land and the sea, both at once, with their docks thrust out over the water and the shoreline strewn with drying racks, where the cleaned and split bodies of fish lay in the sun like some sacrifice made to gods long since forgotten. Further inland sat the clusters of houses, some walled with rough-cut boards, some neatly built of wattle and daub, some thatched, some shingled. And from each of those houses came a column of smoke from a cooking fire, the odor of boiling fish added to the smell of summer, blessed and welcome summer.

It was not that way in Sherborne, twenty-five miles inland. There the breeze, when it blew strong and steady enough, carried on it the smell of the fields and the new-turned earth, an occasional hint of wildflowers. The breeze brought happy relief from the smell of horses and their leavings, chamber pots emptied in the streets, the acrid smoke from the shops of blacksmiths and silversmiths and goldsmiths, bakers and bead makers, brewers and tanners and cordwainers. It wafted away the odor of corruption from the household scraps heaped in piles by the folks' small gardens and left in the sun to turn back into rich, dark soil.

Sherborne, a cathedral town, seat of the bishop, largest of all the towns in Dorsetshire, home to many hundreds of people: laborers and artisans and merchants, freemen and slaves, those who served God in the great church and the abbey and those who made their livelihoods serving those who served. After Winchester, where King Æthelwulf kept court, Sherborne was the most important of all the towns in Wessex.

It sat on high ground, amid a cluster of hills that ran down to the low country beyond. To the south, east and west, another line of hills rose like a defensive wall meant to hold back invaders from the sea, the increasing waves of marauding Northmen who were plaguing the kingdom. Sherborne was partway between two great stretches of water. To the south lay the narrow sea that separated Angel-cynn and Frankia, Frisia, and all the lands to the east. To the north, the body of water known as the Severn Sea thrust like a knife blade driven deep into the western shore, severing the border between Wessex and Wales and pushing right into the left flank of Mercia.

Sherborne was, of course, home to the *ealdorman*, the king's man, the nobleman who ruled the shire. There was no place in Dorsetshire other than Sherborne that was important enough for the ealdorman to make his home. Sherborne was the heart of the bishop's episcopal see, the territory over which he held spiritual dominion. It was the town to which the king traveled when he made his tour of the kingdom of Wessex. It was where people of consequence carried out the important events of their lives.

Such a thing was happening on that fine summer day, with the breezes blowing in from the hills to the south, blowing in through the high windows in the cathedral, bringing some relief to the hundreds attending the ceremony. A wedding. The wedding of the ealdorman. As consequential a thing as was likely to happen on a summer day when West Saxons were not at war with either the people of Wales, or of Mercia, or of Northumbria, or the heathens from across the seas.

The wedding mass was nearing its end. The choir, fifty boys and young men, were singing, heads held slightly back, mouths open, their voices filling the big church, reaching to the upper reaches of the roof, sixty feet above. The people in attendance, their clothing dyed bright and tricked out with gold thread, as colorful and varied as a well-tended garden, stood with admirable patience, as they had for the last hour and more.

The ealdorman was kneeling in front of the altar, his bride beside him. His name was Merewald, and he had been ealdorman of Dorsetshire for a bit more than a year. His father, Osric, who had defeated the Danes when they had come to raid the shire a decade before, had been ealdorman of Dorset for as long as most could remember.

Merewald was young for an ealdorman, no more than thirty-one. Still, he was older than his father had been on assuming that title, and he would be lucky to hold it for as long as the old man had. The chances of his being as beloved by the folk as Osric had been were slimmer still.

An ealdorman needed a wife, of course, because he needed offspring, he needed sons, or one, at least. Merewald had been a bit backward in his efforts to find a bride, just as he had been in most things in life—in his studies and his training at arms and his martial prowess and courage on the field of battle. He was not considered particularly accomplished or impressive. It truth, one of the only things he had managed to do of any value or consequence was to be born the first son of ealdorman Osric of Dorsetshire.

The other thing he seemed to have done right was choosing his bride. Her name was Cynewise and she had blond hair, very blond, yellower than the driest straw, and the willowy, slightly gangly quality that well-bred, fair complexioned women often had. She seemed delicate, a fine thing, easily broken. She reminded Merewald of one of those timid forest creatures that peer out of burrows, fearful of predators lurking beyond.

Cynewise was Merewald's junior by thirteen years. Merewald, out of curiosity, had worked that out after learning Cynewise's age. But thirteen was an unlucky number and so he struggled to put it out of his mind.

Like Merewald, Cynewise's chief recommendation—the thing that made her most attractive as a wife—was the luck of her birth. Cynewise was the daughter of a man named Ceorle, the powerful ealdorman of Devonshire, which sat on Dorset's western border. For Merewald, marriage to Cynewise meant an alliance with Devon. It meant that he and Ceorle would speak with one voice as members of the *witan*, that collection of noblemen who advised the king.

And Merewald was certain that he was clever enough to see that the voice with which they spoke was his, and not that of Ceorle.

In the few months that Cynewise had resided in Sherborne, making ready for the wedding, she had remained generally silent, and Merewald still knew little about her. But that was fitting for the humble wife of a nobleman, and Merewald was certain she could be counted on to remain a quiet but steady and helpful presence.

She had grown up in an ealdorman's home and she knew what that meant. She would run the household, see to the preparations when the king made his yearly appearance, play the gracious host to those of rank who might be passing through Sherborne. She would fill the office of wife, and fill it well, or so it was assumed.

The choir finished, the last note seeming to fade away into the gloomy upper reaches of the cathedral. The bishop himself, a man named Ealhstan, was presiding over the service: it could never have been performed by anyone of lower standing. Now he rose with some difficulty from his throne, flanked by younger, stronger priests ready to assist if needed, and shuffled toward the kneeling couple.

He stepped around the high altar, which was set with massive silver chalices and plates and incensors and candle holders, all inlaid with gold and studded with various glittering gems. The communion set had been a gift from Ceorle of Devonshire, arriving with his daughter Cynewise and her entourage.

Ealhstan, still flanked by the priests, stepped over to where Merewald and Cynewise knelt and he signaled for them to stand, which meant that the service was coming to an end. A sense of relief, clearly perceptible, like the breeze, swept through the nave.

"Rise," Bishop Ealhstan said, making a lifting gesture with his thick arms. "Dearly beloved..." he intoned, and even the importance of the moment, the wedding to the ealdorman of Dorsetshire, could not drive from his voice the weary tone of words repeated many hundreds of times over a lifetime of ecclesiastical service.

Ealhstan had been bishop for more than thirty years; two generations had listened to the monotonous droning of his Latin prayers, the hours-long masses over which he presided in the great cathedral of Sherborne. Ealhstan had grown a bit fat, a bit stooped, with the passing years, and it made his unimposing figure more unimposing still. And that led many, on first meeting the man, to mistake him for someone not terribly clever or formidable. And that was a mistake, indeed. There was a reason that Ealhstan now controlled a diocese that stretched over the shires of Dorset, Somerset, Devon and Cornwall, and it was not from lack of wit or guile.

"Dearly beloved," Ealhstan started in, his jowls and chins quivering a bit as he spoke. "We are gathered here, in the sight of God and our Savior Jesus Christ, to witness…"

Those gathered shifted a little where they stood, leaned in a bit closer. Silks and fine linens rustled, calfskin shoes shuffled in the rushes strewn over the smooth stone floor. These were not the common people, the *ceorl*. They were the elite of the shire. All of them. Because no one of any rank in Dorsetshire would have dared miss this ceremony for fear of angering the ealdorman or finding himself the object of some intrigue arranged in their absence.

At Merewald's side stood his brother, Nothwulf, two years his junior, but taller than Merewald by a good two inches and two stone heavier. It was Nothwulf, not Merewald, who most favored their father, Osric, in nearly every way. But where Merewald had been fortunate in his birth, Nothwulf had been less so, and now he could do little but serve as best man at the wedding of his brother, the ealdorman of Dorsetshire.

There were the churchmen also in attendance, the priests who served at Bishop Ealhstan's pleasure, the men in the highest ranks of the ecclesiastic see. There was Oswin, the shire reeve, who wore a deep green tunic and a red sash and sword as marks of his office. And behind them, standing in ranks, their wives at their sides, stood the more prosperous of the *thegns,* those minor noblemen who formed the base of the ealdorman's power.

While some thegns were little more than peasants, puffed up ceorl who had managed to scrape together five hides of land, others owned considerable property and commanded hundreds of men in the *fyrd*. These were the thegns who were invited to an ealdorman's wedding, and they were not likely to refuse.

Foremost among them, standing in the front rank, was a man named Leofric. Leofric's land, a considerable amount of land, which yielded a considerable amount in rent and taxes, lay to the southeast of Sherborne. It centered on the town of Wimborne, home to a Benedictine nunnery founded by St. Cuthburga, the sister of some ancient king of Wessex, and one of the wealthiest and most influential of its ilk.

Nothwulf stole a glance over at Leofric. The man was wearing his finest, of course, his gray hair swept neatly back, his salt-and-pepper moustache and goatee trimmed to perfection. His face wore no expression. Typical. Leofric was a hard one to fathom.

What do you think of this, old man? Nothwulf wondered. As one of the most influential men in Dorset, and a man close to King Æthelwulf, Leofric's concerns mattered a great deal. That was why both Merewald and Nothwulf, and their father before them, were careful to stay in Leofric's favor.

At the same time, what happened in the ealdorman's house in Sherborne mattered a great deal to Leofric.

"Do you, Merewald, ealdorman of Dorsetshire, take this woman to be your wife?" the bishop intoned, pulling Nothwulf back to the business at hand, though Ealhstan's voice gained no more enthusiasm as he neared the climactic moment of the long afternoon's ceremony.

Merewald straightened a bit, and when he spoke his voice was strong and certain. "I do."

Ealhstan turned to Cynewise. He asked if she would take Merewald for husband. Cynewise spoke, and her voice was soft, carrying to just the first few ranks of the thegns standing in attendance.

"I do," she said.

"Then in the eyes of God and His church, I pronounce you man and wife," Ealhstan said, and he sounded as relieved as any in the cathedral.

Merewald turned to Cynewise. He lifted the veil that hung over her face and she looked up at him, her eyes a good five inches below his. He did not smile as he leaned down and dutifully kissed her, and she did not flinch as he did.

A ripple of applause was just moving through the watchers when the shouting started. It was a sharp scream, a wild sound, and a man named Werheard, a minor thegn from the west, burst out of the second row, a dagger flashing in his hand. He charged at the altar, screaming as he ran, and the shocking sound and the sudden flurry left the others standing frozen and dumbfounded.

It was fifteen feet to the steps where Merewald and Cynewise stood and Werheard covered it in the space of a heartbeat or two, but that was time enough for the others to react. Merewald spun around, a look of horror on his face. Cynewise half crouched, her hands up as if she could defend herself from the wicked blade. Nothwulf spun toward the sound. His hands were coming up from his side when Werheard ran hard into him, shoulder first, knocking him right off his feet and sending him sprawling over the red carpet that covered the dais in the front of the church.

"Bastard! Bastard!" Werheard screamed as he stepped toward Merewald. Now the ealdorman had his hands up as well, palms out, warding off the attack, but he might as well have done nothing at all. Werheard thrust the dagger forward, straight arm, and the stiletto point drove right into Merewald's chest, right into his heart. His eyes went wide, his mouth gaped open, and Werheard pulled the blade free and thrust again, a needless gesture. The knife ripped through Merewald's neck and he toppled sideways, the blood spurting like a fountain from the wounds, already soaking his fine linen tunic.

Werheard turned to the others. "To me!" he shouted, his voice loud, his tone part defiance, part confusion. He looked left and right, eyes sweeping the shocked and frozen thegns from whose ranks he had come.

"To me!" he shouted again and there was more confusion in his voice now, his face more panicked and wild.

The priests who flanked Bishop Ealhstan had pushed him back a few feet and put themselves between him and the killer. The thegns and their wives looked on, stunned, unwilling or unable to move. But Oswin the shire reeve had recovered before Merewald had even come to rest. He drew his sword as he came at Werheard, shouting, "Murder! Damnable murder!"

He pulled the sword back over his head. Behind Werheard, Nothwulf was struggling to stand, and as he did he shouted, "Don't kill him! Oswin, don't kill him!" But if Oswin heard the words he did not heed them. His long sword came sailing around in a powerful backhand stroke. Werheard was still shouting when the blade caught him in the neck and barely hesitated as it passed on through. His head flew off toward the south wall, his long hair whipping as it spun like a falling stone. His body remained upright for a second more, then it slumped down, dropping across the motionless legs of Merewald.

Then everything stopped. The priests, the bishop, Oswin, Nothwulf, the thegns all stood motionless. No one was quite sure what had happened, or what would happen next. Only one sound filled the cathedral, adding another layer of shock and horror to the thing: Cynewise, crumpled on the steps, legs drawn up, shrieking over and over again.

Chapter Two

Little the sand if little the seas, little are minds of men,
for ne'er in the world were all equally wise,
'tis shared by the fools and the sage.

Wisdom for Wanderers and Counsel
to Guests

It was Gudrid who saw the ships first. The morning was well on, a gray and uninviting morning, and the view to the horizon was limited, with the far end of the wide harbor just on the edge of visible. For that reason, the ships were already through the harbor entrance and making for the longphort when he spotted them.

Gudrid saw them because he was the one charged with looking out, a dull task that was shared by all, save for those with eyesight so poor that it was pointless to put them to that job. Gudrid was standing on the top of the earthen wall that surrounded the makeshift longphort at a place that the Irish called Loch Garman, though Thorgrim Night Wolf called it Waesfiord, which meant inlet of the mudflats. It was not a place that Thorgrim loved.

The wall had been built up to a height of fifteen feet. That was high enough for a watchman standing there to see trouble coming from a good distance, at least when the land was not under a blanket of gray fog and rain, which was about half the time. But that morning, despite the hovering threat of rotten weather, a man could see two or three miles in any direction. That was how far away the ships were when Gudrid spotted them.

Thorgrim Night Wolf was not looking out to sea. He could see nothing but the dark planks of his ship *Sea Hammer*, a foot away from his face. He was on his back, the shingle of the beach starting to dig through his tunic, and halfway under the larboard side of the ship, which was pulled up on the beach and resting on its starboard side.

With a hammer in one hand and a caulking iron, like a dull chisel, in the other, Thorgrim was gently tapping a bit of tarred twine between two of the planks where water insisted on seeping through. When *Sea Hammer* had been built, a length of rope was sandwiched between the planks to keep the water out, and it still did its job, mostly. But with the great abuse that the ship had suffered in the months since it had first been rolled into the sea, there were places where she was not as tight as Thorgrim would have wished.

"Thorgrim!" He heard Gudrid's voice clearly over the ring of hammers, the chopping sound of axes and adzes shaping wood. "Thorgrim, ships!"

There was not much Gudrid might have said that would get Thorgrim's attention quicker than that. He dropped the hammer and the iron and rolled out from under *Sea Hammer* and up onto his feet.

Anyone approaching the longphort was a potential threat, but if they were coming from the land, they were undoubtedly Irish, and there was the wall to stop them. There was no such barrier to stop anyone coming from the sea. Ships meant Northmen, Norwegians or Danes, but there was no reason to think they were any friendlier than the Irish.

Thorgrim squinted and looked out over the water, running his eyes from the headland to the north across the wide sweep of horizon. The thick blanket of clouds limited how far he could see, as did eyes that were growing old, and he could make out nothing out of the ordinary.

He turned and jogged over to the wall and up the crude ladder leaning there. All hundred or so men and one woman at Waesfiord had heard Gudrid's cry, and now all work ceased, all eyes turned seaward.

Thorgrim stepped up beside Gudrid. He squinted and turned his head and stared in the direction that Gudrid pointed, but he still could not see them, not at first. Then finally they came into view, four small dots near the edge of the visible world, four ships' sails seen from several miles away. They were just coming through the mile-wide gap between the headland to the north and the sand bar to the south that made up the entrance to the vast harbor, three miles wide east to west and six north to south.

"Well done, Gudrid," Thorgrim said. "Well spotted." There was a flurry of motion below and Starri Deathless scrambled up the ladder and stood at Thorgrim's side. Starri was a berserker, one of those men gifted or cursed by the gods with a madness in battle beyond that of normal men. His senses were sharp, his eyesight, his hearing more acute than that of any man among the crews of Thorgrim's ships. Thorgrim might have used him as a lookout, but Starri could not concentrate on any single task for longer than it took most men to urinate.

"What?" Starri asked, incredulous. "You only just saw those ships, Gudrid? Are you blind? Why, they're all but run up on the beach!"

Gudrid made no reply and neither did Thorgrim. Gudrid would not have suffered such a remark from any other man, but Starri was not like other men, and no one who knew him took offense at his words.

"Four sail, Gudrid, do I see right?" Thorgrim asked.

"Yes, four sail," Starri said before Gudrid could make reply. "I'm happy you can see them, Night Wolf. You've grown half-blind with your advancing age."

Thorgrim grunted. He was not in fact terribly old, just into his fifth decade, but he was feeling the effects of hard years, and he did not care to be reminded of it.

"I suppose," Gudrid said, still ignoring Starri, "that it was only a matter of time before we had company here."

Thorgrim nodded. Gudrid was right. Summer had come to Ireland, the weather warm and as free of rain as it would ever be, the days long and the seas calm. It was the time for raiding, for men from the north to take to the sea, to appear over the horizon and fall on some unlucky town or monastery, to plunder it for valuables and carry off the people as slaves. It was what brought the Northmen swarming to those shores.

It was what Thorgrim and his men should have been doing as well. But raiding meant ships, seaworthy ships, and those things they were lacking.

They did not want for ships. They had four of those. The mighty *Sea Hammer*, which had been built under Thorgrim's watchful eye and skilled hands back in Vík-ló, and *Blood Hawk*, her near sister. There was the smaller *Fox* and *Dragon* as well. They were all pulled up on the beach. They were ships, to be sure, but they were not seaworthy.

A storm in the early summer had rolled over them, just as they were tangled in a sea-fight with a Frisian slaver, and Njord, god of the wind and seas, had driven them ashore and smashed strakes and spars, snapped oars and torn sails to shreds. And so, at a time of year when they should have been driving their ships along the coast, they were struggling just to get them afloat.

Sea Hammer and *Blood Hawk* had needed the bulk of the work. They had been nearly shattered as they were thrown ashore. Since then they had been brought around to this sheltered place, all but sinking during the short passage, and hauled far up the beach on rollers. Broken planks had been cut away and new sections of wood scarfed in, cracked ribs had been pried off and new ones fashioned and pegged in place. New spars had been shaped from pine trees felled further inland. The work had been hard, exacting and extensive, but it was nearly done. Soon the ships would be rolled back into the sea where they belonged.

More men had climbed up onto the wall now and were staring off to the northeast. Thorgrim considered ordering them all back to work but decided against it. They had been hard at their labors for quite some time, with little in the way of distraction, no women and a limited supply of ale and mead. Now here was the most interesting thing to come their way in weeks, and Thorgrim knew he should let them have some pleasure from it.

Harald Broadarm, Thorgrim's son, sixteen years old and strong as any of the men, stronger than most, climbed up the ladder and stood at his father's side. Wisps of his long yellow hair had escaped the thong that bound them and now they danced in the light on-shore wind as he turned and faced seaward with the others.

"Who is this, Father?" he asked. Thorgrim smiled, just a bit. Harald often asked such questions, as if he thought the gods told his father things that other men could not know.

"I'm not sure," Thorgrim said. "Northmen, I have little doubt. The Irish don't go in for ships much, and no trader would be coming on so bold as these fellows."

Harald nodded. Thorgrim wondered if the boy thought that answer was some vision from another realm, some revelation, or just the simple, logical guess that it was.

"Four ships," Harald said. "Four ships to our two."

Thorgrim understood what Harald meant. There were, in fact, four ships in Thorgrim's little fleet, but *Sea Hammer* and *Blood Hawk* were in no condition to take to the water. Only *Fox* and *Dragon*, left on the beach during the storm and the fighting, were seaworthy. They had been missing only their oars, which had been stolen by the Irishmen who found them. For weeks the men at Waesfiord had felled ash trees, floated them down to the longphort, split them with great hammers and wedges and shaped the sections of blond wood into the long, tapering sweeps that would drive the ships when the wind failed them.

The ships could move under oar, of course, but none of them could be considered truly ready for sea until they had sails, which they did not. They had lost their sails to the storm, the fabric shredded in the brutal wind. And while the Northmen could fashion every other part of their ships, they could not make cloth. So, for that they had made a bargain with a nearby monastery at a place called Ferns. The monastery would provide them with the wide bolts of thick, oiled wool they would need, and the Northmen would pay for it with silver.

There were some misunderstandings at first, but once they had sorted out the problems, the cloth had begun to arrive as quickly as it could be produced. Every week or so, nearly, a wagon would roll groaning through the open gate of the longphort, and behind it, an escort of a dozen Irish warriors. The soldiers were led by a monk named Bécc mac Carthach, who had given up his life as a man-at-arms and was known now as Brother Bécc.

He did not look like a man of God, however, on those occasions when he rode into Waesfiord at the head of his small band. The brown robe and long knotted belt were gone, and in their place he wore a mail shirt, polished bright, leather boots and a sword at his waist. On his head was a helmet, shining as bright as the mail. Half of his face was a mask of scar tissue, the remnants of a battle wound that should have killed him, but instead drove him into the service of God.

Even though Bécc was acting the warrior, he was still doing his Christ-God's work, Thorgrim knew. Bécc hated the Northmen and considered them vermin, a curse on the land, and worse, an enemy of his God. His attitude was understandable. Thorgrim had to admit as much, though he thought the Irish would be more justified in their outrage if they spent less time killing one another.

So when Bécc arrived at the longphort, Thorgrim greeted him in a courteous way, with Failend there to translate. And Bécc returned the greeting with his own strained courtesy. But Thorgrim knew he was not really there to see that the cloth made it safe to the longphort. The dozen armed men guarding the wagons did not need his help. He came so he could see what his enemy was about, judge the strength of the fortifications, make certain the *fin gall* were really preparing to leave as they said they were.

It was one of the reasons that Thorgrim maintained a lookout on top of the walls during the day, and at night or in fog sent scouts out half a mile from the longphort to see that no one approached unseen. Though he had given his word that he would not attack the monastery at Ferns, and the abbot whom Bécc served had given his word that the Irish would not attack them, Thorgrim did not trust the abbot or Bécc. And he knew they did not trust him.

"Here, they're taking sail in now," Gudrid said, nodding toward the distant ships. Thorgrim's eye had been sweeping the wide estuary at the mouth of the River Slaney which formed the harbor there. The longphort was on the west side of that harbor, directly opposite the entrance, which was three miles away. The newly arrived ships had cleared the entrance, the light air from the east driving them at an easy pace.

As he stared, Thorgrim could barely discern what Gudrid had seen, the change in shape of the distant vessels as they lowered their wide, square sails and no doubt ran oars out through the oar ports, though it was impossible even for Starri to see such a thing from that distance.

"Here, that one's run aground!" Starri said, nearly shouting with delight. "See how they just stopped? Hard on the sand."

Thorgrim grunted. He could not see that, could not even hope to, but he took Starri's word for it. When the tide was up, which it was, the wide harbor looked like a great unbroken stretch of open water. But in truth it was a hazard of sandbars and mudflats lurking just below the surface. That made it very easy to run aground, though there was little chance of damage hitting that soft bottom, and little problem getting free when you did.

The distant ships continued their slow progress across the harbor, and Thorgrim thought he could make out the grounded vessel backing off the sand and then following behind the others, but he was not certain.

"Do they know we're here?" Harald asked.

"They might be able to see the earthworks," Thorgrim said. "From that distance. But I don't think they'll know who we are." He could not imagine how word of the ad hoc longphort at Waesfiord might have spread abroad, and if it had, he could not imagine why anyone would wish to come there.

If they mean to land here, we must be ready, Thorgrim thought. Four ships, if fully manned, could be as many as two hundred men, twice the number of warriors in Thorgrim's band. If these newcomers came to fight, then the time to hit them, and hit them hard, would be just as they were making the disorganized leap from the sides of their ships into the shallow water.

There was time enough to prepare for a fight. Even pulling as hard as they could at the oars, the far ships would not reach the longphort until well after the sun had passed the noon hour.

But as it happened, they did not come to Waesfiord, and if they did see the earthworks, then they paid them no attention. As all of Thorgrim's men watched across miles of open water, the four ships pulled along the far shore of the bay, then swung north and ran their bows up on the beach. Starri claimed he could see men leaping ashore, but Thorgrim was not so certain.

"They've come to sack Beggerin!" Harald said. "The monastery at Beggerin, that's what they've come for."

Thorgrim grunted again. Harald was probably right. From where the four ships had put ashore it was an easy march over open ground to the small monastery set back from the bay.

"So, what do we do about this, Night Wolf?" Starri asked. Thorgrim knew he hoped the answer would involve battle of some sort, though who Starri hoped to fight he did not know. Probably Starri did not know either, and he probably did not care, as long as there was fighting involved.

"Nothing," Thorgrim said. "We do nothing. It's not our affair."

What became of an Irish monastery was of no concern to Thorgrim and his men. In this case, Thorgrim was not particularly happy at the thought of Beggerin being sacked. They had been purchasing food and ale from the place, the easiest way to keep themselves supplied while they set their ships to rights. If Beggerin was burned and the people there marched off to the slave markets, it would be an inconvenience. But not enough so that Thorgrim felt the need to waste his men's lives defending the place.

Besides that, they were not so far from having their ships repaired and ready to leave those miserable shores, and so would not have need of Beggerin for much longer. And that was Thorgrim's only real concern. Leaving. Back to Norway. Or back to Vík-ló. Whichever the gods decreed.

They watched for a short time more, then Thorgrim called for everyone to get back to their work. The strangers were apparently of no consequence to them, and there was a lot yet to be done; the final repairs on the ships' planks, stitching sails, splicing and tarring rigging, shaping oars, building sea chests and a dozen other things. He sent four men to relieve Gudrid and the other sentries on the wall.

Thorgrim climbed back down to the ground and returned to *Sea Hammer* and his own work. He shuffled back under the hull, picked up his tools and began to tap the old rope into the gap between strakes, but now his ears were alert for the telltale sound of the Northmen launching their attack.

Will I hear it from here? he wondered. Sound traveled easily over water, he knew that, but Beggerin was at least half a mile inland from the bay.

There'll be smoke, for sure, he thought. Great columns of smoke. They were the inevitable marker of a vicious and bloody raid.

Thorgrim finished his work on the seam, all the while keeping an ear cocked toward the north shore, listening for the sound of destruction, the shouting, the screams of terror or agony. He was certain that every other man in the longphort was doing the same. But he heard nothing. He shuffled back out from under the hull, stood, and looked off to the north. No smoke. No sign that anything had changed, save for the four ships on the beach, four tiny dark slashes against the lighter sand, barely discernable to his eyes.

"Nothing, Night Wolf! Nothing at all!" It was Starri's voice, loud and enthusiastic, which was not a surprise. But it seemed to be coming from somewhere over Thorgrim's head, which was a surprise. Thorgrim turned and looked up. *Sea Hammer*'s mast had been unstepped and set on the beach, and the figurehead at the bow removed. Starri was standing where the figurehead was normally mounted, precariously balanced twenty feet above the beach, though it seemed as effortless to him as standing on the ground, as such things generally were.

"What do you see?" Thorgrim called.

"Nothing," Starri said again. "No smoke. I can see men moving on the beach, but they seem in no hurry. I've seen nothing like a raiding party going over the dunes."

Thorgrim turned back, looked north again. *What are they about?* he wondered.

"Wait!" Starri called. "I see smoke now…coming from the beach. Yes, from the beach. A cooking fire or some such. Idiots! They might as well send a messenger to the monastery, announcing that they're there. There won't be a thing left worth taking. Night Wolf, I'm going to go over and slap someone in the head for being such a fool!"

Once again Harald appeared at Thorgrim's side. "What do you think they're up to, Father?" he asked.

"Not raiding the monastery, that's for certain," Thorgrim said, and that was the only thing he knew for sure. But he could not leave it like that. He could not have a band of armed men, outnumbering his own and within sight of the longphort, and not even know why they were there.

He turned to Harald. "In truth, I don't know what they're doing. So I guess we better go ask them."

Chapter Three

But hast thou one whom thou trustest ill
yet from whom thou cravest good?

Wisdom for Wanderers and
Counsel to Guests

There was considerable debate as to how Thorgrim and his men would cross the bay to confront the newcomers on the beach to the north.

They had two ships that could carry them: *Fox* and *Dragon*. Should they take one? Or both? Or should they just take a handful of men in the big Irish boat they used to travel up and down the river? Should they mount figureheads to give a warlike appearance, or should they make an effort to look as if they came in peace? Would that be taken as a sign of weakness?

The debate, however, was entirely in Thorgrim's head, since he was not generally given to asking other men their opinion. And it lasted only as long as it took Thorgrim to turn around and start issuing orders, since he was not the sort who wrestled with indecision.

"We're going over to have a word with these fellows to the north!" Thorgrim called. "Get *Fox* into the water. Leave the figurehead off. We'll take men enough to man her oars, and a dozen more. Shields on the shield rack."

That was a good compromise. The figurehead left off would indicate they did not intend to fight, the shields along the side would show that they were perfectly willing and able to do so if pushed. He did not have to tell his men to bring weapons because Norsemen did not go anywhere without weapons.

Failend appeared at Thorgrim's side. An Irishwoman, she had been Thorgrim's prisoner once, until realizing that she actually preferred the life of a Northman to that of the wife of an Irish lord. She had become Thorgrim's lover, and as an archer, a formidable warrior.

She had Iron-tooth, Thorgrim's sword, in hand, his mail shirt draped over her arm.

"Thank you," Thorgrim said. He took the mail shirt and slipped it over his head, then took Iron-tooth and buckled the belt around his waist.

"Would you have me go with you?" Failend asked.

"Yes, of course," Thorgrim said. "I hope to frighten them, show them how formidable we are as warriors."

Failend smiled. She was just over five feet in height and barely seven stone. She was deadly accurate with a bow and arrow, and quick with the seax she wore at her waist, but the sight of her was not likely to frighten anyone.

"Besides, we don't know who these men are," Thorgrim said. "What language they speak." Failend was generally called on to translate from her native Irish to the Norse she had quickly picked up living among Thorgrim's men. That skill might be needed in the coming meeting.

Of all of them under Thorgrim's command, only Failend and Harald could speak both tongues. Harald, with the nimble mind of youth, had learned the Irish language so that he might pursue an ill-advised courtship with an Irish girl.

"And tell Louis to come as well," Thorgrim said. "Maybe these sorry bastards are Franks like him." Louis the Frank, Louis de Roumois, had been captured along with Failend, lovers fleeing arrest, as Thorgrim later discovered. Unlike Failend, Louis had despised the Northmen. Probably still did. He had escaped, and fate had put him back in Thorgrim's hands, and now he had apparently decided he was just as well off with the heathens as with anyone.

Or so Thorgrim guessed. He never asked Louis. Once, he had looked on Louis as an enemy, a man he wanted to kill, but now he did not really care. If Louis wished to stay with them, that was fine. He was clever, and a skilled and reliable warrior, and he was welcome to share their food and ale as long as he used his sword against the

Northmen's enemies. Now Thorgrim wished for Louis to join them in case these men could speak only Frankish.

"I'll tell him," Failend said.

Thorgrim turned back to where a few dozen men were eagerly heaving *Fox* along the log rollers and back into the water. For the past month their lives had been monotonous routine, and a break such as this was welcome indeed. Thorgrim looked around for Godi and saw him heaving with the rest on *Fox*'s hull. Godi, strong and massive as a bear from his native Norway. Thorgrim did not want to deprive those men pushing the ship of his strength, so he waited until *Fox* was floating free before calling to him.

"Godi, you'll come with us," Thorgrim said as Godi approached, red-faced from the effort of moving *Fox*. For purposes of intimidation, no one could best Godi.

"Very well," Godi said, nodding. Godi was quiet and humble because, like a lot of big men, he did not feel the need to be otherwise.

"Do you still have that banner? The wolf's head?"

Godi smiled and nodded. It had been made for Thorgrim back when he was lord of Vík-ló, a red swallowtail banner with a gray wolf's head. Godi had taken ownership of it, but Thorgrim had not called for it in some time.

"Yes, it's safe," Godi said. "It's in my sea chest."

"Good. We'll bring that as well."

It did not take long, motivated as the men were, to get everything in readiness to cross the two miles of water to where the other ships were beached, and to do so with a sufficient display of strength and confidence. Shields were hung on the shield rack along the ship's side, men in mail or leather armor, helmets on heads, took their places on the sea chests that served as rowing benches, and others stood along the centerline. A pine bough was lashed to the stem where the figurehead would otherwise be, another sign that *Fox* came in peace.

Thorgrim had given command of *Fox* to a man named Hardbein, a good and knowledgeable mariner who had joined with them in Vík-ló. He ran his ship well, but with Thorgrim aboard Hardbein yielded the tiller and command of the vessel to him. Harald was pulling an oar, because he could never be idle while other men worked. Louis de Roumois, in mail and sword, his head, like

Thorgrim's, uncovered, stood aft on the small deck in the stern, but as far from Thorgrim as he could get. He did not pull an oar because, unlike a Northman, he was not raised to the work and was pretty well useless at doing so.

Failend stood halfway between Thorgrim and Louis. And forward, clinging to the stem, as high up as he could get, Starri Deathless stationed himself to keep an eye out for sandbars or any further dangers.

"Starboard, pull!" Thorgrim called and the men along the starboard side leaned forward as one, dipped their oars and leaned back. The ship turned under Thorgrim's feet, a living thing, moving to the drive of the oars, rocking a bit with the small swell coming in from the sea. Thorgrim suppressed a smile but his heart was shouting with the joy of it. Underway. A ship beneath his feet. The land astern, and even if it was only a few yards astern, still, they were waterborne and they were moving and that to Thorgrim was life itself.

They pulled north, skirting the shore, where Thorgrim knew the current from the River Slaney kept the sandbars mostly at bay. They moved with an easy, steady rhythm. The men had not manned the oars of a longship for several months, but the motion was so familiar to their arms and backs that they picked it up as easily as walking.

They crossed the mouth of the river where fresh water flowing from the great watershed to the north collided with the salt water coming in from the south, churning and tumbling along. Thorgrim pushed the tiller to larboard, swinging the bow to starboard to follow the curve of the shoreline.

"Sandbars off the starboard side, Night Wolf," Starri called from his perch on the stem. "But far off, you won't hit them."

Thorgrim nodded. He pretty much knew that even without the benefit of Starri's lookout. He made a frequent study of the shifting sands in the bay so that he would always be ready to navigate those waters if he needed to. And that need, Thorgrim knew, could arise quickly, and at any time.

He shifted his eyes forward, beyond the bow. He could more clearly see the ships pulled up on the beach now. They were of tolerable size it seemed, bigger than *Fox* but not so big as *Sea Hammer*. Still, if they carried the full complement that Thorgrim would expect, their crews would be much larger than the depleted companies of Thorgrim's vessels.

They were half a mile away from the nearest ship when Starri came walking aft, moving down the centerline of the ship with his loose-limbed stride. Before Thorgrim could object, Starri started in. "There's nothing to hit ahead of us, Night Wolf, fear not. You don't need me up in my hawk's nest."

"You were supposed to keep an eye on the men on the beach as well," Thorgrim reminded him.

"And I did. Nothing much there, either. They see us coming, of course, and they're making ready. At least they're standing up and gathering in a mob. Like people watching a bear baiting or some such. They don't look as if they mean to fight."

"Good," Thorgrim said. "Neither do we."

"But see here," Starri continued. "I know these ships, or at least the ones I can see. I've seen them before. You know, Night Wolf, I never forget a face or a ship, and so I'm certain I've seen these before."

Thorgrim made a noncommittal noise in his throat. He and Starri had lived and fought side by side nearly without respite for two years now, but Thorgrim was still never certain how much credence to give Starri's words.

It was true that Starri had surprised him in the past, recognizing men or ships they had seen, but that was no proof that he genuinely did not forget such things. It was also true that Starri had once claimed to be unable to recognize faces.

"Very well," Thorgrim said. "We'll know soon enough if you're right."

They pulled on, and soon Thorgrim could see the men on the beach gathering to meet them. It was as Starri had said; they seemed to be in some sort of loose formation, more like a curious mob than men ready for a fight. Thorgrim could see the bright points of color that indicated that some men held shields, but it was not what he would call a shield wall. Beyond that there was nothing terribly threatening about their posture.

He shifted his eyes back to the ships. Thorgrim had a much better eye for such things than Starri did. Starri was an indifferent mariner while Thorgrim loved the building and sailing of sea craft as much as anything in life. And he could see there was indeed something familiar about the vessels run up on the beach.

They continued on, rowing parallel to the north shore of the bay. Ten strokes more and Thorgrim pointed to a spot on shore and Hardbein pushed the tiller over, swinging *Fox*'s bow north, aiming to run it onto the sand thirty feet away from the ships already there.

That change of course sparked a reaction from the men on shore, Thorgrim could see that. As one they moved closer to the water, forming a line fifty feet up the beach from where *Fox* would touch. There were more shields in evidence now, though *Fox* was close enough that they should be able to see the pine bow, the lack of a figurehead, and the fact that Thorgrim and his men were vastly outnumbered.

Fox closed quickly with the beach. Thorgrim studied the closest ship, which they were fast approaching, and though he could not place it, the feeling of familiarity was even stronger. And the vessel had seen some hard use. Thorgrim could see sections of new wood where strakes had been poorly repaired, and other places where tarred cloth had been nailed over what he guessed were leaking seams. A few of the shrouds had apparently parted, and now they were spliced together.

"One more stroke, then ship your oars!" Thorgrim called forward. The rowers pulled one more time then ran their oars in, held them straight up, then laid them down on the deck like it was some elaborate and well-rehearsed dance. *Fox* continued on, her forward momentum carrying her right up onto the beach. She stopped with a soft grinding sound and a slight jarring motion as her forefoot plowed into the sand.

Godi and a dozen men were on their feet even before the ship had come to a stop. They hefted a long gangplank up and ran it forward over the bow and over the small surf. Godi snatched up the long staff on which he had affixed the banner, held it aloft and made his way down the gangplank, the wood bending ominously under his weight. Behind him, a dozen men whom Godi had selected before they had left the longphort, all wearing mail, followed him down the ramp and formed up as a sort of honor guard, with Godi holding the banner high. Harald was among them, of course, as were Gudrid and Hall.

Starri Deathless was there as well, though he had not been selected by Godi, and to look at, he was one of the least impressive men on board. But it would have been pointless to tell him to stay behind. Even if he remembered the instruction, he would not have followed it.

Once the men were in place on the beach, Thorgrim made his way toward the bow, walking down the length of the ship, followed by Failend and Louis de Roumois. He stepped up onto the gangplank and walked slowly down toward the sand. He would have been perfectly happy to vault over the side and down into the shallow water, as he had done a thousand times, but he recognized the importance of such a display as this. Still, he could not help but feel like a rooster strutting its way around a barnyard.

He stepped off the gangplank and into the soft sand, then through the two lines of men and up the beach. The others fell in behind him, and he could hear the stamping and knocking and jostling of the rest of his men making their way to shore.

But Thorgrim saw none of that. He was looking straight ahead, his eyes on the men waiting for them up the beach. He was looking for some sign of what would greet them, some indication of whether these men were looking for a fight, or an alliance, or just to be left alone.

He could see grim faces, determined-looking faces. Like the ships, the men seemed to have been hard used. He could see grimy bandages, encrusted with dried blood and wrapped around arms and legs. He could see shields with paint flaking and great gouges in the wood. He could see stained, torn clothing. Few of the men were wearing mail.

"Night Wolf! Night Wolf!" Starri had run up from behind and was whispering in Thorgrim's ear, pretty much destroying Thorgrim's dramatic approach.

"What is it, Starri?"

"I know who these men are! These men and their ships!" That caught Thorgrim's attention and he nodded for Starri to continue. Starri had about twenty paces in which to tell his tale, and Thorgrim hoped he could do it in that time.

"You remember Ottar, that great beast of a fellow? You fought the *hólmganga* against him. He nearly killed you."

"Yes, I recall," Thorgrim said. The *hólmganga* was a duel, a formal fight to the death, and Thorgrim had indeed come close to being cut down fighting the massive and powerful Ottar Bloodax. In the end, it was Ottar's corpse that had been carried off.

"Well, after that, you let Ottar's people leave, because you are a soft-hearted fool. And these are those men. Some of them at least. And their ships."

"There were only two of Ottar's ships that sailed from Vík-ló," Thorgrim said.

"And those two are here. Where the others came from, I don't know."

They were fifteen feet from the line of waiting men, and that meant no more time for discussion. Starri stepped back and a man stepped forward from the crowd facing them. A little taller than Thorgrim, with long black hair done up in two braids that hung down on either side of his mail shirt. His beard was long and unkempt and it half hid an unrepaired rent in the mail, just at his shoulder. He had a shield over his back, and his sword was still in its scabbard, but for all that he did not look at all welcoming or even curious as to why Thorgrim had come.

"Here, Thorgrim," Starri whispered. "This is one of them, one of Ottar's men."

The man did look familiar. Thorgrim could see it now. He would not have recalled where he had seen him, but now that Starri pointed it out he knew he had indeed seen him before.

Thorgrim stopped walking and considered the man for a moment before he spoke. "My name is Thorgrim Ulfsson, of Vik—" He got no further.

"I know who you are," the other man said, then spat on the beach, an ambiguous gesture, which Thorgrim decided not to view as an insult. He would not, however, tolerate a second such display.

"Thorgrim Night Wolf, *Jarl* of Vík-ló…former Jarl of Vík-ló," the man said. "I'm Ketil Hrolfsson. I was second to Ottar Bloodax. Until you killed him."

Thorgrim looked to his left and right, up and down the line of men. More than a hundred. A hundred and twenty, perhaps? Still fewer than he would have expected to crew four ships.

He looked back at Ketil who was fidgeting a bit as he waited for a reply. *Jarl…* Thorgrim thought. He had never really thought of himself as a jarl, the jarl of Vík-ló. Generally the title of jarl was bestowed by a king, but there was no king here, and he was, or had been, the unequivocal ruler of the longphort.

He forced those thoughts aside.

"You were second to Ottar," Thorgrim said to Ketil. "And now you are first. I did you a great favor, it seems."

Ketil frowned and his eyebrows came together and he clearly did not know how to respond to this.

"See here," Thorgrim said, saving Ketil from his struggle for words. "I've come here in peace. I have no fight with you, and whatever you're about is not my concern. We have a longphort on the west side of the bay. It's no great defense, since we don't mean to be long there, but it's something. You're welcome to bring your ships there, if you come in peace as well."

Ketil's frown did not dissipate. If anything it grew deeper. This, clearly, was not what he had expected. Thorgrim doubted it was what his own men had expected. But then, there was quite a bit that even his own men did not understand.

Thorgrim had seen the look on Bécc's ruined face when he had accompanied the wagons into the longphort. He had seen the man looking around, silently counting up the number of Northmen behind the walls, judging the strength of the defenses, and no doubt realizing they were no great obstacle. Bécc and the abbot at Ferns had promised there would be no attack on Loch Garman, but Thorgrim knew what such promises were worth. The addition of a hundred or more Northmen to the company at Waesfiord would go far to make the Irish reconsider an attack.

Ketil looked as if he meant to spit again and then seemed to reconsider that gesture. In the end he kept his mucous to himself and instead spit the words, "We did not come looking for friends or for charity, Thorgrim Night Wolf."

Before Thorgrim could reply, Starri chimed in. "Well, if you came to raid the monastery yonder you've done a piss-poor job of it. They'll have carried off anything worth taking by now."

Ketil's eyes shifted to Starri and he stared at him for a moment and Thorgrim could all but hear the thoughts churning around in the man's head. It was clear that raiding was not why he had come, that he had no idea there was a monastery nearby. They had probably come ashore to make repairs, regain much depleted strength, and reckon on what they might do next. They did not look like men who were purpose-driven.

Ketil turned back to Thorgrim. "Why are you here? Why are you not in Vík-ló?"

Thorgrim nodded. "I said before that whatever you're doing here, it's not my concern. Well, the opposite holds true as well."

Ketil did not reply, but his eyes left Thorgrim's and he gazed briefly out into the distance. Again Thorgrim could all but hear the thoughts in Ketil's mind. If Thorgrim and his men were not at Vík-ló, then it was likely Vík-ló was undefended. It did not seem as if luck had been with Ketil and the men under his command. Taking Vík-ló, making himself lord there, that might change Ketil's fortunes very much.

By all the gods, you will not have Vík-ló, Thorgrim thought, and the thought surprised him. He had been ready to make another attempt to sail clear of Ireland. Or at least he thought he was ready. But now the idea of Ketil taking command of Vík-ló, the longphort Thorgrim and his men had worked so hard to put to rights, infuriated him.

"Very well," Thorgrim said at last. "I've said what I had to say. Now you may do as you wish. It makes no difference to me."

He paused before turning, looked up and down the line once again. He saw weary and discouraged men looking back at him. He saw men who were beaten down, men who had the fight driven from them. Men who were leaderless, for all practical purposes.

"Oh, you can be sure I'll do what…" Ketil began, but Thorgrim turned his back and began walking away, the move perfectly timed for maximum humiliation. He heard the tone in Ketil's voice change as he presented his back to the man and began walking away as if his words were of no consequence. Which they were not.

We have a great deal to do, and not so much time to do it, Thorgrim thought.

Chapter Four

I saw that doom-beacon turn trappings and hews:
sometimes with water wet,
drenched with blood's going; sometimes with jewels decked.

The Dream of the Rood

Nothwulf had been raised in the grand home of the ealdorman of Sherborne, the home of his father, Osric, and his brother—his late brother—Mcrewald. He did not live there now. He had not lived there for some time, not since he had come of age and come to realize that it would be a helpful thing all around to have some space between him and Merewald.

His home was still within the walls of Sherborne, of course, about a mile away through narrow, mud-and-filth-choked streets, a town crammed with all the shops and workshops and markets that one would expect to find in the second most populous town on the kingdom of Wessex. It was a grand home, befitting a man of Nothwulf's status. There was a long hall, and connected to it a building with his bedchambers on the upper floors and those of his men below. There was a kitchen and stable, all of them built of timber frames and whitewashed daub, encircling a courtyard and surrounded by a formidable palisade wall, the tall oak gates of which, when closed, could quite cut off the mayhem beyond.

The horses were gathered there now, and Nothwulf's hearth-guard, the warriors who served him and his household, were waiting, milling about in small groups, talking in low voices, because there was much to talk about. They were a dozen men, well-trained and well-equipped, with mail shirts and steel helmets and swords hanging from their waists. All of that Nothwulf had given them, and they in turn gave Nothwulf their considerable strength of arms and their unquestioning loyalty.

The captain of the hearth-guard was a man named Bryning, and he stood off to one side. He did not join in the talk with the others. Bryning knew more than the others did, because Nothwulf told him more, and Bryning in turn would tell no one else. It was one of the reasons that he held his high rank.

Nothwulf stepped through the heavy door from the dim-lit chambers out into the courtyard filled with the dull light of an overcast day. He adjusted his sword belt as he walked and tugged his mail shirt down. Bryning stepped over quickly, intercepting him before he had gone three steps from the door. The two men stopped, standing close, and in a low voice, Nothwulf said, "Well?"

Bryning shook his head. "Not much, lord," he said. "We spoke with Werheard's wife, and those in his household. He had a handful of hearth-guard. We talked with them. Not a one of them had a notion why the man did what he did, killing your brother like that."

Nothwulf frowned. "You questioned them...vigorously?"

"Very vigorously, lord. Very vigorously, indeed."

"Good," Nothwulf said. He wondered just what that entailed, wondered if any of those questioned could still walk. Or breathe. Not that it much mattered. Werheard had pretty much ended the lives of anyone close to him when he had, for some still unknown reason, plunged a knife into the chest of the ealdorman of Sherborne.

"Oswin, that son of a whore..." Nothwulf muttered, as much to himself as to Bryning. It seemed that only Werheard knew why he had committed that foul act, and the shire reeve had cut him down before he could be made to speak. Oswin was supposed to be one of Merewald's most loyal servants, but thanks to his thoughtless brutality the truth of his lord's murder might never be known.

"Is there talk abroad...of me?" Nothwulf asked next.

"Ah, well, lord," Bryning stammered, which pretty much gave Nothwulf his answer, but he let the man arrange his thoughts. "Sure, it's no secret there was no great love between you and your brother. That your father would have been pleased to see you as ealdorman, if that could have been. Tongues will wag, sure, but no one..."

Nothwulf held up a hand, cutting Bryning off, to Bryning's evident relief. The ealdorman was murdered on the very day of his wedding, killed by a man with no apparent reason for doing so? Of course people were going to look for some explanation. They were going to look to the man who had the most to gain from such an unnatural act.

"Well, lord," Bryning said, his tone a bit brighter, "after today I don't think there's much anyone will do, save for kiss your arse good and proper."

Nothwulf gave a thin smile. "Let us hope," he said.

The two men turned and crossed the courtyard to the waiting horses, signal enough for the other hearth-guard to mount up. With a jingling of mail, a clatter of weapons, they swung themselves up into their saddles, wheeled their horses, and fell in behind Nothwulf and Bryning.

There was no need for an armed and mounted guard, of course, to escort Nothwulf the short distance through the peaceful streets of Sherborne, but that did not matter. It was display that was called for, awesome and intimidating. And even that, Nothwulf felt, was not entirely necessary. He was going to claim what God and his father knew should be his—the seat of ealdorman of Dorsetshire—and there was no one who was in any position to stop him.

The stable boys tugged the heavy gates open and Nothwulf led his well-appointed band out of the courtyard and into the narrow, churned streets of the cathedral city. The way was crowded with folk as it generally was at that time of day, but everyone moved briskly out of the way as Nothwulf approached. They made signs of respect to the man on the tall stallion, but their uncertainty was clear in their hesitant gestures. Nothwulf was obviously to be the next ealdorman of Dorsetshire, but he was not ealdorman yet, and the people were not sure what homage to make.

Nothwulf smiled to himself. It was amusing, really. *We'll get this straightened out forthwith, don't you fear*, he thought.

They moved through the streets like a ship through the sea, the people like water parting before them, and soon they were approaching the walls that surrounded the ealdorman's home, Nothwulf's childhood home, a place he knew better than the home he occupied now.

There were guards on the walls and Nothwulf saw one call down to the courtyard below. The big gate swung open and he and his hearth-guard rode through without even having to slow their pace.

A flock of stable boys approached to take their mounts, and at the far end of the courtyard stood Oswin, the shire reeve, with arms folded, and the town reeve standing at his side. Oswin did not look happy, and Nothwulf knew there was little reason that he should. He owed his position to Merewald, and he had cut down Merewald's killer before any tales of a deeper plot could be pulled from him. His new lord, Nothwulf, who had never much liked him, had been beyond furious at the act.

There in the cathedral, standing over the bleeding corpses of his brother and his brother's killer, Nothwulf had upbraided the man. The first thought, the very first thought that came to Nothwulf's mind as he saw the knife plunging into his brother's chest, saw the spout of blood erupting around Werheard's hand was, *They'll blame me for this…* There was no one who needed Werheard's confession more than Nothwulf did.

But soon it would not matter whether he had it or not. He was going to his late brother's house for a coronation, to make official his office of ealdorman. The timing might appear unseemly—Merewald's corpse was not even in the ground yet—but Nothwulf knew that the longer he waited the more mischief might be made. After the shock of the murder, the people needed to know there was a man of proved ability in charge. And once Nothwulf had secured that position there would be no one short of King Æthelwulf himself who might bring about his downfall.

Nothwulf swung his leg over the saddle and dropped to the ground and a stable boy led his horse away. Oswin remained where he was, he did not approach, thus forcing Nothwulf to cross the courtyard to him, a small thing, but one that displeased Nothwulf very much.

Enjoy your office while you can, Nothwulf thought, *though that will not be very much longer. Not much longer at all.*

Oswin spoke first, while Nothwulf was still a dozen paces away. "A sorrowful day, lord," he said. "I share your grief, as does all of Dorset."

"Thank you, Reeve Oswin," Nothwulf said, thinking it better to keep up the pretense.

"The household is in mourning, of course, but we're seeing to the funeral arrangements," Oswin continued.

"Good, good," Nothwulf said. "I am in no doubt you've looked into this matter? Tried to find out what mad plot drove Werheard to do what he did?"

"I have, lord. We visited Werheard's home. But…ah…your man Bryning seemed to have got there before us."

"Yes," Nothwulf said. "That's no surprise. I sent him. I'm as eager as any to find out what's acting here. More so, most likely. Merewald was my brother."

"Yes, lord. But I'm afraid that by the time we arrived the folk there were not… really…in such a way as to be questioned."

Nothwulf nodded. He asked for no clarification. He wanted none. Bryning had been vigorous in his interrogation.

"Nothing seemed amiss to you?" Nothwulf asked instead.

"No, lord. We found nothing. Werheard had land, of course, but for all that, he was not a terribly wealthy man."

"Werheard was a fool, which is why he was not a wealthy man. My brother gave him opportunity enough."

"Yes, lord," Oswin said again. "He was a fool, indeed. Easily led. We found but one thing which seemed out of place." Oswin dug into the leather purse that hung on his belt and extracted a ring, a heavy ring made of gold, with a bright red stone set in the middle. Nothwulf felt his curiosity, his confusion, and his panic rise in equal measures. He took the ring carefully from Oswin's fingers and examined it closely.

"The hart and boar device there," Oswin said, pointing vaguely at the ring. "Those are ones you favor, lord, if I'm not mistaken."

"Yes…" Nothwulf said, still looking at the ring. *How, in God's holy name, did Werheard have this?* he thought. *When did I see this last?* He had not worn it in some time. Many months, at least, if not longer. It could have disappeared anytime since then.

"Might this have been yours, lord?" Oswin asked. "Did you give it to Werheard? A gift, perhaps?"

You know full well it's mine, you perfidious bastard, Nothwulf thought, but when he spoke he did not let his words or his tone convey any of the confusion he felt.

"It's certainly mine," Nothwulf said, handing the ring back. "Or was. How Werheard came to have it, I don't know."

Oswin nodded as he took the ring, his expression unreadable. "Of course, lord," he said. "Stolen by a servant, no doubt. You must be ever on the watch for thieving servants. I'm sure you'll make a lesson of whoever you find who did this."

"I will indeed," Nothwulf said. They were playing a game, him and Oswin, each pretending to accept the other's sincerity. He wondered if he should insist that Oswin return the ring. It was, after all, valuable, and it was his. He genuinely did not know how Wereheard had come to have it, though it did not reflect well on him that he did.

Better to let the whole thing drop, he thought.

"But see here," Nothwulf said. "I have come to speak with Cynewise. My sister-in-law." The last words were just lightly touched with sarcasm.

"Of course, lord, you have much to discuss," Oswin said. "She's been expecting you would pay her a visit."

"Is she in her bedchamber?" Nothwulf asked. "I'll be happy to wait on her, if my men are seen to."

"Yes, lord. No, she's not in her bedchamber. She's in the long-hall, lord. Shall I walk with you?"

The long-hall? Nothwulf thought. *Why is she in the damned long-hall?* The long-hall was the center of the ealdorman's activities: council chamber, courthouse, a space to entertain thegns and kings. A place for feasts. It was a man's realm, the realm of a ruler, and save for those times of feasting, no place for a woman who was not a slave or some doxy of a servant.

Nothwulf said nothing as he followed beside Oswin, a formality, given that Nothwulf knew the place far better than the shire reeve did. They crossed the courtyard and a spearman who stood by the big oak door swung it open and Nothwulf and Oswin stepped through.

The hall was unchanged since the last time Nothwulf had been there, unchanged, in truth, for as long as he could remember it, going back twenty-five years or so. The whitewashed daub of the walls seemed gray in the dim light coming in from outside, the upper reaches of the roof with its heavy beams and ancient thatch all but lost in the dark. Three long tables took up much of the space, running lengthwise down the hall, with heavy benches between them, benches built to not topple over no matter how drunk those seated on them were.

The far end of the hall was raised a bit and another table sat there, perpendicular to the others. It was where anyone of importance sat. It was where Nothwulf always sat when feasting in that place. Not in the center of the table, of course. That place had been reserved for his father, and then his brother. But no more.

To the right of the table was an open area on which sat a heavy chair, with benches around it, like three walls forming a courtyard around a main house. The chair was a throne of sorts, the place from which the ealdorman did his official business, be it doling out justice or succor for his desperate people or making plans for war or taxes. It was heart of the body that was Dorsetshire, and Nothwulf was surprised to see Cynewise sitting there.

A handful of the local thegns were sitting on the benches near her, and they were speaking and she seemed to be listening, but she looked up at the sound of the door opening.

"Oh, Nothwulf, you're here!" she called. Her voice sounded weak and timid, unsure, and Nothwulf felt a small sense of relief. She was, as he had imagined, a frail woman who would be easily cowed.

Nothwulf, unbidden, stepped quickly down the length of the long-hall, his eyes holding Cynewise's, his look of determination unwavering. He took the few steps up to the dais and stopped just short of the ring of benches. Only then did he shift his gaze from Cynewise to the thegns.

"Leave us," he said, jerking his head toward the door. The thegns, who knew their place, were on their feet immediately, nodding their farewells to Cynewise and hurrying off the way Nothwulf had just come. Nothwulf watched them go, and realized that Oswin had stopped at the door and not followed him in. He and Cynewise were alone. So much the better.

Nothwulf turned back to Cynewise. Seated beside her, and a little back from the big chair, was a young woman called Aelfwyn. She was Cynewise's maidservant, and had been for some time, having come with Cynewise from Devonshire some months before. Aelfwyn was younger than Cynewise by a year or so, Nothwulf guessed, lithe and pretty with dark brown hair and a lovely complexion, her skin white with a blush of red at her cheeks. She looked hearty and robust where Cynewise looked weak and frail.

Aelfwyn looked up and nodded and Nothwulf nodded and their eyes lingered a bit more. Then Cynewise said, "Aelfwyn, leave us, please."

"Yes, my lady," Aelfwyn said. She stood from the short stool on which she was perched, smooth and easy as a butterfly lifting off, and with skirts held clear brushed past Nothwulf and was gone.

"Lady, I hope you're bearing up," Nothwulf said, annoyed that he had not prepared words before this.

Cynewise made a weak gesture with her hand, as if she hardly had the strength to indicate how poorly she was. "A shock, a shock…" she said, her voice trailing off. "My poor, poor husband…"

"It was a horrible thing, Lady Cynewise, horrible," Nothwulf said. "We're looking into what drove the murderous…the murderer to do such a thing."

Cynewise looked up at him, her expression touched with hope. "Have you found something out? Do you know why that accursed man did what he did?"

"Ah, no," Nothwulf said. "No, I fear we do not yet know."

Cynewise nodded her understanding. "I hardly feel safe here," she said, her voice faltering and barely audible. "That such a thing should happen to my husband. Sure it might happen to me as well."

Your husband of a minute's duration, Nothwulf thought, but that was not, of course, what he said, but rather, "Your safety, yes, that's in the main what I want to speak about."

"Yes?"

"Well, I should think that my brother was killed because he was ealdorman, because of his office. You might not be safe until the new ealdorman is installed. Until no one could see you as any threat."

"Me? A threat?"

"Well, no, I mean, I understand you are no threat, but whoever was behind the bloody plot that killed my brother, he might see you as such."

Cynewise nodded slowly, thoughtfully. "Of course," she said, her voice just above a whisper.

"So, that's why I've come," Nothwulf continued. "The sooner I'm installed as ealdorman, the sooner you are removed from this danger." Cynewise looked to be a pathetic creature, seated in the chair that was far too big for her, her eyes rimmed red from having been crying through much of the night, Nothwulf imagined.

Marrying you was the only smart thing my brother ever did, Nothwulf thought. Cynewise was pretty in a way, pretty enough to couple with, at least to get a son, and probably more than that. Between her and a mistress there would be enough to keep a man satisfied. What's more, her influence over her father, the ealdorman of Devonshire, was itself reason enough for the match. As Merewald had figured out.

Nothwulf was not yet married. Marriage was a means by which a man could expand his wealth and fortune and standing among the West Saxons. Those were opportunities to be coveted, and not squandered on some shapely little doxy with no wealth or family to speak of. That was what mistresses, servants and slaves were for. As to a wife, Nothwulf had been waiting for just the right opportunity. And he thought perhaps it had come.

"You have come…to…take your brother's office?" Cynewise asked in her weak and hesitant voice. Nothwulf, whose mind had been elsewhere, misunderstood the question. He stammered for a beat or two before he realized she was talking about the ealdormanship, not the bedchamber.

"Yes. Yes, Lady Cynewise," he said. "The sooner we have Bishop Ealhstan proclaim me as ealdorman, then the sooner you will be freed from all this. The sooner you will be safe."

"Proclaim you as ealdorman?" Cynewise said, as if Nothwulf had spoken in some foreign language, the words of which made no sense to her.

"Yes, lady," Nothwulf said, and his words carried an edge of impatience. "Proclaim me as ealdorman. King Æthelwulf will be in Sherborne next month and he can give the appointment his royal blessing then, but until that time the bishop must proclaim me."

"Oh," Cynewise said. Her eyes moved away from him and she stared off into the distance, as if thinking great thoughts, which Nothwulf did not think a child such as this was capable of doing. "Proclaim you as ealdorman…" she muttered again.

"We can summon the bishop now, see to this whole thing…"

"But Merewald was my husband," Cynewise said, looking up at Nothwulf. Her words true though they were, were in no way germane to the discussion and they threw him off balance.

"Yes. Yes, he was." *For one damned minute*, Nothwulf thought again.

"So…if he was my husband, I am not certain…I don't know…but I am not certain that…you think you should sit as ealdorman?"

"Yes, of course, Cynewise. Of course I should." It was a ridiculous thing to ask. He could see now she was confused and he tried for a reassuring tone. "I am Merewald's brother. His only brother." He considered mentioning that their father had always considered him, Nothwulf, to be the son most suited to be heir, but he decided against it.

"Yes…ealdorman…" Cynewise said, her voice trailing off. "But, some of the thegns, they seem to feel that, as Merewald's wife, I should take the office. I don't know. They say such things have happened before, wives serving in their husband's office."

Traitorous bastards! Nothwulf thought. Sure the thegns would want a frail thing like Cynewise to be ealdorman, a child they could bend to their will.

"Of course, Cynewise," Nothwulf said, his tone still soothing. "Sister, if I could call you sister. But remember, your marriage was of short duration. It was not…pray, forgive me…it was not even consecrated."

"True…" Cynewise said, her words weak, as if she was half asleep. "But we were married, you know. We said the words. Bishop Ealhstan called us man and wife. There were many there as witness."

"Yes, of course. But see here, you're still overcome with grief. This is why you must look to me for guidance. Merewald, my brother, he would want you to look to me, just as he would want me to come to your aid."

"Yes, of course he would. And I'm so confused," Cynewise said. "I…I just don't know who to trust…what to do…"

"That's why I'm here," Nothwulf said.

She looked up and gave a weak smile, the sort one might get from a person near death. "God bless you for coming. I'm so tired now. I cried all night, you know, and only near dawn did I finally sleep. Please, will you call on me tomorrow, when I have had some time to think on this? I can't think now…I don't know what to think."

"Of course," Nothwulf said. He made a short bow, then turned and stepped down from the dais and back toward the big door at the far end of the long-hall. It was only when he was halfway across the floor that he thought, *That did not go at all as I had hoped it would.*

Chapter Five

If I were a king who reddens spears,
I would put down my enemies;
I would raise my strongholds;
my wars would be many.

Fragmentary Annals of Ireland

The gathering was held in the great church at the monastery at Ferns. It was one of the few places on the monastery grounds large enough to hold all the men in attendance. But that was not the only reason that Abbot Columb had chosen that site. He had hoped that being in that holy place, in the presence of God, would calm tempers in the same way the Lord Christ had calmed the waters at Galilee.

That did not happen. But at least there was room enough for everyone.

The abbot was seated in a big chair near the front of the church, not on the dais where the altar stood but right near it. At his side was Abbot Donngal, the abbot of the monastery at Beggerin, about fifteen miles due south of Ferns, near the wide harbor at the mouth of the River Slaney.

Father Donngal was shaken, angry, and seemed ailing to the point of being near death, but with Donngal it was hard to tell. He had looked that way for as long as Columb had known him, and he never seemed to get better or worse, he just kept on living and complaining about all things in life. Columb wondered if Donngal would find cause for complaint when he went to his final reward. He imagined he would.

Abbot Columb had not seen Donngal for a year at least. He did not often make the trip from his own monastery of Beggerin. But now he had, as had every other churchman and sister who lived there; all had fled the monastery by the sea for the dubious safety of Ferns. The laypeople, meanwhile, had scattered into the countryside. Because the heathens had come.

Or, more correctly, a new heathen army had arrived. For some months Beggerin and Ferns had maintained a tense but stable peace with the Northmen under the command of a pagan named Thorgrim Night Wolf. The monasteries had provided food and ale, and Ferns had woven cloth for sails, and all this had been exchanged for silver. Thus far both sides had upheld their end of the bargain.

And both Columb and Donngal had been assured that once the ships were repaired and the sails made, then Thorgrim and his heathens would sail off, never to return. The best the abbots could do was hope that Thorgrim was true to his word, never a reasonable thing to hope when the Northmen were involved. But so far Thorgrim had done what he said he would do.

Then, a week past, that awkward standoff had collapsed when four more heathen ships with many warriors aboard had landed on the north side of the bay, less than a mile from Beggerin. Luckily, the hand of God had reached down to stop them from sacking the place and carrying the men and women off to be slaves or worse. Instead the pagan host had remained on the beach long enough for everyone at Beggerin to flee.

Now Donngal sat wheezing and frowning and grumbling at Columb's left hand. On Columb's other side, ten feet away, standing with arms folded, stood Brother Bécc mac Carthach, a former soldier who miraculously escaped death after a Northman's sword carried off his left eye and half his face. Once recovered, he had abandoned the military life for the life of a monk. He was the most loyal, most selfless, and hardest man that Columb had ever known. Brother Bécc did not complain. In fact, he hardly spoke.

The benches that had been brought in for the convenience of the others were now crowded with the more important men of that part of Ireland, the southern and eastern regions of Laigin. There were the *rí túaithe*, the minor nobles, the landholders who controlled the largest swaths of land and owned the biggest herds of cattle. There were the *aire forgill*, the Lords of Superior Testimony, and below them men of the various ranks down to the *aire déso*, the Lords of Vassalry, who had under their rule five free men and five not free and who received five cows per year from each of the five free men.

They were all near panic. All of that part of Ireland was near panic with the arrival of this new Godless horde.

And, like Donngal, they were angry, each speaking in his turn, speaking loud for greater emphasis as well as to be heard over the beating of the rain on the roof, thirty feet above them.

I should have held this gathering out of doors, Columb mused. *That would have shortened it up quite a bit.*

A man named Guaire was speaking. Guaire was one of the Lords of Superior Testimony, though the testimony he was giving at that moment was in no way superior. It was, in fact, a tedious rewording of the same point that had been made several times already.

"Abbot, with all respect due you, this is what happens when you make a bargain with Satan, when these heathens are suffered to remain on our shores, and even provided with cloth, of all things! And now of course more have joined them, just as many of us knew they would. A whole heathen army on our doorstep...."

At that point Bécc, apparently, had had enough. He took a step forward and the arms that had been folded across his chest dropped to his side as if he was going for a weapon. That, at least, was not possible. Bécc was dressed in the long, brown cowled robe of his order, a heavy rope belt knotted around his waist. It was the dress he preferred, Columb knew, though he had found himself more and more often wearing the mail and weapons of his earlier life. Columb wondered—and worried—whether or not the man was starting to think he could better serve God with a sword than a cross.

When Bécc stepped forward, Guaire's harangue came to a quick and awkward stop, as did the general murmuring that had accompanied the drumming of the rain. Bécc glared at the man with his one intact eye. The light of the candles that lit the space around the altar made strange shadows on the hard, smooth scars that formed the ruined portion of his face.

"The abbot did what he thought best to protect the monastery and the lands around," Bécc said, his voice menacing as a growl.

"Oh, I have no doubt..." Guaire stammered, glancing right and left for support.

"Brother Bécc, you too played a part in this," another voice called out, more assured and less intimidated than Guaire. This was Faílbe mac Dúnlaing, the rí túaithe of the lands to the west of Ferns and one of the wealthiest and most powerful men in the area. As he took up the argument, Guaire, with evident relief, sat once more.

"You fought the heathens but you failed to beat them," Faílbe continued. "And for some reason known only to God and the abbot, and perhaps you, they were allowed to return to this fortified place they've set up on the beach. Allowed to repair their ships in peace and even provided with cloth and sustenance. At a fine profit to the monastery, I'm sure, but still, one might wonder why."

Abbot Columb frowned. The heathens had been trapped in the church and surrounded, and it would only have been a matter of waiting until hunger and thirst drove them out. But in the end he had allowed the heathens to go in order to protect a secret mine, a gold mine about which the Northmen had somehow learned. But Columb could not say as much. The mine's existence was a secret, one that, miraculously, had been held for fifty years. He did not wish to bring that miracle to an end.

But Brother Bécc had no qualms about speaking out, at least not about the decision that had been made. It was his nature, and now that he owed allegiance to no one but God and Abbot Columb he felt even less constrained. "You might wonder why the heathens were allowed to leave, Lord Faílbe. You might wonder at the abbot's decision. But do you know why you are so ignorant of the truth?"

"Please, do enlighten me, Brother," Faílbe said.

"You don't know because you were not there. You and the fifty warriors in your house guard, and the hundred or so men you could have called up in your levy. You were so busy guarding your own rath and cattle that you couldn't be bothered to come to the aid of the monastery. You left us to be sacked by the heathens."

Bécc shifted his one eye from Faílbe and let it move slowly over the rest of the seated men. No one spoke, because every one of them was guilty of the same crime. When the monastery had been under threat from the Northmen who landed near Beggerin, each one of them had retreated to their own ringforts to protect what was theirs, rather than bring their men and arms to protect what belonged to God.

Faílbe cleared his throat. "We rí túaithe, and the others here, we have many responsibilities," he argued, his voice calm and even. "We have obligations to protect those who live on our lands. As well as an obligation to the monastery. We do not command great armies. There are choices that need to be made."

This was greeted with a general murmuring from the others, an unspoken agreement, and relief that Faílbe was willing to counter Bécc's arguments when none of the others were.

Bécc opened his mouth. Abbot Columb raised his hand and the undercurrent of sound from the gathered men fell away, leaving only the sound of the rain beyond the church walls.

"Please, I beg of you," Columb said, trying to give his old voice more power than he felt. "We do no good by arguing here. Whether the bargain that I made with the heathen Thorgrim was wise or not, only God can know. But so far the heathens have done what they said they would do, and they've caused no mischief. These heathens that are newly arrived, we don't know about them. Brother Bécc, what can you tell us?"

Bécc looked at Columb, looked at the others, and seemed disappointed that the arguing had been cut short. "We've been watching them, of course," Bécc said. "They've been five days on the beach by Beggerin. They seem to be making repairs to their ships, as Thorgrim says he's doing."

A voice from near the back called a question. "Are they in league with this Thorgrim?"

"Ah," Bécc said. "It does not appear so. My men have seen no one going from the one camp to the other. These newcomers seem to have just arrived out of nowhere."

Silence followed this statement, as each man considered the implications. Faílbe was the first to speak.

"What this means, of course, is that these heathens who have just arrived will not feel bound by any agreement Thorgrim has made. Even if Thorgrim sticks to his bargain, there's no reason to think these new whores' sons will not attack us." Abbot Donngal clucked at Faílbe's coarse words, but Columb hardly noticed. He had much greater concerns.

"I suppose," Bécc began, "that we could just wait here and see what they do. Pray to God they don't attack us."

"We will pray to God regardless of what the heathens do," Abbot Donngal said in his scolding voice and Bécc nodded his agreement.

"Wait to see if the heathens attack?" It was Guaire speaking now. "I hardly think that's the wise thing to do."

Well, you have managed to muster both wisdom and courage today, Columb thought. *It has been a productive afternoon, eh, Guaire?* But he did not say that. Rather, he said, "What course of action would you suggest?"

"Well..." Guaire said, faltering now that he was asked to make a decision. "Well...I suppose we should attack them first, should we not? Attack them on the beach before they march to Ferns."

"Or to your rath?" Bécc asked.

"Well, yes, I would like to prevent that as well. And why not?" Guaire protested.

"Of course. And certainly we would be best to attack them first," Bécc said. "Every soldier knows you're better off choosing the ground on which you fight. But there are only a handful of men-at-arms at Ferns, and the heathens have more than twice that number."

"Oh, dear Lord!" Faílbe said, loud enough to make several men jump. He stood up, looked around, looked back at Abbot Columb. "Yes, yes, yes, we will send men. We'll send our house guards, we'll raise our levies! Anything so we don't have to endure any more of this contrived little bit of playacting that you and Brother Bécc are forcing us to witness."

Abbot Donngal huffed in indignation, but Abbot Columb was forced to suppress a smile. It was true. He and Bécc had worked the whole thing out, planned how to steer the talk around until the rí túaithe agreed to send men-at-arms and think it was their own idea.

Faílbe alone was clever enough to see through that. But it did not matter. Not as long as the soldiers were sent and Bécc allowed to drive these newly arrived heathens back into the sea.

"Very well, Lord Faílbe," Abbot Columb said. "We would welcome your generous and quite unexpected offer."

Chapter Six

[E]ither illness or age of the edge of vengeance
Shall draw out the breath from the doom-shadowed.

The Seafarer
Early Anglo-Saxon Poem

Nothwulf had a great deal on his mind, and it distracted him mightily. He tried to concentrate on the business at hand, the girl in his bed, her smooth, white skin, her slim body, her lovely breasts. He wanted to please her. Nothwulf was not usually very concerned with his bedmate's pleasure, certainly not at the expense of his own, but this girl was different.

She ran her hands down his flanks and guided him on top of her and he moved easily, never putting undue weight on her small frame. Her neck arched back and her legs spread wider and Nothwulf thrust himself inside her. She let out a muffled cry and Nothwulf took great encouragement from that. He began to work in earnest, letting his steady rhythm build in speed while she squirmed and writhed beneath him as if she was trying to push him off, which he was pretty sure she was not.

Finally, with cries that were likely heard throughout the big house, they finished and lay panting, their skin slick with sweat. They stayed like that for a moment, then Nothwulf rolled over onto his back and the girl rolled onto her side and put her head on his chest. Nothwulf wanted nothing more than to climb out of bed now and attend to business. He had a great deal to do. But this moment was the most important of all, and he could not rush it.

He reached his hand down and began to play with the girl's lovely brown hair. "Now, Aelfwyn, my love, won't your lady be missing you?"

Aelfwyn gave a soft chuckle, then rolled over and rested her chin on Nothwulf's chest so she could look into his face. "Lady Cynewise thinks I'm at the market, and she won't look for me this morning. Truly, she's probably forgotten that I'm gone."

"Nonsense, how could anyone ever forget you? I don't. I think of you night and day."

Aelfwyn smiled. "That's sweet, Lord Nothwulf. It's a lie, I know it, but it's sweet of you to say. But my lady, I don't think she's able to think any clear thought at all."

"Is she so simple-minded as all that?" Nothwulf asked. Now they were working around to the information he wanted. They always did. In the past few months, since she had arrived in Dorset with Cynewise—the soon-to-be bride's special companion—Nothwulf had used his charm, position and wealth to lure her into his arms and then into his bed. He found the fornication to be most excellent. Even better, the girl was a flowing spring of information about the goings on in his brother's home.

"No, my lady is not simple-minded," Aelfwyn chided, giving Nothwulf's chest a slap for emphasis, her palm smacking loud on his bare, sweat-covered skin. "But she's had a great shock, her husband brutally murdered by her side, and his killer struck down as well."

"I recall. I was there, you know," Nothwulf said.

"Then you know what a shocking thing it was. So of course, Lady Cynewise doesn't know what to do, who to turn to."

Nothwulf nodded as if thinking deeply. "You know, my brother's death was a great shock to us all. Me mostly. He was my brother. No one loved him more than I did. Not even Lady Cynewise. She might have come to love him as I did, had she known him more than a short time. But they were husband and wife for a few moments, no more."

Aelfwyn laid her head down again and shuffled closer. "It must be very, very hard on you, my beloved," she said, her voice muffled a bit by his skin.

"It is, I won't try to hide that fact," Nothwulf said. "But I have my duties, you know, and they cannot be set aside in my grief. Cynewise is my sister-in-law now, and I have my duty to her. I have my duty to lift the burden of the ealdormanship from her weak shoulders. I wish she could see that, see how I might help her."

Aelfwyn looked up again. "It's hard for her to see anything now, lord," she said. "Her mind is quite addled, and the thegns, they are all there to tell her some story or other, all looking to find favor with her and get her to do this or that just for their own benefit. Oh, lord, I fear my lady will go quite mad."

Nothwulf nodded and looked grave. "I fear that as well. That's why I want my sister to know that I'm ready to help her, ready to take the cup from her hands."

"I can tell her that, lord? Should I tell her?"

"No, no…" Nothwulf said. "Not like that. I don't want her to get the wrong idea, think I'm trying to usurp her place. Perhaps if she thinks it comes from you. Perhaps if you suggest, as her dear companion, that she should turn to me for help in these matters, for direction, perhaps that would be best."

Aelfwyn smiled. "I'll do that, lord," she said. "You are the soul of kindness."

"And I'll see you rewarded," Nothwulf added.

"Oh, lord, the pleasure you give me when I share your bed is reward enough."

Nothwulf smiled as well. "Well said, wench," he said. "Now, I have much to attend to, and you had better get to the market and buy at least one thing to show you have done what you said you would do."

"Yes, lord," Aelfwyn said. She kissed his chest and rolled out of bed and began to pull her clothes back on. Nothwulf indulged himself a moment, watching her dress. She did not try to hide her nakedness from him.

Not a bit of modesty in you, is there? he thought. Then his thoughts moved on to other things and he rolled off the other side of the bed and began to scoop his own clothing off the floor.

Twenty minutes later Aelfwyn had gone off to wherever she was going off to and Nothwulf was stepping into the courtyard of his home, pulling on his leather gauntlets as he walked. The stable boy had his horse, a portion of his hearth-guard were mounted and waiting. Nothwulf swung himself up into the saddle and the gates swung open and he walked his horse over the soft ground and out to the crowded streets beyond.

Once again he was not going far and had no real need of a mounted guard, or indeed of horses at all, but Nothwulf believed that an ealdorman, or even a soon-to-be ealdorman, should not be walking on the filthy streets with the common folk. So once again his horse plowed a furrow through the crowd as he and his men rode to the cathedral, which was less than half a mile from the ealdorman's house in which he was raised.

Bishop Ealhstan and his cadre of priests were there at the door to greet him. Nothwulf had sent a messenger ahead to warn the bishop of his coming, a thing he debated a bit before doing. He would have preferred to catch Ealhstan unawares, speak to him before he had time to think on the subject, and that argued for a surprise visit. But if he did not tell Ealhstan of his coming, then the bishop might not be there when he arrived, and he would be humiliated having to return home after a pointless quest. In the end, the fear of humiliation won out, and he had sent word.

It's not like the old man hasn't been thinking on this already, Nothwulf mused as he slid down from his horse. *I'll venture he's thought of little else.*

"Bishop Ealhstan," Nothwulf said, with all the subdued melancholy one would expect from a man whose brother had just been killed before his eyes.

"Lord Nothwulf," the bishop said, extending a hand so that Nothwulf might kiss the great bejeweled ring on his finger, which he obediently did. "Kind of you to visit us here. Pray, come in."

Ealhstan turned and led the way in through the big door and across the long knave. Nothwulf had not been inside the cathedral since the day his brother enjoyed both the sacrament of marriage and *extreme unction*, the final anointing, all within a few moments' time, though in truth the latter had come a bit too late. As they walked up the dais he could not help but glance down at the floor, but the copious blood that had gushed from Merewald and his murderer had been thoroughly cleaned, and not a trace remained.

The priests trailing behind the bishop departed as Ealhstan led Nothwulf across the dais and into the sacristy. A heavy table with half a dozen chairs around it took up most of the small room. A bottle and two silver goblets, ornate with gold filigree and studded with jewels, sat on a silver tray at the center of the table. The bishop gestured for Nothwulf to sit and he did. Ealhstan picked up the bottle, filled the two goblets with red wine.

"Blood of Christ?" Nothwulf asked.

"No, just wine," Ealhstan said. He sat with a soft grunt and lifted the goblet to his lips.

"You're here no doubt to discuss your brother's funereal mass?" Ealhstan asked when he had swallowed his drink.

"Of course," Nothwulf said. In truth he was not there for that reason at all, had not even thought about it, but he realized in the moment that that was not what he should be telling the bishop.

"All is in hand," Ealhstan said. "Lady Cynewise has made her pleasure known, and we're making the preparations now. It's all something of a rush. Your father, well, he lived to a great age, and his passing was no surprise. We were quite prepared. But a young man like Ealdorman Merewald…" The bishop's voice trailed off.

"Shocking, shocking…" Nothwulf said. "A great shock to all of us. Why would such a thing happen? What might drive a man like Werheard—a man we thought loyal to my brother—to do such a thing?"

"Satan was surely whispering in his ear, just as he did in the garden, and Werheard with no more wit than Eve to fight back."

"I have no doubt Satan's hand was in this," Nothwulf agreed. "But there might be other devils as well. Some who walk among us. I've tried to discover the truth, Bishop. I sent my man Bryning to question Werheard's household, but he discovered nothing."

Ealhstan nodded, drained his goblet, filled it again. He glanced over at Nothwulf's cup and saw that it was still nearly full so he set the bottle back down. "Werheard's folk do not seem to have much to say, but Oswin might get them to talk, by one means or another."

"Oswin?" Nothwulf said, trying to keep the curiosity out of his voice. "He spoke to them already, I thought. Didn't get any more than Bryning did."

"That's true, as far as I hear, and I hear only scraps of rumors, you know," Ealhstan said.

You hear more than that, old man, Nothwulf thought. *There's nothing going on in three shires that you don't know about.*

But that was not what Nothwulf said, of course. Rather, he said, "The truth gets more rare by the day, I fear."

"Indeed it does," Bishop Ealhstan said. "But as I hear it, Oswin has arrested the whole household. He's holding them in the cells at the back of your brother's house."

"He has?" Nothwulf said. This surprised him, and he did not like to be surprised. He did not like to hear things of such importance second hand. He did not like to be less well informed than the bishop.

"Yes, he has," Ealhstan said. "Means to get the truth from them."

Damn that bastard Oswin, Nothwulf thought, and then reconsidered. *It makes no difference. Whatever reason Werheard had for killing my brother, it had nothing to do with me. Even if it is to my benefit.*

"Now, my dear Bishop," Nothwulf said, leaning back a bit and taking a sip of wine. Very good wine, he noted. "Important as all that is, it's not why I've come."

"Oh?" Ealhstan said.

"Yes. I came to confide in you, because you are both a man of God and a man of great influence."

"Influence? I don't know about that," Ealhstan said, but the man's modesty was so contrived that even he was not able to make it sound sincere.

"I'm worried about Lady Cynewise," Nothwulf said. "I fear that some of the thegns have her ear, and they're filling her head with all sorts of wild notions."

"Such as?"

"Such as thinking that she should sit as ealdorman of Dorset."

"And you think…oh, of course…you think you should be ealdorman in her stead?"

Of course I should be, you fat old fool! Nothwulf thought. It seemed as if the idea was just dawning on Ealhstan, which infuriated Nothwulf, but he held that in check.

"Well, naturally," Nothwulf said, once the flash of anger had passed. "I am Osric's second son. It's no secret that my father held me in high esteem. Sure he would wish to see me in Merewald's place."

"Yes, yes," Ealhstan said, leaning back as well. "I see your point. But Lady Cynewise…well, she was wife to your brother."

"For two damned minutes!" Nothwulf said, more emphatically than he intended. He pressed his lips together for a moment, then said, "Forgive me, Bishop. I'm still quite distraught about the death of my brother. My point is simply that they were married for so brief a time. They had not even consummated the marriage. And Cynewise is but a girl. She has no head for such things as being an ealdorman."

Ealhstan nodded his ponderous head. "Of course, of course," he said. "Not that there isn't precedence for a wife of an ealdorman taking the place of her husband on his death. And Cynewise is the daughter of Ceorle, ealdorman on Devonshire. She was raised in an ealdorman's household. She's no stranger to this sort of business."

"Perhaps," Nothwulf said, again feeling a flash of anger. He wondered how a clever man such as Ealhstan could be so damned obtuse. "But I have it on good authority that the girl is not standing up well to all the troubles she's seen. Her husband murdered before her eyes, and herself only just saved from such a death? No one doubts that Werheard would have gone after her as well, had Oswin not killed him. And now she has the matter of ruling all of Dorsetshire? No, my dear bishop, I don't think she will be able to endure all that. I fear she'll collapse under the weight."

Through all this Bishop Ealhstan was nodding and wearing a very thoughtful expression. "Yes, yes, quite," he said when Nothwulf finished. "Well, I've spoken to the girl, of course. We've been working on the arrangements for Merewald's funereal. And yes, she is certainly distraught. Seems to me she's bearing it a bit better than you seem to think, but it's quite possible I'm mistaken in this. I don't have your experience with women, eh?" The bishop grinned at that and Nothwulf dutifully grinned as well.

"So you'll look into this?" Nothwulf asked. "Make certain the thegns aren't filling her head with some foolishness? Help her to see that it's best for the shire if she makes no protest about my stepping up as ealdorman? Of course she's welcome to remain here as part of my household. Or perhaps join a convent, if she would wish."

Nothwulf had been entertaining the idea of marrying her himself, for the same reasons that his brother had, but now he was not so sure. On the one hand, there were many advantages to such a match, most of all the family alliance with Devonshire. On the other hand, Nothwulf was not sure he could stand much of that simpering little tart. Though of course being married to Cynewise would make his access to Aelfwyn all that much easier, and she had a good five years in her before she would grow so old that Nothwulf would have to look elsewhere for entertainment.

"Yes, I will certainly speak to her, and look into her circumstance," Bishop Ealhstan said. He raised his cup. "To the good fortune of Dorsetshire," he said.

Nothwulf raised his cup as well, and when he did, he noticed for the first time the device etched into the side of the silver goblet with its fine gold filigree and jewel studs on the base. It was an intricate design of twisting vines that formed a circle, and at the center of the circle a boar and a cross. It was the device used by the ealdormen of Devonshire. Father of Cynewise.

On a narrow table at the back of the room he noticed ten more goblets, each identical to the one he held.

Chapter Seven

Today Bruide fights a battle
over the land of his ancestor,
unless it is the wish of the Son of God
that restitution be made.

Fragmentary Annals of Ireland

Brother Bécc, sitting his horse in the middle of a wide field south of the River Bann, about a mile from the walls and towers of the monastery at Ferns, and still seething with anger, was nonetheless pleased by what he saw. The rí túaithe and the lesser nobles had been as good as their word, which was not always the case. Rarely the case, in fact, as far as Bécc had ever observed.

Arrayed before him were two hundred or more fighting men. These were the warriors that had been pledged to Abbott Columb in the gathering at the church, after Bécc and the abbot had doled out sufficient humiliation regarding the rí túaithe's past failings. And these were good men-at-arms. Bécc had feared the rí túaithe would honor their pledge by rounding up the most decrepit of the levy, but in fact they seemed to have sent their house-guards, their most skilled and trusted soldiers.

Some were mounted, but those were mostly the captains and the few of the rí túaithe who chose to ride with the army. The rest were on foot, armed with shields, spears and swords. Most wore helmets and mail.

Bécc nodded as he ran his eyes over the gathered men. The Northmen were good fighters, tough fighters. He knew that very well, and it was hard-earned knowledge. But these men were good fighters, too. And they outnumbered the Northmen. And they would have surprise on their side. They would launch an organized attack, and the Northmen would be in chaos. That, at least, was how he intended it to fall out.

Faílbe mac Dúnlaing was one of the rí túaithe who would ride with the men, and Bécc was not surprised. Faílbe was a brave man, and smart, which was why he was the most powerful of the minor nobles in that part of Ireland. He had always found favor with the *rí ruirech*, the high king of Laigin. And now he was here to help rout out the vermin from the north, and to see that the lives of his precious house-guard were not thrown away.

"What say you, Brother Bécc?" Faílbe asked, reining his horse to a stop beside Bécc's.

Bécc made a grunting noise. "The others have come through for us," he said. "I had no doubt you would, lord. You understand the danger here. But I feared the others would not see it, and would not send their best men."

"I made certain they saw it," Faílbe said. "Fear not. Now we have men enough to wipe out the heathens who've landed at Beggerin."

Bécc turned his eyes from the men-at-arms and looked Faílbe square in the face. "We have men enough to wipe out all the heathens for many miles around," he said. He thought this might bring an angry retort from Faílbe, but the man just met his gaze and nodded.

"Yes, Brother Bécc. We have men enough for that. But we won't be doing it. As you know."

It had been a long and unpleasant conversation, carried on by Bécc and Faílbe and the Abbott Columb. The gathering in the church had finished and the others had gone off to their evening meal, but those three stayed behind. Because, the opinions of the others notwithstanding, it was those three men alone who made the decisions.

"This is a chance like we have never had, and may never have again," Bécc argued. "I know that you, Lord Faílbe, will send your best men. If the rí túaithe will do the same, we'll have an army that can stamp the heathens out once and for all."

Faílbe's expression was unreadable, but Abbott Columb frowned. "I've come to agree with you, Brother Bécc, that these newcomers, the ones on the beach near Beggerin, they cannot be suffered to remain. But Thorgrim and his band, they have been true to their word. And you yourself say they seem quite ready to sail from here as soon as they're able. Which apparently is soon. Why waste men's lives fighting an enemy that's leaving anyway?"

"Yes, Abbott Columb, what you say is true," Bécc countered. "But the heathens are like serpents in the garden. They're not to be trusted. And when they turn on us, as they surely will, we will not have the army we'll have now. The heathens can move faster than we can assemble the men-at-arms. We must strike while we have the men."

And that was that. An impasse. Abbott Columb turned to Faílbe, because these were Faílbe's men, mostly, and it would be his decision as to how they were employed.

"These heathens who have come lately, they number somewhere above a hundred men?"

"Somewhere, lord," Bécc answered. "One hundred and twenty, maybe. My men have not ventured so close as to count with any great accuracy."

Faílbe nodded. "So, we will likely outnumber them by two to one. But this Thorgrim has…what?"

"Ninety men, or so, lord," Bécc said.

"Ninety. So now, with Thorgrim and these newcomers combined, we have no advantage in numbers. And even if we bring our best men, we can hope only to match the strength of the Northmen. We certainly will not overwhelm them."

"No, lord. But we don't attack the lot of them at once," Bécc countered. "We surprise the ones newly arrived, stamp them out. Then we are on to Thorgrim's camp, and we bring God's vengeance down on them as well."

"Hmm," Faílbe said and for a long moment he was silent. And then he said, "No, no…I can't countenance it. We can take the one by surprise, but then Thorgrim and his men will be alarmed and ready, while our men will have just suffered what I'm sure will be a bloody fight. And Thorgrim's men have defenses, earthworks. The other rí túaithe, they agreed to send men to meet this new threat, not to fight with men who seem to have no desire to fight with us. I say we fall on those near Beggerin, let Thorgrim and his band of villains depart on their own."

And that was an end to it. Faílbe had men enough and influence enough that his word would be the final word, and all Bécc could do was to bow his head, just a bit, and say, "Yes, Lord Faílbe."

Bécc was still not happy, not at all happy, about the decision.

But Faílbe had kept his promise, brought good men and saw to it that the others did the same, and that tempered Bécc's fury. It had been many years since Bécc had sat at the head of such a respectable force. At first, after having taken his vows, he had loathed the idea of bearing arms again. He had done so when the abbot called on him, called on his special talent, because obedience was one of the vows he had taken. But soon he had come to understand that this, like all talents, was a gift from God and could be used in the service of God. Raising a sword in defense of God and His church was surely as holy an occupation as illuminating manuscripts or brewing ale for the monastery. More so. Fighting put a man on the path to martyrdom.

*Such a waste, such a shameful waste…*Bécc thought. These fine men, and Faílbe would let the vermin infecting their shores live to sack another house of God? It made him wild with anger.

He had tried to shake it off. He had confessed his sins and done his penance. He had prayed about it, and found no relief in prayer. He had shed his monk's robe and replaced it with his padded tunic and mail shirt, his sword hanging at his side. And that was all he could do. He could kill those heathens he was allowed to kill, and try to further discern God's will for him.

"Shall we move, Brother Bécc?" Faílbe asked. "Are we ready to march south?"

Bécc looked up at him. He had been so deep in thought he had all but forgotten Faílbe was there. "Yes," he said. "Yes, let's go."

It was fifteen miles to Beggerin over a muddy track that was called a road. But happily it was an easy country of rolling, gentle hills, an open country where one could see a far way off and not be taken by surprise by some hidden enemy. Bécc led the men south and they covered the miles quickly.

At length they swung off east, skirting the Bog of Itty and then turned south again. It was late afternoon when they arrived at a place just a few miles north of Beggerin. They could see the ocean now when the road crested one of the low hills, and the tang of the salt water filled the air. Bécc held up his hand and slowed to a stop and the other mounted men and the two hundred and more foot soldiers behind him and the wagons loaded with food and tents all stopped as well.

"What is it, Brother Bécc?" Faílbe asked. Some people, Bécc had noticed, when addressing him, put a trace of irony in the word "brother," as if it was absurd that a warrior such as Bécc should consider himself a man of God. But Faílbe did not do that.

Faílbe had been riding at Bécc's side since they had left the field south of Ferns, but they had spoken no more than a few words during that time. Faílbe had not asked Bécc what he had planned, another thing for which Bécc was grateful. But they were close to the enemy now, and Bécc had called a halt to the march, and Faílbe would want to know why.

"We'll stop here," Bécc said. "We'll stop and rest and have our supper."

Faílbe swiveled in his saddle and looked to the west. The sun was dropping quickly toward the distant hills. "Not too much daylight left," Faílbe said.

"That's right," Bécc said. "That's why we're stopping. I intend to attack the heathens after dark."

Faílbe swiveled back and regarded Bécc, and Bécc held his gaze with his single eye. "Attack after dark?" Faílbe said. A nighttime attack was a rare and dangerous thing. It was a hard thing to control. It could easily devolve into chaos.

"Yes," Bécc said. He had thought this all through and did not care to argue, but he knew he could not simply dictate his wishes to Faílbe mac Dúnlaing. Faílbe was a powerful man, and as the one who had brought a great majority of the men-at-arms, he had the most to lose.

"There are reasons, good ones," Bécc continued with all the patience and deference he could gather. "We have to cover a lot of open ground to get to the beach where the heathens are making their camp. Even if they aren't keeping watch, any bastard stumbling off to take a piss will see us coming, and they'll be ready. What's more, you can count on the heathens to be drunk at any time of the day, but once the sun has set they're likely to be stumbling about, barely able to stand."

Bécc nodded his head in the direction of the men-at-arms behind them. They were leaning on spears or squatting on their heels, waiting patiently for their orders. "I wouldn't try such a thing with the scum of the levy, but these are good men, trained men. They're up to a task such as this. We'll cut the heathen swine down like reeds, and hardly lose a man in doing it."

Faílbe listened to this without a word. He looked away for a moment, considering what Bécc had said. Then he turned back. "Very well, Bécc," he said. "Your reasons are good. I trust your judgment and your experience. After dark it is."

Bécc slid down from his horse and Faílbe did the same, and on seeing those two dismount the other mounted men did the same. Bécc could sense a general easing of tension among the men. If Bécc and Faílbe were off their horses, then nothing was going to happen soon.

"Listen to me, you men," Bécc said, his voice loud enough to carry over the crowd. "We'll take our rest here, have supper. When the sun is down we'll move up and we'll attack the heathens when it's full dark. Once the bastards are good and drunk."

This brought smiles all around and nodded heads. None of the men-at-arms seemed at all disconcerted by the thought of a battle in the dark. These were men who fought and killed for a living, and they would understand, as Bécc did, the advantages of waiting for nightfall to drive into the enemy.

The warriors could rest, and as far as Bécc was concerned the captains and the rí túaithe and Faílbe mac Dúnlaing could rest as well, but he had no intention of doing so. He stepped over to where Faílbe was giving instructions to the captain of his men-at-arms, waited until Faílbe was done before speaking.

"When it's near dark I mean to go ahead, scout out the heathens, Lord Faílbe," he said.

Faílbe nodded. "Very good. I'll come with you, if you don't mind."

Bécc did not mind. He trusted Faílbe to not do something stupid. Nor did he have much choice in the matter. So he had a bite to eat and said None, his mid-afternoon prayers, then lay down for a short nap. He woke near sunset, said Vespers, then went off to find Faílbe.

He found Faílbe asleep, because Faílbe, like any experienced soldier, knew to rest when he could. He shook Faílbe awake. Faílbe stood and stretched and scratched himself.

"We're a mile or so from the monastery at Beggerin," Bécc said. "We can ride that far at least."

Faílbe nodded and called to the boy who attended the horses to get his and Bécc's mounts ready. Soon they were riding south again, in the last fading light of day, the road all but lost in the gloom of the gathering dark.

They rode in silence until Bécc saw the bulk of the monastery rising ahead, just barely discernable. He pulled his horse to a stop and Faílbe did as well.

"There's the monastery ahead, Lord Faílbe," Bécc said, nodding toward the cluster of buildings. Faílbe, who apparently had not seen it, stared off into the dark, then made a grunting sound.

"Your sight with one eye is better than mine with two," Faílbe said. "Do you think the heathens are there?"

"Don't know," Bécc said. "I'm sure they've searched the place for anything worth taking. Doubt they found much, since they gave the people time enough to bugger off. There may be a few of the heathens still there...if I were them I'd leave lookouts behind...but most of them will be on the beach. They won't want to be too far from their ships."

"Right," Faílbe said. "So, we'd best go on foot from here."

"That'd be best," Bécc agreed. They slid down from their horses and found saplings sturdy enough to tie their reins to, then continued on on foot. The moon was just starting to make an appearance, casting light enough that they were able to move without stumbling much on unseen obstacles.

The road grew more distinct as they approached the monastery where the path had been more traveled. The two men moved with caution, stepping carefully as they drew closer to the earthen wall that surrounded Beggerin. They looked sharp for any bit of light that might indicate a cooking fire or a lantern, but they saw nothing, and nothing came to their ears beyond the raucous sound of the insects in the marshy ground between the monastery and the sea.

Soon they had left the walls of the monastery behind and were moving along the path through the marsh. Bécc had been to Beggerin often enough in his monk's role to know the place well, and the paths leading in various directions, and that knowledge was a great help now.

They had walked for a quarter of a mile or so when Faílbe stopped and put a hand on Bécc's shoulder, and Bécc stopped as well.

"Do you hear that?" Faílbe asked. Bécc turned his head slightly and listened. And he did hear it. Over the sound of the insects. Singing.

"It's the heathens," Bécc said. "They're well on their way to being drunk. That's what they do, the ungodly swine. They get drunk and they sing."

"Good, that's good," Faílbe said. "It's as you said it would be."

Bécc nodded. He knew about such behavior. He had spent enough nights himself drunk and singing in camps and halls all over Ireland. Drinking and singing and gambling and whoring. All part of a past life he had since cast aside.

"Let's go," he said and he and Faílbe continued on, their eyes searching the dark, their ears sharp for any sound that would suggest they were seen.

They were not too far from the monastery when Bécc noticed a loom of light ahead, a soft glow that edged the dark, grass-covered dunes that blocked their view of the beach. *Fires*, he thought as he and Faílbe continued on. *Fires on the beach*. He could picture the scene well, the big piles of driftwood burning bright, the flames rising high above the sands, the heathens clustered around, drinking and singing their pagan songs.

He put a hand on Faílbe's shoulder. "We should get off the path, in case there's someone watching."

Faílbe nodded. If the heathens had any sense at all they would have sentries posted around. And while it seemed clear they did not in fact have any sense, still it was better to act as if they did.

The two men slipped off the path and into the high marsh grass that lined it on either side. Bécc feared that they would soon be up to their thighs in briny water, but they sunk only to ankle depth and no more. They pushed the grass aside as they pressed forward, stopping now and then to listen, to look toward the beach. If a watchman was standing on top of the dune he would be backlit and clearly visible, but there was no one that Bécc could see. They pushed on.

The ground beneath their soaked shoes grew firmer, and soon they could see the edge of the dunes, not fifteen feet ahead. Still they saw no sentries, and Bécc decided that there were none to be seen.

The singing sounded much louder now, and they could hear the crackling of the fire. The heathens on the beach, Bécc knew, would never see or hear anything beyond the edge of the fire pit.

They crouched as they ran the last dozen or so feet and then fell on their stomachs and edged their way up the dune until they were able to look over the crest to the beach below. The scene before them was exactly the one Bécc had expected to see. A hundred or more of the heathens, all sprawled in a great circle around a big fire in the sand. The ale or mead or whatever they had was flowing, the singing was loud. Off closer to the water six or seven men were engaged in a great brawl, but none of the others seemed even to notice. A dozen men at least were flung out on the sand, sleeping or drunk or dead Bécc did not know or care. If they weren't dead they would be soon.

"Not what I'd call the height of vigilance," Faílbe said.

"No," Bécc said. "They think they have no enemies here, no one who dares attack them."

"We'll prove that wrong tonight, I'll warrant."

"Yes," Bécc said, though in truth his plans went well beyond one night's activities.

This was what Bécc had expected, Godless vermin who were ripe for extermination. But it was more than that. Here was an opportunity, a gift from God himself, laid at his feet. A powerful army at his command and hundreds of heathens to be wiped off the shores of a Christian land.

Bécc would not stop with killing the men before him. Thorgrim and his pagans, they too had to be eradicated. It was the will of God, as clear as His call for Bécc to take up the monastic life. It was a call Bécc would not ignore. He would sacrifice everything if he must, but he would smite the heathens who invaded his land, and no one would stop him.

Chapter Eight

The keen-souled thane must be skilled to sever and sunder duly words and works, if he well intends.

Beowulf

It was the day of Merewald's funereal, a day of great mourning, officially, and the bells of Sherborne rang out in their long, baleful tones.

The streets, which were generally crowded with those folk who did the town's meanest labor, the bakers and butchers and merchants and craftsmen, and with rude carts rolling through the mud and animals driven off to their fates, were crowded now with a different sort. The thegns and the wealthier ceorl, who just days before had gathered at the cathedral for Merewald's wedding, now gathered for his funeral mass.

Horses in fine livery, tricked out with gold and silver, ridden by men in shining mail, paraded through the streets, their wives riding beside them, their well-appointed hearth-guards following behind. The bright-colored wedding finery they had worn just days before was replaced now by the black finery of mourning.

The way was kept clear for this parade, and the lower sorts watched with awe from doorways and windows above the streets. It was no rare thing to see men of power and wealth riding through Sherborne—thegns and bishops, reeves and even the king, once a year at least—but to see so many of such men and such wealth on display, even at a time of universal grief, was unusual indeed.

The Lady Cynewise, grieving widow, clothed in black and audibly weeping, was escorted to the cathedral first. She was borne though the streets in an elegant litter, its usual white silks replaced by black. The litter was carried by four somber slaves, also dressed in black.

The people who watched from the buildings lining the roads strained to see her, but were largely unable to do so. The curtains surrounding her litter were half-drawn, and the litter itself and the bearers were surrounded by the ealdorman's hearth-guard, marching on foot, spears over shoulders. The entire procession was led by Oswin, the shire-reeve, riding slowly on horseback, sword drawn and resting on his shoulder.

News of Merewald's murder had spread through the shire—indeed there was little else that was talked about—and it was generally assumed that Cynewise would have been cut down as well if Oswin had not killed the murdering thegn Werheard first. How deep the plot ran no one knew, and so everyone happily indulged in speculation. It was clear, at least, that Oswin did not think Cynewise was out of danger, and he would not put her life at further risk.

All this Nothwulf watched from a good distance away, far enough that he would not be noticed by any of the people streaming toward the cathedral or those watching them. He was on foot for once, with none of his hearth-guard around, and wearing clothing that, for the man soon to be the ealdorman, would be considered simple and unassuming. He was not exactly hiding behind a building, but his watching place was largely shielded by one.

He frowned and shook his head as he watched Oswin and the well-armed escort conveying Cynewise toward the cathedral, as if drawn by the ringing bells. *Oh, please,* he thought. *Such a great show they make, as if there'll be an attempt on the little tart's life…*

Then he reminded himself that his brother had in fact been killed in a most unlikely manner, and Cynewise may well have been next. And no one knew if there was some intrigue that went beyond Werheard, or who might be involved, and what they might intend now.

And likely we'll never know, thanks to that idiot shire-reeve… Nothwulf thought.

With the sound of the bells and the great parade of men and horses, Nothwulf never heard the soft footfalls behind, and to his embarrassment he jumped when he felt a hand laid on his shoulder. He spun around, and Bryning was there, his hand still extended, but he was too good a subordinate to make mention of Nothwulf's jumpiness.

"Yes?" Nothwulf said, sharp and quiet.

"Oswin's taken all the hearth-guard," Bryning said, also speaking low, though in truth he could have shouted and no one would have been the wiser. "Left a servant to guard the door to the rooms, and no one else around that I can see. No one who would matter."

Nothwulf nodded. "Good, good. Now's our moment."

This was ridiculous, of course. He was sneaking into the home in which he was born and raised, the home that would be his once again, once he had set this ealdorman nonsense to rest. But for the moment he had no choice. If he learned one thing from Oswin's killing of Werheard, it was that he must act fast, before the opportunity was lost.

Nothwulf brushed past Bryning and walked quickly through a narrow space between two buildings, coming out onto another road that led at an odd angle to the ealdorman's house. He could hear Bryning following behind as he moved quickly along the rutted, packed dirt road. It was less crowded here—anything of interest was happening in the neighborhood of the cathedral—and Nothwulf was happy to travel unnoticed.

He could not miss his brother's funeral, of course. Doing that would be a scandal, and would invite speculation he did not need. But if he was one of the last to arrive, that would cause no problems. So grief-stricken he could hardly summon the strength, so weighted down with consideration he could barely tear himself away for the shire's business, any of those were decent and viable excuses.

But he did not have much time. A quarter of an hour and then he needed to join his hearth-guard waiting a quarter mile from the cathedral. From there, with Nothwulf at their head, they would make their approach in grand style.

The big gate in the wall surrounding the ealdorman's house was still open and Nothwulf and Bryning marched through, faces set, eyes up, like men who were there on official, sanctioned and vital business. There were a few servants around, busy at the household chores. They looked up as the men entered, but none of them dared question Nothwulf's presence, or even speak to him as he and Bryning hurried across the courtyard.

For all his determination and sense that he had a right and a duty to do what he was set to do, Nothwulf's face still burned with humiliation. He was the ealdorman, for the love of God, or would be within a day, and yet he felt compelled to sneak around his own home like some thief or cutpurse. It was intolerable. And he thought, not for the first time, that those responsible would pay.

He and Bryning moved around the far end of the long hall to where the lesser rooms in the back, those kept for the servants of visiting dignitaries, opened onto the garbage-strewn space behind. There was a single servant standing there, bored and slumped. He held a spear in his hand, the weapon looking foreign and unfamiliar to him. He looked up sharp when the two men came around the corner. With all of the hearth-guard escorting Cynewise to the cathedral, this sorry creature was the best they could muster for guard duty.

On seeing the men, the servant began to lower the spear, then thought better of it and raised it again. "Beg pardon, lord, but I have instructions from…" he began, stammering the words.

Bryning stepped quickly around Nothwulf's side and in two quick strides came up to the ersatz guard and slapped him hard on the side of the head. The servant yowled, dropped the spear and grabbed his ear, crouching to ward off another blow.

"How dare you, you miserable villain," Bryning hissed. "This is the ealdorman, and you dare speak to him?"

The servant shook his head, made a whimpering noise and tried to stumble away, but Bryning grabbed him by the collar of his tunic and jerked him back. "You don't tell anyone we were here, do you understand?" he demanded.

Again the servant made a whimpering noise as he nodded, but Bryning only shook him, hard, and pulled him closer until their faces were just a few inches apart. "I asked you if you understood," Bryning growled.

"Yes, lord, yes, I do," the servant said and Bryning shoved him and sent him staggering from the door. He backed away, two paces, four paces, clearly unsure if he should abandon his post entirely, but Nothwulf had no more time to spare for him. He grabbed the iron latch that held the door closed, lifted it, swung the door in and stepped into the dim-lit room.

The furnishings were something less than sparse: a small table with a jug and pitcher, a wooden plate with a half a loaf of bread. Crude beds with straw-filled mattresses were shoved up against two of the walls. That was it.

Three people sat on the bed furthest from the door: a woman and two children, a boy and a girl, somewhere between five and ten. Nothwulf was never very good about guessing children's ages, mostly because he didn't care. He was not looking at the children, however, but the woman who hugged them in a protective way and glared back at Nothwulf as he stepped into the room.

Roswitha, the wife of the late Werheard, the man who had killed ealdorman Merewald for some as yet unknown reason. Nothwulf had been trying to speak to her for days now, since he had heard of her arrest. He had not been rebuffed, exactly, but there seemed always to be some reason or other that she was not available to him. She was meeting with her confessor, one of the children was ill, she had had a fainting spell and was not lucid, the excuses came in a great profusion until Nothwulf could see they simply did not wish for him to speak with Roswitha.

He had gone to Cynewise, practically burst into her chambers to demand an explanation. His brother's widow had, as usual, been speaking with two of the more powerful thegns from Dorset's south coast. Nothwulf had sent them away. Cynewise looked afraid. As well she might. Nothwulf was running out of patience.

"Why am I not allowed to speak to Roswitha?" he demanded.

"Who?"

"Roswitha. The widow of the man who killed my brother. She's being held prisoner here."

"Oh…" Cynewise nodded absently. "Yes, yes. Oswin had her brought here. He is still trying to discover what plot there might have been. Against my husband."

My husband… Nothwulf thought. The words sounded more ironic every time Cynewise said them. *My husband…* They had been married for less time than it took him to hump Aelfwyn.

"Yes, your husband," Nothwulf said. His strained patience was near snapping.

"Oh, I don't know what that is all about," Cynewise said, giving a weak wave of her hand, a gesture she did quite often. "Oswin is seeing to her, and he says she's often ill, and the children, too. I can well imagine. I leave it to Oswin. In this time of grief I can't even think about that."

And that was it. Her answer was really no answer at all, and the whole thing was handed back to the shire reeve. Who would not allow Nothwulf to see Roswitha. Nothwulf had thought at first to march down to the rooms and demand the guard step aside. And if he did not? It would be humiliating. He thought of calling out his own hearth-guard and marching them to the ealdorman's house. And he dismissed the idea. He was not ready for such a war.

So instead he chose the most effective, if most humiliating means. He waited until the others were gone and there was no one but a servant to challenge him.

Nothwulf took another step into the room and saw Roswitha draw back and pull the children tighter. Her eyes were on his, and various emotions played on her expression. Nothwulf could see the anger there, and the fear and defiance and confusion.

She did not look good. Her gown was dirty and torn, the hem ragged and mud-stained. There were bruises on her face and arms, some no doubt left by Bryning, some by Oswin and who knew what other inquisitors there had been. Her hair was a great unruly mess.

But her spirit was not broken, not yet, and she stared back at Nothwulf as if daring him to do worse to her than had already been done. He guessed she would still wear that expression when her head was placed on the executioner's block.

"So, you've come," Roswitha said, her voice like the hiss of a cat. "What do you want?"

Nothwulf was startled by the words. He had imagined she would be shocked to see him there, but she spoke as if she was expecting him, as if he was some player in this drama, some part of the grand story.

"You know what I want," Nothwulf said. "I want to know why your husband murdered my brother."

"Ha!" Roswitha said. "*You* want to know? *You* of all people?"

Nothwulf's eyebrows came together. "Yes, me of all people. Merewald was my brother."

"Of course he was," Roswitha said. She took her arms off the children's shoulders, stood, and took a step toward Nothwulf. "And he was the ealdorman. But we've never heard of such a thing as a man conspiring against his brother to gain his place."

Nothwulf cocked his head as he looked at her. He thought he understood the direction this was taking, and he did not care for it. "Conspiring? How do you think I was conspiring?"

"I need not tell you," Roswitha said. "There's nothing about this business you don't know."

"Very well, then," Nothwulf said. "Let's pretend I know nothing of it, and you tell me."

Roswitha glared at him, and it was hatred that he saw now. She crossed her arms and her mouth remained shut and she assumed an attitude of stubborn refusal. Nothwulf knew better than to make a threat against her. Instead, he shifted his gaze, moved his eyes and his head just a bit so that he was looking past Roswitha, looking at the girl sitting on the bed. He let his eyes linger on her for just a moment. Then he looked back at Roswitha.

She had not missed the glance or the threat it implied. "Very well," she said. "My husband was a fool, and he was played for one, and he was played by you."

You are right about the one thing, Nothwulf thought. Werheard was a fool and it was well known. But he was getting the sense that Roswitha was not, that she was far brighter than her husband ever was.

"You were the one who talked him into this great plot and filled his head with notions of the thegns rising up against Merewald, and the favors to be shown them by the new ealdorman," she said.

"How do you know this?" Nothwulf asked. "Did Werheard tell you this?"

"He said it was a great secret, that I was not to know. But I pulled it from him, bit by bit. Usually I could talk him out of any stupid notion he got, but not this time. He was certain this was a plot in which all the nobles of the shire were involved."

"Did he say he met with me directly?" Nothwulf asked.

"No," Roswitha said. "Or at least, he didn't say. He went off to meet with whoever he was meeting with, someplace far from our home." She stopped and thought for a minute. "No," she said at last, "I suppose it was not you with whom he met."

This seemed an abrupt shift, so Nothwulf asked, "Why don't you think it was me?"

"Because whoever it was, he gave him your ring. To prove it was you who was behind all this, that it truly had your blessing. A gold ring, with a red stone, and a device of a hart and a boar. He showed it to me. I knew right off it was yours. He wouldn't have needed such a token if he was talking to you."

Nothwulf turned his head a bit and stared off into the dark corner of the room, seeing nothing, his mind pulling Roswitha's words apart. The room was silent, the only sound the far-off tolling of the bells. Then Nothwulf turned back to Roswitha.

"What…was supposed to happen?" he asked. "What was the plot?"

Roswitha looked at him, more curious than angry now, as if she was wondering how he could be so great a fool. He was beginning to wonder that himself.

"All of the thegns were to rise up against Merewald," she said. "That was why it was to happen at the wedding, when all the thegns would be there, and no one of them could claim innocence. My husband would strike Merewald down just as the ceremony ended, and the rest would step up and join him. You would be ealdorman and then you would see the others well rewarded for their loyalty."

Once again Nothwulf stared off into the corner of the room and let the words roll around in his head. It made sense, sure. It was the only way Werheard might have thought he could get away with such a crime, if all the rest were part of it as well. So, someone wanted him to be ealdorman, and laid out this plot in secret. Someone who could get their hands on the ring that he kept in a small casket in his bedchamber.

A thought came to him. He turned quick and looked at Bryning, thinking if he were the guilty one he might read the guilt on his face. Bryning looked back at him, his eyes wide with surprise, but there was no shade of guilt there.

"Lord?" he asked.

"Did she tell you any of this, when you spoke to her?" Nothwulf demanded, changing direction.

"No, lord," Bryning stammered. "Not a word of it."

"He tells the truth," Roswitha said. "I told no one. Not at first. I thought…I prayed…my husband had not been played for a fool, that I might be rewarded, or at least spared, for what he'd done."

"At first?"

Roswitha frowned and once again the defiance was there. "They beat me, your bastard Bryning there, and Oswin's men, and I said nothing. They brought me here, and then I could see there was no advantage to keeping quiet. You were not going to help me, though my husband died for your intrigues. So I told Oswin everything,

everything I just said to you. Because now my only hope is that I can take you down to eternal damnation with me."

Nothwulf stared at her. At best, he knew, all of Werheard's lands and chattel would be taken as punishment and Roswitha and her children left as beggars. At worst the justices would decide she was part of the plot as well. Then she would die on the block and her children sold as slaves. Nothwulf understood why she felt no need to keep her mouth shut.

It was silent in the room, so quiet Nothwulf could hear the soft sound of Roswitha's breath.

"Lord?" Bryning said, soft. "Lord, the bells have stopped."

He was right. The bells had stopped. The funeral had begun and now Nothwulf would be late and that would certainly set people talking.

"Very well, let's go," Nothwulf said. He turned and pushed past Bryning. He had learned one thing, at least. He had learned that he knew all but nothing about the true nature of this bloody murder.

Chapter Nine

An encampment of the Laigin was overwhelmed by the heathens,
and Conall…and countless others fell there.

Annals of Ulster

Bécc and Faílbe pushed themselves up to a standing position and made their way back toward the monastery at Beggerin. They did not bother hiding themselves in the reeds as they walked. They had seen the heathens' utter lack of vigilance and they were no longer worried that they might be discovered.

They found their horses where they had left them tied, and they mounted and rode back to where the men-at-arms were waiting. Some were eating, some praying, but most were lying down on the cool grass. That was good. Bécc wanted the men rested, fresh. The heathens might be half-drunk, but it never did any good to count on an enemy's weakness. And for heathens, drunkenness might not be a weakness at all; it might well be a benefit.

A few of the captains who knew better than to be caught napping saw the riders approach, and with grunts and somewhat gentle kicks they induced the others to stand and to take up their weapons. Bécc and Faílbe reined to a stop at the head of the rough assembly. Bécc was, of course, Faílbe's inferior in almost every way, but not in matters of warfare, a fact they mutually understood. Bécc did not hesitate or ask Faílbe's leave before assuming command.

"The heathens are on the beach, about a mile from here. They are drunk and they have fires burning so they will be hard pressed just to see their limp members when they take a piss."

That got a chuckle, and Bécc knew it would. He paused, then went on. "We'll march there now. Near the beach we'll divide our men. Faílbe will lead his men and those who serve under Colcu and

Guaire. The rest will be with me. Faílbe will take his men to the east, I will move to the west. I'll strike first, and when you hear me and my men fighting, then you will come up from the other side. Understood?"

He looked out over the men. In the weak light of the moon he could see those closest nodding. They were men-at-arms and they would see right off what he intended, and even if they did not, the captains and Faílbe would.

"Father Niall," Bécc called, waving for the priest who had accompanied them to step forward. "A prayer, please, to ask God for success in our Holy fight." Bécc would have preferred a mass to a simple prayer, but he could feel time slipping away.

Father Niall came forward and stood beside Bécc's horse. He made the sign of the cross and said, "*In nomine Patris et Filii et Spiritus Sancti.*" With a soft jingling sound, two hundred mail-clad arms made the sign of the cross as well in near unison as Father Niall began his prayer. It was thoughtful, reverent, and brief.

There were many reasons why Bécc liked the young priest and took him along when he was campaigning. Niall was clever, he was brave, and he did not complain. When they were away from the abbey, Father Niall would celebrate mass and pray the daily office, in which Bécc would reverently participate. Bécc did not shirk his duty to God any more than he would shirk combat. But sometimes things had to be hurried along. And Father Niall understood that.

The prayer came to an end and once again the two hundred mail-clad arms made the sign of the cross, and that was followed by a more pronounced bustle as the men-at-arms picked up their spears and shields and whatever else they had set aside. They shuffled into loose groups according to their leaders, and once they had done so Bécc wheeled his horse and headed back the way he had just come. Behind him he heard the sound of the men, his men, his army, following along.

It took longer to cover the distance with all the men than it had with just Bécc and Faílbe alone, but Bécc expected that and he didn't mind. *More chance for the heathens to drink themselves insensible,* he thought. He looked forward to the coming fight, the slaughter of those who defiled God's house. His men and Faílbe's would crush them as they surged up from both directions.

Take care, take care, mind your pride and hubris, he thought, and a flush of panic came over him. God did not care for prideful men who felt they deserved victory, even if it was a victory over heathens who worshiped false gods. He crossed himself again and he prayed until the monastery at Beggerin rose out of the gloom and it was time for him to dismount.

He and Faílbe, who was riding beside him, stopped at the same sapling they had used before and once again made their horses fast, and the few other men who were mounted did the same. Bécc and Faílbe continued on, skirting the monastery once more and heading out into the open, marshy ground. He stopped and Faílbe stopped and all the men behind them did as well.

"I think you should take your men east from here, Lord," Bécc said, pointing in that direction. He spoke softly, despite being all but certain the drunken Northmen would not hear him if he shouted, or care if they did.

Faílbe nodded. "Very good, Brother. I'll get my men in place and we'll listen for the sound of you launching your attack. But please, leave some of the heathens for us, will you?"

Bécc gave a half smile and nodded, but Faílbe's hubris made him as uncomfortable as his own. He remained where he was, his warriors in a bunch behind him, as Faílbe led his men down the path and then off to the east. Once Faílbe was well beyond the reach of the firelight he would bring his men to the edge of the dunes and wait, and when he judged the moment right, he and his men would come screaming into the fight, coming in behind the Northmen who would already be engaged with Bécc's men.

At least, that was the plan. Bécc did not see anything that might make it go awry, but he had seen enough careful plans collapse that he was not excessively optimistic now.

"All right, you men, follow me," Bécc growled. "And keep quiet."

He headed off in the same direction that Faílbe and the others had gone, but rather than swinging to the east, he would go west until he and his men were also beyond the light of the fires. And those fires, he could see, were still burning, the edge of the distant dunes illuminated by the flames and a glow of light beyond that.

Like the gates of hell, Bécc thought. His eyes moved along the edge of the dunes as he walked, but there was no one, and the sounds of singing and shouting had died down considerably since he and Faílbe had made their visit earlier.

His eyes still on the edge of the dunes, his ears sharp for any sound of alarm, Bécc was about to lead his men off the path and off to the west when his toe caught something on the ground, something large but not solid, not entirely. He gave a grunt as he pitched forward, arms out, with no way to prevent his falling. He thought vaguely as he went down that it was a humiliating accident, to trip and fall while leading his men.

His hands hit the soft earth and broke his fall, and he rolled onto his shoulder as his body came down, his legs sprawled over whatever it was that had tripped him. And then he felt whatever it was move, and he had a vague thought that he had tripped over some animal asleep on the trail. He heard soft grunting noises from his men as those at the head of the column came to a halt and those behind collided with them.

Bécc rolled over and looked back at what he had tripped over, and in the dim light of the moon, and to his utter surprise, he saw a face staring back, an ugly face, covered with hair, a long beard with what looked like braids, wild eyes gleaming. He was dressed like a Northman.

Bécc opened his mouth to speak, but his surprise was such that no words came out, not right off, and before they did, the Northman scrambled to his feet. And then Bécc understood the danger. He rolled on his back and reached for his sword and called to his men, "Kill him! Kill him! Don't let him get away!"

But the men, as surprised as Bécc, were frozen in place. The Northman was up and Bécc pulled his sword and slashed at the man's legs but found only air. The heathen was running now, running for the beach, and just as Bécc had feared, he was shouting in his ugly heathen tongue.

"Damn! Damn it!" Bécc shouted, words he had not used since he had abandoned the life of a soldier. He leapt to his feet and jerked the spear from the hand of the startled man beside him, spun around and hurled the weapon at the back of the fleeing heathen. He saw the shaft disappear into the dark, but there was no pause in the heathen's shouting, loud and hysterical, and Bécc knew that he had missed, and with the fleeing Northman went their entire plan of attack.

Bécc could not understand the words the man was shouting, but he didn't have to. They could be nothing but an alarm, a call to arms, a warning that a powerful enemy was approaching in the dark.

He doesn't know about Faílbe, Bécc thought. There was still one surprise left.

"Follow me!" Bécc shouted and he turned to his right and began to race through the waist-high reeds, his feet sinking into the marshy ground. The heathens would expect the attackers to be right on the heels of the man they had startled and would be ready for an attack on that quarter. But if he could still bring his men to the west as planned, he might be able to hit them on an exposed flank. There was not much time. The longer he waited, the more sober and organized the heathens would be.

He pushed on. The reeds whipped across his face and the cold water seeped into his shoes, but he did not slow in his race for the dunes, that rampart that God himself had set up between the beach and the marsh. The grass began to thin as he reached the edge of the marsh and the land began to rise slightly. To his left he could see the loom of the fires, the strange glow illuminating the mounds of sand and vegetation.

At the edge of the dune he stopped and held a hand up for the men behind him to stop as well. Better to catch their breath and form up for an organized assault than to rush into the fight like some rioting mob, even if they did lose a small amount of time.

He could hear shouting on the beach, voices calling out in the heathens' tongue, layers of voices as the men there, who, just a moment before thought they had no earthly worries that night, found themselves on the precipice of battle.

"Fland, Imchad, up here!" Bécc shouted and the two captains leading the men under him came jogging over. "Fland, take your men down toward the edge of the water, form them in a line. Imchad, you'll set your men up in a line starting at the dune. See the lines link up. We'll sweep along the beach and shift when we see how the heathens are making ready."

"Yes, Brother Bécc," Fland said, and Imchad nodded. They turned to issue orders, then turned back as a new sound met their ears. The shouting on the beach had risen in volume, risen in pitch, and now the cries of the men there, still unseen behind the dune, were punctuated by the telltale ring of steel on steel. There was more shouting now, and Bécc was certain some of the words were Irish.

"Damnation!" he shouted in his fury. Faílbe must have heard the sound of the heathens preparing for the fight and thought that Bécc was already engaged. He had launched his attack before Bécc's men were even ready to go. Bécc could feel the entire fight slipping away from him. He felt sick and angry and frightened.

Please, God, please guide my hand…

He turned to his right. "Fland, Imchad, hurry! Get the men in line! Go!"

The two captains were already shouting orders, pointing toward the beach, shoving men in place. They, too, had guessed what had happened, or so Bécc imagined. The men-at-arms began to race over the edge of the dune and disappeared from sight as they reached the beach beyond, and Bécc hoped they were forming a line, as instructed, and not just rushing toward the sound of the fighting.

He took a few steps forward and climbed up onto the dune, the highest spot around, the clearest view of what was going on. He could see his own men were indeed making ready, forming a loose shield wall. Good. Nothing could destroy an army faster than a blind rush at an organized enemy.

He looked to the east. There were five big bonfires making a sort of half-circle on the beach. They were still burning well, the flames reaching ten feet or more up into the air. They made it hard to see in that direction, the beach all light and shadow, but in that strange illumination Bécc could see the heathens and Faílbe's men already engaged in a furious fight, knots of struggling men, swords rising up to catch the light of the flames, firelight glinting off of helmets.

Bécc pressed his lips together and tried not to give vent to his anger and frustration. The bastard heathen he had tripped over, probably insensible with drink, had given sufficient alarm for the others to snatch up their swords and shields, to grab spears and axes and get into some kind of order. The warning had come just moments before Faílbe's attack, but it had been enough. Their surprise, their precious surprise, was gone.

No, no… Bécc thought. *The surprise is not all gone. They don't know I'm here.*

He stepped off the front of the dune, half climbed and half slid to the beach below. He strode along the line of men that Fland and Imchad were forming up. He swung his shield off his back and positioned it on his left arm, pulled his sword with his right and raised it over his head.

Good enough, he thought. The men-at-arms were not positioned as he would have most liked, but it would have to do. The time for preparation was over. It was time for killing now.

Chapter Ten

Lugbad was plundered by the heathens…
and they led away captive bishops and priests and scholars,
and put others to death.

The Annals of Ulster

"You men!" Bécc shouted, his voice loud and carrying easily over the crackling of the flames, the sound of the fighting. "In the name of God Almighty let us drive this filth from Ireland!"

The men cheered. They shouted and cheered and cursed the heathens and then they began to move. They stepped off in a line, with Bécc at the center and ten feet ahead of the nearest man. Their speed began to build and their shouting grew louder, because these men knew enough about battle to know that the shouting would confuse the enemy, and frighten him, and that would give them the upper hand even before they were within their weapons' reach.

Bécc blinked his one intact eye and turned his head slightly away from the brilliant flames of the nearest fire. The heathens, as far as he could see, were all on the far side of the bonfires, but it was hard to see past the light. Scattered across the sand he could see the dark forms of fallen men, but he could not tell if they were Norse or Faílbe's men. Both, no doubt.

He moved faster, not running, but a quick walk, closing the distance with long strides. He could see his line of men running nearly from the dunes to the water on their right. They would have been able to hit the heathens in a single line, an unbroken shield wall, if the bonfires had not been in the way. But still they would take the heathens of the flank and drive them back.

Twenty feet from the nearest fire Bécc could feel the heat of the flames on his face. His one eye was tearing up from the brilliant light, and men were slashing and hacking and shouting at one another, moving in and out of the light of the fires. He moved faster and let his battle cry build in his gut and he opened his mouth wide and shouted as he plunged into the fight.

The nearest bonfire was no more than a dozen feet away, the heat almost unbearable, and with the flames and the screaming and the heat it seemed like a preview of hell. One of the heathens came charging out of the light, a battle ax held overhead with both hands, his eyes wild, reflecting the firelight and fixed on Bécc.

Bécc paused, waited for the man to come, his sword and shield held loose at his sides and low, his head and chest open for the strike. The heathen, still shrieking his cry of the damned, hacked down with the ax, and as he did, Bécc lifted his shield and swung it to the left, knocking the ax aside, and using the momentum of the swinging shield to half turn and drive his sword into the heathen's side.

The scream turned from fury to agony and the heathen stopped in his tracks and his mouth fell open and his eyes rolled wide. *Off to hell with you*, Bécc thought as he pulled the sword free, and a great rush of memories came back at him. How many times had he thrust his sword through the side of an enemy, felt the resistance, and then the smooth entry as the point tore through flesh, deflected off bone?

Many times, but not once since he had taken his vows. Sure, he had donned mail and carried weapons in the service of the abbot and monastery at Ferns. But never had he been locked in a real fight like this one. He remembered it now, the rush of energy, the way time and motion seemed to slow down, the pure mechanics of killing a worthy opponent. An enemy who needed killing. He remembered it, and he remembered why he liked it.

Another of the bastard Northmen to his left, and one charging at him on his right. The one on the left had an ax, the one on the right a spear, which was the greater threat, so Bécc turned toward that one and ducked low, shield over his head as if he were warding off rain. He swung the sword in an arc and felt it bite the man's shins and saw him stumble. Bécc straightened and leapt clear as the man came down right where Bécc had been crouching, right in the path of the other man.

The man with the ax stumbled on the fallen spearman, and his arms went out wide to catch himself and Bécc thought, *Praise be to*

*God…*as he drove the sword through the man's neck. He saw the blood, bright in the firelight, as he pulled the blade free again.

But there was something wrong, something amiss. In the rush of the fight, his attention on the heathens before him, he had missed it, but now he could hear it in the sound of the voices, the movement of men.

Oh, damn you, you stupid bastard! Bécc silently chastised himself. He should have been looking to what his men were doing, not taking his own pleasure in the fight. And now he could see the heathens were pushing his men back, the line that Fland had led down to the water's edge, the line that should have been enveloping the heathens, seemed to be collapsing, pushed back by the Northmen. Or so it seemed. It was all confusion on the beach, the madness of a night attack, and Bécc could not tell for certain.

"Stand fast! Stand fast!" he shouted, but he did not think his voice would carry over the sounds of the fighting, nor was anyone listening to him. He started to run toward the water, toward where he saw the men being thrown back by the heathens. It was a frantic melee on the edge of the firelight and it was hard to see what exactly was happening. Men staggering away from the fight, men on knees or tossed down in the sand. Whatever it was, his people seemed to be getting the worst of it.

"Stand fast!" Bécc shouted again, swinging his shield at one who was racing at him, knocking the man off balance. He lifted his sword, saw one of his own men backing away and he hit him hard on the shoulders with the flat of the blade.

"Get back and fight, you damned coward!" Bécc shouted, but the man seemed not to notice as he took another step back, then turned and ran up the beach. Bécc looked around for Fland, but the captain was nowhere to be seen. Dead or run away. Dead, most likely. And more and more of his men, leaderless, were backing away from the wild, screaming Northmen before them.

"Oh, damn you all!" Bécc shouted. He could see the men were ready to break, ready to turn and run. "Stand…" he began again, but it was too late. One after another the men-at-arms turned and fled up the beach, overwhelmed by the drink-maddened heathens, and there was nothing that Bécc could do but stand and die or follow them.

He chose to follow them. He gave it no thought, just turned and ran himself. There was no fear in his heart, just a desire to keep on killing heathens, and he could not do that if he was dead. He had no qualms about sacrificing his life for the defense of Christ and Ireland, but this was not the moment.

They ran past the fires, ran toward the wall of dunes that rose up ahead, reflecting the orange light of the fires. Bécc was sure the men would scramble up the dunes and into the marsh and he did not know how he would rally them again once they did. Nor did he know if they would get that far. With their backs to the heathens, slowed down by the sandy slope of the dunes, they might all be struck down before they made it over.

But the men were not climbing the dunes, not rushing away like rats from a burning barn. They were stopping, turning, weapons ready. Then Bécc heard a voice, a single voice calling orders and he saw men grabbing those who were running and physically stopping them, turning them toward the flames and the heathens on the far side.

It was Faílbe. Bécc could see him, in his bright mail and shining helmet, sword over his head, shouting and pushing the men and making them turn and form a line with the dunes to their backs. Faílbe's captains were there as well, helping form the defense, and as Bécc's men reached the line they turned them as well, extending the shield wall right and left.

Bécc stopped and bent half over and gasped for breath. He was not a young man anymore, and the life of a monk was no preparation for this sort of work, nor was running in the sand an easy thing. He could feel the sweat running down his face and under the padded tunic he wore under his mail. His palm was slick where he held his sword.

He straightened again and jogged the last few yards to where Faílbe stood. He expected the heathens to hit them again, to follow up on their unimaginable victory, and wondered why they had not. He reached Faílbe's side and turned to look down the beach.

The heathens were barely visible down by the water, far back from the fires that were burning high. He could just make them out, the light glancing off their shields, vague forms in the darkness by the water. They were not moving. Bécc sucked in another lung-full of air.

"Where were you?" Faílbe asked. There was an unambiguous note of anger in his voice.

"One of the bastards saw us and raised the alarm," Bécc said. Humility, obedience, those were all part of his vows and he was trying mightily to keep them now. "You heard the heathens getting ready, thought it was us attacking. You came at them too soon."

Faílbe was frowning, but he said nothing. It was a bad situation, mistakes all around. "The heathens, do you think they're making ready to attack?" Faílbe asked.

Bécc turned and looked down the beach toward the water. The half-circle of bonfires were like a defensive ring: it was hard to see past them, and they would once more prevent the Irish from attacking with an unbroken shield wall. And Bécc wondered for the first time if perhaps that was not an accident.

"No," Bécc said. It was hard to see, but the heathens did not seem to be making ready for an attack. They seemed to be collecting themselves, gathering together by the water's edge. He could see a knot of men who seemed to be conferring with one another, the leaders, no doubt, discussing what they would do next. Not that they had much choice.

"They're off balance now," Bécc said. "Now is the time we attack. Let's move down the beach quickly, fall on them while they're in confusion."

Faílbe shook his head. "We're in confusion, too," he said, pointing at the men-at-arms clustered near the dunes. Some were standing, some sitting, some attending to the wounded or dressing their own wounds. Some were carrying the dead clear of the battlefield. Their shields were laid in the sand, swords in scabbards.

"These men, our men, are ready to fight," Bécc said. "They're trained warriors. If I tell them to attack, they'll attack, and they'll kill anyone before them."

"No," Faílbe said. "The heathens are organizing, we will, too." He turned to the men behind them. "You men fought well, but our work is not done. Go to your captains now. Get ready. We must be ready when the heathens attack again."

Slowly the men sorted themselves out, and every moment that passed only added to Bécc's impatience and outrage. An enemy no more than two hundred feet away and Faílbe was dithering in this bizarre standoff. It was driving Bécc to madness.

At last the men-at-arms had sorted themselves out, mostly, standing in knots of men with the captains who commanded them.

Bécc looked past the fires, down to where the heathens stood. They might have been in a disorganized mob before, but they were no longer.

"Shield wall," Bécc said. "They're getting into a shield wall." He hoped he was seeing right. He had only one eye remaining, and the sight in that eye was nothing great.

"Yes," Faílbe said. "They seem to be. And they seem to be waiting for us to come to them."

"Then let us go to them," Bécc said. "We'll form the men into two shield walls, one behind the other. We can push them down to the water, and there we'll kill them. Or drown them. Either is fine."

Suddenly a shout went up from the heathen ranks, a loud, wild sound, voices rising and undulating, and with them the din of swords beating on shields. The whole line began to advance, moving as one up the gently sloping beach, the shields and weapons and bearded faces growing more distinct as they approached the flames.

"Form a shield wall! Form up!" Bécc shouted. "The men with me in the front ranks, Lord Faílbe's men behind! Two ranks! Quickly!" For all Faílbe's efforts, the Irishmen were still in disarray from their ugly retreat and the confusion of the fight, and the heathens would tear them apart if they overran them like that.

The men-at-arms moved fast. They knew what they had to do and they understood the threat and they did not hesitate to form their ranks, Bécc's men in the forward rank, Faílbe's behind them. Their shields clattered as they came together in overlapping order. Bécc and Faílbe stepped in front of the double line and looked down the beach. The heathens were still advancing. And then they stopped.

"What the devil?" Faílbe muttered. Ten feet from the half circle of bonfires the heathen line stopped, shields overlapping, weapons held high. The shouting continued, loud and manic as ever.

"They want us to attack them where they stand," Bécc said. "We'll have to break our lines to get around the fires, and that's what they want. They want our shield wall to come apart, and then they'll attack."

Faílbe nodded. "So what do we do?"

"We attack, Lord Faílbe," Bécc said. "We advance and we butcher them all."

Faílbe frowned. He pulled his gaze from the Northmen and regarded Bécc. "Attack? You just said that was what they want us to do."

"Yes, and we will. We're stronger than them. We outnumber them. And God looks with favor on us."

"I'm not so sure that's a wise idea," Faílbe said. "I think we had better fall back, take up defense at the monastery. In the daylight, when they don't have the advantage of the fires, then we can attack again."

"If we retreat now they'll take to their ships and escape," Bécc argued.

"What of it?" Faílbe said. "We came here to drive the heathens away. If they sail off then we've accomplished that, with no more men's lives wasted."

"No. We don't just want the heathens gone from here!" Bécc said, controlling his voice with some effort. "We want them dead. We want them wiped from the earth. Lord."

"Brother Bécc, I insist—" Faílbe began and got no further.

Bécc raised his sword and shouted, "Shield wall! Advance! Forward! Kill them all!"

"Damn your impertinence!" Faílbe shouted. "I said we will…" But he was too late. That much was clear. The Irish men-at-arms had already begun to advance, and like the heathens they were shouting and banging swords on shields. Their blood was up. The heathens had beaten them once, had killed their fellow warriors, and now they were ready to strike back.

"Go! Go! Kill them all!" Bécc shouted, sword held above his head. He advanced toward the flames. He saw Faílbe hesitate for just a heartbeat before moving forward as well. The man was cautious, but he was no coward. But Bécc was quite done with caution.

The men-at-arms were matching the heathens shout for shout as they advanced on the half circle of fire pits, thirty feet between each. Bécc could see the Northmen clearly now, their mouths open and shouting, the firelight dancing off the faces of their shields. Hard men, but so were the warriors under his command.

He looked left and right. The captains, each with their division of men, were bringing them forward through the gaps between the bonfires, keeping them in as good order as they could. And as they came past the ring of flames, the heathens attacked.

It was like a monumental crosscurrent, wave smashing on wave as the Irishmen and heathens came together. A great clashing of shield on shield, furious shouts and weapons rising and falling. Bécc found himself pressed up against the heathens' shield wall, pushing with his own shield, pushed from behind by his men. He braced his legs in that familiar way and pushed and worked his sword back and forth, jabbing where he could through the gaps in the enemy's shields.

He felt something hit the blade of his sword and he jerked it back, then thrust it forward and felt the tip rip into something, and with that sensation came a scream and whatever his sword had hit fell away. Bécc felt the heathens' shield wall give, just a bit, and he thrust again.

He did not know what was going on along the line of struggling men. His sight, and his attention, was entirely on the few feet of sand he was defending, the three or four men directly in front of him, the Irish men-at-arms on either side. He thrust again and found nothing, drew back and thrust again.

The heathens seemed to fall back, just a step, but Bécc had stood in enough shield walls to know that was a good sign. One step, then another, and soon the enemy's formation would collapse and they would be running. He lifted his voice in a great roar and pushed harder with his shield and lashed out with his sword.

And then it happened, just as he knew it would. The heathens took a step back, quicker now, and then another, and then as if on some signal they turned and ran, fleeing down toward the edge of the water, running in confusion, and confusion would mean death.

Bécc took half a dozen steps forward, turned and faced his men. "Stand fast! Stand fast!" he shouted. If the Irishmen started chasing after the heathens then they too would fall into disorder and all their advantage would be lost.

"Hold your shield wall! Follow me!" Bécc shouted. He turned and began to walk after the fleeing enemy, a quick pace, the rest of the men at his back. There was triumph in the Irishmen's shouting now, the sense that they were going to stamp the vermin out.

The heathens had reached the water's edge. Bécc could just see them in the light of the bonfires at his back, the orange light reaching down to where the sea lapped over the edge of the sand. The

Northmen were up to their ankles, mostly, turned and facing the bloody death that was marching toward them.

"Ready!" Bécc shouted. And then to his utter shock a creature appeared out of the dark, a great arching sea beast, resolving from the black night like it was emerging from the salt water. The orange light of the fires played over its features, its horrible leering snout and arched neck and wicked teeth.

Bécc gasped and stopped and realized in that moment that it was no creature from the sea. It was a ship, a Northman's ship, its carved figurehead leading the way as it raced toward the beach. And then the bow and the rows of oars were visible too as the ship struck the sand and drove ten feet up the beach before it came to a shuddering stop. Behind it, a second ship came looming out of the night.

There was more shouting now, shouting coming from beyond the hideous figurehead, the crew of the longship cheering as they flung themselves over the ship's side to land knee deep in the water.

"Oh, damn these heathen swine!" Bécc roared in fury and frustration. "Where by God did they come from?"

And then in the light of the flames at his back he saw Thorgrim Night Wolf vaulting over the ship's side.

Chapter Eleven

Let a man never stir on his road a step
without his weapons of war;
for unsure is the knowing when need shall arise
of a spear on the way without.

Wisdom for Wanderers and
Counsel to Guests

From the longphort at Loch Garman, the five bonfires on the distant beach appeared as sharp points of light on the dark night, like a tiny earthbound constellation of brilliant stars. They had burned there every night for the five nights that Ketil Hrolfsson and his men had been on the beach. What that sorry gang was doing, what they intended, the gods alone knew.

Thorgrim stood at a distance from the single fire that was burning at his own camp and looked out over the nearly two miles of water toward Ketil's. The air was still, and every once in a while he could catch snatches of singing, or men shouting for some reason or another. This, too, had been a nightly occurrence.

Like any Northmen, in particular those who went a'viking, Thorgrim's men enjoyed a good drunken revel, and did so more often than Thorgrim might have liked. But they had their work as well: ships to repair, sails to make, defenses to fortify, weapons to be cared for. Thorgrim drove them hard, he did not give them the opportunity to sit and ponder any grievances they might harbor. By day's end they were tired. Their revels ended when they collapsed in sleep, which was generally not long, with the anticipation of doing it all again the following day.

Not so Ketil's men, apparently. Every night they lit the fires and the sounds of their carousing drifted over the water.

"What are you staring at so longingly, Night Wolf?" Starri asked, materializing like a ghost out of the dark.

"Ketil. Ketil and his men. I'm wondering when they will run dry of ale and mead."

"They must have had a lot with them," Starri said. "Ale and not much else. They hardly seemed to have one whole suit of clothing between them. But they've been drinking nonstop, it seems."

"I doubt they had ale with them," Thorgrim said. "Probably got it from the monastery. They were too dim-witted to know that the monastery was there, but I guess they looted it well once they found out. The Christ priests would have taken any silver or gold or those books they so love, but they probably left the ale."

"Ale from the monastery?" Starri said. "You mean our ale?"

They had been purchasing food and ale from Beggerin since they had first made peace with the Christ priests. It was simpler than plundering the place and inviting retaliation, and Thorgrim wanted to concentrate on getting the ships ready for sea and nothing else. But they had come to think of the monastery's food and drink as their own.

"Yes, our ale," Thorgrim said. "And if they keep on like this, we'll have to go over and take it from them."

"But they outnumber us, Night Wolf," Starri said. "Sure you're afraid to fight an enemy that outnumbers us?" It was Starri's crude attempt to goad Thorgrim into a fight that he, Starri, desperately wanted.

"Well, we may have to put them to the test anyway," Thorgrim said. "But not tonight. Tonight I'm too tired."

"You're getting old, Night Wolf. What happens when you're too weak to please that little Irish minx who shares your bed?"

"Knowing her, she'll probably kill me in my sleep," Thorgrim said. "But if it comes to that, I'll want her to." He left Starri there and wandered off toward *Sea Hammer*, pulled up on the sand. The repairs to her hull and rigging were nearly done, and Thorgrim had taken to sleeping aboard her, back on the platform in the stern where he felt most at home.

Failend was already there, curled up under the fur they used as a blanket, her small frame making a barely discernable lump in the bedding. Thorgrim reached down to unbuckle his sword belt and remembered he was not wearing his sword because he had spent most of the day lying in the damp sand, pounding caulking into the gaps between *Sea Hammer*'s strakes.

He shucked his tunic and slipped under the fur blanket and instinctively reached for Failend and pulled her close. She made a soft murmuring sound and shuffled against him and he considered waking her for a tryst before sleep.

Too tired... he thought as he felt his weary body sink into the soft furs that made up his bed. He wondered if Failend would indeed kill him in his sleep that night, and he wondered if he would mind so much.

If she puts a weapon in my hand, maybe it would not be so bad...

It was the last conscious thought that he had before sleep swept over him, a deep, dreamless sleep. And then he was awake again. How long he had slept he did not know. It was still dark, the deepest part of night. He did not know what had woken him up, but something had pulled him from slumber and left him fully awake.

He began to sit up and as he did he heard the sound of someone scrambling over *Sea Hammer*'s side. He reached over and laid his hand on the hilt of his sword, and then in the dim starlight he saw the familiar bulk of Harald, coming aft. He was moving quickly, but quietly, trying no doubt to avoid startling his father awake and risk a blade in the gut.

"Harald? What's going on?" Thorgrim called. He saw Harald move faster, looming up beside them. Failend sat up and made some little noise that might have been a word but it was hard to tell.

"I don't know, Father. Starri heard something. And I think I hear it as well."

"Heard something?" Thorgrim asked. "Where? Beyond the wall?" Harald was not always good about giving all the information needed.

"From across the water," he said. "From Ketil's camp."

Thorgrim frowned and stood. The night air was cool on the bare skin of his back and chest. He turned toward the distant beach, looking around *Sea Hammer*'s tall sternpost to get a clear view. The five bonfires were there, as they had been every night since the newcomers' arrival. He cocked his head and he heard something, some sharp sound, quick, and then it was gone.

"What do you and Starri think you hear?" Thorgrim asked.

"Well…" Harald began and his voice trailed off. The boy did not like to be wrong, and he was often hesitant to speak when there was a chance he might be. But he also knew that patience was not one of Thorgrim's virtues. "It sounds like it might be fighting," he said.

Fighting? Thorgrim thought. *Fighting who?* There were only two possibilities. Either Ketil's men had broken into factions and they were going at one another, or the Irish had launched an attack.

Thorgrim picked up his tunic and slipped it on. He picked up his sword and buckled it around his waist as he walked amidships, the easier to hop down onto the beach. He heard Failend climbing out of bed behind him. He stepped up onto the sheer strake and hopped down onto the sand and Harald hit the ground beside him. In the dying light of their own bonfire Thorgrim could see a knot of men standing by the water's edge and looking out toward the north.

He strode over quickly, and the men stepped aside as they saw him coming. He stopped a few feet from where the bay lapped up over the sand and looked north as well. The lights flickered now and again, which might mean men passing in front of them, blocking them from view, just for an instant. If so, it meant there were a lot of men moving around.

There was noise as well; Thorgrim could hear it now. Shouting, to be certain. Sharp pinging noises that could be the sound of steel on steel as heard from that distance. It was far off—nearly two miles—but Thorgrim knew that sound carried far over still water like that.

"There, you hear that, Night Wolf? You hear that?" Starri was at his side, pointing and talking excitedly.

No, I don't hear it, because you're talking in my ear, Thorgrim thought, but in response he only nodded.

"It's fighting. A battle going on there. I can hear it. I could hear it if there was a fight one hundred miles away."

"Has anyone asked the sentries on the walls here if anything's amiss?" Thorgrim asked and heard a shuffling of feet, a low murmur. Then he heard someone, Gudrid, he thought, say, "I'll see…" followed by the sound of running feet.

"When did this start?" Thorgrim asked next.

"Not so long ago," Starri said. "I was asleep, but always with an ear open, you know? That's how I sleep. And I heard someone call out. A single voice, but I heard it clear as a lark in a meadow. And then quiet again. So I came down by the water here, and soon I heard more, like a fight. That's when these others awoke. It was so loud even these drunken fools were roused. It was only you, Night Wolf, who slept through it."

"Hmm…" Thorgrim said. He could hear the sound of the fight more clearly now, clear enough that he was all but certain it *was* a fight. It sounded like one, and in truth Starri was rarely wrong about such things.

He heard feet running on the sand and then Gudrid was at his side, breathing hard. "The sentries…" he gasped out, "the sentries say they've seen nothing unusual, heard nothing at all."

"Good. Thank you, Gudrid," Thorgrim said, his eyes never leaving the five distant flickering points of light.

So…if it's the Irish, then they're attacking Ketil alone, and not us at the same time, Thorgrim thought. That did not surprise him. He would not have thought the Irish would have skill or men enough to launch two attacks at the same time.

He looked to his left. Two of their four ships, *Fox* and *Dragon*, were in the water. Both were nearly ready for sea, lacking only sails, but there was no wind that night in any event.

And in that instant, Thorgrim made a decision.

"We'll take *Dragon* and *Fox*," he said. He pictured the deck of the ships, the room that the rowers would need to work the oars. It would be tight, with the crews of all four ships crammed onto two, but there would be space enough. He did not have many men under his command. "Every man here, save for those on sentry on the walls. Gather your weapons, get aboard. Now."

There was only the slightest pause as the men on the beach absorbed this unexpected order. Starri was first to break the spell as he made a subdued whooping sound and raced off for his battle axes, which were never far away.

Starri's reaction prompted the others to move as well, and the crowd burst like a school of fish startled by a rock thrown in the water. They ran back to wherever they had made their beds, grabbed up swords, axes, spears, shields, helmets and mail, and with barely a break in their stride they returned, splashing out into the knee-deep water and leaping over the low sides of *Dragon* and *Fox*.

Thorgrim did not return to *Sea Hammer*. He already had Iron-tooth hanging from his belt and he knew Harald or Failend would bring his shield and mail and helmet. Instead he stepped into the cold water and made his way to *Dragon*'s side, put his hands on the sheer strake and hoisted himself aboard. He walked after, the few men already aboard moving out of his way, and climbed up onto the small deck at the stern. He looked north again, toward Ketil's camp.

They're fighting, for certain, he thought. He could hear it more clearly now, perhaps because the fight itself had grown in intensity. He wondered if they would get there before it was over, and what they would find when they did.

By the time he turned around once more, the rest of the men were swarming along either side of the ship and tumbling over the rails, and others were boarding *Fox*. Some were pulling the long sweeps down from the gallows and running them through the oar ports. Others were finding places amidships where they could stand and not get in the rowers' way. Some were pulling mail over their heads or strapping sword belts around their waists.

Harald and Failend came after. Harald held Thorgrim's shield and helmet, and Failend had his mail draped over her arm. Both were wearing their own mail shirts. Oak-cleaver hung at Harald's side, the fine Frankish blade that had been carried by his grandfather, Ornolf the Restless. Failend had her seax hanging from her belt, her bow and a quiver of arrows over the shoulder.

Thorgrim took his mail shirt from Failend and pulled it over his head. He looked forward along the length of the deck. Godi was up at the bow. He was looking aft, waiting for orders.

"That's it, Godi!" Thorgrim shouted down the length of the ship. "That's all the men she'll bear. Cast us off!"

Godi turned and cast off the heavy line that ran from *Dragon*'s bow to an anchor set far up the beach. *Dragon*'s bow began to turn, as if the ship itself were eager to get into the fight across the water. He looked to his right and could see *Fox*'s bow line cast off as well.

"Oars!" Thorgrim called. Twenty oars ran out twenty oar ports. "Starboard, pull!" All along the starboard side the men leaned into the oars and *Dragon*'s bow began to swing, the dim shape of the longphort and the earthworks surrounding it sweeping by. Thorgrim grabbed up the tiller. The bow was still coming around, the ship swinging one hundred and eighty degrees.

Thorgrim looked back at *Fox*. Her oars were run halfway out and the rowers were holding them horizontal and motionless.

Thorgrim assumed that Hardbein had taken command of *Fox*, and had sense enough to wait for *Dragon* to get clear before he ordered his men to row.

"Larboard, pull! Pull together!"

On the larboard side the oars came down and swept aft and *Dragon* began to gather way, the wide, shallow hull slicing though the still waters of the bay. Thorgrim said no more. He had no need to. The men were falling into the familiar rhythm of the stroke, each oar double-manned thanks to the abundance of warriors they had aboard.

The ship's speed built with each powerful stroke, moving faster than Thorgrim was accustomed to. The conditions were perfect: no wind, calm water, two men on each oar. Astern of them *Fox* was also underway, moving fast.

We might make it, Thorgrim mused. *We may get there before the fighting is done.*

Louis de Roumois stepped up onto the small deck aft. It was hardly appropriate that he should do so, former prisoner, Frank, the one man with perhaps the lowest status of all in Thorgrim's band. But he probably did not understand that he should not be there, just as he did not understand much about the working of ships.

He stood silent for a moment, looking past *Dragon*'s bow. Then he turned to Thorgrim, and spoke. He was far from fluent in the Norse tongue, but he had spent many months in their company and he was learning quickly.

"You help them?" Louis said, nodding toward the place where Ketil's men were fighting someone: themselves, the Irish, there was no way to know. "Why? Ketil is no friend."

Thorgrim was silent for a moment. It was a good question, and he did not answer right off because he was not certain of the answer. Like so many of his decisions he had made it in an instant, with no clear thought behind it. Just instinct. It was usually after the decision was made that he figured out why he had done it. Usually—not always, but usually—it turned out to be the right decision. He figured that was why men still looked to him to lead them.

Now, faced with Louis's question, he pondered why he had made the decision he had.

"Ketil's men are fighting someone," Thorgrim said. "Maybe themselves. If they kill one another, we can pick up what's left. But I think it's the Irish who are attacking them. Bécc, maybe, from the monastery. And that we can't have."

"Why not?"

"Because if they beat Ketil, they'll probably attack us too, sometime soon. They put up with us, they trade for our silver, but they would rather kill us all. So I want to make certain they know that killing Northmen will not be so easy to do."

Louis made a grunting sound which might have been an acknowledgement of Thorgrim's reasoning. Or not. Thorgrim did not care.

He looked off to the east. There were sandbars lurking beneath the surface, he knew, and if they hit them at the speed they were making they might hang there for some time before getting free. The tide was starting to ebb, and that would make it worse. But he had been over that stretch of water many times in the past month, both in one of the longships and in the skin boat they had acquired from the Irish, and he knew it well and felt pretty certain they would remain clear of the hazards.

He nudged the tiller over a bit and let the ship's bow turn west a few degrees before straightening it out again. He looked astern and saw *Fox* doing the same. The five fires on the beach were growing more distinct, as was the flicker of men passing in front of them. He could hear the shouting more clearly as well, and the clash of weapons. Whoever was fighting, they were going at it hammer and tongs.

Thorgrim considered telling the men to pull harder, but that was pointless. They were pulling as hard as they could. Amidships the men not pulling were straining to see past the bow, to see what was going on on the north side of the bay.

"Night Wolf!" Starri called from somewhere forward in the dark. "It's quiet now!"

Thorgrim frowned and turned his ear toward the beach. Starri was right, as far as he could tell. He could no longer hear the sound of fighting. He wondered if they were too late, and what they would find when they ran *Dragon*'s bow onto the sand. But it did not even occur to him to turn back.

They halved the distance and halved it again. The points of light resolved into actual fires, the leaping flames distinct. The light played over the beach, and Thorgrim thought he could see a mass of men standing down by the water, though why they should do that he could not imagine. He thought to call out to Starri, ask what he could see, but he kept his mouth shut. He knew Starri would be doing that strange jerking thing he did with his arms and his mind would be giving over to the berserker's battle madness and there would be no talking to him.

We'll find out soon enough, he thought.

Ten more strokes and the scene on the beach was growing clearer with every boat length they covered. Thorgrim could see the men now, or at least the outlines of them, framed against the firelight. He saw them move as one, forming up into what he guessed was a shield wall and moving up the beach, and on the heels of that, the battle sounds again, the fight rejoined, and Thorgrim knew he was not too late, not at all.

They were fighting up by the half circle of bonfires, two shield walls slamming into one another. *Dragon* was close enough now that Thorgrim could hear the crunch of shield against shield, and the sharp cries of fighting men. It was one of the oddest sights he had seen, the dark shapes of fighting men against the bright flames. Two shield walls, swaying and undulating like some mighty sea monster in its death throes.

And then the monster was torn apart, the near solid line of men shattering along its length. One of the shield walls had broken, and the men who had been standing their ground were now fleeing down the beach toward the water's edge, where they would be trapped between their attackers and the sea.

"Almost there!" Thorgrim called out, his voice loud enough to be heard the length of the ship. "There are men by the water, but I don't know who they are. If they're Irish we'll catch them between our lines and Ketil's. If they are Ketil's men we push through them to get to the Irish!"

He heard grunts of agreement and swords banging against shields in anticipation. It did not occur to any of them, save for Louis, to wonder why they were joining this fight, or if it did, they did not bother to ask.

And then the beach was there, right under their bow. The men took one last powerful stroke and Thorgrim shouted, "Oars in!" With that the oars came in and were tossed aside as the men who had been pulling now snatched up weapons. Thorgrim stole a glance astern.

Fox was a ship length behind and would be on the beach before his men had even disembarked.

Dragon's bow hit the sand and drove on up the shore, and men fore and aft staggered with the sudden stop. The ship had not yet come to a rest when the first man, which of course was Starri Deathless, launched himself over the sheer strake and into the water. Others followed, eager to get into the fight: Harald, who always wanted to beat Starri into combat but never did, Gudrid and Louis who were no strangers to this sort of work, Vestar, nearly as quick and nimble as Starri.

Thorgrim let go of the tiller and stepped quickly up the deck. Failend was at his side, waiting to join him in the fight, and just forward he could see the looming shape of Godi, holding the wooden pole with Thorgrim's banner lashed to the end.

"Very well," Thorgrim said. "Let's go see who's fighting who." He stepped up onto the sheer strake and pushed off, dropping the six feet to the shallow water below, feeling the impact in his knees as he hit the sandy bottom. He drew Iron-tooth from its sheath as he splashed uphill to the beach. He looked left and right, and forward up toward the bonfires. He still had no certain idea what was going on, but the story was revealing itself.

It was Ketil's men who had been driven to the water's edge. Thorgrim recognized a few of them, and the clothes and weapons of the others marked them as Northmen. They had been taken by surprise, Thorgrim could see that as well. Few wore mail or helmets, many had no shields. They did not look like men who had gone into battle prepared to fight.

He looked past them at the shield wall formed further up the beach. It had been sweeping down on the disorganized men in the surf, and would have swept them away, but the sudden appearance of the longships seemed to have stopped them in their tracks. As well it might. A longship was a frightening thing to see come charging out of the night. Thorgrim had counted on that.

They were Irish, those men facing them, but with their backs to the fires they were little more than shadowy figures, hard to see. Not that it mattered. He had come to rescue Ketil's men, and to make clear that there would be a price to pay for attacking Northmen, and so whoever they were they had to be driven from the beach.

He thought for an instant about getting the Northmen into a shield wall to advance on the Irish and dismissed the idea just as quick. The moment was hanging in a balance—the Irish were unsure, confused, surprised. Their line was wavering, and lunacy would push them off the edge.

"At them! At them!" Thorgrim shouted, holding Iron-tooth aloft and pushing through the men between him and the open ground between the combatants. Even before the last syllable had come from his throat the Northmen let out a great roar that rolled up the beach ahead of them, and like a storm-driven wave they came roiling over the sand, weapons held aloft, shields in front, screaming like the half-wild men they were.

Starri led the way. He moved like a deer, opening the gap between himself and Thorgrim's advancing line, ready to take on the Irish by himself. And, indeed, in the grip of a fight, he seemed quite unaware of anyone or anything other than his weapons and his enemy.

Just as Thorgrim was leading his line of men, so one of the Irish men-at-arms stood a few paces ahead of his waiting shield wall. Thorgrim saw the man react to Starri's approach, saw him shift to the right to place himself right in Starri's path. The light of the fires at his back flickered off the steel of the sword he held aloft.

Thorgrim watched the moment unfold. So many times he had been certain that Starri would run right onto a blade: a sword held out at arm's length or a spear thrust from a shield wall or a seax darting like a snake's tongue. It had happened only once, had nearly killed the man, but still Thorgrim could not help but think it would happen again.

He'll go over him, Thorgrim thought. It was what Starri loved to do. He would launch himself in the air, vault off whoever was in front of him and launch himself at the rest of his foes. Thorgrim was sure he would do it again, and now there was the glittering blade there to greet him.

But Thorgrim was wrong. Starri, to Thorgrim's surprise, flung himself down onto the sand and Thorgrim thought he had tripped on something. But Starri did not come down in a heap. Rather he tucked his two axes against his side and rolled right into the man's shins, swept his legs out from under him. Thorgrim heard the man grunt as he was flung down on the sand and Starri rolled back up onto his feet and continued to run as if nothing had happened, charging at the shield wall again.

"At them!" Thorgrim shouted once more. The Norsemen's advance had built to a run, their shouts like crashing surf. Thorgrim did not know if Ketil's men had joined them, but he guessed they had. The man whom Starri had knocked down was up again, sword and shield ready, and Thorgrim shifted sideways and charged at him.

The man was ready. Thorgrim was five feet away when the warrior swung his shield sideways, as if swatting Thorgrim away, and behind the shield came his sword, the thrust fast and straight.

But Thorgrim was ready as well. He caught the blade with his own shield, knocked it aside, and counter-thrust, only to feel the shock of steel hitting steel, the man parrying his blow. Thorgrim stepped back, looked up at the man he was facing.

Bécc.

Of course… Thorgrim thought. Bécc was a cunning one, a true warrior, and hatred of the heathens burned in him, pure and hot as fire. Of course he was here. Thorgrim wondered if Bécc had made peace with Ketil and his men and then betrayed them as he had done to Thorgrim and the others.

Bécc snarled, an animal sound, and stepped forward, once again sweeping with his shield and looking for an opening with his sword. On either side of them Thorgrim's men and Ketil's men raced past as they ran screaming at the Irish shield wall. Thorgrim risked a glance past Bécc and he could see the Irish taking the smallest of steps back, their courage wavering in the face of this terrifying surprise.

Then Bécc's sword was back, whistling around, and Thorgrim got his shield up just in time to catch the blade with an impact he felt though his whole body. He pushed Bécc's blade aside and stepped forward and his foot caught some imperfection in the sand: a piece of driftwood, a stone, something of the kind. He felt himself stumble and his arms reached out for balance and he knew he was going down.

And he knew that Bécc's sword would follow him. He raised his shield as he fell, tucked his sword arm under him, and hit the sand with his shoulder. He felt the impact of Bécc's sword against the shield's wood and leather face and he rolled off to his right, away from Bécc. Shield held up, Thorgrim came up onto one knee, Iron-tooth ready to parry the blow that he knew would come.

But it didn't. He looked over the edge of his shield. Bécc was gone.

With a grunt Thorgrim pushed himself to his feet. The Irish shield wall was no more, the men-at-arms broken and running and those Northmen with breath enough chasing after them. Thorgrim wanted to call for them to stop, but he knew that he was gasping too hard to yell, and anyway he would not be heard.

Where Bécc was he did not know. Off with his men, he guessed. He must have seen the collapse of his line and decided he did not care to be left behind. Bécc was no coward, Thorgrim knew, but he would see little point in being cut down for nothing.

Louis de Roumois came ambling over, looking as if he were going for a stroll in his garden, save for his tousled hair and a rip in his chainmail and the blood glistening on his sword. He looked at Thorgrim with that vaguely amused look he seemed to favor.

"Well done," he said, his words barely distinguishable through his thick Frankish accent. "You beat them. Easy."

"Not so easy," Thorgrim said.

"You think they'll learn? Not to fight heathens?"

It was a good question. The most important question of the night. "That was Bécc, leading those men," Thorgrim said. "They called him Brother Bécc. You remember."

Louis nodded. Of course he remembered. Brother Bécc came within moments of burning Louis and Harald at the stake.

"Brother Bécc is not the kind who's willing to learn," Thorgrim said. "Not from this sort of thing."

Chapter Twelve

So becomes it a youth to quit him well
with his father's friends, by fee and gift,
that to aid him, aged, in after days
come warriors willing...

Beowulf

The funeral mass for the late ealdorman Merewald had not been a pleasant experience. By their nature, of course, funeral masses were not generally pleasant, but in this instance it was worse than usual. For Nothwulf, at least.

He had been late, unable to pull himself from his surprising, confusing interview with Werheard's wife, Roswitha. The bells had long stopped ringing by the time he slipped in through the big doors at the back of the cathedral, and the covey of priests had begun to swing their incensors as Bishop Ealhstan watched from his great carved oak chair on the dais.

Had Nothwulf been just one of the thegns he might have slipped unseen onto one of the benches near the back of the church. But of course he was not a thegn; he was the brother of the deceased, by his own lights the rightful ealdorman of Dorsetshire. His place was at the very front of the church, on the bench reserved for those of the noble house. And so he had no choice but to walk the full length of the massive cathedral, past the curious and condemning glances of those already seated, and take his place beside the sniveling, half-crumpled form of his sister-in-law, Cynewise.

Oh, dear Lord! Nothwulf thought as he settled himself on the upholstered bench and met the bishop's disapproving gaze with an unflinching stare of his own.

Dear Lord, Cynewise, you pathetic tart, will you stop this playacting grief?

Nothwulf did not believe that Cynewise felt any great sorrow, and he did not think anyone else in that great house of God did either. Not Bishop Ealhstan, who had often found himself at odds with Merewald. Not the thegns, at least not most of them, who looked on the late ealdorman as a tight-fisted, weak, poor imitation of his father. Not Nothwulf, who had always resented the fact that the happenstance of his and Merewald's birth order had bequeathed the ealdormanship to his less able brother.

And certainly not Cynewise, who had been Merewald's wife for less time than it took for the ealdorman to bleed out on the cathedral floor.

Nothwulf let those thoughts ramble through his mind as he set his face in an expression of stoic mourning. The voice of the priests' chanting and the bishop's prayers and the choir's songs and Cynewise's soft weeping all passed unnoted through Nothwulf's ears. He had more to think about now than his dead brother, who was now of no more importance to anyone than a stone in a field. Less, in fact.

He had endured the mass, longer even than was the bishop's usual wont. When it was over Bishop Ealhstan and his retinue of priests and altar servers and Cynewise's guard—unarmed now, as was fitting for attendance at mass—escorted her through the parted crowd of sorrowful-looking mourners. Nothwulf, as was befitting his station, followed directly behind, and he could not help but note the looks of sympathy directed at Cynewise changed to expressions of curiosity, or anger, or disgust as he moved past.

Nothwulf had gone from the cathedral directly back to his home. He had instructed Bryning to see the hearth-guard was kept alert, with men armed and ready throughout the night. Nothwulf did not know what, exactly, he was defending against, and that made him particularly uneasy.

But that would change, and soon.

"It's clear to me, clear to anyone, really," Nothwulf said to Bryning, "that the simpering tart who calls herself my late brother's wife has no intention of giving over the ealdormanship to me."

"No, lord," Bryning said. They were seated at a table in the outer room of Nothwulf's sleeping chamber. It was three days since the unpleasant spectacle of the funeral mass. The dull light of an overcast day filled the room, the windows uncovered in the warmth of early summer, the fireplace empty and cold.

"Some of the thegns…some, not all, mind you…have her ear," Nothwulf continued. "And of course that bastard Oswin, the shire reeve. They see a chance here, mind you. Convince her to put herself in as ealdorman and they can play her like she was some sort of puppet. Bastards. If they can't be ealdorman themselves then they can have a pet ealdorman to play with. Whore's sons."

"Yes, lord," Bryning said. Bryning was, in truth, of no consequence. There was no point in telling him any of this. But Nothwulf felt an absolute need to say these things out loud, to hear if they sounded reasonable, or rather like some flight of fancy, and Bryning was the only man whom Nothwulf trusted entirely.

"But is doesn't much matter, do you see?" Nothwulf continued. "Because these decisions are not hers to make, regardless of what she might think."

Bryning nodded.

"The King of Wessex will make these decisions, not her," Nothwulf continued. "Æthelwulf will decide who will be ealdorman, and he will be here in a fortnight."

"You reckon when King Æthelwulf gets here he'll set this straight, lord?" Bryning asked. "Put you in your rightful place?"

"Yes, I do," Nothwulf said. "But I won't leave it to chance." He held a letter in his hand, folded and sealed with his own seal, a shield with the hart and boar device, vines twisting around the edges. He had sealed it just moments before, and now he touched the wax to see that it was sufficiently hard, which it was. He handed the letter to Bryning, who took it reluctantly, as if the paper itself might cause him some harm.

"This is a letter to King Æthelwulf," Nothwulf explained.

"Asking that he see you are made ealdorman?" Bryning asked.

"No," Nothwulf said. "Telling him that as ealdorman I look forward to serving him in any way I can." Nothwulf knew better than to ask for something. A request could be denied. Better to work from an assumption of authority, to let the king know that he, Nothwulf, took it for granted that he was to be ealdorman.

And of course it would be easier for Æthelwulf to swallow such an assumption if Nothwulf provided something to ease it down his throat.

"You'll take this to King Æthelwulf yourself," Nothwulf said. "Along with a tribute to the king, by way of showing my appreciation for all the favor and justice he has shown Dorsetshire during the rule of my brother and father."

"Yes, lord," Bryning said. "Tribute, lord?"

Nothwulf made a dismissive wave of his hand. "It's no great thing, some silver and a few cartloads of flour and beef. Some wine."

Bryning nodded. Nothwulf wondered if the man knew he was lying. It was in fact a great thing, nearly all the silver Nothwulf had in his possession and enough of the produce given him as rent to nearly empty one of his storehouses. But it was a gamble worth taking. The risk was great but the potential reward much greater.

"This is all being assembled at my farm near Somerton," Nothwulf said. "The fewer who know of it the better. My people at Somerton don't know what it's about. Only you and me."

Bryning nodded, but he did not look comfortable. He was not a man who was much inclined toward intrigue, nor very good at masking his feelings, which was why Nothwulf trusted him and put him in command of the hearth-guard.

"You're to assemble half the hearth-guard, your most trusted men, and you're to escort the wagons to Winchester, to King Æthelwulf. He's still there, as I hear it. If not, you'll deliver the tribute and then find the king to give him my letter. Do you understand?"

"Yes, lord," Bryning said.

"Good," Nothwulf said. "Then, off with you."

"Yes, lord." Bryning stood, the letter held in both hands, as if he was afraid of dropping it. He nodded his respect, then turned and stepped through the outer door, closing it behind him.

Nothwulf sighed. He had put considerable thought into this, and for all his doubts he still felt it was the best approach. Sure, he could go to the thegns, the wealthier ones who held the most sway, convince them of what should be obvious—that he, Nothwulf, should be ealdorman. But why try to win the loyalty of a dozen men when he needed only the backing of one, King Æthelwulf?

He had known Æthelwulf for many years. His father and then his brother had entertained the king and his retinue at Sherborne when Æthelwulf had made his annual visit, and they in turn had resided at Winchester when the family traveled to see the king.

Æthelwulf held him, Nothwulf, in high esteem, or so Nothwulf believed, and he had no reason to doubt it.

Still, the uncertainty nagged at him, and it was a new sensation. His life, which thus far had moved along a well-defined route, now seemed to have become lost in some sort of wilderness.

"We'll get this straightened out quickly enough," he said, softly and to himself. He did not think this current confusion was any great problem, just a little snag. Still, he could not rid himself of the idea that there were things happening which he did not understand, important things to which he was blind and ignorant.

He stood, stared blankly for a moment at the door which Bryning had closed, then turned and stepped back into the bedchamber. A drape had been pulled over the one window, leaving the room in a twilight of darkness.

Aelfwyn, reclining in the wide bed, half-covered by the blankets, stirred as he came in and propped herself up on her elbow with her usual lack of inhibition. Her dark hair tumbled around thin, naked shoulders, her breasts, quite exposed, looked firm and well-defined, if not overly large. She was smiling her sleepy smile.

"Lord Nothwulf, I thought you had forgotten me," she said with a thoroughly insincere pout. "I would have been most put out if you had. I would not have returned to your bed, depend upon it."

Nothwulf gave her a half smile. He thought his dealing with Bryning and the consideration of his mounting troubles had thoroughly killed his passion, but the sight of Aelfwyn, naked and waiting in his bed, rekindled it like dry straw on glowing embers.

"Never, my beloved, never would I forget you," he said, casting off the brooch that held the collar of his tunic closed. He grabbed the hem of the garment and shucked it off over his head and was rewarded with a smile and soft approving sound from Aelfwyn.

"Come here, and at least pretend to love me," she said.

Nothwulf smiled, took a step toward her, then stopped. Aelfwyn had been in his bedchamber for some time, she had been there alone while his letter to King Æthelwulf had sat, unsealed, on the table pushed against the far wall. Nothwulf felt the first gentle nudge of suspicion assert itself.

"What, my love?" Aelfwyn asked.

"Oh," Nothwulf said. "It's just, I recalled, I wrote you a poem, my darling." He stepped over to the table where a deed to property east of Sherborne lay open. The property bordered land owned by the thegn Leofric, and Nothwulf was in the process of making Leofric a gift of it, it seeming like a good time to keep in the good graces of that influential man. Now he snatched up the deed and brought it over to Aelfwyn, who took it from him with undisguised confusion.

"A poem," Nothwulf said. "I wrote it to express my appreciation of your beauty. Pray, read it, tell me what you think."

Aelfwyn's gaze shifted from Nothwulf to the paper she held in her hand, and she looked as if she could not tell which of the two was more odd. "I don't know letters, lord. I can't read this," she said.

"Ah, more's the pity," Nothwulf said, taking the deed from her hands.

"But you must read it to me, lord, please? I would be delighted to hear you speak of my beauty. And in a poem, no less. No man has ever written me a poem before."

"I find that hard to believe," Nothwulf said. He put the deed back on the table, turned and approached the bed, undoing his trousers as he did. "But it truth, my poetry is terrible. Let me show you instead what I think of your beauty." And that seemed enough to please the girl. She gave a small laugh and rolled onto her back, spreading her arms in welcome.

The candles which had been left burning on the table were mere nubs when Aelfwyn finally rolled out of bed and collected her gown from the floor. "I must go, my lord," she said, struggling into the garment. "My lady will surely miss me by now."

"Your lady...the lady Cynewise," Nothwulf said, trying to sound casual, as if he had only a vague interest. "How does she do?"

"Oh, not well, lord," Aelfwyn said. She picked up a mirror from the small table that held the wash basin and angled it to see her reflection. She frowned and ran her fingers through her hair.

"Not well?"

"No, lord. She has no idea what to do. I think she wants nothing more than to return to her father's home and be done with Dorset. I would too, were it not that I must leave you. She thinks one thing, the thegns tell her another. She's like a leaf blown about in the wind."

"Indeed? Does she think at all that she'll give up this notion of being ealdorman?" Nothwulf could hear the suppressed eagerness in his voice as he asked that, and he hoped Aelfwyn did not. And it did not seem that she did.

"She doesn't want to be ealdorman," Aelfwyn said, deftly tying the cloth of her headrail around her head and tucking the ends in place. "She wants you to be ealdorman. But there are some thegns, I think, who try to convince her that she should be."

"Who? Why would they do that?" Nothwulf asked.

"I don't know who. Many of the thegns speak with her, but in private, and I don't know who says what. But my lady tells me that she thinks some of those men hope to control her." She stepped over to the bed and kissed Nothwulf one last time, a lingering kiss.

"But they know they could never control you," she added. "And when you're ealdorman, you'll forget all about me."

"Nonsense," Nothwulf said. He slapped her on the bottom and she let out a shout of mock outrage, then turned and was gone.

Nothwulf lay in the bed for some time longer. Aelfwyn's scent lingered in the warm air and he breathed it deep, enjoying it.

*I'll miss her, once she and Cynewise are sent packing back to Devonshire...*he thought. But no sooner had the thought occurred to him than he recalled those damned gold goblets owned by Bishop Ealhstan. And following on the heels of that image, a memory of Cynewise's father, whom Nothwulf had met once. Powerful, commanding, Ceorle, the ealdorman of Devonshire. And with that he felt his warm, luxurious post-coital glow melt away like snow on a warm spring day.

Chapter Thirteen

Alas, o holy Patrick
That your prayers did not protect it
When the foreigners with their axes
Were smiting your oratory!
Annals of Ulster

After all the men-at-arms had scrambled up and over the dune, there were, save for the dead and wounded, only two Irishmen left behind on the sand: Faílbe mac Dúnlaing and Brother Bécc.

When the shield wall collapsed they had rallied the men for a rearguard, a line of the most trusted warriors to hold off the heathens long enough for the others to get away. Faílbe and Bécc, as fitted their station, had stood at the center of that defense, and once the bulk of the men had gone up and over, only then did they think to follow.

They were in deep shadow, far from the fires, which were starting to burn low. They were not fighting, because there was no one to fight. It seemed that the heathens did not even know they were there. When the last of the Irish shield wall had collapsed, when the last of the men-at-arms had raced off into the night, the Northmen had given up the battle. They had won. They apparently saw no need to chase their enemy off into the marsh.

It had been a disorganized assault, the heathens flinging themselves at the Irish. If Bécc and Faílbe's men had not been thrown off by the surprise appearance of the ships, they would surely have turned the attackers back. But the men-at-arms were disorganized as well, tired from marching and fighting, dispirited by the sudden turn of fortune, and there was no way that Bécc could rally them for a stand.

He knew that. But it did not make him any less furious.

The shield in his left hand was half shattered, and the grip of his sword was slick with either blood or sweat, he was not sure which. He dug his heels into the sand and looked left and right for the next attack, the next enemy he could beat down. But there was no one. The nearest of the heathens was fifty feet away, near the closest of the fires, and if he or any of his fellows could see Bécc and Faílbe in the shadows, they did not seem to much care.

That truth heaped more coal on Bécc's fury, a fury that already burned hot. He had abandoned his fight with Thorgrim, given it up at the very moment he might have struck the bastard dead, because he felt it was his duty to be with his men, even as they were running off. He regretted that now. He regretted preserving his own life when he might have sacrificed it to send the heathen Thorgrim off to hell.

Faílbe, standing on his left side, hit Bécc's shield with the pommel of his sword. "Come on," he said, jerking his head toward the dune behind them. "Our men are safe, let's go."

Bécc scowled, looked at Faílbe and then at the heathens. Then back at Faílbe. He did not know what to do.

"Let's go!" Faílbe said, more emphatically. He turned and began to climb the steep dune and Bécc followed. He did not think about it, he just followed, as if his legs were obeying Faílbe's order even as his mind was still debating it.

They crested the dune and looked out over the silent expanse of the marsh, then Faílbe stepped down off the rise and began heading north where the monastery at Beggerin lay unseen in the dark. It was there, Bécc was sure, that the men would have stopped their retreat. It was there they would have collapsed in exhaustion on the ground, too tired to defend themselves if the heathens had pursued them, and thankful to the Lord above, and the saints and angels, that they had not.

Bécc looked down at his shield, and in the dim light he could see that the wood slats were hanging in pieces from the iron rim, so he tossed it aside. He wiped the blade of his sword on the hem of his tunic and slipped the weapon into its sheath. The only sounds were his and Faílbe's soft footfalls and the jingle of their mail, and, muted and far back, the sounds of the Northmen in the aftermath of the fight.

They walked on. Bécc was exhausted to the point of near collapse, and at the same time his rage drove him on like he was being prodded with a dagger point—a strange sensation indeed. His head was swimming, his steps were both determined and unsure. His thoughts had spun off to some place he did not recognize.

Victory had been pulled from his grasp, and Bécc's anger had grown and transubstantiated into something much worse, something much more profound. Fury, perhaps, but that word did not quite encompass all that Bécc now felt. His entire life, from boyhood until the moment he had given himself to God, had been one of anger and violence. But he had never felt anything such as he felt at that moment.

It's the righteous anger of the Lord, Bécc thought. *I am God's weapon here, and His anger flows through me like a river.*

They walked on, side by side, the soft sounds from the beach receding behind them. Finally Faílbe spoke, and his voice sounded odd and out of place.

"You fought well, Brother Bécc. Of course you fought well…what I mean is that you did well in leading the men. All that anyone could do."

Bécc made a grunting sound. "I failed," he said. "I failed the men, and I failed the Lord my God."

"You failed no one," Faílbe said. "You…no one…could have guessed those damned ships would arrive when they did."

Bécc made another grunting sound. The Lord knew the ships would arrive when they did, sent them to test him, Bécc was certain. A test he failed. But it was not too late for redemption. As long as he lived, it was not too late for that.

"We have some time before first light," Bécc said. "Time enough for the men to rest, and then we can move them over the marsh before the sun's up. We can fight again at dawn. Not try another night attack. The heathens will surely be drunk by then, and never expecting our return."

Faílbe stopped in his tracks and turned toward Bécc. "Are you serious?" he asked.

Bécc frowned. It was an odd question. If anything, he thought that suggestion was too obvious to be worth making.

"Of course I'm serious," Bécc said. "The heathens are still here, and we have not done our duty to God until we've driven them off."

"It's not always clear what our duty to God is," Faílbe said. "We did what we thought God wanted, and we failed. Perhaps that means God does not wish us to throw away any more Christian lives."

Bécc shook his head. He was not even sure how to approach this. "We cannot suffer heathens to pollute our shores, not one moment more," he said. He could hear the note of desperation creeping into his voice, but there was nothing for it. "Those whores' sons are near spent, and they're close at hand. We have the men, good men, trained men. We would be pissing on God's gift to let this chance pass."

Faílbe shook his head, and though Bécc could barely see his face in the dark, there was a quality of finality to the gesture. "Our men are spent, more spent than the heathens. They're hurt and many are dead, or will be soon. There's no fight left in them. We're done here."

"Done?" Bécc said. "What do you...?"

"We'll make our way back to Ferns at first light. Protect our homes if the heathens mean to come inland, which I'm not sure they do. They've not moved from the beach in a week. We'll speak with the abbot, see what he thinks of all this."

Those words were like a knife in Bécc's gut. *We'll speak with the abbot...* It was bad enough, this failure in the eyes of God, but God at least rarely made his displeasure immediately known. Not so the abbot. Bécc had already failed the man once, made a great festering mess of dealing with Thorgrim and the renegade *rí tuath* Airtre mac Domhnall. And now this. How could he return to the abbot with yet another tremendous failure to his name?

He couldn't. It was as simple as that.

"No," Bécc said. "No."

Faílbe was quiet for a moment, apparently trying to decipher that single word. "No?" he said at last. "No to what? Speaking to the abbot?"

"No, we will not leave the heathens in peace. Not when we have an army here to crush them."

"Brother Bécc," Faílbe said. "You fought well, and I appreciate that. And the abbot will as well. But these are my men. I am the rí túaithe, I command here. I've made my decision."

He turned back the way they were heading but Bécc's hand shot out, grabbed him by the shoulder and turned him around so they were once again facing each other. He saw Faílbe's head turn to look at the impudent hand still gripping his shoulder, and Bécc removed it. Not quickly, but he removed it.

"See here, lord," Bécc said. He was speaking low, teeth clenched, trying to control the animal that was raging inside him. "I will not allow us to make such a mistake."

"You will not allow it? You?"

"This is not my affair, it's God's affair, and I will..."

"God?" Faílbe said, incredulous, the sound of the Lord's name on the man's lips infuriating to Bécc. "See here, *Brother* Bécc, the Lord saw fit to place me above you in the order of things, and so if you wish to do His bidding..."

Bécc's mind was a whirl, he felt as if he were trying to see in a smoke-filled room, to make sense of any of this, to form a single thought. He felt his arm reach around behind him, his hand fall on the grip of the seax that hung from his belt.

They were just moving shadows in the dark, Bécc and Faílbe, but Faílbe did not fail to see the gesture. "You bastard, you dare..." Faílbe cried, his voice loud with surprise and outrage.

Bécc jerked the seax from its scabbard and brought it around from behind his back. There was no thought, no decision made, he was just moving now.

But so was Faílbe. His shield was still gripped in his left hand and he moved it in front of him as Bécc brought the seax around. The iron rim of the shield hit Bécc's forearm and knocked it aside and Bécc saw the man twist as he reached for a weapon of his own.

But it was too late for that. Faílbe's time on earth was finished. He had defied Bécc, God's chosen weapon, and so he would be smote like the armies of old. Bécc grabbed the edge of the shield with his left hand and jerked it aside, throwing Faílbe off-balance as he did. Faílbe made a small, strangled sound, surprise and recognition of the end, and Bécc drove the seax into Faílbe's chest.

The point of the weapon was sharp, the blow delivered with tremendous power. The steel parted Faílbe's mail and the point went right on through, right into the man's chest. Bécc heard the gasp and expulsion of breath as he drove the weapon in until it was stopped by the hilt. He felt the liquid warmth of Faílbe's blood as it poured over his hand.

They stood like that for the few seconds it took Faílbe to die, they remained fixed in that place until Bécc felt the dead man's knees buckle and he let Faílbe slip to the ground, the seax drawing free as he fell.

For some moments they remained motionless, Bécc listening, Faílbe dead. There was nothing out of the ordinary that Bécc could hear, no sounds that were different from what he had heard just moments before. He had no sense for how loud his struggle with Faílbe had been, how far Faílbe's outraged cry had carried, but it seemed that no one had heard it but Faílbe and him. And neither of them would be telling tales.

Bécc bent over and found the hem of Faílbe's tunic and wiped the blade of the seax clean and slipped it back into his scabbard. He would need no explanation for the blood that covered his hands and sleeves: every man there was covered in blood, his own or his enemy's.

He grabbed Faílbe's legs and dragged the man off the trail and into the high marsh grass until he felt he was sufficiently hidden. Not that he was terribly concerned about that, either. Even if Faílbe's body was found, Bécc doubted that anyone would even think to be suspicious. Dead men were no surprise in the aftermath of a battle, even when found where one might not expect.

That done, Bécc trudged back to the path that led to Beggerin, and only then did the thought occur to him, *My Lord, what have I done?*

He had killed Faílbe mac Dúnlaing, struck him down where he stood. Murdered him.

I did not mean to, Bécc said. *Didn't think to do it.*

He had not planned to do what he did. His hand had moved as if moving on its own. As if some other force had directed it. As if God himself had directed the arc of the seax.

Bécc fell to his knees and then lay prostrate on the ground. He felt the tears flow from his one good eye. He begged the Lord to tell him why he had done what he had done.

And then, from behind, from down on the beach, he heard the heathens cheering, a multitude of voices calling out in the barbarous language of the North. And Bécc knew.

God had directed his hand because God needed Bécc to fulfill his mission. He needed the heathens driven from those shores. The God of old did not hesitate to lay waste to cities, to armies, to nations, when his Holy Name was profaned. And surely these days were as dark and perilous as any written of in the Old Testament.

Surely these heathens were as great a threat to the True Faith as any Philistine or Pharaoh.

Bécc got to his knees and then to his feet. God had given him his answer, though in truth he had known it all along. And God had given him this army, and the means to see His will done. And that was what Bécc would do, or he would die in the attempt. He began to make his way along the path once more, and he felt a renewed power in his step.

Chapter Fourteen

My sword was stained with gore,
but the Odin of swords
sword-swiped me too...

The Saga of Gunnlaug Serpent-Tongue

It was not entirely clear to Thorgrim Night Wolf just when the fight ended. The Irish had drawn back to the dunes lining the beach and it seemed there was fighting there, but by the time Thorgrim managed to make his way over the sand, it was done. The Irish were gone, and none of Thorgrim's men had followed, at least not that he could see.

He could hear no fighting anywhere, just the familiar sounds that followed a battle: the moans of the wounded, the laughter of men who had lived through the fight, the bitter sobs of Starri Deathless who had once again missed his chance to be visited by the Choosers of the Slain.

Thorgrim and Louis de Roumois turned and walked back toward the nearest of the fires, still burning, though no longer the roaring blaze that had been visible from Loch Garman. Thorgrim's men were gathering there, and Ketil's men as well, some of whom Thorgrim recognized, some he did not.

Off in the night he heard men cheer, a ragged cry. He had no idea why they were cheering. Perhaps because the Irish had been run off. But he himself did not feel much like cheering, because he knew that the tenuous peace he had with the Irish was now shattered, and his whole world had just become considerably more complicated.

Thorgrim paused by the fire and looked left and right. He saw Harald, around the other side of the pit. There was blood on his face, but it was probably not his. He was smiling, talking to a knot of fellow warriors standing near the flames. Thorgrim was relieved to see the boy, but he had other concerns, and continued to glance around.

"Failend," Louis said, with a hint of a smile. "I saw her, over there." He nodded off into the dark. "Not hurt."

Thorgrim grunted. "Good," he said. Louis's smile grew, just a bit, a knowing smile that Thorgrim found infuriating. He wished, once again, that he had killed Louis long before.

Godi came looming out of the dark, an ax still held in his right hand, the pole with Thorgrim's wolf-head banner in the left. He jammed the butt of the pole into the sand deep enough for it to stand on its own.

"A half-dozen of our men wounded, as far as I can count," he said as he wiped the edge of his ax on the hem of his tunic and thrust the handle into his belt. "Hallorm took a sword in the belly. He won't be long for this life. The rest should mend if the rot doesn't set in."

Thorgrim nodded, but before he could reply, another man emerged from the night, and this one Thorgrim did not know.

"Jarl Thorgrim?" the man asked. "Thorgrim, the one they call Night Wolf?"

"Yes," Thorgrim said, his tone neutral. The man was a little taller than Thorgrim and maybe ten years younger. His hair hung long from under a steel helmet and his beard, just as long, was twisted into two braids that hung down over a mail shirt. There were a half-dozen silver arm rings on his right arm and a fair amount of blood clogging the links of the mail and drying there.

"My name is Jorund. I was second to Ketil. I suppose."

"Was?" Thorgrim asked. "Where's Ketil?"

"Dead," Jorund said. "Don't know when he was killed, or who killed him."

"Wasn't it the Irish?" Thorgrim asked.

Jorund shrugged. "Might have been," he said. "His body was down by the water." He held up a small leather bag. "This is his purse, it was on his belt." With no further comment Jorund tucked the purse into his own belt.

"So you command here, now?" Thorgrim asked.

Jorund looked left and right, as if searching for the answer. "I suppose," he said. "I command that longship," he said, jerking his head in the direction of the four ships pulled up on the beach. "Next to last. The big one. Called *Long Serpent*. The ship beyond it is *Oak*

Heart. We were sailing together and we joined up with Ketil and his men."

Thorgrim nodded. "Why?" he asked.

"More men, the greater the places we might raid," he said. "And we thought Ketil might be a lucky man."

"Was he?"

Jorund shook his head. "Ketil was not a lucky man," he said.

Thorgrim nodded. From the bedraggled, shattered look of the men he had seen on the beach the day of their arrival, they did not look as if luck had been with them.

"You didn't come here to sack the monastery just over the marsh there?" Thorgrim asked. There were a number of things about which he had wondered, and now it seemed he would be able to get answers.

"No," Jorund said. "We came to repair our ships, tend to our wounded. We didn't even know there was a monastery there."

"I see," Thorgrim said. *Not a lucky man.*

"We didn't think there was any around here who would dare attack us like that," Jorund went on. "Particularly at night. I don't know who those men were."

"I do," Thorgrim said. "Irish men-at-arms, from a monastery nearby."

"The one over the marsh?" Jorund asked.

"No. Another. Called Ferns. About fifteen miles to the north."

Jorund shook his head, as if astounded at the number of things Ketil had not known.

"They're led by a man named Bécc," Thorgrim went on. "One of these Christ priests, but he used to be a man-at-arms and he knows his business."

"He surely does," Jorund said. "He'd have killed us all if you hadn't come. Though only you and the gods know why you did, with the words Ketil spoke to you when you were here last. But anyway, you did come and fight, and we owe you our lives."

"You owe me nothing," Thorgrim said. "I didn't come for you. I came because I didn't want Bécc to think he could kill Northmen and pay no price."

"Whatever the reason, you have my thanks. And that of my men. Ketil's men, too, I reckon."

More men were gathering around now, Thorgrim's men and the others. Failend stood off by the edge of the fire. She had a torn bit of cloth wrapped around her left calf. Blood had soaked through the fabric, making a dark and irregular shape, but she did not seem much hurt beyond that.

Thorgrim turned back to Jorund. "Where were you going, after you had repaired your ships here?" he asked.

Jorund grunted. "Vík-ló," he said. "We heard from some others that there were only a few folk left there, mostly just the ones you left behind. Ketil had a mind to go there and make that his own longphort. That's why he wasn't happy to see you. He had an idea to be a lord there." He paused, then added, "Ketil was no lord. Didn't have it in him to be lord of a pig sty. We were just figuring that out."

Thorgrim nodded, but his mind was elsewhere.

Vík-ló...

He had been thinking about Vík-ló, thinking about the longphort more and more over the past few weeks. They had fought hard to make it theirs, and spent a brutal winter working on the neglected defenses and the houses and halls within those walls. By the time they sailed away, Vík-ló was a small but substantial and well-found ship fort.

And why had they left it? For no good reason, other than Thorgrim's frustration with staying in one place, and the difficulty of keeping men such as those he commanded satisfied without the lure of raiding and plunder. The gods had told him to go, and so he went. But it was clear—had been clear for some time—that the gods did not intend for him to leave Ireland. He seemed no more able to leave that accursed island than a dead man was able to free himself from Niflheim.

All this Thorgrim had been thinking about as he worked on *Sea Hammer*, shaping planks and caulking seams to make the ship ready to take to the water again. It was his destiny to stay in Ireland, he knew that now. But he and his men could not just sit idle in some port: men, like ships, would rot and molder away if they were not put to the task for which they were intended. But going a'viking did not mean they could not have a home to which they might return.

Vík-ló. He had made it his home, seen it rebuilt to his own standards, just as he had seen that *Sea Hammer* and the other ships were repaired to his satisfaction, and he was a demanding overlord when it came to such things. So why not return to Vík-ló, make it his home once more, just as his farm in East Agder had once been his home?

He had all but decided that very day, and if ever he had hoped the gods would give him a sign that he had decided well, then here it was. Ketil and his men, more men than Thorgrim commanded, had been on their way to take Vík-ló for themselves. But the gods had flung them up on the beach and sent the Irish after them, and seen to it that Ketil was struck down in the bargain.

"This might have been better for Ketil, a quick and honorable death," Thorgrim said. "You see, we're bound for Vík-ló as well. I intend to take my place there once more."

He heard a muffled sound of surprise from Godi and saw Gudrid, who had also joined them, give a quizzical look, but both men knew better than to say anything. Thorgrim was glad that Starri was not there, as he would surely have voiced his surprise.

"You...were bound for Vík-ló?" Jorund asked.

"That's right," Thorgrim said. "We've been raiding along the coast, but now it's time we returned. Once we've refitted properly and taken our rest at Vík-ló, then we'll see what other places hold promise."

Jorund nodded. He seemed hesitant, and he looked around as if for support. A few men, Jorund's men, Thorgrim imagined, were standing by him, and that seemed to inspire him to speak further.

"Here's the truth," Jorund said. "Since you showed up the other day, there's been a lot of talk here, among the men. My men and Ketil's. Most weren't happy that Ketil didn't accept your offer to shift over to your longphort. Even Ketil's men weren't happy. 'Cause Ketil, like I said, was not a lucky man. But Thorgrim Night Wolf...your name is known along this coast. You *are* known as a lucky man. And I think Ketil hated you for it."

"I see," Thorgrim said, and thought, *Me? A lucky man?* He could not imagine how anyone would think that, but here it was. Before he could inquire further, Jorund was speaking again.

"There were some here who thought we should join with you. Swear an oath to you. Of course Ketil threatened to kill any man who spoke that way. But he couldn't stop them talking. And he might not have stopped them from doing it, if the Irish hadn't come."

Godi took a step forward. "Doesn't much matter now what Ketil wanted," he said. "I suppose Jarl Thorgrim might accept your oath, if you were to ask."

Jorund nodded. "Ketil's men have no leader," Jorund said, "and I guess they would be happy to join you."

"And you?" Thorgrim asked. "You command the crews of two ships."

"I swore no oath to Ketil, and I don't care to swear an oath to any man," he said.

Thorgrim nodded. He could appreciate that sentiment. He had sworn an oath to Jarl Ornolf once, and had been loyal to him for as long as Ornolf lived, but he would never swear an oath to another.

"If you want to join with me, I'd welcome you. You need swear no oath. If you want to part ways any time, that's your decision."

"I'd hoped you would say that," Jorund said. He turned and called to his men, and they came over, shuffling toward the fire, wounded men, exhausted men, dispirited men. And with them came the remnants of Ottar's men, those who had sailed with Ketil when they left Vík-ló with Ottar's stiff, pale corpse aboard their ship.

But not all of Ottar's men had left. Many had stayed and sworn allegiance to Thorgrim, and some of those now greeted their old shipmates, or ignored those with whom they had quarreled. It was like the households of two brothers coming together after a long estrangement.

"Listen to me," Jorund said in a voice loud enough to carry to the edge of the firelight. "Jarl Thorgrim and I have been talking."

Jorund had the attention of every man whom Thorgrim could see, and he recounted to them the conversation they had just had, the talk of how some had wanted to shift over to the longphort, how Ketil had feared Thorgrim, how Thorgrim intended to return to Vík-ló, where he had been jarl before. He told them how he himself intended to join with Thorgrim, and how Thorgrim said he would take the oath of any man who wished to give it.

It was a good talk, and mostly accurate, and Thorgrim could see nodding heads and determined looks on the faces of those who listened. When Jorund finished his speech he called out, "Who would join with Thorgrim Night Wolf?"

They cheered. The men gathered around the dying fire cheered and raised weapons and yelled as loud as they could. Exhausted as they were, wounded as they were, they cheered because they were stuck on a foreign shore, and they were surrounded by enemies, and they had no agreement among them as to what they would do, or who would lead them, and now they saw an answer, they saw a path. It was Thorgrim Night Wolf, who, apparently, had a reputation as a lucky man.

Thorgrim knew he should say something, but he could think of nothing so he just nodded as the men yelled.

There it is, he thought. *I have just doubled the men and ships under my command.* And there was a great deal he could do with such an army, if Bécc did not return first to slaughter them all.

Chapter Fifteen

He minds him of hall-men, of treasure-giving,
How in his youth his gold-friend
Gave him to feast. Fallen all this Joy.

The Wanderer
Early Anglo-Saxon Poem

A road ran north out of Somerton, an ancient road, rutted and uneven. Dry now, though in the winter and spring it was often a muddy quagmire. It had been built in ages past by the Romans, and Oswin imagined it had been a marvelous thing then, like all the marvels that the Romans had left in their wake.

He imagined the road had been smooth and even and paved over in some fashion. Some parts of the old road showed signs of that. But there was no one now who had the skill, wealth, or will to keep the roads up as they had been.

The shire reeve's gaze was resting absently on the long, straight stretch of the ancient way, which he could see from his place at the crest of the hill over which it climbed. His gloved hands rested on his saddle, the reins of his horse held loosely in his fingers. Behind him he could hear the restless sounds of the other mounts, four horses bearing four men, the best of his troops.

For some time he had watched the small caravan approach. There were five wagons which, from a distance, appeared to be no more than dark points moving slowly along, drawing closer, always closer. They were still more than a mile and a half distant, and at the rate they were moving he wondered if they would reach him by nightfall.

Heavy loaded... he thought. They moved slowly because they were bearing a considerable cargo. And that was good.

123

Oswin had seen them for the first time an hour before, but he knew who they were and what they carried. He was the shire reeve. Nothing of any size or significance moved in Dorset without his knowing it.

He wasn't worried about anyone in the distant caravan seeing him and his men. They had been careful to position themselves near a stand of trees which would make them all but invisible from that distance. But they would have to move soon, and Oswin did not want them seen when they did, so he waited.

The road, the ancient Roman road, ran mostly straight, jogging left or right only when it met some impassable obstruction, and even then it only altered course a little.

How did they do that? Oswin wondered. He tried to picture the men who had staked out that road, and who had built it, and he wondered what sort of geniuses they must have been, what now-lost knowledge they held. But he could not imagine it.

When the road had first been laid down it no doubt ran through open country, and if it met with forests Oswin imagined that the Romans had cleared the woods away. This land was home to the savage Britons then, and the Romans would not have left them cover from which to stage an ambush.

But no more. Now stands of trees had grown up along the road, some mere patches of wood, some all but forests.

The road at the bottom of the rise on which Oswin and his men were waiting was engulfed by a quarter mile of such forest before emerging again and rising up to where the shire reeve sat his horse. It was why he was there.

They waited for some time longer, waited until the riders who road ahead of the wagon train disappeared from view in the woods below, and then the first of the wagons was similarly swallowed up, and then the next behind it. Oswin had a sudden fear that he had waited too long.

"Come on," he said to the men behind him. He kicked the flanks of his horse and the animal, startled after having remained motionless for so long, leapt forward, heading down the hill at a trot. Oswin could hear the others following behind.

They entered the woods at the bottom of the hill, the light of the overcast day yielding to the deeper gloom of the forest. Here was one of the few places that the road made a long, gentle curve, and that prevented Oswin from seeing more than a couple hundred feet ahead. But that was no matter, because anyone approaching from the opposite direction would be equally blind until it was too late.

He reined his horse to a stop once again and heard the others behind him do the same. He looked left and right, his eyes piercing the woods as best they could, but he could see nothing. He strained his ears. He could hear the creaking of the carts not too far away down the road. He could hear birds in the trees. Nothing else.

Good…

It was not long after they reached their position that the first of the riders appeared around the bend, a couple hundred feet away. Oswin saw them rein to a stop, surprised to see men on the road, men who seemed to be waiting for them. He could see the riders turn and confer with one another, and Oswin could well imagine the discussion they were having.

Finally one of them wheeled his horse around and disappeared, heading back toward the unseen wagons.

That's right, Oswin thought. *Back you go, tell the wagons to stop where they are.*

The other two riders continued on, closing with Oswin and his men. They were fifty feet away when Oswin knew for certain that one of the men was Bryning, the captain of Nothwulf's hearth-guard. Which was no more a surprise than any of it.

Bryning approached to twenty feet distance and stopped. "Oswin," he said, with a touch of surprise, a touch of wariness. He would have no reason to fear the shire reeve, though neither would he have expected to encounter him at that place. "What business have you here?"

"Anything that happens in Dorset is my business. That's why I'm the shire reeve, and not, say, the privy reeve." That got a short laugh from one of the men behind him, but not Bryning.

"And I'm on Nothwulf's business," Bryning said, an edge of uncertainty in his voice. "We have a few carts back on the road, and we're accompanying them to Winchester. There's no toll here, I'm certain, and even if there was, Nothwulf pays no tolls in this shire."

"I see," Oswin said. "What do you carry, that you need such an armed guard? Do you think these roads unsafe?"

"What I carry is Nothwulf's business, not yours," Bryning said. Oswin could tell the surprise was wearing off, and Bryning was asserting himself. Bryning was no coward, of that Oswin had no doubt, and his men outnumbered Oswin's. As far as Bryning could tell.

"I'm not so sure this isn't my business," Oswin said, and then, as if he had given a signal, a man screamed from somewhere down the road, somewhere back where the wagons were hidden from view. It was a scream of surprise and agony, the kind of scream a man might make if he had been shot with an arrow by an archer crouching unseen in the woods. Which, Oswin knew, was exactly what it was.

The scream died off as abruptly as it came, and there was a moment of silence, a heartbeat or two, no more, and then chaos, as if a minor battle had erupted just beyond their sight. Men shouted, horses stamped and they could hear weapons being drawn. Someone else screamed, the same sort of scream: shock and pain.

Bryning had turned toward the sound and now he turned back. His calm of a moment before was gone, and in its place Oswin could see confusion and rage. Mostly rage, he guessed, because it would not have taken Bryning long to understand what was going on.

Oswin drew his sword and Bryning did the same and Oswin thought Bryning was going to charge, but he did not. Instead he pulled his horse's head around, spinning the animal in place and kicking its flanks hard, while the man at Bryning's side did the same. Bryning might have wished to thrust a sword through the shire reeve, but his duty was to protect the wagons at any cost, and that was what he would attempt to do. And, Oswin knew, he would fail.

Sword in hand, Oswin spurred his horse to a run, flying down the road on Bryning's heels, his men pounding behind him. The sound of shouting and the unseen clash of weapons and the stamp of horses seemed to build to a high point and then die away as Oswin followed Bryning around the bend.

The first of the wagons was there, the oxen pulling it standing motionless and dumb, as if waiting patiently for the men to finish with their foolishness. Two riderless horses were prancing around, the once-mounted warriors sprawled on the hard-packed road, arrows standing like banner staffs from their chests. On the carter's seat the wagon's driver lay slumped on his side.

Bryning did not pause over his dead but raced on past, charging back along the road down which he had just come. Oswin stayed on his heels as best he could, but Bryning's horse was fast and the distance began to open.

"Stop him! Stop that bastard!" Oswin shouted to whoever might hear, whoever was in a position to help. He saw an arrow streak through the air and embed itself in a wagon's side, but Bryning had long since ridden past.

Oswin reined his horse to a stop, as did his men, but Oswin shook his head and pointed up the road and shouted in his anger, "After that son of a bitch! Get him! Kill him, or not, I don't care, but stop the bastard!"

The orders were unnecessary. Oswin's men knew what to do. They did not hesitate as they raced off after the fleeing Bryning, and Oswin paid them no more attention. They were good men, reliable. They would bring Bryning's bleeding corpse back to him.

The shire reeve turned his horse in a half circle. A dozen more of Oswin's men were moving around the wagons, seaxes in hand, bows slung over their shoulders. They had been hidden in the woods, waiting for the wagon train, while Oswin and the others had been waiting at the crest of the hill. They crouched among the trees until Oswin forced the carts to stop at the place they had arranged for them to stop. Then they let go a flight of arrows, too fast for the eye to follow and utterly unexpected. Two arrows each, and then they had attacked with their blades, but Oswin doubted there had been many left standing by then.

The fight had been short and it had been one sided and it had been exactly as Oswin had planned.

He slipped down off his horse. He felt the muscles in his legs protest as he walked slowly back along the line of wagons. He stopped at the second from the end. The driver had fallen forward, bent nearly double, an arrow sticking out of his back, a great blossom of blood soaking his tunic. The arrow had struck at such an angle as to drive itself right into his heart, a near instant death.

You're a lucky bastard, Oswin thought and he pulled himself up and stood on the seat beside the dead man. The bed of the cart was fully loaded, a heavy canvas cloth covering the lot of it. Oswin pulled a knife from his sheath, cut one of the cords that held the cloth in place, and peeled it back.

Barrels. The cart was loaded with barrels. Wine, Oswin guessed. Good wine. Nothwulf would not send anything less than that for the pleasure of King Æthelwulf. Doing so would be counterproductive.

He pulled the canvas back further and inspected the top of each barrel. Then he stepped onto the side of the cart and worked his way around until he could see the bottoms. No marks, nothing to indicate the wine had come from Nothwulf. That surprised Oswin. An oversight. But a good one, as far as he was concerned.

He hopped down from the wagon and continued forward, making a cursory inspection of each wagon as he passed. More barrels, and also some stacks of bags made of course fabric. Flour, rye, oats, he imagined. He stopped by the lead wagon. Strewn around the vehicle were four of Bryning's men-at-arms, all quite dead. It seemed they had been gathered around that one wagon in particular, giving it special protection. Oswin was not surprised.

He climbed up onto the wagon. The wagon driver had made it to the far end of the seat before the arrows in his neck and chest had put an end to him. Now he lay half-slumped and motionless over the edge of the wagon. Oswin spared him a glance, no more, then once again drew his knife, cut the canvas tarpaulin free and peeled it back. There were bolts of fine cloth beneath, and smaller barrels that contained some luxury or other to grace a king's table. And a small, elaborately decorated casket made of polished wood and tricked out with silver filigree.

"Ah, there you are," Oswin said. He picked up the casket. It was disproportionately heavy, a good sign. He tilted the lid back. The casket was filled with mostly coins, some gold, most silver, that gave off a dull gleam in the muted light. It was a significant horde. Oswin did not know exactly how wealthy Nothwulf was, but he guessed this had put a pretty big hurt on his treasury.

Holding the casket in one hand, Oswin extracted a half dozen coins and tucked them in a purse hanging from his belt, then shut the lid and returned the casket to its spot in the wagon's bed. Next to the casket was a leather pouch. Oswin lifted it gently and flipped the cover back. There was only one document inside, which Oswin extracted, turning it over in his hands. On the face of it was written in a flourishing hand, *His Most Benevolent Majesty, King Æthelwulf, Beloved Sovereign of Wessex.* On the back side of the letter was a wax seal, and pressed into the wax was Nothwulf's device, a shield, hart, and boar, entwined with vines.

Oswin broke the seal and unfolded the letter. *My beloved Majesty King Æthelwulf, most benevolent sovereign…*he read, his eyes moving quickly over the familiar sycophancy and on to the substance of the letter. In truth it really didn't matter what the letter said, but Oswin was curious.

With the tragic and sorrowful death of my brother, Merewald, one who was revered by his people and much esteemed by me, I ask now how I might best serve Your Majesty in my office of Ealdorman of Dorsetshire…

Oswin smiled. "'My office of Ealdorman of Dorsetshire,'" he said to himself. "Presumptuous bastard, aren't you? And I have no doubt you're inconsolably distraught over your idiot brother's death. Well, we'll see about *your* office."

He tucked Nothwulf's letter into a leather pouch of his own, which hung on his belt, and drew another letter out. It was very much like the one Nothwulf had written, but the hand that had addressed it to King Æthelwulf was more feminine, and the seal showed the boar and a cross of Devonshire. This Oswin put in Nothwulf's pouch and replaced the pouch beside the casket.

He felt the wagon move under him and he looked up. Two of his men were dragging the body of the driver off the seat. Oswin looked down the road as far as he could see. Others were hauling the corpses of Bryning's men, both waggoneers and men-at-arms, off into the woods, where they would be lost in the bracken. They might have given the men Christian burials if they had time, and if Oswin cared in the least, which he did not.

Oswin hopped down from the wagon and strode back down the road as his men came thrashing their way out of the woods. The men-at-arms, part of Merewald's old hearth-guard, were mounting their horses, while the others whose job it was to drive the wagons were climbing up onto the seats and picking up the oxen's reins.

A man named Alnoth, who had led the ambush, approached him now. "All of Bryning's dead are off the road, and I don't reckon they'll be found," he said.

Oswin nodded. The road was not much traveled, and those who did travel it were not much inclined to start wandering through the woods. The foxes and wolves and crows would take care of Bryning's men before any human eyes lit on them.

"Those two you sent after Bryning, they're not back," Alnoth continued.

"Doesn't matter," Oswin said. "They'll catch Bryning and do what they must." Oswin did not think Bryning would let himself be taken alive, and that was fine. Preferable, actually. "Then they'll catch up to you."

Alnoth nodded. "Very well."

"Very well, indeed," Oswin said. "Now, get on your way. It's a bloody long trip to Winchester, you know."

Chapter Sixteen

I am a sinner, a simple country person, and the least of all believers.
I am looked down upon by many.

St. Patrick's *Confessio*

Brother Bécc mac Carthach thought himself a humble man. But he also saw how such a thought could lead a man into danger. To consider one's self humble might well be an act of hubris. But there was no way around it. He could not eschew humility for fear of that. There was nothing he could do but seek authentic humility and let the Lord decide how successful he was.

Part of authentic humility, a large part, was admitting he was wrong. Which he did. And admitting that Faílbe mac Dúnlaing had been right, which he did as well.

The men were indeed spent, as Faílbe had insisted. They had no fight left in them. Bécc realized that as he made his way back along the path, back toward the deserted monastery at Beggerin. He expected to be challenged, to hear a voice call out to him, some indication that someone was watching the approaches for a possible counterstroke by the heathens. But there was nothing. Even the insects and night creatures were still.

Bécc did not realize he had reached the remnants of the army until he came upon the first of the dozing men. He could just barely make out their forms in the dim light, sprawled on the beaten earth near the outer wall of the monastery. If they had been dead, Bécc would not have been surprised. They looked no different from dead men.

They're soldiers, and the call of battle drives them, Bécc thought. *Not the call of God.* And that was why these men had collapsed in their exhaustion, while he, Bécc was ready to launch another attack on the

131

heathens. But even Bécc in his passion understood he could not renew the battle on his own, and he could not get these men to fight until they had slept and eaten and dressed their wounds.

Not all the men were asleep. Bécc saw a figure coming toward him, a phantom in the dark, and his hand fell on the hilt of his sword. Then he recognized Father Niall, the young priest.

"Brother Bécc!" he said, speaking softly and making the sign of the cross. "God be praised! When the others came back and you and Lord Faílbe were not with them, I feared the worst."

Bécc grunted. "Faílbe is dead," he said. "But I am here."

"Oh, my dear Lord..." Niall said. "You're quite certain? It's too late for me to administer the last rites?"

"Too late," Bécc said. "I saw him die."

Brother Bécc felt no great remorse about killing Faílbe mac Dúnlaing. It was not so different from killing heathens—both were obstacles to God's plan, and any such obstacle must be eliminated. But he would have to confess the killing, nonetheless. He was certain that his actions were justified in the eyes of God, and not sins that required forgiving, but again it was God, and not he, who would decide.

He looked at Father Niall and considered asking the man to hear his confession, then and there. Niall, of course, would tell no one what he heard. Such was the sanctity of confession. But it would still be a terrible burden for the young man to carry, and Bécc knew the priest would never again look on him the way he did now, with love and respect. And that would only be another obstacle in the way of his mission to drive the heathens from those shores.

"What is it, Brother Bécc?" Father Niall asked, and Bécc realized he had been staring wordlessly at the man while those thoughts played out in his head.

"Nothing, Father, nothing," Bécc said. "I'm very weary, is all. The men are asleep? Have any run off?"

"I don't know for certain, Brother," Niall said, "but I don't think so. Those who came back from the beach, they've gone no further than this place. I don't know if they would even have the strength to go further."

Bécc nodded. "There's nothing more to be done now, at least not until they've recovered their strength. You get some rest, and I will, too."

Niall gave Bécc a weak smile. "I'll confess, I'm weary, too, though I've not had a night of battle like you and the others."

Bécc put his hand on Niall's shoulder, a gesture of genuine affection. "Every day you fight for the Word of God," he said. "And that's the greater fight, and the more important. Now, go."

Niall smiled again, turned and headed back up the path, off to find some place to sleep, Bécc guessed. Bécc himself had no intention of sleeping. There was still an enemy out there, one that might muster the will to launch an attack, unlikely though that was. Bécc would not be caught unawares.

He turned and headed back the way he had come, a quarter mile or so from the sleeping men-at-arms. If the heathens attacked, then he was far enough that he could give sufficient warning, and close enough that his voice might be heard.

Satisfied with his position, Bécc dropped to his knees and pulled his sword, holding it in front of him, the hilt and the cross guard and blade serving as a makeshift crucifix. He made the sign of the cross and began to pray.

It was some time until the sun came up, illuminating the ceiling of cloud to the east, and Bécc remained in prayer until that time, until he could just barely see the ridge of dunes in the distance, God's own rampart between him and the heathens.

He crossed himself again and stood and his legs nearly buckled under him from the stiffness in his muscles. He turned and worked the tightness out as he walked back toward the monastery. No heathens had come in the night, and Bécc did not think they would come in the day. To kill Northmen, he would have to go to them.

He reached the first of his sleeping men right at the place where the marshy ground yielded to the trampled earth surrounding the monastery like a wide, brown moat. He looked down at the man's face, pale, tinged almost blue in the predawn light. He was sleeping on his back, his eyes closed and his mouth gaping open, and Bécc might have thought he was dead if he had not been audibly snoring. He also recognized the man as one of Faílbe mac Dúnlaing's captains, perhaps the man who was second to Faílbe in command.

Which meant he was now first in command. Of the men Faílbe had brought, anyway. Bécc knew who was in overall command now, and he would make certain the others did as well.

Bécc nudged the sleeping man with his toe, then nudged him harder when he failed to wake. A third and harder nudge got his eyelids flickering. He sat up and glanced around, a look of dumb confusion on his face.

"Come on, get up," Bécc said. "Near dawn, we have to get ready to move."

The man looked up at Bécc. His confusion seemed undiminished. He looked around again. "Where's Lord Faílbe?" he asked.

"Dead," Bécc said. "What's your name?"

"Bressal," the man said.

"You were Lord Faílbe's captain?"

Bressal nodded.

"Were there any men over you?"

"No," Bressal said. "I was second to Lord Faílbe. I was captain of all his warriors."

"Well, you're captain still," Bécc said. "But now you answer to me, because Lord Faílbe is dead and he and the Lord our God have put me in command." That was not entirely true and Bécc knew it, at least where Faílbe was concerned. But he was certain about God's wishes, and there were no others that needed to be obeyed.

"Is that clear?" Bécc asked Bressal.

Bressal nodded.

"Good. Get your men up and under arms. We have little time before the sun is up. We must be ready to go over the dunes at the very moment there's light enough." Bécc, in his humility, was also willing to admit he had been wrong to think they could succeed in a night attack.

We did succeed, he thought, *or would have, if the devil had not sent his most loyal servant, the heathen Thorgrim.*

Bressal cast off the blanket that covered him and struggled to his feet. He looked around once more, then faced Bécc. "Under arms?" he asked.

Bécc frowned. "Yes, under arms. We'll advance across the marsh and attack the heathens when the sun begins its rise."

"Are you mad?" Bressal asked. "The men are near dead with weariness. Many are wounded. There's no fight in them."

"So are the heathens, near dead with weariness. And likely drunk to boot. We'll never have a better chance."

"Brother Bécc, I don't think you…"

Bressal got no further than that. Bécc grabbed the collar of Bressal's mail shirt and jerked him close, their faces just inches apart. Bécc knew from long experience that men found his scarred, half-ruined face with its missing eye unnerving, and more so when they were forced to confront it so close.

And Bécc knew how to command men.

"You listen to me, Bressal," he said, his voice a low growl, an animal sound. "We'll attack the heathens now. Now! God wills it. And I demand it. And if you'll not get your men to arms, by God Almighty I'll have your head and find another who will."

Bécc held Bressal's gaze with his one remaining eye and he could practically hear the man's reluctance melting away. Finally Bressal nodded, a weak and defeated gesture, and Bécc shoved him away.

"Get Lord Faílbe's men ready. I'll see to the rest. Be quick but don't make a lot of noise."

Bressal nodded again and moved off with just enough alacrity to keep Bécc from rebuking him again. Bécc hurried off in the other direction. One by one he kicked the sleeping men, not hard, just hard enough, and ordered them to get up and under arms. He came across some of the other captains and ordered them to begin rousing their men. He found Brother Niall, walking but as dumb with exhaustion as the rest, and he sent the priest to help gather the men-at-arms.

Soon, what had been a silent and motionless landscape was filled with grunting, moaning, murmuring and cussing warriors. The morning was growing brighter and Bécc could see them more clearly and he was not encouraged by what he saw. They were weary and dispirited, and even those not wounded were feeling the ill effects of their hard use and little sleep. They had not eaten since just past midday the day before.

Never mind all that, Bécc said to himself. *These aren't a bunch of God-forsaken farmers, they're fighting men, real men-at-arms. They'll do what they must, when they must.*

"Men, hear me," Bécc said, as loud as he dared. The men-at-arms made a collective sound, a sort of groan, touched with the sound of affirmation, and they moved a bit closer, *en masse*.

"God has laid before us a great opportunity," Bécc continued. "The heathens are here, prostrate, like Isaac laid out on the altar for sacrifice. But God will not stay our hand, as he did Abraham's. Now is our chance to rid our shores of this filth!"

It had been many years since Brother Bécc had spoken in that way, words to prompt his men to fight. Indeed, it had been his habit, since taking his vows, to say very few words, knowing what mischief words could cause. In his earlier life he might have inspired the men with visions of plunder and women, but now he inspired them with their duty to God. He felt alive, like there were tiny bolts of lightning shooting through him. He felt the power of the Holy Spirit lifting his soul, and with it, his words.

"You are tired, you're hurt, you're hungry!" Bécc continued. "But the heathens are as well, and no doubt dead drunk and fast asleep. We'll sweep over them, kill them all before they are able to stand. It is the will of God and he drives us on with His righteous power! Are you with me, men?"

He did not expect great cheers and he did not get them. And that was fine. He was still concerned that the heathens might hear them. But the men-at-arms did cheer, after a fashion. They had been stirred by Bécc's words, despite their exhaustion. They were standing straighter, holding their shields and spears and swords with more enthusiasm. Some managed something akin to a smile.

"Father Niall, a prayer," Bécc called, and the young priest stepped forward and made the sign of the cross and as one the men-at-arms did the same. Niall led them in prayer. His words were powerful, full of hope and the glory of the Lord, and brief, just the way Brother Bécc liked them in such circumstances.

"Amen," Bécc and the rest said as Niall finished entreating God for victory over the heathens from the North. "Let's go," he said next, and turned and hurried off down the now-familiar path through the marsh. Behind him he heard the sound of nearly two hundred men-at-arms moving with him, their speed building to match his, not running, but something faster than walking.

Up and over the dune, up and over and right at them, Bécc thought. No careful plans that would invariably become a misguided nightmare. Straight on. Catch them by surprise, put them to the sword. Thorgrim and the rest, they would never imagine that Bécc and his men would have the stomach to launch another attack so soon after the first. They probably thought the men-at-arms had retreated back to Ferns. They would realize their mistake and it would be the last realization of their lives.

He could see the dunes now, quite clearly. He looked off toward the east, out over the sea. The clouds were too thick to see the sun, but the light on the horizon told him it had just come up. Perfect. His men would be able to see with no limitations, and the heathens would still be asleep.

Fifty feet remained between Bécc, at the front of the lead rank, and the dune that shielded them from view. No heathens on lookout, none that he could see, because the heathens did not expect an attack and there were none willing to forgo their drinking to keep the watch.

Bécc thought about a war cry, letting go with a shout that would make the heathens understand that the wrath of God was about to descend on them.

Wait, wait... Bécc thought. It had all been timed so well, he could not ruin it now. Once he crested the dune, and was ready to race down the far side, once he was only a few paces from striking one of the bastards dead, only then would he let loose his cry.

The dune was just a dozen yards away now, and the men-at-arms' pace was closer to a run than a fast walk, but Bécc saw no problem with that. In other circumstances he might have wished for a more coordinated attack, but now they were looking to overwhelm their enemies.

He felt the ground beneath his feet rising as he raced up the landward side of the dune and he felt the cry build in his gut. Three more paces and he was at the top, bursting though the tall grass and the battle cry issued from his throat like Gabriel's horn. He held his sword aloft and looked at the scene below him, looking for Thorgrim, who he intended to kill first.

And there they were. The heathen army, the host of Satan. Visible, just over the dunes, as he knew they would be. Visible, crowded aboard their ships and half a mile away, pulling for the beach behind their earthen walls at Loch Garman.

Chapter Seventeen

Then sang on her head that seemly blade
its war-song wild. But the warrior found
the light-of-battle was loath to bite, to harm the heart.

Beowulf

Nothwulf felt in equal parts angry and foolish. Foolish because he was standing just outside his own bedchamber, wearing only a loose undertunic, and peeking in around the curtain that hung over the entrance, like some sort of pathetic voyeur. Furious because of what he was witnessing.

Aelfwyn was standing by the table on which he kept his papers. She had just climbed out of his bed completely naked, the brazen thing. The room was lit by a single candle burning on the table. Its light fell on Aelfwyn's perfect skin and she seemed to glow in that illumination.

Nothwulf shook his head, though he was not sure why. Various reasons, really. Aelfwyn was so damned beautiful, he had to admit it. The shape of her young body, the great tussle of her hair spilling down her back—it was all flawless. That was why he had decided to have one last go at her, before he put her to the test, before he brought it all down on her head.

Some creature—a mouse, most likely—scurried by, making a sound that was disproportionately loud in the quiet chamber. Aelfwyn gave a small gasp and looked up quick, looked right at the place where Nothwulf stood, but he knew she could not see him. She remained frozen in place, just her eyes moving side to side. Silent and listening. The hour was late, most of Sherborne asleep.

A short time passed and Aelfwyn turned back to what she was doing. She lifted the letter that Nothwulf had left, half-written, on the table and angled it toward the candle. She remained that way for a moment, and though Nothwulf could not see them, he could picture her lovely brown eyes scanning the words.

He ran his eyes up and down her body one last time. *God, I'll miss this,* he thought, then stepped around the curtain and back into the room.

"My dear, what interests you so?" he asked. His voice was soft, gentle, but still he saw Aelfwyn visibly startle. She turned quickly, setting the letter down as she did.

"Oh, lord, you frightened me!" she said. She glanced down at herself, as if just noticing that she was naked, then threw Nothwulf a coy smile and scurried over to the bed, jumping onto the mattress and half-burying herself in the blankets.

"Have you finished the business you were on?" she asked. Nothwulf had made some weak excuse for leaving her alone in the bedchamber. Then Aelfwyn added, in a tone that seemed to drip honey, "Are you ready to attend to me again?"

Nothwulf stepped further into the bedchamber. He stopped at the table and picked up the letter that Aelfwyn had been holding, a prosaic message to one of the thegns under his rule concerning grazing lands. He glanced at it, then set it down again. He looked over at Aelfwyn, still regarding him seductively.

"I thought you couldn't read," he said.

"I can't," Aelfwyn said. "It's just...I love the look of letters, do you see? They are such a mystery to me, and I love to look on them, the lovely swirls of ink on the page." Her words sounded like a genuine confession, though Nothwulf was sure it was counterfeit.

"I see..." Nothwulf said, and he meant it. He had only recently suspected, but now he knew for certain. He took a step toward the bed. He saw something flash in Aelfwyn's eyes, something behind the carnal enticement.

Nothwulf stopped just a few feet short of the bed. "When you came here, did you see Bryning?" he asked.

"Of course, lord," Aelfwyn said. "He showed me up here, as he always does."

"Were you surprised to see him?"

"No, lord, why should I be?" Aelfwyn said, and she sounded confused now, or at least like someone trying to sound confused. "He's captain of your hearth-guard. I see him whenever I'm with you, which isn't often enough. Now, pray, lord, give up this questioning and come to bed. I want to show my esteem for you. You won't be sorry."

Nothwulf nodded. "You see, my angel, Bryning was nearly killed just days before. Did you not hear? He and some of my best men were escorting a half dozen wagons bringing tribute to King Æthelwulf. The rest were all killed, but Bryning got away. He has a fast horse, a damned fast horse. He would be dead were it otherwise."

Aelfwyn looked shocked, and a bit afraid, and Nothwulf thought that perhaps they were getting down to real emotions now. "That's terrible, lord!" she said. "Thank God in heaven that Bryning was not hurt. Was it bandits, lord?"

"No...not bandits," Nothwulf said. "Actually, it was Oswin. Oswin and his men."

"Oswin?" Aelfwyn said. "Not Oswin the shire reeve? Surely not."

"Yes, Oswin, the shire reeve. Upholder of the law. The shire reeve who serves your lady Cynewise, I suppose, since she seems determined to stand on as ealdorman."

"Well, this is dreadful!" Aelfwyn said, louder and more emphatic. "But of course my lady had no knowledge of this. She would never allow such a thing. Is Oswin plotting some terrible deed?"

"I don't know," Nothwulf said, taking another step toward the bed, noting how Aelfwyn shrunk back, just a bit, as he did. "I don't know if Cynewise knew of this or not. But here's the thing. No one knew of the tribute going to the king. No one save for me and Bryning. Even the men protecting the wagons did not know where it was going. There was, however, a letter addressed to Æthelwulf, and it was lying on this table." Nothwulf gestured to the table where Aelfwyn had been standing just moments before.

"You were alone in the bed chamber with that letter," Nothwulf continued.

"My lord! No! I..." Aelfwyn began, but Nothwulf cut her off.

"There's been a certain amount of suspicion cast on me, concerning my brother's death," he continued. "In part because Werheard was given a ring that belonged to me...had my crest on it...and it was supposedly given as assurance of my support. That ring came from this same bedchamber. Now, who might have had the chance to steal such a thing from my bed chamber?"

"Servants, lord?" Aelfwyn asked, and that was an end to Nothwulf's much-taxed patience.

"Servants?" he shouted. "You lying bitch, you know full well it wasn't servants!" He lunged at her, hands reaching for her throat, her delicate white throat that he so loved to kiss. He felt his fingertips brush her skin as she rolled clear of him, rolled off the far side of the bed and landed on her feet, a long, thin dagger in her hand.

Where the devil did she get that? Nothwulf thought, and a part of him was admittedly impressed.

He circled around the foot of the bed, wary now, eyes moving from Aelfwyn's face to her knife and back. He had thought that Aelfwyn was one sort of girl, and now he saw she was something else entirely, and he was humiliated by his mistake. He wanted to kill her, the traitorous whore, and he knew it was because of his own shame at having been so easily duped.

"My lord!" Aelfwyn cried. "What are you saying? What lies have people been telling you?" She held the knife in front of her, turning as Nothwulf rounded the foot of the bed.

"You know what lies I've been told, you bitch, you told them," Nothwulf said. He noticed that Aelfwyn's hands did not tremble, that her grip on the knife was strong and sure.

"Was it Oswin who put you on this? Or Cynewise?"

"Lord, I'm sure I..."

Nothwulf lunged, darting around the end of the bed, reaching for Aelfwyn's knife hand with his right, her hair with his left. As he did, Aelfwyn lunged, the knife darting at Nothwulf's chest with terrible speed. Nothwulf leapt back and Aelfwyn was on the bed and over it in two strides, coming down on the far side. She stumbled, regained her footing and raced for the bedchamber door.

Aelfwyn was fast, but Nothwulf, still not yet thirty years of age and fit from a lifetime of martial training and sport, was fast as well. He raced around the bed once more, grabbing a floor-standing candle holder as he did and swinging it like an ax as he ran. He missed as Aelfwyn twisted to avoid the blow but he reached the entryway before she did and stood there, candlestick in hand, as Aelfwyn backed away, still naked save for the knife.

"Let me go, lord, or by God I'll stick you, I swear it!"

"'By God?' That's rich. I don't think God will look to save a treacherous wench like you. But if you tell me who you told about the tribute to the king I might let you live, do you hear? Your life. It is mine to give or take."

At that Aelfwyn smiled. She actually smiled and the expression was sincere. "Do you really think so?" she asked. "Do you really think you have any power at all in this shire? Are you such a fool?"

Nothwulf frowned. He did not like Aelfwyn's words, but of greater concern were the sounds coming to him from beyond his bedchamber, muted sounds of shouting, running feet. Something was going on, something that should not be going on at that late hour. He tried to ignore it, concentrate on the business at hand, which was certainly worthy of all his attention.

"I have no power?" Nothwulf asked, taking a step forward, brandishing the iron candle holder. "Then, pray tell me, who does? Oswin? That simpering fool you call your lady?"

There were footsteps now, running, coming closer. Nothwulf could not ignore that fact any longer. Assassins coming to kill him? Oswin and his men? They had killed half his hearth-guard. Now Nothwulf's household would be easy enough for them to overrun.

"I asked you a question," Nothwulf said, "and you'll answer me now or by God I'll break your head." He took another step, raised the candlestick.

But Aelfwyn had heard the footsteps as well, and she stepped back and smiled once more.

Does she know who's coming? Nothwulf wondered. Or did she just understand, as he did, that whoever it was, whatever reason they were running toward the bedchamber, it was likely to change everything in the space of a heartbeat.

"Someone's coming," Aelfwyn said. "If you're going to kill me you better do it fast."

Nothwulf pressed his lips together. Aelfwyn was making an ugly joke, but she was not wrong. If he was going to do this, he had to do it now, while there were no witnesses, no one to hear Aelfwyn's pleas of innocence.

He took a step toward her and held the candlestick higher and Aelfwyn gasped and took a step back and the sneering smile on her lips vanished. Then the footsteps grew louder and stopped and a fist pounded on the door.

"My lord! My lord!" Bryning's familiar voice, with an unfamiliar note of urgency.

"Come!" Nothwulf shouted. He heard the latch on the door lift and Bryning's footsteps behind him, then heard Bryning's intake of breath.

"What the devil?" he said. Nothwulf spared a glance at him, saw his wide eyes staring at Aelfwyn, naked and brandishing a knife. "What is going on?"

"He's gone mad!" Aelfwyn shouted. "Pray, save me! He's trying to murder me and I don't know why!"

Bryning did not move.

"Give it up," Nothwulf said. "Bryning won't fall for your whore's tricks." Nothwulf straightened and lowered the candlestick. He stepped back, next to Bryning. "This whore's betrayed me, but I don't know who she's betrayed me to. We were just discussing that."

"Yes, lord," Bryning said, and then he seemed to recall why he was pounding at the door in the late hours of the night. "Lord, the hearth-guard at your brother's house—Cynewise's house—they've been called out, lord, and it's said they are coming to arrest you. Oswin is leading them."

"Arrest me?"

"Yes, lord." Nothwulf did not bother asking how Bryning knew this. Bryning had his ways, and that was why Nothwulf kept him well paid in whatever currency Bryning wished.

"Lord, half our hearth-guard are dead, killed with the wagons," Bryning said, his voice somewhere between pleading and panic. "We can't fight the ealdorman's guard, beg your pardon…" Bryning knew better than to refer to anyone save Nothwulf as the ealdorman, but there was nothing else he could call the men coming for him now.

"What are you saying?" Nothwulf asked.

"We must flee, lord. I've turned out what's left of our hearth-guard. They're mounted and ready, but we must hurry, lord. I beg you."

Nothwulf nodded. There was no choice, he could see that. He turned to Aelfwyn. "Get your gown on, you'll come with us."

"No!" Aelfwyn cried. "No, never!" she turned the dagger over and held the needle-sharp point to her breast. "I'll kill myself first."

"Very well, then, get on with it," Nothwulf said.

Aelfwyn's eyebrows came together. "What?"

"Get on with it. Kill yourself. I haven't much time." He handed the candlestick to Bryning and hurried across the room to where his tunic lay in a heap. He grabbed it up and pulled it over his head, certain that Bryning would keep Aelfwyn from plunging the knife into him.

He pulled the tunic down and grabbed his trousers and pulled those on, then took up his sword belt and belted it around his waist, adjusting the hang of the weapon. He looked over at Aelfwyn. She had made no move to end her life. In fact, she had not moved at all.

"As I thought," Nothwulf said. He crossed the room and Aelfwyn followed him with wide eyes, but still she did not move. He wrapped his fingers around her hand and pulled the knife free and tossed it aside.

"We'll have the truth, or my men will have their pleasure, but either way we'll find some use for you." He grabbed her arm and jerked her toward the door.

"Lead on, Bryning," he said. "I trust you already have some idea of where we'll go."

Chapter Eighteen

I sing 'neath the shields, and they fare forth mightily
safe into battle, safe out of battle,
and safe return from the strife.

The Song of Spells

Starri Deathless, recovered at last from the bitter disappointment of once again surviving battle, had settled himself at *Dragon*'s masthead. It was his given place in such circumstances, rowing across hazard-strewn waters, enemies lurking on every shore.

He was not, however, keeping a lookout for any of those potential dangers. He was looking in the one direction from which there was no danger: the beach astern, from where they and the late Ketil's men, now Thorgrim's men, had just shoved off.

"Ha! I see them now, Night Wolf!" Starri cried down at the deck, then twisted back until he was again facing aft and called to the Irish men-at-arms ashore. "You're too late, you dumb bastards, and you may thank your God we have gone, or we'd be adorning ourselves with your guts!"

Thorgrim had been quite certain that Bécc would return, and it would not take the man long. He felt like he knew Bécc now, knew how he thought. He even respected him, at least the warrior in him. Most men would have turned for home, leading their wounded, exhausted warriors away from the fight. Not Bécc.

Nor was Thorgrim averse to fighting. But he would not fight when it was pointless, and fighting Bécc that morning would have been pointless. Ketil's men had been drinking hard, and then fighting hard, and even the ones who were not wounded were ready to drop where they stood. His own men were in much the same condition. And while Thorgrim was sure they could have beaten the Irish men-

145

at-arms a second time, there was nothing to be gained from fighting them again. It would be a hard fight, and the Choosers of the Slain would carry off many of his own men.

And that was a concern. Bécc could replenish his forces from the countryside; he could probably raise two or three times the number of men under his command, if the need was great enough. The Northmen had no such luxury. There were precious few ways to augment a heathen army in Ireland.

"We'll cross back to the longphort," Thorgrim announced, soon after Ketil's men and Jorund's men had agreed to serve him. "Collect up whatever's worth taking and get it aboard the ships, and the wounded and the dead as well, and we'll put off."

There were nods of approval. The men on the beach did not look as if they wanted another fight that day. They moved as quickly as they could, collecting up the food and the ale and the weapons on the beach, carrying the wounded men aboard the vessels as gently as they could and laying them on the deck boards amidships.

They took the dead as well, the Norse dead, in any event. On Thorgrim's orders they were hefted aboard *Dragon*, laid around the mast like cordwood ready for a burning at the stake. There were not too many, seven or eight men, but it would not do to leave them for the crows and wild pigs. They would be given a proper send-off, not for their sake, but for the good of the living. It did a man's attitude no good to think his own body might be left to be torn apart by scavengers on a foreign land.

The sky to the east was just showing hints of gray when the crews of each ship arrayed themselves along the sides and heaved their vessels back into the calm water of the bay. There was nothing to hear but the soft lapping of the sea on the shore and the thump of soft shoes on deck planks as the men climbed aboard, and the gentle grind of long oars thrust through oar ports larboard and starboard.

Six ships, and from them six voices gave the muted order to give way. Twelve banks of oars came down in the water and the ships moved silently away from the beach. One by one they spun in their length and with *Dragon* in the lead began the two-mile pull to Loch Garman.

They had opened up a half-mile of water between them and the shore when Bécc and his men appeared, just as Thorgrim had guessed they would. He could not see them of course. Even if he had been at the masthead like Starri, he would not have been able to see that far. But Starri could, and he whooped with delight.

"Come on, Bécc, you great Irish sheep-buggerer!" Starri shouted. "I'll wait for you on the other shore!" And then, in a display of balance and coordination that was stunning even for him, Starri stood with his feet on top of the shrouds, turned his back to the Irishmen on the beach, dropped his leggings as far as they could go and exposed his narrow, hairy posterior to the morning light.

The men on deck laughed and groaned, caught between amusement and disgust. Starri began to wiggle and gyrate and the groans grew more pronounced. Thorgrim happened to look up at that moment, caught a glimpse of Starri's antics, and quickly brought his eyes back to deck.

I could have happily lived my whole life without ever seeing that, he thought.

It was not long after that Starri called down, "There they go, Night Wolf! Those Irish dogs are slinking away, tails between their legs!"

Thorgrim risked a glance aloft and was relieved to see Starri's leggings were back up and he was in his usual perch.

"Glad to hear it, Starri!" he called up. "Now would you keep an eye out for sandbars?"

"Of course, Night Wolf!" Starri called, shifting his position to see forward. Thorgrim did not actually care what Bécc and the Irish were doing right now. He did not have to care, because he had ships and the Irish did not. With ships the Northmen could cover the distance to Loch Garman in very little time, whereas it would take Bécc a day at least to get there. Such was the advantage of being water-borne, and such was the reason that the Northmen were able to unleash such devastation on the Irish.

They crossed the bay without incident and closed on the beach at Loch Garman, where *Sea Hammer* and *Blood Hawk* still sat on rollers, where woodchips mixed with the shingle, and makeshift tents and smoldering fire rings dotted the place, all enclosed by the wide arc of the earthen wall they had thrown up for defense.

Thorgrim walked forward along *Dragon*'s deck and the men parted for him. He skirted the heap of dead men amidships, covered over with an old tarpaulin, and hopped over the bow and down onto the damp sand. One by one the other ships pulled for the shore, running their bows aground at even intervals, oars coming in like great birds folding their wings.

The only men who had been left in the longphort were those unfortunate enough to be on guard duty on top of the walls when Thorgrim made the decision to go. They came ambling over now, eager to hear of the fighting they had missed.

They certainly would have been able to hear the fight, Thorgrim mused. It must have driven them to madness to hear a battle so close, but to have no way of joining in. He wondered if they had soothed their disappointment with mead. He saw red eyes, mussed hair, sallow complexions and he guessed they had done just that.

Thorgrim walked further up the beach. Behind him he heard his men climbing over *Dragon*'s side and following him ashore. He ran his eyes over the longphort, the all too familiar longphort. It had a look of semi-permanence, the sort of ingrained, settled look of a place whose occupants have been there for a while, and intend to remain a while longer.

Thorgrim shook his head. *Time to go*, he thought.

Jorund's ship, *Long Serpent*, had followed *Dragon* in and now Jorund came ambling over. The long twin braids in his beard, weighted down with beads at their bitter ends, bounced off his mail shirt as he walked. He stopped at Thorgrim's side and joined him in scanning the area enclosed by the earthen walls. He nodded his head.

"You've done a lot," he said. "You and your men. You didn't mean to stay here?"

"No. Just to keep the Irish out, long enough for us to fix our ships."

Jorund nodded. "That's your ship there?"

"Yes," Thorgrim said. "*Sea Hammer.*"

Jorund nodded again. "Nice ship. Nice lines. Not too narrow at the beam, like some."

"Thank you," Thorgrim said. Other than saying kind words about Harald, there was little Jorund could have said that Thorgrim would find more pleasing.

The two men walked further up the beach and Thorgrim indicated where Jorund's men could make their camp, setting up sail tents for shelter and digging pits for fires. Thorgrim told Jorund to have his men and the late Ketil's men bring what supplies they had and deposit them with those already stacked near the big fire ring, those that Thorgrim had bought from Beggerin and Ferns.

The implication was clear: they were all one army now, and they would share supplies like one army. Thorgrim paused to see if Jorund would object, if he was unwilling to join his forces with Thorgrim's so completely. But Jorund only nodded once more and made no comment about that arrangement.

The rest of the day was spent in setting up a temporary camp for the new men, and off-loading the four new ships, new at least to Thorgrim's fleet. Jorund's ships, like Thorgrim's, had seen some hard use. That was chiefly the reason, Jorund explained to Thorgrim, that they had sought the shelter and the convenient beach at Beggerin. They had meant to haul the ships ashore and attend to their increasingly needed repairs.

Once Jorund's ships had been off-loaded of supplies, they were also stripped of oars, sea chests, deck planks, masts, yards, sails, rigging and anything else of significant weight. That done, rollers were set on the beach and ropes run through the oarports. Once the tide had reached its high mark, every man in the longphort tailed onto the ropes, and one by one the ships were hauled, groaning, creaking and dripping from the water until they sat propped up and land-bound on shore.

With the vessels settled propped up and dry, they made an inspection of them: Thorgrim and Jorund and the captains of the other three ships and crews.

A man named Asmund commanded *Oak Heart*, the second of Jorund's ships. He was tall and thickly built and not much given to talk, which Thorgrim appreciated. The two ships which had been under Ketil's command were *Black Wing* and *Falcon*. *Black Wing* had been Ketil's ship. After his death, courtesy of an Irish sword, command fell to a man named Halldor. He was shorter than Thorgrim, young and talkative, with a broad, quick and easy smile. In that way he seemed the opposite of Asmund, but Thorgrim was inclined to like him as well, though he would not form any real opinion until he had something on which to base it.

Falcon was the smallest of the four new ships, forty or fifty feet long and pierced for eight oars per side. It was commanded by a man named Hrapp, a regular sort of man with a thick black beard and black hair bound up in a long, braided tail.

Once Jorund had made introductions all around, the men went from ship to ship, inspecting hulls from inside and out, discussing what needed to be done and what could be done, there on the beach, with only the tools and resources on hand.

They wasted little time with talk. Once decisions had been made, once priorities had been set and tools and materials allocated, they set to work, each of the crews to their own ships. Thorgrim was satisfied with the knowledge and skill the captains seemed to possess—more than satisfied with Jorund, who seemed to know as much as any shipwright about the ways of longships—and he did not think it would be so very long before all the vessels, those that had been long in his fleet and those just joined, would be ready to take to the sea.

The rain held off, despite the heavy layer of clouds, and they worked until the first hints of darkness fell over Loch Garman. Thorgrim relieved the men walking patrol on the top of the walls and replaced them with some of the men who had been with him for a long time and with some of the men who had just become part of his army.

Two pigs, recently purchased from Ferns and butchered that morning, had spent the day roasting over low flames in the big fire pit in the center of the longphort, the smell driving hungry men to near madness. Now the well-cooked beasts were taken down and the flames stoked up until they rose taller than the tallest man there, and the men tore into the pigs with a will. Evening turned into night, barrels of ale and mead were broached, and the tired men settled around the pit, some talking, some singing, but most silent.

Thorgrim sat on a short length of log just far enough from the fire so that the heat was bearable. Failend, Harald, Godi and Starri were with him and they ate and drank in silence and stared into the dancing flames. Soon Jorund appeared out of the dark, and with him the captains of the other ships: Asmund, Halldor and Hrapp.

"We brought mead," Jorund said, indicating a small barrel that Asmund held in his arms. "Not the goat piss we've been drinking, some genuinely fine stuff we've saved."

"In that case, you're welcome to join us," Starri said, gesturing toward unoccupied spots on the logs. Asmund broached the barrel and Thorgrim made introductions for those who had not met and soon they were dipping cups into what was indeed superior drink.

"Do you mind if I ask," Jorund said, "why did you leave Vík-ló? There are stories that pass around, ship to ship."

Thorgrim shrugged. "It seemed time to go. The gods told me it was time to go."

"And now the gods have told you it's time to go back?" Jorund asked.

Thorgrim considered the question. In fact, he had been considering it quite a bit as of late, though he kept his own council. And he had come to a conclusion: he was tired of trying to guess what the gods intended for him.

There seemed to be only one thing that was certain, and that was that he would never leave Ireland. And so be it. If he was to stay, then he would make for himself in Ireland what he had lost in his home in Vik. Land and wealth and slaves and men to command. All those things, he realized, he could have as jarl of Vík-ló. And so he had decided.

"Thorgrim Night Wolf is beloved by the gods," Starri offered. "That's why they test him so."

Thorgrim smiled to himself. *I could do with a little less love of that sort*, he thought.

"Starri Deathless," Jorund said. He said the name slowly, as if trying it out. "There are tales told of you, too, on this coast. They say you can't be killed."

"Don't know that I can't be," Starri said. "I know only that no one has killed me yet. But I stay close to Thorgrim Night Wolf, and I'm sure that means I'll be killed by and by."

"Odin keeps Starri alive," Godi said. "He likes him. Starri makes certain they have plenty of company in Valhalla."

Jorund smiled and nodded his head. "That's how I understand it." He turned back to Thorgrim. "And now you intend to return to Vík-ló? To hold the longphort and be lord over it? To launch raids from there? I don't mean to pry into your business, Night Wolf, but it's now my business as well, and that of these men." He nodded toward Asmund, Halldor and Hrapp.

"It is all of our business," Thorgrim said. "So, we'll return to Vík-ló and we'll take the place back, and with any luck we won't even have to fight for it. We'll see to the defenses, rebuild the walls if we must. We'll see that our ships are in the best condition. And from there we'll go a'viking, wherever there's good hunting to be had."

He looked from man to man and saw each nodding slowly. "That's what I intend, anyway," Thorgrim added. "But a man's intentions are not always the gods' intentions."

"We do the best we can," Jorund said. "We try to make ourselves worthy of the gods' respect."

They turned to their cups and drank in silence for some time, and then Jorund asked, "When do you reckon you'll be ready to sail from here?"

"We've been some time setting our ships to rights," Thorgrim said. "But now we're ready. A day or so, and we'll be ready."

Jorund nodded. "I think my ships…the ships that are just joined with you, the other ships, they'll be ready in a few days as well. It was hard to get men to work when Ketil was in command, but now I think they'll work hard. They're eager to get to Vík-ló and make that their home."

"Good," Thorgrim said. And it was. He, too, was eager to get to Vík-ló, to take hold of it again, to build it back into the fine place it was when he left it.

For two more days the men labored through all the daylight hours, finishing the last of the repairs. Thorgrim's ships and Jorund's ships were made seaworthy again, and then they were pushed back into the water, the great heaps of gear and supplies loaded back aboard, and Thorgrim remained eager to go.

And then he saw the smoke.

Just after dawn, two days after he and Jorund and the others had talked and drunk mead at the fire's edge, they saw the dark streaks rising up from some unseen source. It was to the west, not too far from the walls that encircled the longphort. Columns of smoke. Not thick columns, just tendrils, but a lot of them.

There was an ugly, threatening, unsettled quality to the morning, even before the smoke appeared. Sunrise, it seemed to Thorgrim, was late, as if the sun had overslept after a hard night of drinking. And when at last it came staggering over the horizon it was all but invisible, lost behind a solid dome of black cloud, made just a bit brighter by the sun on its far side. The wind was from the northwest and cold for that time of the year, and grew bolder as the sky grew lighter. Not light, just lighter.

Thorgrim had slept aboard *Sea Hammer*, delighted that his ship was now floating. He reveled in the gentle motion of the ship in the small waves of the bay after so long feeling his beloved craft lifeless and immobile beneath his feet. He woke with the thought, barely formed, that something was wrong. He looked to the east, the black and foreboding dawn, felt the cold wind on his neck.

Godi was there, lumbering aft. "What do you make of this, Thorgrim?" he asked. Some of the men, Thorgrim knew, thought he had a supernatural sense for the weather, but he didn't. He just observed, and remembered what he observed, and that told him much about what was to come.

"It's not a pretty thing," Thorgrim said. "It'll get worse." In his mind he was cursing the weather, and at the same time trying to figure what it meant. They had intended to sail that day, but if the growing storm went the way Thorgrim thought it might, then going to sea would be akin to asking the gods to crush them.

Do the gods mean for us to stay here? Thorgrim thought. *For how long?*

He turned slowly, as was his wont, carefully observing everything around him: the other ships, the men walking up in the longphort, the walls arcing around in a great half circle.

That was when he saw the smoke. It was hard to discern against the dark sky, and the wind was pulling it apart, but by then the sun was providing sufficient light, even behind the clouds, to make it visible.

"Look there, Godi. Failend. What do you see?" Thorgrim said, nodding to the west. The two were silent for a moment.

"Looks like smoke," Failend offered and Godi grunted his agreement.

"Smoke, yes," Thorgrim said. "Small fires. A lot of small fires."

Some farmer burning a field, or a raider burning his neighbor's home, would have made for a single thick column of smoke. But this was many columns, thin columns.

"Cooking fires," Thorgrim said.

"Could be," Failend said. She sounded as if she was not certain, but Thorgrim was. Cooking fires. Men cooking their breakfast. A host of men who had appeared since the sun had gone down the night before.

"Come," Thorgrim said. He strode forward with Godi and Failend behind, and they were joined on the way by Harald and Starri. Thorgrim stopped before hopping over the bow, and said to

Gudrid, who was looking at him though eyes bleary with sleep, "Go get Jorund and the other captains. Have them meet me on the wall."

Gudrid nodded and stood and Thorgrim jumped over the side into the shallow water under the bow and headed up the beach, the others following behind. They crossed to the center of the earthen wall and climbed up the ladder, spreading out so they could all look out to the west. Soon Jorund and the others joined them.

"What is it, Thorgrim?" Jorund asked. He was looking in the direction that Thorgrim was, but his tone suggested he did not know what he was looking at. "Is it the storm coming?"

"No," Thorgrim said. "Look there. Smoke. Do you see it?"

For a moment Jorund said nothing. The wind was rising and it was blowing the smoke away before it rose much above the tops of the trees. "Yes…I see it now," Jorund said at last. "What of it?"

"It's an army," Starri said with undisguised excitement. "It has to be. They must have arrived last night, made camp. They're cooking their breakfast now."

"An army?" someone said, a voice Thorgrim did not recognize. He turned to see who had spoken. It was Hrapp, captain of *Falcon*. "What army?"

"Bécc. The Irishman who attacked you a week past," Thorgrim said. "I'll wager anything it's him."

Jorund made a grunting sound. "Don't give up easy, does he?"

"No," Thorgrim said.

They watched in silence for a moment longer. Then Halldor spoke. "Well, he's too late. Dumb bastard. We're ready to sail this morning."

Thorgrim heard grunts of agreement. But not from everyone. Not from his people, and he wondered if they felt as he did, or if they just knew what he would say.

"Storm coming," Godi said. "And it looks bad. Not the time to go to sea."

"We don't have to go to sea," Jorund said. "All we have to do is cross back to the beach at Beggerin. That whore's son Bécc won't be able to get to us for a day or more. By then the storm has blown out and we're off to Vík-ló."

It made sense. Perfect sense. Thorgrim shook his head.

"No," he said. "No. We don't leave until we've fought him and beat him."

That statement was met with silence. Finally Jorund spoke.

"We left them on the beach at Beggerin," he said. "You thought there was no good to come in fighting him then, and you were right. There's still no good in fighting him."

Jorund, of course, was right. There was no good reason to stay and fight. But Thorgrim did not care.

"We can't leave this. We can't let Bécc drive us off, or think he's driven us off. He's done us enough hurt."

There was an uncomfortable murmuring now, and it was from Jorund and his people. Thorgrim's men, and Failend, felt as he did. Or at least he thought they did. If they did not, they were not likely to say so.

"You think it's worth losing men for this?" Jorund asked.

"There's no worth to be weighed, like this was some sort of merchant's trade," Thorgrim said, patient as he could be. "This is a thing that must be done."

It was pride, and Thorgrim knew it. Pride would not let him leave if it meant letting Bécc think he won a victory. But pride was not a bad thing. The gods expected a man to have pride.

As if reading his thoughts, Starri chimed in. "Look at the sky! Feel the wind! Do you think the gods want Night Wolf to slink away? Wouldn't they have brought fair winds if they wanted that?"

It was a hard thing to argue, and like all berserkers Starri was thought to have a special insight into the desires of the gods. Men listened to him, at least in that regard.

Here is your test, Jorund, Thorgrim thought. He and his men and Ketil's men had thrown in with Thorgrim. Would they stand with him still, if he was doing something they thought foolish? Or would they take to their newly repaired ships and leave their newfound allies on the beach?

"When do you think these Irish might attack?" Jorund asked next. "Should we get the men under arms now, or do we have time for breakfast?"

Chapter Nineteen

*The wine-halls crumble; their wielders lie
Bereft of bliss, the band all fallen
Proud by the wall.*

The Wanderer

True to his word, Bryning had Nothwulf's hearth-guard mounted and ready to move. The horses, made skittish by this odd turn of events, this unorthodox activity at that dark hour, stamped and pawed restlessly at the courtyard ground and twisted nervously as their riders worked to control them.

Bryning flung open the big door of the residence and stepped aside. Nothwulf shoved Aelfwyn ahead of him and as she stumbled into the courtyard he took that moment to pull his cape over his shoulders and fasten the brooch that held it in place. Aelfwyn was now half dressed: Nothwulf had given her just enough time to pull her gown over her head, no more, but that would have to do.

He took two long strides and grabbed Aelfwyn by the arm just as she was recovering from the push, and continued to pull her protesting behind him. As far as he was concerned, the girl should consider herself lucky. Nothwulf's first instinct had been to drag her naked into the courtyard.

Second from the last in the line of riders was a big man named Tilmund, an unsympathetic brute and a good man in a scrape. Nothwulf paused there.

"Tilmund," he said. "We're taking this whore with us. Bear her along, will you?"

"Aye, lord," Tilmund grunted, too disciplined or incurious to ask why. He leaned over and grabbed Aelfwyn's arm and hoisted her up. Nothwulf's use of the word "whore" would be enough to indicate to

Tilmund that there was no need to treat the girl with much consideration. Aelfwyn gave a short cry of pain and protest, but said nothing more as Tilmund settled her in front of him.

Nothwulf strode on. His own mount was beside Bryning's at the head of the line. He could hear sounds now from beyond the walls of his home, an undercurrent of disturbance at an hour that was generally quiet as the grave. Something was happening, someone coming.

Nothwulf swung himself into the saddle and Bryning did as well and the grooms handed them the reins.

"Go," Nothwulf said, just loud enough to be heard, and the men at the big gates swung them open. Nothwulf nudged his horse and the animal moved forward, Bryning at his side, a dozen men of his hearth-guard, all that were left, following behind. They had meant to ride off before the ealdorman's guard arrived, but they were too late.

"Hold up," Nothwulf said, raising his hand and reining his horse to a stop.

"Lord?" Bryning said, an anxious tone. The ealdorman's guard, sent to arrest Nothwulf, were just one hundred yards distant and marching fast down the road, their armed parade lit by two torches held by the men at the front of the column. The captain of the guard led the way, backlit by the flickering light. Nothwulf sat calmly, watched them approach.

"Lord, perhaps we best go," Bryning said.

"We won't run off like we're thieves caught in the barn," Nothwulf said. His pride would not stand for that. What's more, there seemed to be only ten men coming for him, and they were on foot.

The guards' steps made muffled footfalls on the soft earthen road, but no more sound than that. They wore no mail and carried no shields.

Thought you'd catch me a'bed, didn't you, you miserable bastards, Nothwulf thought. He was surprised that Oswin was not there, at the head of them.

No, he thought, *Oswin will want to keep clear of this dirty business*. He waited as the guard approached and Bryning and the others fidgeted and the horses shuffled side to side. The torchbearers stopped ten feet short of Nothwulf's horse, and the others drew to a halt behind them.

"Lord Nothwulf," the captain of the guard spoke. His name was Herelaf, and Nothwulf had known him for many years. "What business have you abroad at this late hour?"

Nothwulf paused a moment before speaking, and when he replied his voice was quiet and even, but his tone carried the implied threat of a drawn sword. "What possible concern is that of yours, you miserable little whore-monger?"

Herelaf's mouth opened but nothing came out for what seemed an abnormally long time. "Well, lord, I…"

"You what? You pathetic turd."

"I…" Herelaf stuttered, then found his footing again "I have orders to…to…the lady Cynewise asks you attend her."

"The lady Cynewise?" Nothwulf asked. "Surely she's still too grieved by her husband's death to speak with me. And at this hour, as you say. You may tell her no, I have other business to attend to."

"Well, lord…I…" Herelaf began again. "I have orders, lord, to bring you to the ealdorman's house…"

"And how do you propose to do that?" Nothwulf asked. He saw Herelaf's eyes move down the line of mounted and well-armed men. Nothwulf's men, unlike Herelaf's, wore mail and carried shields and were considerably better-trained warriors.

Then something else caught Herelaf's eye. "Is that Aelfwyn? My lady's handmaiden?"

"Yes," Nothwulf said. "She chooses to go with us. Is there a problem with that?"

"Ahhh…" was all that Herelaf managed to get out in reply.

"No, I thought not," Nothwulf said. "Now see here. I have pressing business in Shaftesbury and I must be off. Pray tell my beloved sister-in-law that I'll speak with her on my return. That is if she's not still overcome with grief."

With that, Nothwulf was done with Herelaf. He kicked his horse into motion and led his men off in the direction opposite of the ealdorman's house, leaving Herelaf and the guard to watch them go. And there was nothing Herelaf could do to stop them, short of using force, in which case he and his men would die, a thing they did not choose to do just then.

Nothwulf led his guard down the wide road that cut like a river through Sherborne and ended at the big gates built into the walls around the town. There the guards pulled the gates back because

Nothwulf still commanded considerable respect in Dorset and because word had apparently not been sent to them that Nothwulf was not to be allowed to leave.

They rode through the gate, the dark countryside spread out before them. Nothwulf wondered if Aelfwyn would scream, her last desperate attempt to keep from being carried off, but he heard nothing. He wondered if Tilmund had his massive hand clamped over her mouth, but he did not take the trouble to turn and look.

They rode south and west, which was not the way to Shaftesbury because they were not actually going to Shaftesbury. That had been a minor deception, which might or might not have won them a little time from pursuit.

The air carried on it a strange smell, a damp and oppressive smell, that Nothwulf noticed once clear of the stink of the city. It made him uneasy. It was very dark, no moon or stars to be seen, but Bryning had had the forethought to bring a lantern, which he now lit and rested on his saddle. The light, feeble as it was, was enough to show their way along the road, an old Roman road, wide and level as the Romans had built them and the Saxons could not.

They rode in silence. Once, they heard the sound of furtive movement ahead, a rustling of brush, soft voices, perhaps. Robbers most likely, lying in wait. But the thud of a dozen horses' hooves, the jingle of mail, the scraping sound of half a dozen swords being drawn from scabbards seemed to dissuade anyone who might be inclined toward violence and theft, and the riders never saw who or what had made the sounds.

They had ridden for some time when the morning light made an appearance, grudgingly, revealing an ugly sky. It was thick overcast to the east, and to the north the clouds were black and roiling, a portent not of rain but of something much more threatening. It looked Biblical, like something that might have prompted Noah to get a move on. The wind began to rise with the sun, a cold wind from the north. Nothwulf wrapped his cloak around him and cursed.

With the coming of day, Nothwulf was at last certain of where he was. It was a road he knew well, the road from Sherborne, where he had been mostly raised, to Blandford where he owned a manor which had been given him by his father upon reaching his majority. It was a prosperous holding and provided him with a tolerable portion of his income, and he spent a fair amount of time there in the warmer seasons, when the hunting was good.

They continued on, until Nothwulf's thoughts of breakfast overshadowed even his worries about his present circumstance and the threatening weather. He knew it was time that he and his men stopped, but only as long as needs must be.

Another two miles further they came to a small hamlet, a cluster of houses really, around a large, two-story inn which owed its existence to the well-traveled road. Nothwulf had stopped there often. The food was serviceable, the grooms fairly competent and the innkeeper, a fat man named Bedwig, was jovial and pleasant to all who had silver in their purse. On the upper floor, accessed by a ladder through a hole in the ceiling, Bedwig kept a whorehouse of above average quality, which Nothwulf knew from the reports of his men and his own frequent experience.

But there would be no time for that now, nor was Nothwulf in the right frame of mind for such things.

When at last they reached the inn, Nothwulf led the way into the yard. The weary men climbed down from their saddles with various groans and curses as the stable boys came out to take their mounts. They shuffled toward the inn, a solidly build structure of heavy beams and daub walls and a split shingle roof. Bedwig was there, standing in the doorway and looking to the north and the dark and mounting clouds. He turned to Nothwulf and his hand went up in a half-hearted gesture, part wave, part salute.

"Lord Nothwulf!" he said, and again there was a false note in the greeting, but Nothwulf was far too weary to think beyond recognizing its strangeness. He has spent the previous evening humping Aelfwyn, and spent the night riding to safety, and he was near collapse, with an empty stomach and another five miles or more to ride.

"Bedwig, feed these men. And ale, as well, and be quick about it, we're in a hurry."

"Yes, lord!" Bedwig said and with that he led the way into the inn's big front room and started shouting orders to the serving girls, who scattered like a flock of birds. Nothwulf followed him in and deposited himself in a chair by the fire, a nice fire that lit the dark room and filled it with a pleasant warmth on the chilly summer morning.

Tilmund stepped up to him, his big hand holding Aelfwyn by the arm. He seemed to be both supporting her and dragging her along. "What shall I do with her, lord?" he asked.

Nothwulf looked Aelfwyn up and down. It had not been a good night for her, he could see. She wore no headrail, and her hair was in a disorganized tangle. Her fear and outrage had been outstripped by her exhaustion, which was all Nothwulf could see on her face now.

He nodded toward a stool by the fire. "Set her down there," he said.

Bryning came into the room and sat on the other side of the small table at which Nothwulf sat. The tavern girls were moving among the other tables now, setting down wooden tankards filled with ale, while in the kitchen behind the building Nothwulf imagined roast beef was being carved, loaves of bread tossed into baskets, potatoes roasted over an open fire. He felt his mouth watering.

Bedwig himself delivered tankards to the table at which Nothwulf and Bryning sat. "There you go, lord, best in the house!" Some of the joviality had returned to his voice, and Nothwulf imagined that he had figured out what he might charge for feeding all these men, and he liked the number he had arrived at.

"Best? You're sure? Not the dog piss you sell to the other travelers?" Nothwulf asked.

"The best, lord. Like you say, the dog piss is reserved for others."

Nothwulf nodded. He did not doubt Bedwig's claim. The land on which the tavern stood was Nothwulf's land, and all the hundreds around it, and Bedwig would not try to pawn off spoiled ale on the presumptive ealdorman of Dorset. On the other hand, Bedwig's best was not so terribly great.

"How are things about here?" Nothwulf asked. "I know you hear everything, and I'm sure you know I've not been to my manor in some time."

"Oh, things are much the same," Bedwig said. In the past Bedwig might well have pulled over a chair by now, but he remained standing. "All the folk around here are struck with grief over your brother's murder, lord. We can hardly believe such a thing."

"Yes, my brother was well loved throughout Dorset," Nothwulf said, with just enough gravity to hide his sarcasm.

"Yes, he was," Bedwig said. "But now the people thank God in his heaven that you are here to take your brother's office."

"Is that what the people expect?" Nothwulf asked.

"Well…yes, lord. Whatever else could they expect?" The fat man's eyes shifted toward the fire. "The lady, lord, should we get her food and drink?"

"Her?" Nothwulf said, looking over at Aelfwyn sitting on the low stool and slumped against the wall. "No, I've brought her to you, Bedwig. A new whore. You may show her her duties and then set her in a room above."

"Lord?" Bedwig said. Nothwulf was sure the man did not know what to make of Aelfwyn. Her gown was no whore's or peasant's garment, though her appearance was certainly not that of a lady.

"I'm jesting, Bedwig," Nothwulf said. "Get her bread and water, that will do well for her."

Bedwig nodded and withdrew and seemed glad to do so. Nothwulf stared into the fire. He and Bryning exchanged a few words, and when their food arrived they ate ravenously and in silence. It was not long before all of the men had eaten and drunk their fill, which greatly rejuvenated them, and soon they were mounted and riding southeast once more.

The road ran through open country, the farmland from which taxes and rent poured into Nothwulf's purse and tithings into the church. The day was well on, but the sky grew more threatening by the hour and remained as dark as it might be in the moments before dawn. It gave an ominous cast to a day that had never been too promising to begin with.

From atop his horse, Nothwulf could see for miles now, and this country was even more familiar to him than the land between Sherborne and the tavern. Everything about it was familiar, in its place and as it should be, save for the column of black smoke they saw rising up ahead before it was torn apart by the breeze.

Nothwulf could hear muttering behind him. Whatever was burning was hidden from view by the low rolling hill ahead of them. But Nothwulf did not need to see it to know what it was. He knew what was on the other side of that hill, the only thing substantial enough to create such a column of smoke, and that was his own manor.

He felt sick, like that time as a boy he had seen one of his father's servants crushed under the wheel of a cart, something so horrible he could hardly make sense of it. But the servant had been of little consequence to Nothwulf, and the feeling soon passed. But this was something different. This was his manor, his refuge after being driven from Sherborne. It seemed as if his whole life was being crushed under a wagon's wheels, or obliterated between grindstones.

He spurred his horse, and tired as the animal was, it worked itself up to a trot. Down the road, into the dip between the hills, then up over the far hill. At its crest Nothwulf could see the countryside all around, the swath of wood to the north, the road winding its way down to fertile fields. From that hill he had always had the finest view of his manor with its great hall and it's church, it's barns and stables and smaller houses, all enclosed by a high palisade fence.

And there it was still. Save for the great hall and the barn, which were just blackened patches on the ground, the smoke still roiling up from their charred remains.

He rode down the hill, the rest of the hearth-guard still in line behind him, and up to the gate in the palisade wall. It was closed, and a man's head appeared over the top of the wall to the left. He stared at them for a moment, uncomprehending. Nothwulf did not recognize the man and it occurred to him that he might be one of those enemies, whoever they were, who had burned the place, that he might have led his men right into a trap to which his anger and despair had blinded him.

Then the man said, "Oh, Lord Nothwulf!" He looked down at someone hidden behind the gate. "It's Lord Nothwulf, open the damned gate!"

Nothwulf turned in his saddle. "Ready, men, we don't know who's at home." The fact that the man on the wall recognized him was no proof that he was a friend, nor did the fact that Nothwulf didn't recognize the guard mean he was an enemy. There were plenty of men in Nothwulf's service whom he would not recognize.

The gate swung open and a man came striding out, and this man Nothwulf did recognize. He was Siward and he commanded the manor's hearth-guard, just as Bryning commanded the guard at Sherborne. But that did not make him Bryning's equal, since Bryning had command of all the guard that served Nothwulf, a considerable force. At least it once had been.

Nothwulf slid down from his horse. "Siward, what in the name of God has happened here?" He could see people shuffling like sleepwalkers around the charred heaps of building beyond, the people who worked at the manor, the smiths and cooks and laundresses and grooms.

It occurred to Nothwulf that this might have been an accident, that some spark might have caught in a pile of straw and next thing you know the long hall was gone and the barn with it. It happened all the time. He found himself, in those seconds before Siward responded, hoping very much that such was the case.

"Raiders, lord," Siward said and Nothwulf felt his hope crumble, his sense of desperation flare like coals under a bellows.

"They come, I don't know, a little before dawn," Siward said. "Over the wall with ladders, I guess. Just a few, to open the gate." The explanation came haltingly, and Nothwulf was not surprised. Siward was in charge of seeing that sentries were posted, that people did not climb silently over the walls. Siward was finished in that office, but Nothwulf would wait before doling out any punishment.

"Opened the gate?" Nothwulf asked.

"Yes, lord. Opened the gate. Of course we turned out the hearth-guard, but to a man they were asleep, save for the sentries, of course."

Of course, Nothwulf thought. *The sentries weren't asleep, they were drunk.*

"So the long hall, it was already burning by the time we were to arms. Then they went for the barn."

"Who?" Nothwulf asked. "Who went for the barn? Who were these men?"

"I dunno, lord," Siward said. "They were mounted, and most had mail, so they weren't just bandits or such. A dozen men, maybe?"

Nothwulf had heard enough. He brushed past Siward and approached the still burning mass of timber that had been his long hall. His personal apartment had been in the east end of that building. His weapons, his jewelry, his clothing, his papers.

He felt a gust of breeze like a draft from a tomb and it chilled him. He looked up. The sky was blacker still, with lower, gray wisps of cloud racing past. Not a good day to be without a long hall.

Siward was following a few steps behind, eager to show some level of competence, Nothwulf imagined, eager to save his position, though he had to know it was a hopeless quest.

"What happened after the raiders set the fires?" Nothwulf asked without taking his eyes from the destruction.

"Once the building was burning well, then they rode off. They were gone by the time we turned out, lord."

"I see," said Nothwulf. "So, how did you know how many there were? And that they wore mail?"

"The hostler saw them, lord. That's what he said."

Son of a bitch, Nothwulf thought. If they had killed one, or better yet captured one alive, then he might find out who had sent them. Not that there was much doubt in his mind.

"Did you follow them? The raiders?" Nothwulf asked.

"No, lord. Our horses weren't saddled, and with the hall and the barn burning we reckoned we better to stay here and try to put the fires out then go chasing around in the dark."

That made just enough sense that Nothwulf could not accuse the man of cowardice or neglecting his duty. "Very well. Get your men together and mounted. We'll see what we can find of the bastards that did this. And find someone to lock up that little bitch that Tilmund has with him."

There was the slightest hesitation before Siward said, "Yes, lord," and hurried off, shouting orders and trying to sound like a man who was never backward in his duties.

Too late for you, Nothwulf thought. He turned and hobbled back to Bryning and the hearth-guard from Sherborne, who had dismounted and were stretching sore, weary arms and legs. His mind was squirming. The exhaustion, the agony of losing his long hall and barn, the strange, violent weather brewing, were all working on him. But he forced himself to think, to see the next move.

"Let's mount up," Nothwulf shouted to the men and he thought he heard a low and collective groan, though nothing so explicit that it could be attributed to any individual. But that was the extent of the protest, and then the men climbed back up into their saddles.

They waited a few moments more until Siward and his men came riding from the stable to join them. There were fifteen men in the manor's guard, good men, and added to Bryning's dozen they made a formidable force. Enough to overpower the raiders, Nothwulf imagined, if they were lucky enough to find them.

They whirled their horses around and headed back up the road and Nothwulf called, "Siward, get up here!" The sound of horses' hooves on the hard packed rode and Siward was riding beside him. "Did you see what direction they rode off? The raiders?"

"Well…we were pretty busy with the fires, lord. But I think they went off to the east."

Nothwulf frowned and looked off in that direction, as if he might see the raiders, riding away. "That's Leofric's land."

"Yes, lord," Siward agreed. "But there was nothing to say the men was Leofric's men. But that doesn't mean they weren't. Seeing as how they did head off that way, lord."

Nothwulf nodded. They continued on, keeping their horses at a walk. Nothwulf watched the edge of the road, looking for some sign of where a dozen riders might have turned off into the open country, but he saw nothing. Bryning was searching the other side, and he reported nothing as well. Finally Nothwulf reined his horse to a stop and nodded off to the east. "That way, do you think?"

"I should, think, lord," Siward said. "Like I said, I didn't see where they rode, exactly, and it was still night, but I thought I saw them ride off that way. One of them had a lantern," he added, as if just remembering. "I watched that from the wall, saw the light going off to the east."

Nothwulf nodded. The cold breeze gusted and lifted his cape and he thought he heard the distant sound of thunder. "Let's go," he said.

He spurred his horse to a walk and left the road, Siward on one side of him, Bryning on the other, the combined house guards following behind. They moved across the open country, the grass up to the horses' bellies, and toward the great swath of woodland to the east. If the riders had found a path through those woods, Nothwulf knew, there would be no catching them.

They rode a bit longer and Nothwulf felt the exhaustion washing over him. His eyes closed and his head lolled forward and then he jerked awake and shook his head. And understood the sheer futility of what he was doing. He pulled his horse to a stop and turned to Bryning.

"This is pointless," he said. "If I was thinking straight I would have realized as much. Let's return to the manor."

"Yes, lord," Bryning said. Nothwulf swiveled around to make certain that Siward had heard as well and to his surprise he saw Siward reaching across his belly and wrapping his fingers around the grip of his sword.

"Siward, what the devil..." Nothwulf said, but before he could continue Siward pulled the long blade from its scabbard, and behind him, Nothwulf heard the rest of Siward's men doing the same.

Chapter Twenty

[D]reary I sought hall of a gold-giver, Where far or near I might find
Him who in meadhall might take heed of me,
Furnish comfort to a man friendless, Win me with cheer.

The Wanderer

Nothwulf, stupid with fatigue, twisted in the saddle, turning his back on Siward, looking to see what threat was coming, why the man was drawing his sword. Half-formed thoughts tumbled around in his head. He wondered why only Siward and the guards from the manor were drawing weapons.

Oh, you bastards! he thought as the truth of the matter struck him.

From behind someone shouted, "My lord! Keep a care!" Nothwulf turned back. Siward was urging his horse forward over the few feet between them. His sword was raised high, his eyes were fixed on Nothwulf. No time to draw his own weapon, Nothwulf drove his spurs into his horse's flanks. The animal leapt forward, crossing in front of Siward's mount, out of reach of his blade.

Siward cursed and twisted his horse around, and then another rider was there, his horse slamming into Siward's, throwing Siward off balance. Not one of Nothwulf's men but one of the manor guard. He looked at Nothwulf, eyes wide, and shouted "Run, lord! Run! They'll murder you all!"

Nothwulf was still having trouble understanding this, comprehending what was taking place. Siward was turning to come at him again and Nothwulf took that instant to look around. One of his hearth-guard was down, sprawled in the high grass and thrashing about. Bryning had his sword out and was hacking at riders on either side of him. Horses were twisting and rearing and swords flashing in the dull light.

Even as he took that in, Nothwulf pulled his sword and wheeled his horse around, aware that Siward was coming for him. He heard the clash of swords and saw the guard who had warned him to run meeting Siward's blade. One stroke, another, then Siward thrust and caught the man in the shoulder, sinking the point in deep as the man screamed and twisted.

Nothwulf pushed his horse forward, two stride to come up with Siward and he slashed down at the man. But Siward's blade was free and he caught Nothwulf's sword, deflected the blow with a force that sent a shudder through Nothwulf's arm.

"Bastard!" Nothwulf shouted in fury, but rather than renew the attack he rode past Siward, clear of the man. He had to see what was happening, if his men were putting up a fight. If everyone save Bryning had betrayed him.

The field was a chaos of horses, swords, spears, shields in the dark light of the growing storm. It was hard to tell who was who, who was fighting whom, but as best as Nothwulf could see his hearth-guard was standing with him, and the men from the manor had turned. Two men were down in the grass, but he could not tell who they were, friend or foe.

Siward was coming on again, pushing his horse to close with Nothwulf's. Nothwulf felt rage displace his confusion, his surprise. "Bastard!" he shouted again and plunged at Siward, his horse bolting forward. They came at each other, right side to right side. Siward was a trained man, but for all his training he was still the sort who relied more on strength than skill. And Nothwulf was trained as well, very well trained. Trained like an ealdorman's favorite son.

Siward was shouting as he came on, but the words were lost in the general noise of the battle. He had his sword raised as he had before, more like an ax than a blade that might be wielded with any agility. He slashed down, and as he did Nothwulf swung his own sword left to right, meeting Siward's blade and knocking it aside. A tiny turn of the wrist and the point of his blade was in line with Siward's chest and Nothwulf could just feel the amount of force he would need to drive the point right through the links of mail.

He thrust, and as his arm shot out he heard in his head a warning: *Don't kill him!* An image of Oswin hacking Werheard down, the man dead and all that he knew dead with him. Nothwulf felt the point of his blade pierce Siward's mail, felt the resistance and the pop as it broke through, but he stayed his hand there, delivering a wound, painful and deep, but nothing that would kill him. Not immediately, anyway.

Nothwulf reined his horse around, sure that Siward was no threat now, and would not be for the next few moments, at least. It was still a whirl of madness, riders charging back and forth, wielding weapons, shouting and striking and deflecting blows with shields.

And then Nothwulf saw the others. More riders, breaking from the tree line. How many he could not tell, but more than he had. Twenty at least. They were fifty yards off, close enough for Nothwulf to see weapons drawn, shields on arms, the dull-looking silver of helmeted heads. One of the riders was carrying a banner, though coming straight on there was no way for Nothwulf to see it. But it did not matter. Siward had led them here for a reason, and this was it. The second part of the trap.

"Bryning! Men of Sherborne! With me! Follow me!" Nothwulf shouted. It was pointless to make a stand there. There came a time in a man's life, often enough, when he had to stand his ground and die on it, if it was God's will. But this was not such a time, at least not as Nothwulf saw it. To die just then meant victory for someone else. Someone nefarious and wicked.

"With me!" Nothwulf shouted again and he spurred his horse and charged off the way they had come, racing along the trampled grass like it was a road. He looked over his shoulder and was relieved to see Bryning and the others, his men, riding in his wake. He would not have it thought that he meant for himself alone to escape. He would take death over accusations of cowardice.

Twisted in the saddle, jarred by the heavy footfalls of his horse, it was hard for Nothwulf to see clearly what was going on behind him. His men were breaking off from the fight. The men they had been fighting, Siward's men, were not chasing, but seemed to be in some confusion. And beyond them, the fresh riders were coming on fast.

Then another thought came to Nothwulf. *Siward didn't lead us here, I did...* This could not have been a trap of Siward's making because Siward did not know Nothwulf would bring the men that way.

It was all very confusing, at least it was to Nothwulf's mind, dulled by exhaustion and the sudden exertion of fighting. He slowed his horse and turned and stopped. His men were overtaking him fast, but Siward's were not following. Indeed, they seemed to be turning to meet the new arrivals. Nothwulf could make no sense of it.

There was no more than twenty feet between Siward's men and the unknown horsemen when Siward seemed to understand his danger. Nothwulf heard him shout something, saw him drive his horse forward, saw the rest of Siward's men, those still mounted, turn as well and try to kick their mounts to a gallop.

It was too late for that. The newly arrived men came swarming over them, weapons raised, and through his confusion Nothwulf realized that whoever these people were, they were enemies of Siward, not him.

The riders broke like a wave over Siward's men, slashing at them even as they tried to break free. Once again Nothwulf found himself witnessing a chaos of fighting in the tall grass, but now he was a watcher, like this was some entertainment put on for his benefit. For a moment he remained motionless, observing, as his men reached him and slowed and turned as well, so that they, too, could see.

Bryning reined to a stop beside him. "Who's this, lord, come to help us?" he asked. Nothwulf shifted his gaze. Bryning had a cut on his cheek that was bleeding down his face and there was a rent in his mail, but he did not seem hurt beyond that. There was blood on his sword.

"I don't know," Nothwulf said.

"Friends?" Bryning asked.

"I suppose," Nothwulf said. He turned back. The riders outnumbered Siward's men two to one, and they were fresh and unwounded and they were hacking down Siward's men in quick order. And then yet another thought emerged through the fog of Nothwulf's brain.

"Don't kill them!" he shouted and spurred his horse to a run. "Don't kill them all!" He charged at the fighting men and he heard Bryning following behind. Whoever these men-at-arms were, Nothwulf had to assume they were allies. But if in their enthusiasm they slaughtered all of Siward's men, then Nothwulf might never discover what had happened. Once more he thought of Werheard, dead on the cathedral floor.

The fight did not last long. By the time Nothwulf reached the place of battle, it was over. A dozen riderless horses milled about or charged off in panic. The victorious men moved slowly through the grass, making certain that those on the ground posed no further threat.

"If there are any alive, let them live," Nothwulf shouted, well aware that he was in no position to give these men orders. He did not even know who they were. Then one of the riders replied, his voice friendly and familiar.

"Lord Nothwulf, you are the soul of forgiveness."

Nothwulf looked in the direction of the voice. The rider had removed his helmet and was wiping his brow with the back of his gloved hand. Leofric of Wimborne. Nothwulf smiled.

"Leofric, my friend," he said, hoping Leofric was indeed his friend. It was becoming hard to tell. "Your arrival was timely, though of course me and my men pretty much had won a victory by the time you showed." He smiled to show he was in jest.

"Indeed, lord," Leofric said, smiling as well. "Just hoping to catch a bit of your glory." He looked down at the men sprawled in the grass. Nothwulf's men, and Leofric's, but mostly Siward and his company.

"That's your man Siward, if I'm not wrong," Leofric said, nodding to someone Nothwulf could not see in the grass. "Now why would he be trying to cut you down?"

"I hoped you might answer that," Nothwulf said. "I'm sure I don't know. But you must understand what's going on, if you were coming to our aide."

"Nothing of the sort," Leofric said. "We weren't coming to fight. We saw the smoke and it seemed to be coming from your manor. Seemed like it might be trouble, so we came to find out. Thought maybe the damned Northmen were back. Then we heard all the commotion here."

"How did you know it was me fighting? How did you know to engage Siward?"

Leofric shrugged. "I didn't at first. But I can't pass up a good fight, you know."

Nothwulf smiled. Most men as old and wealthy as Leofric were content to remain in their long halls and get fat. But Leofric, despite his white hair and close-cropped white beard, had the physique of a much younger man, and the restlessness to boot. He was indeed the sort who could not resist a good fight.

"We'll ask Siward what this was about, why he turned on us," Nothwulf said. "We'll have the truth from him eventually."

Leofric looked back down at the grass. "No, I fear not," he said. "Someone seems to have split the man's skull quite open. I don't think he's in the mood for talking."

Damn it all! Nothwulf thought, but he knew it would sound like ingratitude to voice his frustration. "Well, surely you did not kill them all. Sure one can be made to talk," he said.

"I should think," Leofric said. And somewhere off to the north the thunder rolled over the open ground, and with it came a gust of cold wind.

"Pray, you and your men, come shelter in my hall," Nothwulf said before he recalled the circumstance that had started all this. "Or, my chapel, I suppose. It'll have to serve in the hall's stead."

"Is that what the smoke was?" Leofric asked. "Your hall?"

"Yes. And my barn."

Leofric shook his head, a gesture of disgust and sympathy. "Who did it?"

"I don't know," Nothwulf said. "But if any of these men still live we'll bring them back to the manor, and there we'll have the truth out of them."

Leofric nodded. "I don't doubt you will. But see here…your long hall is burned and the people at your manor seem determined to kill you. Which makes me think we had best go to my manor instead."

Far off a clap of thunder sounded, the noise rolling over the summer fields, and a cold gust of wind enveloped them all.

Twenty-One

The haughty unshaven horde
Began to traverse the harbours;
Birds' bills with bearded heads were seen
Coming from the churches of Ulaid.

Annals of Ulster

Brother Bécc mac Carthach removed his helmet and turned his scarred face up to the sky. It was a sky such as he had never seen before: black, roiling clouds dancing and twisting against a backdrop of clouds blacker still. It was midday but the land was dark as if it were near nightfall. It was the kind of sky he might expect to see at the end of days.

Perhaps this is it, he thought. *Perhaps this* is *the end of days.*

That would be fine, he thought. It would not be so bad to die just then, to have the entire world destroyed, and the dead lifted bodily from their graves. He was ready. Because he would be doing God's work that day, whether he lived or died.

He turned his eyes back to earth. Bressal was heading toward him now, the cold wind blowing his hair sideways as he walked. He, too, glanced up at the dark skies and he looked troubled and Bécc guessed that Bressal could also sense the presence of God's wrath. But if he was worried by it, it meant he did not understand.

Bressal had retained command of Faílbe mac Dúnlaing's men-at-arms since Faílbe's unfortunate but necessary death in the tall grass near Beggerin. Faílbe's men had once made up a majority of those under Bécc's command. But no more.

The heathens' escape had angered Bécc, but only for a short time. He had yelled and cursed and screamed for Thorgrim and the rest to come back and fight, but the ships were already too far off for the men aboard to hear him.

When his equilibrium returned he stood for a long time and watched the six vessels growing smaller in the distance and he hated them. The ships were the thing that made the heathens so hard an enemy to fight. They would be at Loch Garman before the sun had climbed much higher in the sky, while it would take him the better part of the day to march his men around, and by then they would be too tired and the day would be too far gone for them to attack.

Ships... Bécc thought. Ships brought the heathens from across the seas and ships carried them easily up rivers and into the heart of Ireland. Ships allowed them to disappear over the horizon, beyond the reach of his vengeful sword. He hated ships. They were the work of Satan. He knew his Bible and he knew that nothing good ever came about because of ships. What was one of the Lord's greatest miracles? Walking on water. Shunning the frail vessel that held the terrified apostles.

He shook himself out of that pointless reverie. The men were lined up along the dunes and watching in silence as their enemy rowed off to the safety of their fortifications. And they expected Bécc to do something. God expected Bécc to do something.

Which he did. He ordered the men back to Beggerin. There was a great circle of a wall around the monastery, but the gates had been left unbarred when the terrified occupants—priests, nuns, monks, servants, slaves, artisans and laborers—had fled at the first report of heathens landing on the nearby beach.

Now Bécc led his men back through the gate. All the people of the monastic city had left before the heathens attacked, but the heathens had come soon after, that was clear. Doors hung open, carts were overturned, barrels were smashed on the ground and sacks torn open and left scattered like dried leaves. The people had taken anything of value, and the heathens had come for the rest.

Bécc turned to Bressal. "Get the men bedded down in any place you can find. Post a watch. I doubt there'll be any threat, but post one anyway. And look around, there might be some food or drink left. If not you'll have to find some."

"Yes, Brother Bécc," Bressal said. "But...are you leaving us?"

"For a time," Bécc said. "I'm going to Ferns. I'm going to make sure this vermin is crushed."

Exhausted as he was, Brother Bécc left Bressal in command, found his horse, and rode off to Ferns and the wise council of Abbot Columb. Whom Bécc did not entirely trust, not anymore.

The abbot was a holy man, of that Bécc had no doubt. But even holy men could make mistakes, and Columb had done just that, making a bargain with the heathens, suffering them to remain at Loch Garman, trading food and ale and cloth for silver. Silver plundered from some other unhappy monastery. It had been a mistake and it had come apart just as Bécc had known it would.

Bécc did not intend to lie to the abbot. That was a sin, and he was not sure even Father Niall would give him absolution if he confessed such a thing. Besides, he had yet to confess to the killing of Faílbe mac Dúnlaing. But Bécc also knew that there were ways to tell the truth that still gave the impression one wished to give. And that was what he intended to do. Because it was essential, absolutely essential, that Abbot Columb understand that the heathens were a threat that had to be wiped off the face of God's earth.

He went directly to the abbot's quarters. He was filthy and bloodstained and visibly exhausted. He still wore his sword at his side and his mail, the links caked in patches with dark brown dried blood. His appearance, he was sure, would give the moment the gravity it deserved.

Bécc did not miss the shock on the abbot's face as he looked up and saw God's battered warrior enter the room. And the abbot did not fail to understand the gravity of the situation, as Bécc informed him of the bloody fighting, of how it had resulted in the tragic death of Faílbe mac Dúnlaing and many others. Bécc explained how the heathen Thorgrim had betrayed them, had stolen God's victory right from their hands, and had brought death to Christian soldiers. He explained how the heathens had joined forces, how they had plundered Beggerin and how they would next come for Ferns.

He told no lies about the fierceness of the fighting, the grave threat the heathens posed. He did not have to. The truth alone was enough to create the proper fear in the abbot's heart, and the hearts of those other men of rank whom the abbot summoned to hear Bécc's tale. Bécc may have left some facts out, he may have left it to the others to reach certain conclusions, but he told no lies.

He was near collapse when at last he staggered off to his familiar cell. He managed to remove his sword belt and his mail, that was all, before he lay down on the coarse mattress and fell immediately asleep. He told himself he would wake for vespers and compline—he always did, the habit was ingrained—but to his shame he slept right through the night, waking only when the bells rang for lauds the following morning.

It was not long after the morning prayer that the first of the men-at-arms began to arrive, and with them the *bóaire* and *fuidir*, the lower sort, tenant farmers who owed military service to their lords. They came with spears and shields and an odd assortment of leather armor. They provided little in the way of military prowess, but they came in numbers, and Bécc knew he could make good use of them. Even untrained men could do damage to an enemy, if there were enough of them.

By the following day the *ad hoc* army had swelled to well over a hundred men, closer to one hundred and fifty, and more kept coming until there were at least two hundred souls, armed and ready to move. The abbot and the rí túaithe of the lands around had been made to understand that their property, cattle, people and lives depended on crushing the heathen threat. They had responded. And now Bécc had the instrument he needed to fulfill the will of God.

He marched them south from Ferns, linking up with Bressal and the others at a ford on the River Slaney. Nearly four hundred men, four hundred Christian soldiers, off to drive the heathens back into the sea.

They crossed the Slaney and marched south, closing with Loch Garman. Bécc sent scouts out ahead to make certain that the heathens were still there, which they were, and not waiting to spring some trap, which they were not. Bécc set up the *dúnad*, the encampment of an army on the move, less than a mile from Thorgrim's earthen walls. He had the men eat and rest. He had Father Niall celebrate mass and he ordered that enough bread and wine be provided so that all the men there could receive communion. If ever there was a time to look for the Lord's blessing, and to be prepared to meet him, it was now.

The next morning dawned black and ominous, as threatening a sky as Bécc had ever witnessed, a sure sign from God that today would be a momentous day, a Day of Judgment for many. A day that would see untold numbers of heathen souls cast down into hell.

"Brother Bécc," Bressal said, coming to a stop at Bécc's side. He was nervous, Bécc could see that. Most of the men were, the captains included. It was not the pending fight, he knew that. Bressal and the others, the men-at-arms, anyway, were trained warriors. They were not afraid of going into battle, even against Northmen.

It was the weather. The low, black clouds, the cold gusts of wind from the north and, increasingly, the far off rumble of thunder had them on edge. It was frightening, there was no doubt about that. But it did not frighten Bécc because, unlike the others, Bécc knew that he was reading it right.

"Yes?" Bécc said.

"The men...they're ready. Ready to move as you ordered. But...the fires...from the cook fires this morning. Sure the heathens must have seen them, even with this wind. They must know we're here."

"Good," Bécc said.

Bressal squinted, looked away, looked back at Bécc. "Won't they be ready then, for us to attack?"

"They will," Bécc said. Bressal's expression suggested he expected Bécc to further explain, which Bécc did not intend to do. Instead he said, "We'll have Father Niall offer one last prayer. He knows how to be brief. And then we move."

Father Niall was indeed brief. When he was done he raised his hand in blessing, and all the soldiers there made the sign of the cross and knew that this holy man had brought God's blessing down upon them.

"Let's go," Bécc growled to Bressal. Bressal turned and relayed the orders to the other captains, a dozen of them, leading the contingents sent by the many rí túaithe who stood to lose a great deal if the heathens were allowed to range over the countryside.

Bécc led the way. He was on foot and he walked with Bressal a little behind him and some of the more senior captains behind Bressal and the men spread out in three columns behind them. Bécc felt like the tip of the arrow, the deadly point that would be thrust into the heart of the heathens. He liked that. Overhead the thunder rumbled, louder and closer, and the wind picked up, hitting him nearly head-on and making him stagger a bit. He liked that as well.

The earthen wall surrounding the heathens' makeshift seaport was a couple hundred yards away when Bécc stopped at the edge of the tall grass that may or may not have hidden them from the men watching from the wall. If there were any. He could not tell.

"Bressal," he said, and Bressal appeared at his side. "Are there any sentries on the wall, that you can see?"

Bressal paused and scanned the distant earthworks. "Two, maybe, that I can see, Brother Bécc."

"How well can you see?" Bécc asked.

"Very well," Bressal assured him.

Bécc grunted. He might have expected the heathens to be more alert, if they had seen the cooking fires. Which of course they might not have done. They might have been too drunk, or engaged in some other debauchery. He turned and looked behind him.

Three divisions of men, each with their captain leading them on. In the center division the men held a ten-foot section of log, a foot thick, with a series of ropes lashed along its length by which they were holding it. A battering ram, one that would make short work of the sorry lash-up of a gate that was built into the heathens' earthen wall.

"You know your duty!" Bécc shouted, his voice carrying over all the hundreds of men arrayed behind him. He nodded to one of the young men in the center division who held in his hand a long wooden shaft with a banner wrapped around the end. The young man stepped up to stand beside Bécc. He unwound the banner. The cloth stood out immediately in the stiff breeze, a pure white background, and on it a simple cross, deep red, the color of blood.

"Forward!" Bécc shouted. He stepped off and behind him he heard the men moving as well, a great army, as great an army as he had ever led, moving toward the heathens' camp, that blight on the shores of sacred Ireland.

He moved a little faster, but not too fast, because he did not want the men to break into a run. Now even he could see men on the walls. More than the handful that had been there before. The Northmen, when they saw the Irish coming at last, must have sent more men to defend the earthworks. Now they were pointing and running and apparently shouting to those on the far side. They were scrambling to make ready, it seemed, because they had been caught unawares.

We shall see, Bécc thought. The heathens would be fools to think their pathetic defenses would hold anyone at bay for long. But he had learned long ago not to underestimate an enemy, any enemy. And the devil, the cleverest enemy of all, whispered in the Northmen's ears. And no one seemed to hear and heed the devil's cunning advice more than the heathen Thorgrim.

There were more men on the wall now, armed with bows, a weapon not much used by the Irish. Bécc half turned his head to the men behind him. "Shields!" he shouted, and the men obeyed as they had been told to do, lifting shields up high to defend against the coming arrows, while the men-at-arms who flanked the battering ram held their shields to cover those laboring under that burden.

Bécc, too, raised his shield, but just a bit, just enough to set an example. He did not feel the need for such protection. He was in God's hands. Which did not mean he thought God would shield him from death. Not at all. He might well be struck down that day. But regardless of what happened, it would be God's will, not his.

Overhead, as if to reinforce the notion of God's omnipotence, the thunder rolled and the lightning flashed. Bécc stole a look up at the sky and shook his head. *Here is the power of God's wrath*, he thought. The sky was so black, the clouds swirling so that he would not have been surprised at all to see them part and see God Himself descend to His creation.

There was nothing Bécc would have more liked to do than sink to his knees and revel in the glory of the Lord, but there was God's work yet to do. Thirty feet from the earthen wall and the arrows started to come, streaking down from above, thudding into shields or embedding in the soft ground or finding a mark that was followed by a grunt or a shriek.

Not so many... Bécc thought. He would have guessed the heathens would have more archers and spearmen on the wall. The best chance they had for stopping the attack was to prevent the Irish from breaching the defenses. Once Bécc had his men past the wall, the heathens were done for, and he had to imagine Thorgrim knew as much.

He stepped aside, his flag-bearer still with him, despite two arrows standing out from his shield. Bécc reached up and jerked the arrows free and tossed them aside and the men with the battering ram and those protecting them with shields hurried past. They crowded around the gate and Bécc could not see what was happening through the press of men, but he heard the sound of the ram's blow against the gates, heavy and substantial. A pause and then another blow, and with it a cracking sound.

This will not take long, Bécc thought.

He could hear shouting now from behind the walls, the sounds of confusion and panic. The heathens seemed as unprepared as Bécc had hoped they might be, and now they were trying mightily to organize for a fight. The battering ram pounded, then pounded again. The sound of shattering wood grew louder.

Bécc looked up, ran his eyes along the top of the wall. There were only two archers left, and they were being met with a shower of spears from the Irish gathered at the foot of the wall. He saw one of the heathens take a spear in the shoulder, the impact spinning him around and knocking him off the far side. That was enough for his partner who disappeared after him, putting the earthen rampart between himself and the Irish army.

There was another thump of the battering ram and the sound of rending wood and a shout from the crowd of men and Bécc knew that the gate had come apart, and now his men-at-arms could flood unimpeded into the longphort and start that morning's real work.

"Follow me," Bécc said to his flag-bearer, and he headed for the edge of the wall, slinging his shield over his back as he did.

The wall, of course, was built as vertical as it could be, but since it was essentially just a great mound of earth it could only be made to stand if there was a considerable slope to the sides. Once such a wall was grown over with grass which held it together it could be made steeper, but this one was new, and still bare earth.

Bécc led the way down into the ditch from which the dirt of the wall had been dug and up the far side, then up the slope of the wall. It was not an easy climb, and anyone trying it would have been an easy victim for defenders on the top, which was the wall's chief purpose. But there were no defenders now, as Bécc had seen, and using feet and hands he managed to get up the steep slope and pull himself onto the flattened top of the barrier.

He straightened just as his flag-bearer came up beside him. He opened his mouth to admonish the flag-bearer to make certain the flag was restrained and not flying in the wind, but the boy, a clever one, had already done so, holding the cloth against the wooden shaft with both hands.

Bécc turned and looked out across the longphort. It was a place he knew well, since he had insisted on accompanying every delivery made from Ferns to that place. He told Thorgrim it was to be certain that nothing was stolen along the way, but he doubted Thorgrim believed him. Bécc came to observe the defenses, the number of men there, the state of the ships. To seek out any potential weakness. It was not to assure the safety of the deliveries, though for the sake of peace he and Thorgrim pretended that it was.

What he saw now, from his perch fifteen feet above the ground, made him smile. It was not a smile of pleasure, but one of appreciation. Appreciation of his enemy. Because Thorgrim had not been caught off guard, not at all.

The heathens had built makeshift walls out of the logs they used to roll their ships in and out of the water. Not tall, no more than four feet high, but enough to give them a considerable advantage. The walls flanked the main gate and stood perpendicular to the earthen wall, forming something like a long, narrow pen, and the space between them narrowed as they reached into the longphort.

The heathens, with spears and swords and axes, stood behind the barriers. The Irish would be trapped between the two walls like deer driven into an enclosure and cut down. It was what Thorgrim had hoped would happen. It was why he had not really tried to defend the wall.

But Bécc had guessed Thorgrim might try something like that. He had not guessed at the walls exactly—that was more clever than he had thought the heathens would be—but he suspected there would be some trickery. That was why he had arranged things as he had. That was why the center division, going in through the gate, was made up mostly of the farmers, the bóaire and fuidir. Better to sacrifice them than the men-at-arms, who were of much greater value in a fight. It was an unhappy fact, but a fact nonetheless.

He waited for a moment, watching as the first men burst through the gate and ran into the longphort, flanked by the log walls on their right and left. He saw their enthusiasm for battle fade as they realized the trap, and the first men in the column were cut down by spear thrusts and arrows. He saw the woman, Failend, standing on top of the log wall, nocking and shooting arrows faster than he would have thought a person could.

The men pushing through the gate were slowing, hesitating as they saw their companions fall and understood the trap into which they were charging. But the men who were still outside the gate, who could not see into the longphort, were pushing forward, driving the reluctant farmers into the gauntlet of the Northmen's weapons. It was a butcher's yard, the center of the fighting, and it held the attention of every man there.

Bécc turned to his flag-bearer. "Now," he said. The flag-bearer released the cloth and the flag stood out in the growing wind and overhead the thunder rolled in God's powerful voice. The flag-bearer raised the staff and waved the flag back and forth in a great sweeping arc, and continued to wave it.

The fighting below was a bloody mess, but Bécc lifted his eyes from that and looked off to his left, and then his right. Nothing. He wondered if perhaps the flag could not be seen. But then he saw something: a man, climbing up onto the semi-circular wall on which he stood, but far off, closer to the far end of the wall where it met the bay.

"There," Bécc said, nodding toward the distant figure. "What do you see?"

The flag-bearer did not pause in his waving, but answered, "It looks like Bressal, Brother Bécc, but he's far off."

Bécc grunted. It should be Bressal. He looked to his right and now he could see more men coming up over the wall on the other side. In the twilight dark of the building storm, and with his poor eyesight, it was hard to be certain, but they appeared to have shields and helmets on their heads. The men-at-arms. The left and right divisions. While the poor bastard farmers fought it out in the pen the heathens had built, the real fighters were coming unseen over the walls behind them.

Just as Bécc had planned.

He looked back to his left-hand side. Bressal was over the wall and half climbing, half sliding down to the trampled ground below, and behind him more of his division were following, while still more were climbing up over the edge of the wall. One hundred and fifty men following Bressal, another one hundred and fifty in the division to the right, led by a man named Fergal, an experienced old campaigner.

Bécc looked down at the slaughter below him. The farmers and the few men-at-arms among them were fighting back, facing the heathen enemy on either side. There were quite a few dead among the Irishmen, lying bloody and sprawled at the feet of the fighting men. But there were dead and wounded among the heathens as well. And still no one seemed to have noticed the warriors coming up from behind.

Bécc looked up again. The two divisions were over the walls and formed up into loose shield walls, but they were not wasting a lot of time making their lines nice. Speed and surprise were their chief weapons.

"Now, kill them! Kill them all!" Bécc shouted, but in that same instant a great boom of thunder rolled down from heaven and obliterated his words.

Twenty-Two

Spear screeched in his wound
sorely — I cannot be sorry.

Gisli Sursson's Saga

Standing on the earthen wall, the storm building, a cold wind whipping their hair out like tattered rigging on a ship at sea, Thorgrim had said to Jorund, "Breakfast. Before we make ready for Bécc. But be quick about it. We have much to do."

Jorund had nodded and called out to his men to eat now and eat quickly and Godi and Harald did the same and soon the men were scrambling to fill their stomachs. Thorgrim could not know when the fighting would start, but he did not think it would be until the morning was well along, and he knew men should not fight on empty stomachs if it could be helped.

He himself did not go for his morning meal, but remained on the top of the wall, staring out at the columns of smoke. They were more difficult to see as the wind continued to rise and blow them away, and as the men in the distant camp finished with them and let them die.

Thorgrim could picture what was going on now in the Irish camp: the men-at-arms shuffling into mail and running stones over the edges of swords. The Christ priests chanting their chants and going through their magic rituals. The country folk that the Irish called up for fighting trying not to look as afraid as they were.

In Thorgrim's homeland every man was trained with weapons from a young age, whether they fought for their king or went a'viking or spent all their days in farming. They would make a formidable enemy. But not the Irish. For the Irish, the farmers who were put under arms were little more than an obstacle to be placed between the enemy and the real warriors.

How many men do you have, Bécc? Thorgrim wondered as he looked out over the land. The sky right down to the hills in the distance was awesome and frightening. It looked the way the sky would look during Ragnarok, the final battle and the end of Midgard, the world of men. It made Thorgrim wonder if he was indeed witnessing the start of it, the beginning of the world's end.

He saw movement beside him and turned as Failend came walking up. She held a wooden bowl full of porridge that steamed in the cool morning, a wooden spoon half buried in the mush. She handed it to him and he took it and nodded his thanks.

"You send the men to eat, but you don't eat yourself," Failend chided.

Thorgrim smiled. "The other men don't have you to bring them their breakfast."

"You were so sure I would serve you in that way?" Failend asked. Thorgrim shrugged. In truth he had not thought about it one way or the other, had not considered eating at all. He had other concerns.

He took a spoonful and ate it. There was honey in it and it was warm and sweet and wonderful. "I never know what you'll do," Thorgrim said to Failend and meant it. "But I thank you. And I'm grateful for you." And he meant that as well.

For a moment they were silent, looking out over the dark countryside, while Thorgrim finished off every bit of the porridge. He was hungry and had not even realized it. Finally Failend spoke.

"Jorund was right, you know. We can just row away. We don't need this fight." That was the truth, and Failend alone among them dared to say such a thing. Jorund had brought it up as a practical matter, but once Thorgrim had spoken his mind, Jorund would say no more. None of them would. They would not risk being thought cowards.

But Failend knew no such fear. She was a woman and so did not jealously guard her reputation as a warrior as the men did. Besides, she had proven herself often enough that no one would have thought to question her courage.

"We don't need this fight, but the gods demand it," Thorgrim said. "Look at the sky. Do you hear the thunder? The gods would never favor a man who was so backward in his courage as to flee before the fighting starts. That's what they're saying now."

"I see," Failend said. She was quiet for a moment, and then said, "You know, Bécc is out there somewhere, and he's certain that the sky is a sign that God...his God...my God...wishes him to drive the heathens from Ireland."

Thorgrim looked at her. This surprised him. "You think so? You think Bécc sees this as a sign from his God?"

"Yes. I'm sure he does."

Thorgrim made a grunting sound. How odd. How odd that a man could read the heavens so wrong.

"How will you fight him?" Failend asked after some time. Another question that no one but her would have dared ask, not even Harald.

"There are two ways that Bécc can get at us," Thorgrim said. "Over the walls or through the gate. If he has a great number of men, and he attacks along the whole length of the wall, then we won't be able to fight them all off. But Bécc will lose a lot of men doing that. So I don't think he will."

"But if he comes through the gate, won't he also lose a lot of men?"

"He could. But if they're bold and quick it won't be so bad for them. Or Bécc might do both, come through the gate and over the wall as well. So we'll make ready for that. We'll make ready for anything."

They climbed down off the wall as the men were eating the last of their breakfast and bundling up their gear and getting their weapons in order. Thorgrim called Godi and Jorund and the other captains to him, along with Harald and Louis. And Starri, of course, who would have come anyway.

"They'll attack soon, I would think," Thorgrim said. "They'll come over the wall or through the gate or both. Here's what we'll do."

The others listened close as Thorgrim laid it out, step by step, how they would defend the longphort and beat back the Irish, so that the Irish would not think the Northmen weak, and the gods would not think them cowards for slinking away. And then they set to work.

The morning was well along, and the rollers that had been used to move the ships piled into makeshift walls extending out from the gate, by the time Bécc and his men finally made their appearance. It was Starri, positioned on the top of the wall and scanning the countryside, who saw them first. He had asked Thorgrim—begged him—for leave to go down the far side of the wall and scout out Bécc's movement, but Thorgrim had refused. He did not trust that Starri would limit himself to looking and reporting back, and he did not want Bécc to think they were in any way prepared to counter his attack.

"Ah, here we are, Night Wolf!" Starri said, pointing off into the distance. "The rabbits are showing themselves, peeking out from their burrows!"

Thorgrim looked in the direction Starri was pointing, but he saw neither man nor rabbit nor much of anything beyond grass and trees. He turned to Harald.

"Do you see them?" he asked.

Harald nodded. "Yes, I see some men. Not many. Just to the left of where those tall trees stand."

"Bécc and his captains," Godi suggested. "Come to see what they're up against."

"I'd wager you're right," Thorgrim said. He turned and looked down at the men clustered on the ground. "You men for the wall, come up here now!" he called and a couple dozen men swarmed up the ladders to the top of the wall. They had already been told of their part: to defend the walls, but also to feign surprise and confusion at the sight of the enemy. The more excessive confidence they could inspire in Bécc, the better. The more likely that Bécc would do something stupid.

Thorgrim did not necessarily think that Bécc would do something stupid—he knew Bécc well enough to know he was no fool—but it was worth tempting him. Because he knew this would not be an easy fight. Bécc would not have come back unless he had considerably more men than the Northmen had. He would not attack if he did not have reason to think he might win.

Overhead the thunder rolled again and another gust of cold wind, stronger this time, hit Thorgrim on the back and nearly made him stagger. He thought about Bécc out there, across that open ground, certain that it was his God who was calling for blood that day. It gave him an odd, unsettled feeling. He had seen much of the Christ God during his years in Ireland, and he wondered how powerful He was.

Then a general murmur ran through the men along the wall and Thorgrim was pulled from those pointless thoughts to more immediate concerns. A few hundred yards away, where the more trampled earth yielded to a field of taller grass, the Irish had appeared. Not the handful who had shown themselves earlier, but the army, Bécc's army, the horde he had led here to drive the heathens out. There were a lot of them.

Harald and Godi and Jorund had joined Thorgrim on the wall and for a moment the four men watched in silence as more and more soldiers appeared from the field and formed up into three divisions.

"Three hundred men, at least," Harald said.

Godi grunted. "At least. I would make it more like four hundred."

"More like four hundred," Jorund agreed.

"They'll be tripping all over themselves," Thorgrim said and that elicited grunts from the others. "Now go. You have other places to be."

They left him on the wall, took their positions with the men behind the barricades. The men picked for standing on the wall—the men and Failend, with her deadly bow—were spread out along its length, watching the Irish as they began their slow advance, but they were not motionless or silent. Rather they were rushing back and forth in a lovely imitation of panic, and pointing at the Irish and shouting to the men below them in the longphort.

Thorgrim smiled. "Archers!" he shouted, and the men on the wall armed with bows, began to draw and fire on the enemy, now just a few hundred feet away. Failend, too, had dropped to one knee and was pulling arrows from her quiver and firing into the oncoming enemy, taking her time, taking her aim, which was bad luck for any man she picked out of the line.

The Irish did not hesitate. In fact, their pace built as they came on, and almost as one the front ranks raised shields, clearly reacting to some order Thorgrim could not hear. Men were falling here and there, victims of the Northmen's arrows, but still they came on.

How will you do this? Thorgrim wondered. Bécc's men were still in their tight groups. If they were going to assault the walls he would expect them to attack as many points as they could, to make the Northmen spread their defenses so thin as to be useless. But that was not what they were doing.

Then Thorgrim saw the center group moving forward, shields up, protecting the cluster of men in the center, and he knew. "They're using a battering ram!" he shouted. "They're coming through the door!"

He turned and looked down the length of the wall. "You men, get behind the barricades, get ready to meet them when they drive through!"

The archers and the spearmen on the wall obeyed, and turned, climbing and sliding down the slope to the ground. Thorgrim grabbed two men before they could make their descent.

"You two, stay on the wall. Keep clear of their spears but keep an eye on what they're about. If it looks like they're going to make an attack somewhere along the wall as well, you let me know, and be quick about it!"

The two men nodded and crouched down, making smaller targets of themselves, and Thorgrim clambered down to the ground below. The bulk of the men were lined up along the two barricades. Once the Irish smashed the flimsy gate in and poured through, they would be caught between the log walls and the shield-bearing men behind them and they would be cut down.

Thorgrim took a position a dozen feet back from the men lining the log walls, a spot where he could see all that was going on in one sweeping glance. He looked at the grim and patient men standing there, and as he did, the battering ram took its first solid blow against the gate. It was a deep and substantial sound, the sound of a heavy log wielded with considerable force, and with the sound of the impact came the sharper, softer sound of shattering wood.

This will not take long, Thorgrim thought.

The men along the barricades shuffled closer and raised their shields a little higher and refreshed the grip on their weapons, but they were not silent. As Thorgrim had instructed them, they were yelling out to one another, shouting words of confusion, bordering on panic. It made a comical sight, these men standing firm and stoic, weapons at the ready, eager for the coming fight and screaming like frightened children

Starri was shirtless and spinning around in place, his twin battle axes in hand. Harald was at the center of the far barricade. Those men who had been with Thorgrim and those who had just thrown in with him seemed tossed together in no particular order, and that was good. Cohesion was good. Factions were not.

The ram struck again and the sound of breaking wood was considerably more pronounced. It struck again. "Stand ready!" Godi bellowed, his big voice carrying over the faux panic.

Thorgrim looked up at the wall. The men he had left to keep an eye on Bécc's movements were gone. He looked down at the ground. One was lying at the base of the wall, a spear jammed in his shoulder and he was kicking his legs and twisting and holding the shaft of the spear, trying to summon the nerve to pull it out. The other man was nowhere to be seen. Thorgrim frowned and cursed under his breath. He could not afford to be blind to Bécc's movements. The assault on the gate might be just a diversion.

He turned to order two more men to take their place when the gate gave way and the screaming, triumphant Irish came pouring through.

The change was quick and startling. The Northmen at the barricades stopped their silly playacting and took up their battle cries, calculated to bring terror to an adversary. The Irish in turn came pouring through the gate, rushing forward with shields and spears, shouting as if they had already won. But those cries of exaltation wilted on their lips as they realized they were trapped between the two low barricades, with armed men on either side and more of their own pushing in behind them, driving them further into the jaws of the trap.

The confusion had not yet left their faces when they began to die in earnest, the Northmen thrusting out with spears and swords, hacking at the crowd of men with their long battle axes. And the Irish began to scream—in pain, in terror, in fury—but to their credit they turned and fought. Shields up, spears driving over the barricades, they struck back as hard as they could.

These are not the men-at-arms, Thorgrim realized. There were only a few with mail, a few with swords. Most wore the simple, rough clothes of working men and they carried simple weapons. Bécc had sent the dispensable men in first, with a smattering of men-at-arms to boost their courage. He wanted to weaken his enemy as much as he could before sending in the real fighting men to finish the job.

It was a good plan, Thorgrim had to admit, and it might have worked if they had not built the barricades to pen the attackers in.

These farmers, Thorgrim knew, would not overpower his warriors. They would not even do them much hurt. If they turned and fled and tried to get back out through the gate, they would run smack into the others pushing forward, and the result would be a tangle of panicked men. If they stood and fought they would create a third barrier with their bodies as they fell.

You are not so clever after all, are you, Bécc? Thorgrim thought, and that thought made him uneasy. The gods were apt to punish such pridefulness. He pulled his eyes from the fighting and looked back up at the wall. There were two men there now, but they were not his men. One looked thin and lithe, a young man, apparently. He held a pole with a banner at one end, though he held the cloth folded against the pole.

The other was stouter, solid-looking. There was a look of permanence to his stance, a posture of command.

Bécc... It had to be. Bécc had mounted the wall so he could watch the action below.

Why are you not in the fighting? Thorgrim thought next. He and Bécc had crossed swords not long before. He knew the Irishman was not shy about taking his part in a fight, putting himself in danger.

Then the young man beside Bécc released the banner and the wind grabbed the cloth and whipped it out straight. He raised the staff high and began to wave it side to side in a wide, sweeping motion.

What, by the gods...? And then the thunder boomed overhead and Thorgrim understood. A signal.

"You bastard!" Thorgrim shouted at Bécc, but his real anger was with himself. He turned around again. The fight at the barricades had not slackened off, but now at the far end of the longphort, near to where the earthen wall met the water, he could see men-at-arms coming up over the top. They wore mail and helmets and carried shields, because they were the real warriors whom Bécc had held in reserve. Now they were pouring over the wall while his men were distracted by the useless farmers.

Thorgrim drew Iron-tooth from its scabbard, a reflex gesture. He had no immediate need of the weapon; there was more to do before he could cross swords with the men-at-arms. His own warriors, fighting at the low log walls, had to disengage and turn to face this new threat, but at the same time they could not turn their backs on the spearmen in front of them. His own trap had been turned on its head.

He ran at the line of Northmen ahead of him, grabbed the nearest man and pulled him back, then grabbed the next. "Step back! Step back! Back!" he roared, loud as he could, and pulled a third man from the wall.

Harald, fighting at the opposite barricade, was nearly opposite him. At the sound of Thorgrim's voice he looked up and their eyes met across the mass of struggling men and Thorgrim pointed with Iron-tooth at the coming threat. He saw Harald turn his head, saw the boy's eyes go wide, saw him begin to push his own men back from the log wall.

The Northmen backed away from the barricades, eyes shifted toward the wall, swords and spears pointed in the direction of this new threat. Thorgrim could see both confusion and relief on the faces of the Irishmen caught between the barricades as the enemy inexplicably broke off the fight. He could see his own men pointing to a place behind him.

He turned once again and saw what the others had seen. Bécc had not sent one division of men over the north wall, he had sent two: one over the north wall and one over the south. Thorgrim had not seen the second division, coming in behind him, but he did now. A lot of men. More than one hundred, certainly, and the same number coming in over the north wall. His own men were outnumbered, and even the spear-armed farmers would be able to do considerable damage now that the Northmen had the men-at-arms to contend with.

This does not look good, Thorgrim thought. And indeed it did not. But his men were already divided into two battle groups, and that would help. On the far side of the barricade Harald and Godi were already pushing the men away from the log wall, getting them turned and formed into a shield wall of sorts, while the Irish men-at-arms did the same.

Thorgrim turned back to the men on his side of the barricade. "Make a shield wall! Make a shield wall! They'll be on us quick!" Gudrid was there, and Jorund and Halldor and they were pushing the men into line and echoing Thorgrim's orders.

Failend came rushing past, nearly colliding with Thorgrim as she did. She ran two dozen paces out ahead of the nascent shield wall and dropped to a knee, in the same motion whipping an arrow from her quiver and setting it on the bowstring. She drew, shifted her aim a hair's breadth and let fly. She was already reaching for a second arrow when Thorgrim saw the first take one of the men-at-arms square in the neck and send him reeling back, arms flung out, shield and sword flying off in either direction.

He heard the familiar clatter of shield on shield as his men overlapped the iron-bound disks to form a wall. He looked behind him. The farmers in the barricades were all but motionless: surprised, confused and grateful for their unexpected salvation. But soon someone, one of the men-at-arms among them, would push them over the log walls and back into the fight.

"Forward! Forward!" Thorgrim shouted, Iron-tooth raised high. He stepped off, making for the Irish who were also forming a shield wall, and the rest of his men followed. Failend let off another arrow, then dashed out of the way of the advancing line of men.

Thorgrim looked off to his left. Harald's men were moving forward his were, putting distance between them and the spearmen behind them, advancing on this new threat. Four shield walls, two Irish, two Northmen, converging on one another like ships on course to collide. And then the rain began.

It was only a few drops at first, big, heavy drops that made dark spots on the brown trampled earth. Then more. Then lightning flashed and the thunder came right on its heels and the dark, ponderous clouds seemed to open up.

It fell like no rain Thorgrim had ever felt before. It fell with a force and weight that seemed like an assault, as if the gods were set on using the deluge to inflict hurt on the men below. In the space of three steps the world around them went from dry to soaked. The rain beat down on iron helmets and mail shirts, it drenched tunics, it turned the ground into a viscous mess. Thorgrim opened his mouth to shout an order and it was instantly full of water and he spit and choked. He wiped the water from his eyes, a useless gesture.

"Forward! Move it!" he managed to call, but the words had a gagging sound to them. The rain was disorienting, blinding, it was hard to think. The ground, instantly muddy, pulled at his soft leather shoes. "Forward!"

He pushed on, angling the line toward the water. He wanted to get as close to the ships as he could, in case Bécc's men had some designs on them. At least now he knew they would not be setting them on fire, even if that had been their plan.

The Irish were surging forward, a row of round shields coming directly at Thorgrim and his men. Thorgrim blinked and resettled his grip on Iron-tooth. Thirty feet. Something brushed past him and he thought for an instant it was Failend again, but it was not, it was Starri Deathless, screaming louder than the rain, louder than the near continuous rolling thunder as he raced for the enemy's shield wall. He had been thoroughly covered in blood from the fighting at the barricades. Now the blood and driving rain made streaks and swirls down his back and chest, as if he had been painted by some mad, blind painter, and it made him more frightening still.

Thorgrim saw the men at the center of the Irish line pause as Starri charged and the line fell out of order. A spear flew from over the shields, straight and true at Starri's chest, but Starri batted it aside with an ax as if he were playing some game, and then he was on them, axes swirling so fast they seemed like little more than dark blurs in the rain.

The blade of one ax embedded itself in an Irish shield and Starri yanked down, pulling the shield away, revealing the surprised soldier behind it, surprised for just an instant, and then the second ax was down on his helmet, cleaving the iron plate in two and continuing on.

The Irishman fell, probably dead on his feet, and Starri jerked the ax free but the helmet was still embedded on the blade. He swung it sideways like a club, hit the man next to the dead man in the side of the head, sent him staggering into the next in line. The shield wall was just starting to come apart when Thorgrim's men slammed into it, head-on.

With a grunt Thorgrim felt his shield hit that of the man in front of him and his forward momentum stopped. Down the line he heard the familiar sound of shield slamming shield, the shouting, the clang of weapons, the nearly pointless orders called out over the din. He pushed against the man in front, felt his feet sliding on the slick ground. He looked over his shield as the big Irishman facing him raised a sword and thrust it right at Thorgrim's face.

The move was no surprise. Thorgrim leaned to one side and the blade slid past. He knocked it aside with his mail-clad arm, then straightened the arm as he thrust Iron-tooth back at the man. The tip hit the Irishman's helmet with a clanging sound and glanced off and Thorgrim jerked his arm back.

Thorgrim had no sense for time passing—moments, hours—it might have been either. The rain beat down and blinded him and soaked him and the dirt was churned to mud as the two lines pushed against one another to no effect. The weapons rose and fell, thrust and block and counter-thrust. The shouting and the noise seemed to be coming from some other place, close but not very close.

And then something did change. The noise. The shouting. Now it was coming from some certain place, and that place was behind them. Thorgrim chanced a quick glance over his shoulder. It was the farmers, those who had survived the barricades. Rallied by some experienced man-at-arms, inspired or threatened to plunge back into the fighting, they were massed and rolling forward. A disorganized mob, but they had shields and spears and they were shouting their blood lust as they charged right for the backs of Thorgrim's men, who were now caught between them and the men-at-arms.

Thorgrim pressed his lips together. He had to do something, but he genuinely did not know what.

Fight... That was all that came to mind. Fight, die, there in that makeshift longphort. Because sometimes that was the only choice.

He slashed at the man-at-arms in front of him, the one with whom he had been exchanging blows for more time than he could remember, though he knew it must have been moments, no more. He stepped back, calling for the others to do the same, hoping they would see his move and follow. They could not just let the farmers drive spear points into their unprotected backs. Perhaps half his line could fight the men-at-arms, half the farmers, but he had no way of organizing that.

He held his shield up, half turned to see the men from the barricade racing toward them, screaming now, spears held low like lances. He saw his own men doing as he was doing, trying to fight both sides at once, trying to gauge which was the biggest threat, and how they could avoid being crushed between these two Irish lines.

Through the driving rain, across the open ground, he saw Harald, standing like a tree-trunk, shield in front, his grandfather's sword, Oak Cleaver, held level with the ground. He was shouting something, but Thorgrim could not hear it. The Irish spearmen from the gate were charging the backs of his men, too, while the men-at-arms in the shield wall were pushing forward, hitting Harald's line again and again, like waves pounding a beach.

And then the Northmen did the one thing Thorgrim had not even considered they might do. They broke and ran.

Chapter Twenty-Three

Woe for that man who in harm and hatred hales his soul
to fiery embraces — nor favor nor change awaits he ever.

Beowulf

Harald Thorgrimson, known as Harald Broadarm, felt his feet slipping as he pushed against the Irish shield wall. He tried to dig his toes into the muddy ground for more grip, but it did no good. None of his considerable strength of arm and leg could be directed toward pushing his enemy. But neither was he himself being pushed, so he knew the Irish were having difficulty, too.

What now, what now? he thought even as he thrust Oak Cleaver at the man-at-arms he could only glimpse between the gaps in the shield wall. *How to end this?*

This shield wall was his to command, his and Godi's really, and the new men, Halldor and Hrapp, who also ended up with them. It was a little unsettled, actually, this question of who among them was in command. But that uncertainty did not much matter to Harald, who was not really one for nuance anyway.

Son of Thorgrim Night Wolf, he would assume a leader's place because he was born to it, and his father would expect it, and because the only thing on earth he really feared, other than elves and spirits and such, was disappointing his father.

He and his men were pushing against the Irish shield wall, hacking and thrusting with swords and axes and spears. The Irish were pushing back, wielding weapons as furiously and as skillfully as were the Northmen. Neither was gaining, neither was staring at defeat. But the Northmen were outnumbered, and Harald knew that might soon make a difference.

198

His mind was tumbling over how to change things up, how to gain an advantage. He was trying to think clearly, but it was hard, with the shouting and the clash of weapons and the need to fight and the rain pouring down like he had never seen before, even after two years and more in that remarkably rainy country. The water ran down his face, cascaded into his eyes. He blinked furiously, but it did little good.

And then something changed. There was a new layer of sound, a new surge of human voices. Harald looked back over his shoulder, the quickest of glances, but long enough to see the spearmen from the barricades formed up and charging him and his men from behind, spears leveled, shields up.

He had forgotten all about them. Not the most formidable enemy, but an enemy nonetheless, quite capable of driving an iron spear point into the Northmen's backs, and he had quite forgotten they were there.

Oh, by the gods... he thought. They had to turn and face this new onslaught, but if they did, the men-at-arms would cut them down. He did not know what to do. He secretly wished that Godi would take charge, would give some order that would get them out of this intractable mess, and then he felt a flush of guilt for thinking such a thing.

He stepped back, holding his shield at arm's length to ward off any attack from in front, turned sideways so he could see this new threat. A spear point came sailing over the iron rim of the shield and Harald instinctively leaned back as the shaft flew past, inches from his face and he knew he could not turn his eyes away for much longer.

"Watch your backs! The spearmen! Watch your backs!" he shouted, but he could think of nothing more constructive to say, no firm orders he might give. And if he tried, no one would hear him anyway. He did not know if his warning had even been heard.

But apparently it had, or perhaps the others in the line had heard, as he had, the shouting from behind. He could see men half turning to the new threat, fighting, twisting, unsure what to do. Godi was bellowing something, but Harald could not make out the words.

I'll charge at them, Harald thought. *I'll run right at these bastards and see if the others follow.* Maybe scare the spearmen, maybe put some distance between his men and the shield wall, win them a moment to fight clear. It was the best he could come up with.

And then it was over. It was as if some signal had sounded. One moment the Northmen were fighting for any advantage against the Irish shield wall, bracing for this new attack from behind, and then the next they were in flight, racing away over the muddy ground, leaving the Irishmen watching in surprise as they fled for the ships, floating and tethered to the beach.

"No! You bastards! No!" Harald shouted, but there would be no turning the men back now. He had seen routs before, seen them from both sides, and he knew once men started running there was no stopping them.

He looked to his right. Godi was there, like some giant of legend, shouting and wielding his ax and slamming men sideways with his shield. The Northmen were streaming around him. Some were tossing weapons aside as they ran.

The Irish shield wall was still more or less intact—they had not had time to react to the collapse of the Northmen's line—but Godi was battering his section of the wall. But he could not keep that up long. Soon the spearmen would be on him, and the men in the shield wall would envelope him and even the mighty Godi would go down under their combined weapons.

"Godi!" Harald shouted. "Godi, we must go!" He looked off to his left, toward the other fighting men. Like his, Thorgrim's men had fled for the ships, leaving only the startled Irishmen in their wake. He looked for his father but could not see him, lost in the chaotic press of men.

"Godi!" Harald shouted again, but they had waited too long. The spearmen were on them now, a hoard like stampeding animals racing forward, spears leveled. It was too late to turn and run. He would get a spear in the back if he did that. So instead he stood, feet as firm as he could make them in the soft earth, and raised his shield and sword.

It was like standing on the edge of the sea and waiting for a cresting wave to break over him. The Irish rushed on, mouths open, screaming in triumph and something else. Madness. They were blinded by the sight of an enemy in flight, driven by their vision of an easy slaughter.

The first spear reached out toward Harald as its bearer rushed forward, but the man did not seem even to be trying, as if he expected Harald to just stand still and be skewered. Harald, however, had a different vision. He batted the spear aside with his shield and as the startled Irishman took another step forward he thrust Oak Cleaver right through the man's throat, then jerked it free before it became stuck there.

The Irishman made no more than a gurgling sound and his momentum carried him right past where Harald stood, spraying blood as he stumbled. Harald did not see him hit the ground as he was already bracing for the next man who was also charging at him with a blind insanity.

This time Harald took the point of the spear right on the face of the shield, which stopped the weapon dead, but not the man holding it. He careened forward and slammed into the shield with a blow that visibly jarred him. Harald pushed hard, pushed the man back so there was space enough to use his sword, and then he did just that, driving the tip right into the spearman's gut. He wore no mail—he was no man-at-arms—and the sword went in and out with the slightest of effort.

And then Harald was alone. All of the other spearmen had raced past in their headlong pursuit of the fleeing Northmen. Where a moment before there had been a great crowd of armed men, now there was only the familiar dirt walls of the longphort and new made barricades and the smashed gate and a great litter of dead and wounded men.

He looked to his right. Godi was still standing in the same spot, three dead spearmen at his feet, a confused look on his face. The Irish shield wall was gone now, the men-at-arms having followed the spearmen off in their rush to get at their fleeing enemy.

Harald looked to his left. Men racing for the ships, more dead and wounded. And his father, lying on the ground, half propped up, cradled in Failend's arms, Louis de Roumois kneeling beside him.

"No! Oh, no!" Harald shouted. "Godi, here!" He raced off across the open ground. He tossed his shield aside and slid Oak Cleaver into his scabbard as he ran. Failend was supporting Thorgrim as he sat up, his legs sprawled at odd angles, his head lolling back. She looked so tiny next to him.

The rain had not eased, not a bit, but Harald did not notice it now, in his panic. There was something odd about his father, but he could not make it out until he had closed half the distance, and then he saw. There was a spear embedded in his gut and lying across his legs. Harald could see the red blood coming from the wound and joining the rainwater as it flowed to the ground.

"Harald!" Failend cried, a note of desperation in her voice. Harald ran the last few feet and fell to his knees at his father's side.

"We didn't know...what to do..." Louis said, his tone both worried and apologetic.

Harald nodded, but his eyes were on his father, his mind whirling. Thorgrim groaned and rolled his head and Harald made himself look at the wound. It was not in Thorgrim's stomach, which was good, but it was just to the side and it was deep, the spear point sunk in nearly to the socket.

"Very well, very well..." Harald said. "We'll...we'll..."

Then Godi was there, looming over them. He looked down at Thorgrim and frowned. "We'll have to carry him," he said. "The spear has got to go."

"Sure," Failend said, "But we thought..."

Godi did not let her go on. He reached down and wrapped a massive hand around the shaft of the spear and yanked it free. Thorgrim shouted and gasped and his eyes flew open, but the reaction gave Harald hope. There was still life in his father; it had not all washed out with the blood.

"I'll carry him," Godi said. He straightened and looked toward the water and the others looked that way as well. They could see their fellow Northmen clambering up over the low sides of the ships. Many, but not all of them. The Irish had reached the water's edge and now there was more fighting as the Northmen tried to climb aboard without being killed in the process. "We'll have to cut our way through, and quick, or we'll be left behind."

Harald and Louis stood and they helped Thorgrim to his feet and Harald was relieved to see that his father was able to help in that effort, that he still had strength in his legs.

"Starri!" Godi roared, loud enough to be heard over the rain and the thunder and the shouting. Twenty feet away Starri Deathless was slumped on the ground. Harald had not seen him there, and now that he did he wondered if the berserker was at last dead.

But he was not. At the sound of his name Starri looked up with a quizzical expression. He looked around as if he had come to in some strange land.

"Thorgrim's hurt!" Godi shouted. "We have to get to the ships!"

Starri nodded and leapt to his feet, his two axes still in his hands. A gust of wind slammed into his side and made him stagger and the rain, blown sideways, lashed them all. Starri regained his balance and trotted over to where they stood.

The storm, intense from the start, had turned into a gale and Harald had to speak loud to be heard even by those around him.

"We'll try to reach *Sea Hammer*," Harald said. He knew his father would want to be aboard his own ship, and the men on *Sea Hammer* were not likely to leave without him.

"Good!" Godi said. He had already discarded his shield, and now he thrust his ax in his belt. He leaned over and wrapped an arm around Thorgrim's waist and stood with Thorgrim over his shoulder, as easy as if he were taking a lamb to be slaughtered.

"You bastard, put me down, I'll rip your lungs out!" Thorgrim yelled, and though his voice was weak, there was still force in it, and genuine anger, and Harald was happy to hear it.

"Just stand fast, Father," Harald said and realized that was a silly thing to say, but it was too late. Of course his father was not happy. It was not the most dignified way to board one's ship, but it was also necessary. They would have to hack their way to the water's edge, and they could not do that if they were supporting Thorgrim as well.

Harald turned to Failend to tell her to retrieve Iron-tooth, but he saw that she already had the sword in hand, holding it by the grip as if she intended to put it to use, which he guessed she did. He felt a moment's hesitation, unsure if his father would approve of someone else, and a woman at that, wielding his sword. But he also knew of Thorgrim's affection for Failend, and his respect, and guessed it would be all right.

"Keep a good hold of that; don't lose it," he said to her, and then to all of them, "Let's go!" He hurried off toward the water's edge at a jog, Starri on one side, Louis on the other, Failend and Godi behind. Just five of them to fight their way through four hundred or more Irish warriors to get to their ship.

But they had a few things at least in their favor. The Irish did not see them coming. They had their backs to Harald and the others as they fought with the men struggling to get to their ships. The other was that the fighting madness seemed to be building in Starri once again.

Bécc's men and the water's edge were only a few hundred feet ahead of them when Starri could control himself no longer. He howled and burst into a run, axes held over his head. Even over the sound of the battle in the surf and the screaming of the building wind, Starri's cry was both piercing and terrifying.

The Irishmen closest to him turned at the sound and Harald saw their eyes go wide. They had seen Starri in battle already and they wanted no more. They began to back away but in the press of fighting men they could not go far, and in an instant Starri was on them, howling and slashing with his axes. A spear reached out, it's black point aimed at Starri's chest, but Starri snapped the shaft in two with a stoke of an ax. The spearman died with the remains of the weapon in his hand, and the man beside him went down as well.

Panic was sweeping through the packed men, at least those who had turned to see Starri attack, and they were trying to shove their way clear even as Harald and Louis reached the line. Oak Cleaver came down on a raised sword, one of the men-at-arms with the courage to stand fast. The Irish warrior tried to sweep the blade aside, but Harald pulled it back quick and drove it straight in, straight through the tight links of mail until he felt the tip hit something softer. The man gasped and staggered away and Harald did not know if he was badly hurt or not, but it did not matter. Either way, the man was out of the fight.

To his right Louis was driving into the men already terrified by Starri's attack, the Frank's quick blade moving faster than the poor Irish soldiers could counter. He was not killing the Irish standing against him, but rather wounding and terrifying and spreading more panic on the beach. Louis had not forgotten that their goal was just to get through, just to reach the ships.

And it worked. The sudden, unexpected and brutal attack on that single point in the Irish line sent the panic rippling out. The Irish spearmen shoved and pushed themselves out of the way of Starri and Harald and Louis's attack and suddenly a gap appeared, a clear path right to the water's edge and the ships beyond. The manic north wind gusted and made Harald stagger as he drove into the opening. Starri was still at it, on Harald's left-hand side, and Harald grabbed his arm as he ran through, jerking Starri away.

Starri screamed and raised his ax and Harald met his eyes and shouted, "It's me, Starri! We have to go!" He saw a hint of recognition in Starri's eyes and he saw the arm holding the weapon relax and Starri stumbled after him, Louis on their right, still swinging his long straight sword.

Harald looked behind him. Godi was there, Thorgrim draped unceremoniously over his shoulder, and Failend, with Iron-tooth, which looked as long as she was tall, held high, cocked over her shoulder, ready to come down on anyone who might oppose them.

"Here! Here!" Harald shouted as he ran, pointing toward *Sea Hammer* off to their left. The ships were crowded with men and more climbing up over the sides, but the wind had them now and it was driving them back against the shore. Harald could see that *Sea Hammer* was slamming her larboard side against *Fox*'s starboard, and on the far side *Blood Hawk* was slamming against *Sea Hammer*. It would be a nightmare just trying to get the ships clear of the shore, but before they did that they had to reach them first.

Which apparently would be easier than Harald thought. The panic they had brought to the center of the line had spread, and men were pushing away in either direction, unaware, apparently, that the attackers had been just five strong. It was the first bit of luck the gods had offered them.

Harald, with his left hand still gripping Starri's arm, Oak Cleaver in his right, splashed into the shallow water, stumbling as he raced to reach *Sea Hammer*'s side. He stopped and pushed Starri forward and yelled, "Get aboard, Starri, get aboard!" and happily Starri did just that, running past Harald, grabbing on to *Sea Hammer*'s sheer strake and swinging himself over.

Godi came charging past next, his thick legs kicking up a wake as he ran through the water. He stopped at the side of the ship and anxious hands reached down to grab up Thorgrim and haul him aboard, as Thorgrim in turn cursed and shouted and threatened their lives if they did not unhand him.

They were still pulling Thorgrim aboard when Harald turned back to face the enemy lining the shore and standing ankle-deep in the water. The panic they had unleashed with their surprise attack was just starting to dissipate, the disorganized men on the beach just beginning to see that the threat had passed. But it was too late. The Northmen, those who were not dead on the ground, were all aboard the longships and now the oars were coming out and the vessels starting to back away from the shallow water.

Failend and Louis were at his side as well, weapons held ready, eyes waiting for some threat from the shore. "Go, go," Harald shouted and the two of them turned and splashed the last dozen feet to *Sea Hammer*'s side.

And then it was Harald alone left standing in the water. He turned Oak Cleaver around and slid the weapon into its scabbard and was half turned toward the ship when one of the Irish men-at-arms came bursting out of the crowd, sword in hand. He wore mail that hung loose from a big rent in the shoulder and his face was splattered with dirt and blood that had been streaked by the rain. But that was not all. There was something else wrong with his face, but Harald could not quite tell what that was.

He was not a small man, but he charged through the shallow water with surprising speed, sword held high, his mouth open as he shouted something incomprehensible. And then Harald realized who it was.

Bécc... Bécc of the ruined face, Bécc who had been scouting out the longphort for months now, who had led this unwarranted attack against them. Bécc who would not suffer them to get away.

Harald's hand fell on Oak Cleaver's hilt and he drew the weapon as Bécc closed the last few feet and swung his sword at Harald's head, a wild and uncoordinated move. Harald leaned back and the tip of Bécc's blade passed his face inches away. Harald could see a spray of water coming off the blade as it sliced through the sheets of torrential rain. He lunged, but Bécc knocked the blade aside and drew his own sword back to counter the attack.

"Thorgrim!" Bécc shouted. "Thorgrim, you bastard, son of the devil, fight me!" Bécc shouted over Harald's shoulder as he drove the point of his sword at Harald's chest. Harald knocked it aside, but before he could do more, Bécc raised his foot and drove it into Harald's stomach and sent him staggering back.

Harald struggled to regain his footing as Bécc came at him again and he heard, from behind, his father's voice. "Bécc, you bastard, here I am! I'll come and cut your heart out!"

Bécc took a step forward and swung at Harald once again and Harald ducked low and let the blade pass over.

He doesn't understand... Harald thought. He was thinking about what his father had said, that Bécc would not understand the Norse words, but he realized, as the thought came to him, that Thorgrim must not have understood Bécc's Irish words either. But their words both spoke of hate and revenge, and that they both understood.

Harald was squatting on his heels, having ducked Bécc's blow, and must have looked quite helpless to Bécc who drew his sword back, ready to give the final blow. But Harald was not an easy kill. He leaned back and lashed out with his right foot. He felt the soft sole of his shoe connect with Bécc's knee, and despite the rain and the wind and the shouting he heard the sickening snap of bone.

Then every sound was drowned out by Bécc's scream of agony and rage as his leg collapsed under him and he fell in a heap into the shallow water. Already his men were charging into the short surf after him, but Harald could give them no more thought. He turned and sheathed Oak Cleaver as he did and raced toward *Sea Hammer*'s side.

The oars were out and the ship backing away from the beach, but the howling wind was holding it back as if Odin's shoulder was pressed against it. Five great strides and Harald was at the ship's side, hands on the sheer strake, pulling himself up as more hands grabbed onto his mail shirt and his belt and hauled him over the side.

He fell in a heap on the deck planks and sat there, heaving for breath. Godi and three others were holding his father back while Thorgrim thrashed and fought, but the sight of his son seemed to calm him. He ceased his struggling and the others let him go as he shook them off.

"Vík-ló!" Harald shouted. "We go to Vík-ló, but we'll be back!"

Thorgrim nodded. Harald could well imagine how furious he was about everything that had just happened there at the longphort at Loch Garman, but he seemed to take some comfort in the thought of Vík-ló. And of their return.

Chapter Twenty-Four

A shower of honey rained upon the fort of the Laigin.
A shower of wheat, furthermore, rained on Othan Becc.

Fragmentary Annals of Ireland

The rain lashed the town of Sherborne, the wind doled out its punishment, ripping thatch from roofs, sending barrows tumbling down the streets, overturning carts and tearing apart lesser structures. The sky was nearly black at midday, a darkness few had ever witnessed. The bells on the cathedral tolled and tolled. They were driven by the wind, saving the priests the trouble of doing it themselves, calling the wicked to repent their sins at what might turn out to be the end of time.

And the wicked came to do just that. Those who dared left the dubious safety of their homes, soaked through even as they struggled to close doors behind them and stagger down the streets to the cathedral. They knelt and they prayed and Bishop Ealhstan stood in clouds of incense and chanted the prayers that might bring them some relief from the storm. And, if not that, then salvation when the end finally came thundering down, which it seemed most inclined to do.

Cynewise was on her knees as well, kneeling on the hard, stone floor, the cold working its way through her linen underdress and the fine, heavy wool of her gown, dyed a deep red. It was not an appropriate color to wear to the mass, but Cynewise was not at the mass. She was kneeling on the floor of the long hall, what she had come to think of as *her* long hall. She was holding the cold, boney hand of King Æthelwulf, and she pressed his ring to her lips and gave it the most delicate of kisses. Then she stood, straight and tall as she could stand, her face nearly level with that of the old man, and looked him in the eyes.

"Welcome, my dear King Æthelwulf," she said. "I give thanks to the Lord that you were able to find shelter in my hall before this wicked storm was upon us."

Æthelwulf sniffed. "Not exactly 'before,'" he said. But Cynewise knew that. The men who stood behind the king, his guards and the ealdormen who had come with him, and his courtiers and sundry human detritus, were soaked through, their clothing black with wet, regardless of the color it had been before the rain, and hanging in sodden folds and dripping thoughtlessly on the floor.

I don't know what you're complaining about, Cynewise thought. Æthelwulf was perfectly dry. The others had clearly taken pains to see that no rain fell on the king, even if it meant their own soaking.

"Well, my lord, the fires are blazing in your rooms, I can assure you," she said with an ingratiating smile. "Pray, let me show you to your apartment, where you might rest and refresh yourself. We have a banquet planned which we hope will do honor to your majesty."

With that she rested her hand on Æthelwulf's arm and guided him back down the length of the long hall. He would have to step outside once again and cross the now muddy courtyard to the residence, but Cynewise knew there would be servants there with a portable awning to keep the man dry. She had given specific orders for such, and Ulger, the chief steward, was not likely to forget. Such an omission could prove fatal to a man like Ulger.

Cynewise led the way through the big door at the end of the hall. The awning was there, as she had assumed, and eight servants were struggling to hold it in place against the powerful wind. Æthelwulf looked up at the flogging cloth with vague disapproval but said nothing. Cynewise remained silent as well, but the ferocity of the storm surprised her, even after having listened to the wind and the rain beating on the long hall all that morning.

Lightning flashed, washing the dark courtyard in light, and thunder clapped overhead, so near and loud Cynewise could feel the earth tremble with it.

The hand of God is in this, she thought, glancing up at the sky beyond the edge of the awning. It was in some ways a foolish thought. The hand of God was in all things, of course. But this was different. More like a warning, a hint of punishment, and Cynewise felt a flush of guilt, and fear.

This storm is upon Wessex and many lands beyond, she thought. *Sure there are people more wicked than me that God means to warn.*

They made it to the residence with no further sign of God's retribution and Cynewise deposited Æthelwulf in his apartment, which had been made so comfortable that Cynewise thought even the old man would find nothing of which to complain.

She took the liberty of giving him a soft hug, a liberty she knew he would not mind, and she stayed pressed against him long enough for him to run his gnarled hand over her ass. Æthelwulf, for all his piety, liked women quite a lot. Flattery and a willingness to endure his impotent groping went far toward winning the royal favor. She had learned that at a young age in the court of her father, Ceorle, ealdorman of Devonshire. Her relationship with King Æthelwulf went way back.

With the king tucked safely away for the time, Cynewise returned to her work, which was plentiful. Æthelwulf had not been expected for another fortnight. She had counted on that, counted on having things more in order by the time he arrived. But a courier had appeared just two days before to announce that the king had altered his plans, that he would bypass Glastonbury Abbey for the time and make right for Sherborne. Why, Cynewise did not know, but she had her ideas.

For the rest of the afternoon, with the storm still raging and the thunder making her jump with each terrifying crash, Cynewise moved through her duties. She directed the preparation of the long hall for the royal feast, looked in on the cooks laboring in the kitchen, and met with the ealdormen who would be present. She returned to her chambers and sent her servants away with instructions to send for Oswin. It was not long before the shire reeve was at her door, giving a shallow bow.

"Come, Oswin. Shut the door," Cynewise said. Oswin stepped into the room and closed the door behind him. He knew what she wanted, so he did not wait for her to ask.

"I've heard nothing from the borders, Lady Cynewise," he said. "If your father's men passed into Dorsetshire they did so unseen, but I'm hard pressed to believe that's the case."

"No," Cynewise said. "They did not come over the border. As you say, if they did they would be seen. Word would spread. I'm not confident that we have the complete loyalty of all the thegns whose lands they would have to pass through."

"You have the loyalty of the thegns, lady," Oswin protested.

"The complete loyalty?" Cynewise asked. The question hung in the air. Oswin did not make an answer.

"The thegns are like dogs," Cynewise said. "They're loyal to whoever is feeding them. And we don't know who truly sides with us, and who still thinks Nothwulf will come to power. So my father decided to send two hundred of his best warriors. But not overland. He's sent them by ship, around to Christchurch Priory."

"Christchurch Priory?" Oswin said. "That's Leofric's land. Leofric's loyalty is the most suspect of all, my lady."

"I know that," Cynewise said. "My father's men-at-arms will secret themselves in the priory. It's remote enough that they should be able to keep their presence a secret. Then, when the time comes that we must take control, complete control of the shire, then they'll be ready to move. And ready to take down that bastard Leofric first of all."

Oswin nodded. A gust of wind hit the building and it shuddered. They could feel the floor tremble beneath them.

"Your father's men…went by sea?" Oswin asked.

"Yes," Cynewise said. "When, I don't know. I don't know if they are at Christchurch now, or if they have yet to leave. But let's hope they're not out at sea in this hellish weather."

"Let's hope," Oswin said. "There's no ship could live through this."

All through the afternoon the storm blew with full fury, but by nightfall it was a shadow of itself, with only the occasional flash of lightning, and thunder far enough away that it seemed like an echo of the earlier blasts. The long hall was lit by torches lining the walls and the long oak tables were crowded with the men and women who had been invited to the royal banquet.

Cynewise was on the dais, at the center of the head table, surveying with satisfaction all that lay before her, when the horns sounded the arrival of Æthelwulf and his entourage. They processed into the long hall with the slow, solemn dignity one might expect of a king, though Cynewise suspected that the old man was not trying to be solemn, he just could not move any faster.

"The king looks well," Bishop Ealhstan said. He was standing beside Cynewise, standing at his place at the head table, the seat of third highest honor. Not even the threat of the end times and the second coming would keep the man from attending to the king.

"He does look well," Cynewise agreed. *Like a well-preserved corpse,* she thought. But her smile did not dim in the least as Æthelwulf ascended the dais to the rest of the guests' enthusiastic pounding on the tables. She turned her cheek for a demure kiss which Æthelwulf gave her, still smiling even as he discreetly ran his hand down her side and over her posterior. She thought of how happy Æthelwulf must be that she, and not Nothwulf, was there, how the king would certainly rather grab her ass than Nothwulf's. And then she wondered if that was indeed true.

The servants flanking Æthelwulf's chair pulled it back and the king sat and Cynewise pushed such thoughts from her mind. The wine was poured and she led a toast to the king and they drank. Then the bishop led a prayer, then a toast, and then the food was served out: roast beef and venison and a multitude of summer vegetables, fish from the villages of Wareham and Swanage, pheasants and fine white bread. It was damned expensive putting on a feast for a monarch and all his lackeys, but Cynewise felt certain that it would ultimately be enough to her benefit that she did not begrudge the drain on her stores.

For some time Æthelwulf concentrated on eating, and Cynewise was surprised how much he could put away. She had seen him eat many times at her father's table but had never noticed that before. Finally the king leaned back.

"Terrible, terrible thing, what happened to Merewald," he said. "Bloody murder. And in the cathedral, no less, on his wedding day."

It was the first mention the king had made of that event, and all Cynewise could think was, *I know, you damned fool, I was there.* She opened her mouth to speak, but Æthelwulf leaned forward so he could see past her to Bishop Ealhstan.

"Bishop, a bloody business, the murder of young Merewald. He was a good ealdorman. Not the man his father was, but good enough. Are you quite recovered from that shock?"

"Yes, my lord," Ealhstan said, making the sign of the cross. "A bloody business indeed."

"I imagine Nothwulf is not so pleased with…" The king paused, looked right and left. "Where is Nothwulf?" he asked. "I certainly would have expected him to be here."

"Ah," Cynewise said. "Nothwulf I believe is at his estate at Blandford."

"Really?" Æthelwulf said, turning his eyes toward her. "At such a time as this? What business has he there that's of greater import than what's happening here at Sherborne? A royal visit."

"I'm sure I don't know," Cynewise said. She took a small bite of carrot, chewed it contemplatively. "He may not have felt as welcome in Sherborne as he might hope," she ventured.

"Oh? And why would that be?"

"There are some…oh, my lord, these are only stories going about. Gossip, mostly, I'm loath to even say it."

"Go on, child, go on," Æthelwulf said in a way that Cynewise found particularly annoying. "I would hear what you have to say."

"Well, your highness, there are some who suggest that Nothwulf was not so sorry to see his brother murdered. That he had ambitions…ambitions to set himself up as ealdorman of Dorsetshire."

"Humph," Æthelwulf grunted. "He might indeed have become ealdorman. Might still. It's a strange situation. Not really settled, I'd say, though you sit in that chair and your father has spoken in your favor."

"Of course, lord," Cynewise said. "A very unsettled situation. But there is also talk abroad…and let me say I believe none of it, and I hate to even speak it…that Nothwulf had some hand in my husband's murder."

At that Æthelwulf frowned and his bushy black and gray eyebrows came together. "Some hand in Merewald's murder?" he said, sounding as incredulous as Cynewise would expect him to be. "I've known Nothwulf since he was a boy. He rode with me when we drove the heathens from London not four years ago. He's a hothead, sure, but murder?"

Cynewise shook her head. "I'm loath to believe it. But there was some evidence, or so Oswin tells me. Some token of Nothwulf's that was found among the murderer's things. And testimony by his wife. Concerning Nothwulf's involvement."

Æthelwulf's frown deepened to a scowl. "This is monstrous," he said. "Is this why Nothwulf won't show his face here?"

"It might well be, sire," Cynewise said. "We've not heard from him for days now. I have word he's gone to Blandford, but I don't know with any certainty."

"Humph," Æthelwulf said again. "Well, I shall talk to Oswin, and we'll find Nothwulf and I'll talk to him as well. I have a knack for sussing out the truth, and we'll find it, rest assured."

"I'm pleased to hear that, sire," Cynewise assured him.

"And I'm pleased that you were here to put a steady hand on Dorset. This sort of thing can be a bloody business, you know. It already is, with your husband's murder, but it can get much worse. Blood running in the streets as they fight for the ealdormanship."

"I'm only pleased that I can bring your highness some comfort in that regard," Cynewise said. "My only desire is to see peace in Dorset...in all of Wessex. The dear Lord knows we are beset enough with enemies, what with Mercia to the north and the heathens attacking our shores. We don't need to be fighting amongst ourselves."

"Amen," Bishop Ealhstan said and crossed himself and Cynewise and Æthelwulf did the same, if a little less enthusiastically.

Æthelwulf turned to Cynewise and his expression suggested that his thoughts had moved on, that he was done for the time with Nothwulf and the intrigues of Sherborne. "I did not thank you, dear, for the generous gift you made me and my court. Five wagonloads, meat, wine, cloth. It must have cost you dearly."

Cynewise gave a dismissive wave of her hand. "I'm happy to do what I can to support the king's estate in Winchester. It's you, sire, who gives so much for this kingdom."

"Hmm," Æthelwulf said, a sound to indicate that Cynewise had said the right thing. "Your father is a good man, Lady Cynewise, and he's taught you well, I see."

"Thank you, sire. He's taught me to love my king, that's for certain." He had also taught her that Æthelwulf was greatly moved by even the most baldly insincere flattery, and that advice had already done her much good.

Gifts as well. The king loved gifts, gifts of any kind, as long as they were the finest to be had. She guessed that the five wagons that had been sent to the king under her name had been loaded with the finest. Oswin had assured her that was the case. Nor would Nothwulf, who was no fool, have sent anything less to win the king's favor.

Cynewise nibbled on her carrot and thought, *Thank you, Nothwulf, you sorry bastard, wherever you are…*

Chapter Twenty-Five

[Y]our new-tarred ship by shore of ocean
faithfully watching till once again
it waft o'er the waters those well-loved thanes.

Beowulf

Thorgrim felt as if he were being engulfed by fire. His fury was blinding, utterly consuming, his vision distorted as if he were looking through heat and flames. Bécc had beaten him. Not once, but again and again. Tricked him, led him by the nose, tricked him once more. Killed his men, taken his longphort. He himself had been carried off the battlefield, wounded, defeated, while Bécc still lived.

Four men were holding him fast on *Sea Hammer*'s deck as he fought against them. The wound in his side was rippling pain and he could feel the warm blood under his wet tunic, but his passion was driving him past all that. He was desperate to vault over the side and charge back at the beach and finish the fight with Bécc that had started months before. The fate of the ships, the men, himself, were of no concern to him now.

And then two things happened nearly at once that quenched the fire, at least for the moment. Harald climbed aboard, pulled over the sheer strake by his fellow warriors and dumped on the deck. The sight of his son brought Thorgrim partway back into the land of reason. And just as that happened, Thorgrim became once more aware of the howling wind, the black sky and the flashing lightning and thunder just overhead. His ship—his fleet—might still be within the protective arms of the bay at Loch Garman, but it was nonetheless in grave danger.

His ship in danger.

Thorgrim reacted to the thought the way a mother reacts to the crying of her child. He shook off the men holding him and they let go and stepped back, not sure what would follow. The shaking motion tore at the wound in his side and he gasped, but he still did not know how bad the wound was.

Nor did he have time to worry much about it. His mind had already left the fight on the beach and turned to matters of seamanship. He was near *Sea Hammer*'s bow, looking out past the stem toward the swarms of Irishmen on the beach. The ship's oars were out and moving and *Sea Hammer* had already pulled far enough from the water's edge that none of the Irish could have reached her if they wanted to, which in any case they did not seem too eager to do.

Thorgrim turned and looked aft. The oars were haphazardly manned, some double-manned, some not even run out. He headed aft, hunched over just a bit, moving fast down the ship's centerline, hand pressed against his wound, calling orders as he did.

"Two men on each oar! Quickly, now, you sorry bastards! Move! Hall, Godi, get the rest of the oars down from the gallows! Come along, we'll be driven back on the beach before you whores' sons get another stroke in!"

He reached the small after deck and stepped up, then leaned over the side and looked out over the water. The wind was from the northwest now, and blowing harder than he had felt it blow in a long time, whipping his long, wet hair against his back and face. He could see his ship was being set down to leeward even as the men strained at the oars to drive the ship into the wind.

He crossed the small deck and looked over the starboard side. The other ships were also pulling away from the beach, opening up the gap between themselves and the Irish warriors ashore, and they, too, were having a hard time of it, struggling to counter the strength of the wind.

"We've got to turn, got to turn," Thorgrim said to himself. They were backing *Sea Hammer* away from the beach, but the men at the oars could not put half as much power into the stroke pushing the oars to go astern as they could pulling them to go forward. He had to swing the bow around, but it would not be easy.

He stepped to the edge of the deck. His wound was throbbing terribly and so painful that it seemed as if the spear point were still embedded in his flesh, but he ignored it as best he could.

"Listen to me!" he bellowed, and there was power enough in his voice to be heard over the shriek of the wind. "We must turn to starboard, get her bow into it! On my command, larboard will back water, starboard will pull! You sons of bitches had better row like Loki has you by the balls or we'll be on the beach for the Irish to cut our throats!"

He saw eyes locked on him, grim faces, some men nodding even as they kept up the stroke. They were already straining at the oars, and it was about to get worse. Thorgrim looked out to windward. *Fox* was about fifty yards away, right on their starboard side, and it would only be with the best possible luck that they did not collide as *Sea Hammer* made her turn. He looked back at the men.

"Now!" he shouted. "Larboard, backwater, starboard stroke!"

And they did as Thorgrim commanded. Each one of the men, raiders of long experience, had spent countless hours pulling oar, and now they reaped the benefit of that mindless labor. Their muscles were hard and taut and the motion of the stroke deeply ingrained. Backwater, stroke, they understood the commands as if by instinct. Every hand was pulling an oar, even Starri Deathless, who longed to die in battle but was terrified of dying at sea.

Thorgrim took two steps aft and laid his hands on the tiller, as familiar to him as the stroke of an oar was to the others. He pulled it aft to help *Sea Hammer* in her turn to starboard, but it was the oars that were driving her now.

Or not. Thorgrim looked past the bow and he could see that the ship was not turning, that the force of the wind was holding her in place as she turned broadside to it and pushing her down toward the beach. Once her keel touched it was over, and Bécc's army, his overwhelming army, would swarm over the sides.

Pull, pull, you bastards, pull, Thorgrim thought, but he did not bother speaking the words because he knew that the men forward were pulling with every last bit of strength they had left.

And then the balance of forces shifted. Oar stroke and gale winds had held one another in check, but now the power of the oars began to win out. Thorgrim saw the stem begin to turn, the beach seemed to shift to the left as *Sea Hammer* began to turn to the right.

The men saw it as well. Looking after, they would see the sea and land beyond the sternpost moving in the opposite way and they would know they were gaining in their struggle. Thorgrim saw a few smiles here and there among the grimacing, red, straining faces.

Don't smile yet, he thought.

The ship continued to swing, moving faster as the oars gained power, and Thorgrim felt the wind shift from the starboard beam forward as the bow turned up into the storm. The hair that had been whipping the left side of his face now began to stream aft, and beyond the bow the land turned faster and faster.

Good, good, good, Thorgrim thought. They were doing it, turning the bow through the eye of the wind, and soon *Sea Hammer* would be pointing northeast, with the wind on her larboard side, and then they would be able to claw their way across the wide bay to the beach near Beggerin, where at least they could run ashore with Bécc's army a good day's march away. Let the storm blow out, get to sea, back to Vík-ló, build his army again….

"Larboard, pull! Starboard, pull!" Thorgrim shouted. *Sea Hammer*'s bow had made it through the wind. They needed now only to row, to drive the ship forward, and with that speed through the water Thorgrim could use the steerboard to set the course.

As one, the men on the larboard side lifted the blades of their oars from the water, paused to get in time with the rowers to starboard, then dropped their oars and pulled, leaning back into the stroke, the muscles of their arms and legs bulging with the strain, the rain washing over them as if they were standing under a waterfall.

Thorgrim could feel the tiller bite, could feel *Sea Hammer* begin to gather momentum. He looked out past the bow as the ship turned. *Sea Hammer* had been the last of the ships to leave the beach, the crew waiting for Thorgrim, Godi, Harald and the rest to get aboard. The other seven ships were already underway, struggling to get sea room, to pull clear of the beach and out into wider water. They fanned out ahead of *Sea Hammer* as they fought their way into the wind.

Fox was closest to them, just off the larboard bow and about a hundred feet ahead, and her men seemed to be having a hard time of it. They were still trying to make the turn through the wind, but their rowing was uncoordinated, and not all the oarports had oars thrust through. There had been no organization as the men flung themselves back aboard the ships, and Thorgrim guessed that some of them were well manned, and some were not.

He looked to the starboard side. *Oak Heart* was about two ship lengths upwind, and Thorgrim thought he could make out Asmund's large frame standing on the afterdeck. His rowers were hard at it, the blades rising and falling, driving the longship into the wind and the increasingly steep chop. *Oak Heart* would pass ahead of *Sea Hammer* comfortably. But only if *Fox* was able to get clear.

Thorgrim looked back over the larboard bow and he saw what he feared he would see. *Fox* had failed to get through the wind and now she was falling back, spinning out of control, her men unable to drive the ship through the punishing wind. She was blowing down toward *Sea Hammer*'s path, but Thorgrim was not worried about that. *Fox* would pass ahead of *Sea Hammer* and not hit her. But she would hit *Oak Heart* if Asmund continued on his course. And with the rain and *Sea Hammer* blocking his view, Thorgrim was sure that Asmund could not even see *Fox* and the danger he would soon be in.

"Oh, by the gods…" Thorgrim muttered. They had almost made it clear. But now disaster was forming under his bows, and there was nothing he could do. Shouting a warning would be pointless. He could barely be heard aboard his own ship over the howling storm.

Fox was drifting fast, her oars moving sporadically, and Thorgrim guessed that most of the rowers had dropped from exhaustion. *Oak Heart* was still pulling hard, shooting ahead, Asmund, unable to see *Fox*, was thinking that his only concern was passing in front of *Sea Hammer*.

And then Asmund saw the danger. With one stroke *Oak Heart* shot ahead, one hundred feet beyond *Sea Hammer*'s bow, far enough ahead of *Sea Hammer* that he could see *Fox* drifting down on him. Thorgrim saw *Oak Heart* turn to starboard, turning away from the oncoming ship, but it was not that simple. There were sandbars downwind of *Oak Heart* and if she turned too hard she would be set down on them and the wind and seas would beat her apart. The short chop was already breaking white on the shallow water over the bars. Asmund did not have much room to escape.

In fact, he had no room. Before the crew of *Oak Heart* had given one more pull *Fox* slammed into her, bow to bow, their stems locked like men arm wrestling, and they began to drift downwind. And now they were directly in *Sea Hammer*'s path.

There was only one reasonable thing for Thorgrim to do, and that was to push the tiller away, turning *Sea Hammer* to larboard and letting the two disabled ships drift down onto the sandbar. There was nothing he could do for them, and there was no reason to lose *Sea Hammer* and the men aboard her as well.

It was the reasonable thing to do, so of course Thorgrim dismissed it out of hand. Instead he pulled the tiller a bit toward him, aiming *Sea Hammer* at the bows of the two ships ahead, aiming like an arrow at the point where they were locked together. The men at the oars pulled and *Sea Hammer* shot ahead and Thorgrim was glad that they were looking aft, that none of them could see what he was about to do.

"Harald!" he shouted. "Harald, come here!"

Harald was pulling an oar, but he looked up at Thorgrim's call and without hesitation stood and bounded aft. He stopped at the break of the afterdeck and looked up at Thorgrim, blinking rain from his eyes.

"Yes, Father?"

"We're going to hit those ships," Thorgrim said, nodding forward. Harald turned, hesitated for a second, then turned back, eyes wide with something that looked like panic.

"*Fox* is disabled, undermanned," Thorgrim shouted over the wind, loud, before Harald could protest. "When we pass by, you throw them a rope and we'll take them in tow, you understand?"

He glanced down at his son. Harald nodded and then dropped to his knees to fish a rope out from under the afterdeck. It was insane, of course. The men of *Sea Hammer* could hardly drive the one ship against the wind. Towing another vessel would likely be impossible. But Thorgrim was curious now to see if it could be done. If not, they would all be pounded to death on the sandbar, but with the reckless madness on him, Thorgrim did not much care about such things.

The rowers leaned forward and pulled back and *Sea Hammer* drove grudgingly into the wind. The rain was coming down so fast it was filling the ship's bilge, the water starting to lap over the deck boards. That meant considerably more weight, the keel deeper in the water, the vessel more sluggish and hard to row. Not good.

"You men!" Thorgrim called out. His throat was starting to ache with the effort of shouting over the storm and the water that choked him every time he spoke. "You get ready to pull your oars in fast when I give the word! You hear?"

Heads nodded, the stroke never altered. If they hit the two ships with the oars out, the shafts would be snapped like twigs and then there would be no hope at all. Thorgrim looked over at *Oak Heart* on his starboard side. Asmund, reliable, competent, had seen *Sea Hammer* coming, had seen the danger to his own ship, and had ordered the oars in on his larboard side.

You must wonder what stupid thing I'm about to do, Thorgrim mused, looking at Asmund's tall figure aft. *You must wonder if I've lost my mind.*

It was a fair question. One Thorgrim himself could not answer.

Chapter Twenty-Six

West over water I fared
Bearing poetry's waves to the shore
Of the war-god's heart.
                    Egil's Saga

Harald, rope in hand, leapt up onto the aft deck and stood leaning against the ship's side. He had snatched up a battle ax and tied it to the end of the rope to give it more heft for the throw. Now he stood poised, waiting, the ax swinging back and forth in little arcs.

Thorgrim looked forward. Less than a ship's length until they hit. He waited as the men at the oars gave one last pull, until he was as sure as he could be that *Sea Hammer* carried enough momentum, and then he shouted, "Oars in! Oars in! Now! Now!"

There was no confusion. The men forward were accustomed to handling the oars and accustomed to Thorgrim's unexpected and unorthodox commands. They pulled the oars in quick and smooth, the long shafts reaching across the deck and resting on the opposite side.

Heads turned right and left. They could see *Oak Heart* and *Fox* now, close on either side, and it was clear to all that they were going to hit. Thorgrim saw men turn on the sea chests on which they sat, stare forward, stare from side to side.

Fox, to larboard, was no more than thirty feet away, locked bow to bow with *Oak Heart*. Thorgrim could see Hardbein standing at the tiller, but he could make out little detail, could not even tell if the man was looking his way. Though he probably was.

"Hardbein!" he shouted. "We'll send a rope, take you in tow!" There was little chance that Hardbein heard him, but Harald was standing tall and holding the coil of rope up high and swinging it, and that Hardbein seemed to understand. He waved his arm and then apparently shouted something forward to his diminished crew.

Thorgrim wiped rain from his eyes and looked forward at the very instant that *Sea Hammer* drove into the bows of the other two ships. He felt the shudder run down the length of the longship and he stumbled forward and grabbed hard to the tiller to keep from falling. He shouted in pain as he felt the impact jar his still bleeding wound but happily no one could hear him over the roar of the wind.

They could most certainly hear the sound of wood shattering with the impact, however. *Sea Hammer*'s bow struck right at the vertex of the angle formed by the two fouled ships and drove right on through. *Fox*'s tall stem, caught around that of *Oak Heart*, was wrenched clean off, taking part of *Oak Heart*'s with it. Thorgrim wondered if any of them would suffer damage below the waterline, which would put one or both ships on the bottom.

We'll see…

He looked to larboard. *Fox*, free from *Oak Heart*'s embrace, was swinging toward them. He could see men running along her length and oars resting on the sheer strake to fend *Sea Hammer* off before they struck. Harald was poised with his rope, swinging the ax back and forth, and then he drew back his arm and with a wide, straight-arm swing he heaved the ax and line away.

Thorgrim watched the weapon fly through the air, a beautiful, perfect arc that dropped the ax and the line made fast to it right amidships on *Fox*'s deck. Men aboard the smaller ship grabbed it up and raced it forward, while Harald took the other end, the end still aboard *Sea Hammer*, and made it fast to the heavy cleat mounted on the larboard side.

Sea Hammer shuddered again and again, a series of blows as she bounced off *Oak Heart* and *Fox*. *Oak Heart* had pivoted with the impact on her bow and swung alongside *Sea Hammer* and now the two ships were smashing one into the other as *Sea Hammer*'s momentum drove her forward. Thorgrim could see sections torn from *Oak Heart*'s sheer strake and his as well, but it was minor damage compared to what might have been if *Oak Heart* and *Fox* had gone up on the sandbar.

He looked at *Oak Heart*'s afterdeck, with which he was closing as *Sea Hammer* bashed down the other ship's side. Asmund was still at the tiller, looking back at him, with no more than twenty feet separating them. Asmund raised his arm in greeting, as if the two of them had happened across one another on either side of a street, and Thorgrim raised his arm as well. It was odd, very odd.

Then Thorgrim recalled that *Sea Hammer* was only drifting, that they would soon have the weight of *Fox* pulling behind them and they had better start rowing again, and quick. He looked forward, but Godi had already thought of that, and was moving from forward aft, ordering the men to run their oars back out the oar ports as each drew clear of the ships on either side.

Thorgrim looked to his left, where Harald stood by the cleat. Harald was a good mariner, and one of considerable experience, even at seventeen years of age. He had taken a turn of the rope around the cleat, which would allow him to keep hold of the line when it came tight, but he did not tie it off for fear it would snap if *Fox*'s weight came on it all at once.

*Well done, well done…*Thorgrim thought. He looked forward. Most of the oars were out now, the men pulling like lunatics. *Oak Heart* had her oars back out as well, and Asmund was driving his ship as directly away from the sandbars as he could without running afoul of *Sea Hammer*.

"We're taking *Fox* in tow!" Thorgrim shouted forward to the men working the oars. "You better row like you mean it, now!" He wondered if they had the strength enough left to move *Sea Hammer*, and *Fox* as well, after driving the longship off the beach.

He felt *Sea Hammer*'s aft end began to slew around and he knew that the tow rope was coming tight, the smaller ship starting to exert drag on his own. He looked aft, craning his head around the sternpost. *Fox* was directly behind them now, the rope between them rising from the short chop, dripping and straining. But Hardbein had had sense enough to drive his men back to the oars, and now one and another and another of the long shafts emerged from the row ports to drive *Fox* under her own power as much as they could, and help the men of *Sea Hammer* in their efforts.

Forward the men fell back into their steady rhythm: arms down, lean forward, arms up to dip the blades, lean back to pull. Their faces were still set and grim, but they were driving against the wind, making headway. They could see it, and it gave them more encouragement than any words Thorgrim could speak.

"Father, can I return to my oar?" Harald shouted. It was a torment for the boy to see other men working harder than he was, but Thorgrim could not let him go.

"No, I need you to tend the tow rope!" he called without moving his eyes from the bow. He could picture the look on Harald's face—he had seen it often enough—but Harald would do as he was ordered and would not argue.

Thorgrim looked back over his shoulder and he was surprised to see how far astern the beach was already. He felt as if they had been rowing for hours and had made no progress at all in that time, but in truth it had been just a few minutes and they had already put a couple hundred yards between themselves and Bécc's army.

He looked forward, past the bow, toward the shoreline to the north, which appeared as little more than a dark line through the driving rain, and he did not like what he saw. He was steering *Sea Hammer* in a straight line, but the distant shore seemed to be moving, right to left. That meant the wind was pushing the ship sideways, driving it and the others down onto the sandbars. If they touched, they would be stuck fast and they would be beaten apart before the storm blew out.

Thorgrim pushed the tiller away, turning the ship's bow more into the wind, and he saw the other ships adjust as well. Eight ships working against the gale force winds. He looked to starboard. The water was piling up and breaking over the sandbars, more obvious now with the still mounting wind, and he could see they were being pushed down that way.

Row...all of you sons of whores...row... His thoughts were not just with the men of *Sea Hammer* but all the hundreds of men now under his command. His army, his fleet. Would their saga consist of a single defeat at the hands of the Irish, then death in the waters of Loch Garman? It was too much to bear. He wondered if there was still room enough to turn the ship and run back to the beach and die fighting Bécc. A proper death. He would try it, if the sandbars got much closer than they were.

Foot by foot the ships clawed their way to windward, the shallow water lurking downwind, the breaking whitecaps like arms beckoning them. But they kept ahead of the sand and the breakers, kept to their agonizing pace, fathom upon fathom, pulling for the northern shore and the beach at Beggerin.

Thorgrim had no sense for how long they had been at it—hours, days?—when the realization came to him, obvious as a rune stone at a junction of two roads: *We won't make it.*

Sea Hammer was still at the end of the line of ships pulling for the shore. She had been last to get off the beach and she had *Fox* tethered astern, half rowing, half under tow. From where he stood, Thorgrim could see how things would play out. The ships were trying to go north, but they were being driven off to the east as the wind and the short, choppy waves pummeled them on their larboard bows.

He could see his own men were tiring rapidly, as of course they must. Every man was at the oars; there were no replacements, no fresh arms waiting. The men pulling oar on the other ships would be as tired as well. Like *Sea Hammer*, the other ships would be half filled with water, making them harder to row, more susceptible to the power of the wind. If they kept on the way they were, the men's strength would desert them, and soon. Even the most powerful rowers could only keep at it for so long in the teeth of such a wind. And when that happened, the ships would be up on the sandbars in minutes.

Thorgrim swept his eyes along the horizon. If his current plan would not save them, then he needed to think of something else, and fast. To the north there were the beaches at Beggerin, safe havens where the wind would keep the ship off the sand, keep them from being beaten to death. But they could not reach them. To leeward were the sandbars and beyond them the spit of land that formed the ocean side of the wide bay. They could reach those easy enough, and they would be destroyed once they did.

And just to the northeast, and all but downwind, was the wide gap in the shoreline, where the bay of Loch Garman emptied into the sea beyond.

Thorgrim pressed his lips together. It was madness, and it was not likely to save them, but it was the only chance that he could see. He pulled the tiller to him, just a bit, and swung *Sea Hammer's* bow off to the northwest. He looked beyond the starboard rail at the water breaking over the sandbars. It would be a tricky thing, heading off on that course while keeping clear of the shallows. He had no way of gauging it beyond his gut feeling, and his gut feeling said they would make it, and that was good enough. It had to be good enough.

He pulled the tiller a bit more toward him, and as the bow turned further from the eye of the wind, the ship began to heel and the rowing became much easier. He could see exhausted men looking up in surprise at the sudden easing of their burden. He felt *Sea Hammer*'s speed increase as the wind began to aid, not hinder, her motion.

Oak Heart, not burdened with a vessel towing astern, had managed to claw her way upwind of *Sea Hammer*. A couple hundred yards to windward, she was little more than a dark shape through the rain and the heavy clouded sky, as were the rest of the fleet. They had all been moving in the same direction, but now *Sea Hammer* had turned away, heading off on her new course.

Do they see what I'm doing? Thorgrim wondered. There was no way, no way at all, to communicate from one ship to another. Thorgrim could only hope that the others would notice him and follow his lead. Or not. What he had in mind was as likely to kill them all as anything else, and he was happy to let the others choose their own watery grave.

They passed downwind of *Oak Heart* and Thorgrim could see the next ship ahead, which he thought was *Blood Hawk*, though it was impossible to know for certain. She, too, was still struggling to row to windward, and *Sea Hammer*, the wind helping her now, began to catch up with that ship as well.

"Father!" Harald shouted. He was still standing at the windward rail, the tow rope in hand, keeping careful watch on the degree of strain that came on it. "*Oak Heart*, they're following! I think they're following!"

Harald, of course, had guessed at what his father intended, and understood the dangers as well. Thorgrim turned and craned his neck to look astern, and he could see Harald was right. The big ship had indeed turned to follow in *Sea Hammer*'s wake, and Thorgrim was now looking at her bow as she followed after.

Well, Asmund, you'll see soon enough if I've killed us all, Thorgrim mused.

Sea Hammer continued on her course, turning ever more toward the east as she skirted the sandbars on her leeward side. Whereas once they had been rowing straight into the wind, now with their change of heading the wind was mostly behind them, driving the ship along, until at last the men at the oars could not row as fast as the wind was pushing them, even with no sail set. The long sweeps were run in and laid across the deck and the men collapsed over them, hunched over and resting on the looms of the oars, too exhausted even to look up.

Thorgrim was looking up. His eyes were everywhere: on the shoreline to north and south, on the breakers off the starboard side, on the other ships of the fleet. Like Asmund on *Oak Heart*, they, too, had seen what Thorgrim had in mind and had turned in his wake, following behind. The tow line running from *Sea Hammer*'s cleat to *Fox* astern was slack now and Thorgrim told Harald to cast it off. The smaller ship was no longer in need of towing.

"Night Wolf!" Thorgrim looked up to see Starri Deathless moving aft, performing an odd sort of dance as he tried to keep his footing on the sharp rolling deck. He stepped up onto the aft deck by Thorgrim's side and took a moment to look around.

"I'm not the great seafarer that you are, Night Wolf," he said at last. "But I thought we were making for the beaches at Beggerin, and I'm all but certain they're that way." He pointed over the larboard quarter to the strip of land astern of them.

"They are," Thorgrim said, nearly shouting to be heard, though Starri was only a few feet away. "But we wouldn't have made it. Couldn't pull against the wind. And if the rowers gave out we'd have been on the sandbars, and knocked to pieces."

Starri nodded. "So now where are we going?"

"Only place we can," Thorgrim shouted. "Out to sea!"

A look passed over Starri's face that suggested discomfort with this idea. Starri Deathless was not at all certain that a man who drowned would be taken up to Odin's corpse hall.

"And you think that's a good choice?" Starri said.

"It's the only choice," Thorgrim said. "That doesn't make it good."

The motion of the ship changed under them, the stern lifted higher, the bow twisted around as Thorgrim worked the tiller to keep her on course. They had been closer to land before, but now there was several miles of open water behind them, the full width of the bay at Loch Garman, and the wind was building the waves up to a respectable height.

Thorgrim looked aft, larboard and starboard. The other seven ships were behind him now, some close by and clearly seen, some only shadows in the rain and dark. But they were all on the same course, the same track.

The stern lifted again and the ship corkscrewed under him. The exhausted men at the oars began to lift their heads and look around, and Thorgrim wondered if any of them had guessed what he was doing, or if they were so happy to not be rowing that they did not care.

Off the larboard side, directly abeam, Thorgrim could see the point of land that formed the northern entrance to the bay, a beach he knew well, having walked it several times. To the south, also abeam, was the long sandy spit that made the southern entrance, which he had only seen from a distance.

The seas lifted the ship once more, the wind drove her forward, and the land to the north and the south passed astern of them. Thorgrim looked forward, past the bow. There was nothing there but the sea, the open sea, and the massive breaking waves rolling off toward the dim horizon.

Chapter Twenty-Seven

Many nobles sat assembled, and searched out counsel
how it were best for bold-hearted men
against harassing terror to try their hand.

Beowulf

The thunder rolled, the long hall shook as if something massive and solid had struck it, and Nothwulf could no longer contain his curiosity.

"That will do for now, Tilmund," he said to his man, standing at his side. "Sit, have a rest, we'll get back to it in a minute. You, too," he added to Bryning, standing off to the other side.

Tilmund grunted and sat on the bench behind him. Bryning remained standing. Nothwulf strode down the length of the long hall, which was all but empty, and pushed open the tall oak door at the far end. He was struck immediately by the wind, a cold, powerful blast that drove the rain before it. Rain like projectiles, like weapons of some sort. The howling sound, muted by the thick walls and thatch roof of the long hall, came at full volume now, a deep moaning sound such as Nothwulf had never heard and never expected to hear this side of the grave.

Heavy as the door was, Nothwulf had to hold it with both hands to keep the wind from smashing it open. He looked out across the courtyard. The roof of the stable was gone, and beyond that the entire bake-house had collapsed into a heap. A couple of carts, quite substantial vehicles, had been flipped on their sides. Clumps of wet thatch torn from roofs lay half drowned in the pond-like puddles that covered the ground.

Nothwulf had no idea what time of day it might be. Near evening, he guessed, but there was no telling from looking at the sky, which had been a preternatural black since early morning.

*Dear God…*he thought. *Surely, this marks the end of creation.*

Nothwulf did not really believe that. Still, upon seeing that sky, and the destruction wrought by the epic wind and driving rain, rather than just hearing from inside the hall, he did not entirely disbelieve it, either.

There have been enough unnatural acts these past weeks, he thought. *It might well herald the end of times.*

Of course, people had thought the same with the coming of the Northmen which had begun a generation ago—that they were God's punishment on a wicked people. And, savage heathens that they were, they had seemed to be just that. But the men of Wessex had fought back, and driven the Northmen into the sea. His father had been foremost among them, as had the king, Æthelwulf. Nothwulf himself had played his part. The Northmen could not have been sent by God, he reasoned, since a punishment from God would not be defeated by mortal men.

*Not defeated…*Nothwulf thought. *Driven off, but not defeated. They could return.* He was not sure which was more frightening: the storm he was witnessing or the thought of heathen raiders overrunning the shire.

With some difficulty he pulled the door shut against the wind and made certain it was properly latched. The doorway had sheltered him somewhat, but still his clothes were pretty well soaked through as he turned and walked back to where he and Tilmund and Bryning had been at work.

Leofric and his men had retired to the apartments at the far end of the long hall, or to their own quarters in one of the smaller buildings within the palisade fence surrounding the manor. Leofric wished to give Nothwulf privacy to do as he wished, or so he said, and that was true enough. But Nothwulf was also sure that what he wished to do was not something Leofric cared to witness.

There was one other man in the room and his name was Wulgan and until the distraction of the storm he had commanded the others' attention. He was seated on an oak chair, his head lolling forward on his chest. There was blood on his tunic where it had flowed from his mouth and his nose. His legs were splayed out haphazardly in front of him. At least three fingers were broken.

Wulgan had, as of that morning, been one of Nothwulf's men, one of the hearth-guard who served under Siward. He had been a loyal servant, or so Nothwulf thought, right up until the moment he had drawn a sword against Nothwulf and his men. That had been a bad decision. Living through the ensuing battle, remaining whole enough to be questioned, had been worse.

Tilmund stood as Nothwulf approached. Nothwulf stopped in front of the slumped man and looked at him for a moment. He wasn't sure if he was even conscious at that point. He kicked Wulgan's leg and the man let out a little moan and shifted his head. Nothwulf had not kicked him hard. The moan, he guessed, was more in anticipation of further punishment from Tilmund and Bryning.

Nothwulf reached over and grabbed a fistfull of Wulgan's hair and tilted his head back until they were face to face. From the nose down Wulgan's face was covered in blood, his beard matted with it. He looked up at Nothwulf through half-closed eyes and it was not at all clear that he was still aware of what was happening. Nothwulf sighed and let go of Wulgan's hair and the man's head slumped down again.

"I think we're done with him," Nothwulf said and the other two grunted their agreement. Wulgan was the third man they had questioned, the last of the hearth-guard who had been taken prisoner and were still whole enough to talk. And he, like the others, had talked. They had talked even before the beatings had begun. The punishment was to make certain they were telling the truth. And it seemed that they were.

Of course, they had no reason to lie, Nothwulf soon came to understand, because they did not know anything. They had all said pretty much the same. Siward had gathered them together and told them of treachery in Sherborne, that he, Nothwulf, stood accused of his brother's murder. Siward had said the king himself would come to Sherborne to see justice done, and that given the chance they were to kill Nothwulf's hearth-guard and place Nothwulf under arrest.

Who had given Siward these instructions they did not know. Who had set fire to the long hall they did not know either, and no amount of punishment that Tilmund could dole out could get them to change their stories. And that made Nothwulf pretty sure they were telling the truth, useless as their knowledge was.

"Very well," Nothwulf said. "Tie him up and toss him outside with the others. If any of them are still alive in the morning we'll...I don't know. We'll think of something to do with them. And find one of Leofric's servants to clean up this mess."

Bryning and Tilmund set to work on Wulgan and Nothwulf left them to it, walking down the length of the long hall and through the door at the far end that led to the apartments and various sleeping chambers. Leofric had given him the largest of the rooms that was available, which was none too large, but tolerable and welcome. They had arrived fresh from the fighting the day before, and Leofric had ordered up a banquet, which even on such short notice was wonderfully done.

Nothwulf had always considered Leofric a friend, and something of a mentor, and he was proving to be those things once again. He trusted Leofric, and felt that the old man's affection was genuine. What's more, Nothwulf would likely soon be ealdorman of Dorsetshire, and that fact would do much to raise him in Leofric's esteem. Still Leofric was wealthy and powerful enough already that he did not feel the need to curry favor.

He sat on the edge of the bed and looked around. A single candle set on the table was casting its weak light around the space. Nothwulf pulled his shoes off. He was exhausted. Tired as he had been the day before, sleep had come only grudgingly, hardly a surprise given the way his life had been turned on its head. He lay down and listened to the storm battering the thick walls of the long hall and closed his eyes.

A knocking woke him and he opened his eyes and saw nothing and was not entirely certain where he was.

"Lord Nothwulf?" a timid voice called out, muffled by a door, and he remembered. The candle on the table had gone out, leaving in its wake an impenetrable blackness.

"Yes?" Nothwulf called out.

"Lord Leofric's compliments, lord, and he asks would you join him for supper in his chamber?"

Supper? Nothwulf had no idea how long he had been sleeping, but that gave him a clue.

"Yes, yes, I'll be there directly," Nothwulf called out, swinging his legs over the side of the bed. "And fetch me a candle, do you hear?"

It was not long after that Nothwulf was welcomed into Leofric's apartment, the outer room that he used when he took his meals alone, or with a few intimates. There was no question of Nothwulf's dressing for supper: he had nothing in which to dress save for the clothes he wore. He was very aware of the splatters of mud and the various rents and tears in the fabric and the dark spots of blood that speckled his tunic.

"Ah, Lord Nothwulf, so happy you could join me!" Leofric said, standing as Nothwulf entered. There was nothing insincere in the greeting, no insinuation concerning Nothwulf's appearance. "Please, sit. Some wine, with you. You look as if you could use some wine."

Nothwulf sat. He accepted a cup with pleasure. Leofric was correct. He could use a cup of wine. More than a cup. Considerably more.

The servants brought cheese and soft, white bread and the two men tore pieces from the loaf and went at the cheese with their knives as if it were their mortal enemy. "I hope you don't mind the lack of company, lord," Leofric said, gesturing at the otherwise empty room. "I had a thought it might be best if we were to dine in private. Talk in private."

"A good thought, indeed," Nothwulf said. He had hardly been in the mood for the banquet the night before, was in no humor to make idle chat, particularly when it meant yelling over the raucous and mostly drunk crowd. But at the same time he could hardly refuse to appear at his host's table. Now he welcomed the chance for a more civilized meal.

"I was going to say, we should send for your clothes," Leofric said, "but then I remembered your hall was burned down, and you lost all you had there, I would imagine."

"Nothing but a vast black patch of ground left," Nothwulf said.

"Hmm," Leofric said. "And did you learn anything today? From your...interviews?"

"No," Nothwulf said. "Nothing. They said only that Siward told them I was to be arrested. They didn't know why. Weren't sure Siward did. Didn't know who put my hall to the torch."

"Hmm," Leofric said again. The cheese and bread was removed and the bulk of the supper brought in: roast beef and summer greens, potatoes and, not surprising, an abundance of fish, Leofric's lands encompassing the villages Swanage and sundry other villages that made their living from the sea.

They served themselves and for a short time ate in silence. Then Nothwulf said, "Each of the prisoners we spoke to, they all said that King Æthelwulf would be coming to Sherborne soon, to see for himself what's going on."

"Not coming, my boy," Leofric said. "He's already there."

Nothwulf set his knife down and looked up at Leofric. "Already there? He was not expected for a fortnight."

"Seems to have changed his plans. He arrived just as this storm was coming in. Trust me, I'm certain of it. I'm careful to know such things."

Nothwulf looked off at the tapestry hanging on the wall, but his thoughts were back at Sherborne. This was bad news, very bad indeed. It had been his intention to be at Sherborne when the king arrived, or better yet, to meet his party on the road, before they reached the cathedral town. To make certain that his, Nothwulf's, version of events was the first that Æthelwulf heard.

"He's…he's lodging at my brother's home?" Nothwulf said.

"Oh, yes," Leofric said. "They've set out quite a welcome for him. Fit for a king, as it were."

Nothwulf could feel the emotions welling up like the storm blowing outside, an ugly stew of anger and fear and humiliation. He was thwarted in every direction he moved, and he did not know who was responsible. Oswin, perhaps, but did the shire reeve really have that much sway? Nothwulf had never thought so. One of the thegns? Few had power or wealth enough, save for Leofric.

"So, who is seeing to the king's entertainment?" Nothwulf asked. "Who is giving him the welcome he would expect?" The question made him hopeful. Failure in that regard, by whomever was pulling strings, would make it clear to Æthelwulf that the shire needed Nothwulf's hands on the reins.

"I understand Cynewise is seeing to all that," Leofric said, and there was a note of hesitation in his voice.

"Cynewise? That simpering little fool? Please. She could hardly look me in the eyes, I don't imagine she's seeing to the entertainment of a king."

"I don't know," Leofric said in a tone that suggested he did know, or at least knew more than he was saying. "I doubt I've said more than a dozen words to Cynewise. And she did always strike me as…reticent. But I know her father, Ceorle, quite well. There's a clever and powerful man. You must know him, surely?"

"I do. Not well. I've been to his manor, and he's visited my father and my brother." Nothwulf felt a growing unease springing up from this line of talk, but he did not want Leofric to see it.

"Then I must go to Sherborne," Nothwulf announced casually, as if he was suggesting a hunt or some such trifle. "If the king is there, it's only fitting that I should be there. I am, after all, the rightful ealdorman."

"Of course," Leofric said and for the first time a patronizing hint crept into his voice. "But see here, I believe they tried to arrest you, last you were in Sherborne. And again just here at your manor, as well. Arrest you or worse."

"Would they dare, with the king in residence there?" Nothwulf asked. He considered it a rhetorical question—with Æthelwulf in Sherborne, whoever was behind this would not dare commit such bloody murder—but Leofric frowned and raised his eyebrows to suggest it was not an impossibility.

"There is a great deal happening, my boy," he said. "And even I do not understand very much."

"Ah, but if you were with me," Nothwulf said, his mind moving down a different track. "If we were to ride in together, my hearth-guard and yours, ride in with all the proper ceremony, then there would be naught anyone could do." Nothwulf knew that was true. He was still well loved by the people, even if that love was mostly light reflecting off his father. Whoever was behind all this trouble, he would not dare make so public a move. There was a reason that Herelaf and his men had been sent to take him in the dead of night.

Nothwulf looked at Leofric and Leofric met and held his eyes. *Well?* Nothwulf thought. *Will you stand with me? Risk your own neck? Or are you part of this thing?*

Finally Leofric sighed. "I suppose I was a fool to think I could hide out here and not get involved in all this intrigue. Of course you're the rightful ealdorman and of course I'll ride into Sherborne with you."

Nothwulf felt himself relax. He had been holding his shoulders tight and clenching his fingers and had not even realized it. "Thank you, my friend," he said. "It's a comfort to have at least one soul I can count on. One man I can trust."

"Humph," Leofric said. "I'm not sure I would trust myself. But in any event, I think this storm will blow itself out soon, and then we shall collect our men-at-arms and be off to give our respects to Æthelwulf. I look forward to seeing him again. I'm always pleased to be in the company of someone even older than myself."

Nothwulf smiled. Leofric seemed never to worry much about anything. He wondered if that was his nature, or a function of the power he wielded in the shire, or his wealth or his age. Or some combination of the four.

By the following morning the storm had indeed blown itself out, but the men did not leave Wimborne. The destruction wrought by the manic wind and rain needed Leofric's attention. It was more than Leofric could turn over to a subordinate. For all of that day, from first light until after the sun was well down, Leofric was in his saddle, touring his holdings, his manor, the town of Wimborne, all the places for which he was responsible and which had suffered greatly from the apocalyptic weather.

Nothwulf, for lack of anything better to do, accompanied him on his rounds. Later, exhausted, Leofric barely managed dinner with Nothwulf before excusing himself and stumbling off to bed. It was the first time Nothwulf had seen the man show his age, but Leofric still had energy enough to promise they would leave for Sherborne on the following morning.

When the sun rose the next day there was still much to do, but happily nothing that absolutely demanded Leofric's attention. He passed the word for his hearth-guard to fit themselves out with their best mail and red capes clasped with broaches at the shoulder in preparation for making an impressive, showy, and very public entrance into the cathedral town.

Nothwulf called on Bryning to assemble the remainder of his men. Had they been in Sherborne, with their own gear close at hand, they would have made a considerably more regal display even than Leofric's men did. But as it was, they looked like what they were—a handful of beaten fugitives, forced to flee their homes in the dark hours of night, forced to run and to fight. Men being blown about by events like the loose thatch in the storm.

But that would not do for Nothwulf. He could not ride into Sherborne looking as if he had been dragged behind his horse, as if he was already a defeated man. Leofric loaned him a fine shirt of mail and a clean tunic and leggings, a fur-trimmed cape and new-made shoes. He mounted Nothwulf on one of his finest horses, seated in a saddle worth more than the year's pay for one of the hearth-guard.

Nothwulf was pleased to be dressed in fine clothes again, and grateful to Leofric. In order to secure Æthelwulf's support for him as ealdorman, Nothwulf knew he had to look like an ealdorman, and a successful one at that.

By midmorning, two days after the last gasp of the storm had blown itself out, the combined hearth-guard of Nothwulf and Leofric were mounted and waiting. Nothwulf, standing by his horse, was enjoying the warm sun spilling down on him. He imagined that this was how Noah felt when the waters had subsided and set the arc down on Mount Ararat. The weather brought hope with it.

The big door to the long hall swung open and Leofric stepped out of the gloomy interior and into the daylight, the sun glinting off his polished mail. With is white hair and short, gray beard he looked more like a wise and just ealdorman than Nothwulf did, Nothwulf had to admit as much.

Leofric looked over and smiled and said, "Good morrow, Lord Nothwulf. Shall we go see the king?"

Nothwulf smiled back. "Nothing would delight me more."

The wide manor gate was open, ready for the men-at-arms to depart, but before Leofric and Nothwulf could mount, a man on the wall above the gate called down, "Lord Leofric, a rider's coming, coming at a gallop!"

Leofric frowned. Riders did not generally gallop without good reason. "Just the one?" he called back.

"Aye, lord, just the one!"

"Well, I suppose one rider will not present any great threat," Leofric said to no one in particular. "Leave the gate open!" he called to the men stationed there, who were looking over at him, awaiting orders. Leofric turned to Nothwulf. "I wonder what new horror this portends."

Nothwulf had his guesses. The king dead, an army marching to arrest him and Leofric, war with Mercia, any number of possibilities ran through his head as he listened to the beating of the horse's hooves grow louder.

The rider came in through the gate, still riding hard, and reined to a stop only when he was well into the courtyard. He swung down from the saddle and looked around. He spotted Leofric and hurried over, bowing as he did.

"Lord Leofric," he said.

"Yes, what is it?" Leofric said.

"Lord, I just come from Swanage. Lord," he said between gasps. "The Northmen have landed there, lord. A great army of them!"

Northmen? Nothwulf thought. *Northmen?*

This was the one thing he had not expected. Northmen, arriving on those shores as if conjured up by the sea. It was a surprise, to be sure. And it changed everything.

Chapter Twenty-Eight

Together we twain on the tides abode, five nights full till the flood divided us, churning waves and chillest weather, darkling night, and the northern wind ruthless rushed on us: rough was the surge.

Beowulf

Thorgrim had to admit, to himself, anyway, that he felt profound relief when the rising sun revealed a long, low coastline to the north and east.

They had been at sea, beyond the sight of any land, for two and a half days by Thorgrim's reckoning, though he was not entirely sure. It should have been a simple thing to know: the sun rose, the sun set, and you count the number of times that happens and that is how many days you are at sea.

But in practice it was not so clear. The skies had been near black with clouds even during the hours that they guessed were daylight. There seemed to be no time at all, just wind and massive seas and misery, the near presence of death, the unending struggle to live.

Which coast it was he did not know. He did not even know which country it was: Ireland, Engla-land. Even Frankia or Iberia were possibilities. He knew only that it was land, and land meant a beach on which they could pull their ships ashore. It might take some looking, but there was always a harbor somewhere.

He looked up at the sky, the blue sky overhead, so clear it seemed he could see right into Asgard. As if that would help divine the gods' intentions in this. It was not at all clear to him if the gods had come to his aid, or tried to kill him, or were testing him once again. Some of each, it seemed.

Once Thorgrim had realized, back at Loch Garman, there was no reaching the north shore of the bay, he was faced with a simple choice. He could head out to sea, with the great likelihood of their being swamped and drowned, or remain in the harbor, with the absolute certainty of being smashed on the sandbars and drowned. He had swung his ship around on an easterly heading, nearly running before the wind, the only course he could hope to hold, and made for the open ocean.

Thorgrim did not ponder the situation. In truth, he made his decision without even thinking much about it as he turned *Sea Hammer's* bow toward the mile-wide gap that made up the entrance to the harbor. With the wind over the larboard quarter, *Sea Hammer* had been building speed as the shores of Loch Garman moved past and the massive seas became visible, rolling off to the horizon.

Might be able to turn south… Thorgrim thought. *Maybe beach the ships on the south shore…* With the wind blowing off the land, there was reason to hope that the waves breaking on the beach would not be so big as to put the ships in danger. But it would also mean rowing against the wind to reach the shore, and Thorgrim was pretty certain that was not going to happen.

So they would go to sea and discover what Njord had in mind for them.

He looked over his shoulder, left and right. The other ships had turned as well, following astern of him. He wondered if the other captains were just following his lead, or if they had realized, as he did, that going to sea was the only choice they had. Either way, they were all entering into this together, and they could only wait to see who if any would come out the other side.

The headlands swept past and *Sea Hammer* was scooped up by the open sea, her stern lifting and twisting as Thorgrim pulled the tiller, pain radiating from his wound with the effort.

"Harald!" Thorgrim shouted, and though his son was only a dozen feet away he had to call twice to get the boy's attention. Harald leapt to his feet and staggered as quickly as he could to Thorgrim's side.

"Harald, lend a hand with the tiller!" Thorgrim shouted, nodding toward the wooden bar in his hands. Harald nodded, and as he grabbed on, Thorgrim could see the concern in his face. He, Thorgrim, had never asked for help steering the ship before.

"My wound!" Thorgrim shouted by way of explanation, but he did not know if that would cause Harald to worry more or less.

The two men held the tiller fast as *Sea Hammer*'s bow drove down into the trough of the waves. The stem hit with an impact that sent a great spray of water up on either side and made the vessel shudder. Thorgrim could see men looking around, some pulling capes over their heads in a near pointless effort to ward off the spray and the driving rain.

He pulled his eyes from the seas ahead, looking for Harald and Godi, but instead he saw Failend, heading aft. Not walking, but crawling on hands and knees, her long, soaked hair hanging down like vines and dragging along the deck behind her. She pulled herself weakly up onto the afterdeck and sat there, leaning against the side of the ship, her head lolling back. Her eyes were closed and her skin was a color not generally seen on living humans. Had she not been moving on her own only moments before, Thorgrim would not have thought she was still alive.

He took his eyes from her, looked forward and shouted, "Godi! Gudrid! Armod!" Shouting was pointless, but the three men were at that moment looking back in his direction, waiting for orders no doubt, so he waved them aft. They moved carefully, grabbing handholds where they could find them, stopping to maintain their footing as the ship pitched and rolled.

It took an absurdly long time for them to walk the forty feet aft to the stern, but they made it at last, holding on to the sheer strake and crouching a bit as they looked up at Thorgrim. Thorgrim opened his mouth to shout out his orders when the stern lifted again, higher than before, and *Sea Hammer* twisted below them.

The bow hit the seas ahead with just the right amount of force, at just the right angle, to scoop up a great mass of cold salt water. Thorgrim saw the seas break over the bow and come rushing aft. The mass of water struck men and sea chests and the mast and gallows and burst upward in welters of spray, looking exactly like storm-driven waves breaking on a rocky shore.

"Hold fast!" Thorgrim shouted and the men grabbed the sheer strake with both hands and braced their feet and then the water struck. It hit with malevolent force, slamming into their legs, trying to knock them off their feet, making a seemingly conscious effort to sweep them away.

Thorgrim and Harald grabbed the tiller with both hands, planted their left feet back, right feet forward and braced as the wave rolled over them. Thorgrim felt the water tear at his leggings and tunic, felt his grip on the deck slipping as the seas drove past him.

The ship's bow rose as the seas passed under her. She rolled to the side and a great torrent of water poured back over the sheer strake and into the sea. Thorgrim looked down and to his left. Failend was gone.

"No!" Thorgrim shouted. "No!" He twisted around to see if he could see her in the ship's wake, aware as he did that there would be no retrieving her even if she managed to keep herself afloat.

She was there. Not in the water, but jammed up against the sternpost in the very aft end of the ship, left like wrack where the boarding sea had deposited her. Thorgrim felt relief sweep over him, more than he might have hoped. He had tried to keep from feeling too much about the odd Irish girl, and he knew he was failing.

"Harald!" he shouted. "Lash her to something!"

Harald nodded. He let go of the tiller, fished out a length of line and climbed up onto the afterdeck and staggered aft, past where Thorgrim stood.

Thorgrim shifted his eyes between the ship's bow and the seas building up aft and Harald's progress. His reaction to Failend's disappearance, momentary though it was, surprised and unsettled him. He liked Failend and respected her. He enjoyed her company and enjoyed her sleeping with him. But he had no deep feelings for her, because he did not allow himself to have deep feelings for anyone, save Harald. Or so he thought.

Harald bent over, with one hand still gripping the sheer strake, wrapped an arm around Failend and lifted her with as much effort as one might use to pick up a cat. He shifted her forward and leaned her against a wooden cleat mounted to the side, normally used to make the ship fast to a dock. He crossed the rope back and forth between the horns of the cleat and across Failend's chest and belly, tight enough to hold her in place, not so tight as to limit her breathing.

Failend made no protest. She did not even open her eyes. But her head moved by what was apparently her own volition, and she opened and closed her mouth to breath and moan, and Thorgrim was relieved to see that.

Well, she's alive, anyway, he thought. *If she dies now, it'll probably be because the whole ship has sunk from under us.*

"Good job, Harald!" Thorgrim shouted, and Harald nodded and took his place at the tiller once again. Thorgrim gestured for Armod and Godi and Gudrid to come closer. They huddled on the after deck and Thorgrim shouted, "She's too tender! Too much weight up high!" The others nodded their understanding.

"Knock the gallows down and lower the yard to near the deck!" he continued. "About five feet above the deck! Lash it there!" The others nodded again.

The yard, with the sail lashed to it, had been lowered down onto the gallows where it was normally stowed. But that left it ten feet above the deck, and all that weight and windage were making *Sea Hammer* tender, making her roll too much in the seas. They had to get the weight down, but not too far down, or then she would not roll enough, but rather snap upright and possibly tear the mast right out of her.

Armod, Godi and Gudrid headed forward again, once more making their slow, labored way along the deck. Thorgrim waited until *Sea Hammer* was rising on a following sea, and then he leaned over the side to look aft, first to larboard, then starboard.

He could afford no more than a quick glance, but in that time he was able to see five of the seven other ships, spread out over half a mile of ocean astern. Some were cresting the seas and he could see them entirely from the waterline up. Others were mostly hidden by the big seas, and Thorgrim could see just the masts rising above the waves, and a bit of the lowered yards and sails. He did not know where the other two were. Still in Loch Garman, or out of sight astern of *Sea Hammer*, or settling on the bottom of the ocean, Thorgrim had no idea.

What he did not see was the coast of Ireland. When *Sea Hammer* had first led the fleet from the sheltered bay, Thorgrim harbored a dim hope that they would be able to land on one of the beaches to the south and ride out the storm there. But he abandoned that hope the moment he felt the seas under the keel, and the power of the wind whipping the spray over the deck.

The moment they had broken out into the open ocean they were completely at the mercy of wind and wave and whatever gods were stirring them up. The ships were runaway horses now, and all that their crews could do was hold on and hope the gods tired of all this before the fleet was destroyed. Where they were bound Thorgrim had no idea, and there was nothing he could do about it even if he did.

He gripped the tiller and pulled it back to straighten the ship's bow to the seas and Harald followed his lead, lending his strength. Even with no sail set, the wind against the mast and shrouds was driving the ship fast enough through the water to give her steerage, the one thing that might possibly save them. *Sea Hammer* felt right on the edge of destruction, and Thorgrim wondered if the other ships were fairing any better. He wondered who was in command of them. He had seen Asmund aboard *Oak Heart* and Hardbein driving *Fox*, but in the chaos of the rout on the beach he had no idea who else was aboard what ships, if every vessel even had a competent master at the helm.

Then Thorgrim forced his mind to work on another problem. He twisted the steer board to keep *Sea Hammer* stern to the waves and tried to picture what few drawings he had seen of the oceans in that part of the world. He had a sense that the great island of Engla-land lay to the east of Ireland, at least twice Ireland's size, and if they were blown anywhere from south-east to north-east they would pile up on those shores.

So what direction are the gods driving us? he wondered. The wind had been from the northwest as it swept them away from the Irish shore, but he had no way of knowing if it had shifted. The sky was gray and black, as dark as he had ever seen it during the daylight. If it was still daylight.

Must be... Thorgrim thought. Dark as it was, there was still light enough to see the ship and the seas around. But there was no chance of seeing the sun, not through the great and impenetrable blanket of clouds overhead, the driving rain that blinded him and choked him whenever he looked up. And without seeing the sun he had no way of knowing in what direction they were being set.

The likelihood of their wrecking on the distant shore would depend on how long the storm blew, and how far Engla-land was from the east coast of Ireland. The first of those Thorgrim could not know. The second was nearly as much of a mystery. He seemed to recall mariners telling him that Engla-land was a few days' sail in a fair wind, at most.

It doesn't much matter, really, he concluded. They had no control at all over their course and speed. Either they would be wrecked on the coast of Engla-land or they would not, and all they could do now was try to keep on the right side of the ocean's surface.

He looked forward. Godi and the others had lowered the yard to about five feet above the deck and lashed it there to keep it motionless. They had taken down the gallows and laid them flat and secured all the oars on the deck. Thorgrim could already feel the change in the ship's motion, the more sea-kindly roll of the hull in the steep seas. Nearly every man who was not helping with the yard was using a bucket or a helmet or a vessel of some sort to scoop water from the ship and throw it over the side.

All except Starri Deathless. At first Thorgrim could not see him, though he ran his eyes over the full length of the deck. He was growing concerned when he finally looked up, and there was Starri, in his familiar perch at the top of the mast. As the ship rolled and pitched, Starri was whipped through a great arc, at least ninety degrees side to side, the motion so extreme that Starri was actually using arms and legs to hold on, a thing Thorgrim had never seen.

Thorgrim shook his head. He was certain that Starri, if asked, would claim to be serving as a lookout, though there was no chance of his calling anything down to deck. Thorgrim had to shout to make himself heard from five feet away. Starri had gone aloft because he could not resist the urge.

He wondered if Starri had decided a death at sea, in such conditions, would earn him a place in the corpse hall. Probably. That was pretty much the only reason that Starri Deathless did anything.

Time crept by, moment by agonizing moment, inching along like Failend crawling aft. With the yard down and the ship as free of water as she was going to get and her motion as easy as it could be made—violent as it was—there was nothing for any of them to do now save for hunkering down and trying not to reflect on the misery and terror of such a storm.

This will ease off, Thorgrim thought. *As the sun goes down, the wind will calm some. It usually does.* And that was true, in Thorgrim's experience. The setting sun often brought with it an easing of the wind. Still, Thorgrim cursed himself for thinking such a thing, because it was also his experience that the gods were likely to punish a man for foolishly guessing at their plans and believing that the wind would ease.

And now it seemed the gods were doing it again. Thorgrim had no way of knowing, of course, if the gods were punishing him or not. He only knew that as the day grew perceptibly darker, the wind, far from easing, rose to a new level of force, well beyond anything Thorgrim had ever experienced at sea.

This will not do, he thought as he and Harald fought the tiller with aching arms.

Night was definitely approaching now. He could see the deep blackness on the horizon to the east. Once the sun was down and the night had completely closed in he would no longer be able to see the waves coming up astern. He would not be able to steer one direction or another as the stern slewed off to larboard or starboard. And if, in his blindness, he drove *Sea Hammer* the wrong way, then the seas would grab the ship and spin her broadside to the waves and roll her over before any one of them had time to call for Odin's succor.

No, they could not ride out the night that way. And Thorgrim knew that he could not keep at the tiller much longer in any event. Even with Harald's help, he felt himself weakening. He was beyond exhaustion, with a deep wound in his side. He had lost a lot of blood and he knew he was going to pass out soon.

They would have to do something else. He looked forward, hoping to catch someone's eye, to wave them aft, but each man was furiously bailing, or collapsed in exhaustion, or huddled under their cloaks, and no one was looking his way. He thought about sending Harald, but he did not trust himself to hold the tiller alone, not even for a few moments.

He looked down at his feet. The tail end of the rope binding Failend to the cleat, about twenty feet of it, was washing around the deck. He reached down quick and snatched it up, made a coil as best as he could with one hand and flung it at Vestar, who was sitting aft, closest to the stern.

The rope hit Vestar on the side of the head, which was good because Thorgrim did not think anything less would have garnered his attention. Vestar's eyes jerked open and he looked aft and Thorgrim waved him over.

"Go get Gudrid and Godi and send them to me!" Thorgrim shouted when Vestar had made his way back to the tiller. Vestar nodded and began working his way along the pitching deck, and soon Gudrid and Godi were coming aft, staggering up to the break of the afterdeck.

"We can't keep running before the storm!" Thorgrim shouted. "Once it's dark, we'll broach and roll over, for sure!"

Gudrid and Godi nodded. Their faces looked grim.

"We need a sea anchor!" Thorgrim shouted next. "Get two of the stoutest ropes we have, walrus hide, and bind up a half dozen oars! Toss them over the stern and we'll pay it out and then make fast! Carefully, so we don't rip the whole stern out of her!"

The two men nodded and Thorgrim was certain they understood, understood all the nuance of what he was asking, all the things that had to be done to make this work. They would intuit the things Thorgrim could not convey over the howling wind, the seas crashing on either side of the ship, the rain slapping down. They were smart men, and more to the point, they were mariners. They understood these things in their guts.

Godi turned and began making his way forward, slapping men on the shoulders as he did, waving for them to follow him. Gudrid dropped to his knees and began fishing ropes out from under the afterdeck. They had cordage made of various materials, mostly hemp, but the strongest and most expensive were those made of braided walrus hide. It was two of those that Gudrid dragged out from where they were stored and laid them down on the deck. He found the bitter ends and began to coil the ropes down in such a way as to assure they would pay out smoothly and not tangle as the sea anchor was streamed astern.

He was just finishing with the second rope when Godi came aft once more. A half-dozen men were with him and they were moving slow and deliberately, carrying a bundle of half a dozen oars between them. They staggered as the ship rolled and once the three men at the back of the line fell in a heap, but they managed to regain their feet and make it to the stern.

Thorgrim looked down at Failend, tied to the cleat. Her eyes were still shut, but there seemed to be a bit more color in her face, which was encouraging. "We'll need to move her," he said, loud enough to be heard. "We'll need that cleat!"

The others nodded, but none of them save for Harald would dare to manhandle her, so Gudrid took the tiller from him and

Harald untied the rope and lifted her and set her in the very stern, leaning against the sternpost. "I think she'll be safe there!" he shouted and Thorgrim nodded his agreement. Once the sea anchor was set he had reason to hope there would be no more great boarding seas.

The others had set to work on the oars. They laid them down and lashed them together at various intervals, then Godi began to tie the two walrus hide ropes securely to the center, but Thorgrim stopped him.

"Tie one to each end!" he shouted. "So we can adjust the angle we're dragging them!"

Godi nodded and did as Thorgrim instructed. As he did, Thorgrim looked out over the larboard side. *Blood Hawk* was there, nearly abeam of them, a quarter mile away and rolling and pitching in the same manic way that *Sea Hammer* was. Thorgrim could just make out figures moving along her deck. Then he had an idea.

"Godi!" he shouted. "Before you send the oars over the side, lift them and wave them! Wave them side to side!"

Godi looked confused but he knew better than to question Thorgrim, particularly in that situation. He grabbed the bundle of oars and lifted and the others joined him to help, though Thorgrim imagined Godi alone was bearing nearly all the weight.

The oars came up vertical and Godi and the others waved them side to side, which would have been tricky even if the ship was on an even keel and not bucking and twisting. But Thorgrim wanted to attract the notice of the men aboard *Blood Hawk*. They may have already thought to put out a sea anchor, but if they had not, he wanted to give them the idea.

"Good!" Thorgrim shouted. "Now, get it overboard!"

The men lowered the bundle of oars, resting one end on the edge of the ship. Harald stood with one rope around the larboard cleat, and Hall stood with the other to starboard. Godi lifted the oars and slid them overboard into the chaotic sea. The ropes lifted off the deck as the strain came on them and were instantly straight as iron rods. Harald and Hall began to ease away, paying the rope out as the sea anchor was swept astern.

"Start to check it, slowly, now, slowly!" Thorgrim shouted and Hall and Harald gripped their ropes tighter, slowly stopping them from paying out over the side.

"Good! Hold there!" Thorgrim said. For a moment everyone remained as still as they could on the heaving deck, feeling the motion of the ship underfoot. Thorgrim looked forward to gauge the angle of the ship's centerline to the set of the waves.

"Hall, ease your line, just a bit!" he shouted, then, "Good! Hold there!"

Once more they stood frozen, seeing how *Sea Hammer* would respond. Thorgrim could already feel the difference. With the oars dragging behind, the ship was going just a bit slower than the waves pushing her. Rather than racing down the crests and slamming into the rollers ahead, the big seas were moving under her, lifting her stern and rolling forward to lift her bow in turn. Up and down like a teeter-totter, but there was a controlled feeling to it. They no longer felt as if they were right on the knife edge of destruction.

Thorgrim nodded. "Good!" he shouted. The others were smiling and they wore expressions of relief. It was, in truth, way too early to feel anything of the kind, but Thorgrim kept his mouth shut and let them have their little victory.

He looked across the water at *Blood Hawk*. She was passing ahead of them now, not having the drag of a sea anchor as *Sea Hawk* did. But hopefully they had seen what Thorgrim was up to and would follow his example. Hopefully all the ships would see, or at least think of the idea on their own. Thorgrim did not think there was any other way they could hope to live through the night.

With the ship pulling at the sea anchor, the steering board had no effect, so Thorgrim let go of the tiller and lashed it in place. His wound throbbed and his arms were stiff and aching, more than he realized, and once he lowered them it was hard to lift them again. But with any luck he would not have to, not for some time.

"Now what?" Harald shouted.

Thorgrim shook his head. "Night's coming!" he said. "Nothing more we can do! Let's try to sleep, and if any of us are still alive come morning, then we'll think of what to do next!"

Chapter Twenty-Nine

[S]hort is the ship's berth, and changeful the autumn night,
much veers the wind ere the fifth day
and blows round yet more in a month.

Hávamál

When morning came at last, *Sea Hammer* and all her crew still lived. That was how it seemed to Thorgrim, though he was not certain, and he was also not certain he was glad of it. He woke sometime after first light and pulled aside the oiled cloth he had used to cover himself and Failend and looked out at the same thick blanket of cloud, the same howling wind and driving rain that had been with them at nightfall.

He was all the way aft, jammed into the narrow wedge at the stern of the ship. Failend was pressed up against him and they had managed to dry a bit under the makeshift tent. A gust of cold wind blew in under the cloth and Failend stirred and made a moaning noise and opened her eyes. She looked much improved from the night before. There was color in her cheeks and less misery in her expression.

"Are we still alive?" Failend asked.

"Must be," Thorgrim said.

"How do you know?"

"I don't think Valhalla looks like this," Thorgrim said. "And even if it does, they certainly would not welcome a Christ worshiper like you there."

"Fine. I'll happily take my heaven over yours. And I know this isn't it."

"How do you know?" Thorgrim asked.

"Too wet to be heaven," Failend said. "It could be hell. That's where I would expect to see you heathens. But it seems too cold for that." They were quiet for a moment and then Failend said, "I'm hungry."

That announcement was both surprising and welcome. Thorgrim pushed the cloth off of them and stood with more difficulty than he had anticipated. The muscles of his arms and legs were cramped and stiff and sore and they bitterly protested the movement he demanded of them. His wound was tight and he took care as he straightened. He held on to the sternpost with one hand and stretched as best he could.

"I'm hungry, too," he said. "But whether any of our food has survived this storm, I do not know."

Once he trusted his muscles to work as they should, he began to make his way forward. First he checked the ropes holding the sea anchor astern. Harald and Gudrid had wrapped them in cloth where they ran over the sheer strake to keep them from chaffing through, which they would have done, quickly, despite the strength of the walrus hide rope. They seemed intact, but Thorgrim eased each one out a few feet so that they would rub on a different section and then repositioned the cloth.

That done, he looked out toward the horizon, moving his eyes slowly from stern to bow. The seas were still enormous, rolling and breaking and cresting, but *Sea Hammer* was riding them easily enough, her stern, sharp as her bow, cutting through the waves as they rose around her. Somewhere behind them the sea anchor was still straining at the lines, checking the ship's drift and holding her at such an angle that she could live in that wild ocean.

And *Sea Hammer* was not the only ship that lived. Some ways off Thorgrim could see what he thought was *Blood Hawk*, rising and falling on the seas as his own ship was doing. He guessed from her motion that they, too, had set a sea anchor, and he wondered who had assumed command of the vessel.

Further off and a bit astern he could see another ship that he thought was *Oak Heart*, and another that was too far off to make out: just a small, dark point on the dark gray sea. He turned and crossed the deck and looked over the starboard side. One of the smaller ships, *Fox* or *Dragon* or *Falcon*, was astern. So at least three of the ships, along with *Sea Hammer*, had also lived through the night, and

Thorgrim was glad of that. It was still possible that the others floated as well, and were just beyond his sight. He nodded to himself and continued on forward.

Most of the men had found some sort of cover: scraps of the old sail or cloaks or the cloth from the tents they would set up when ashore. *Sea Hammer*'s deck looked like the wreckage of a cloth merchant's shop, with sundry bits of fabric lumped here and there. But the men under them were starting to move, starting to pull their covers back and peek out at the day. They were happy no doubt to find themselves still alive and floating. Not so happy to find that their conditions had not changed much.

Godi and Harald and a few others were pulling themselves to their feet as Thorgrim approached. He was about to call to them when a heap of oiled cloth at his feet seemed to burst into life and Starri Deathless kicked himself free of his cover. He leapt to his feet and looked wildly around. For a moment Thorgrim thought he was in one of his berserker rages, and he did not like to think what would happen if that was the case. Then he saw the recognition creep back into Starri's eyes.

"Night Wolf! When by the gods will we get something to eat and drink? Are you trying to starve us all, now that you've failed to drown us?"

"There's still a good chance you'll drown, never fear," Thorgrim said. "As to food, I was just coming to look into that myself."

The mention of food and drink sparked more activity among the men. They began to shuffle to their feet and work their way around the heaving deck, walking as best they could, and crawling when they could not. They pulled up deck boards, looking for provisions that had been stored down in the shallow bilge and inspecting the barrels and bundles that were lashed in place on deck.

There had not been much food aboard to begin with, as they had only intended to sail for Vík-ló, and of what little there was, most was ruined. Fresh water casks had been bashed open with the wild motion of the ship, their contents mixing with the salt water coming over the sides. Bags of bread had been reduced to a soggy, inedible mess. The same with bags of oats.

But it was not all gone. Two small barrels of salted pork were found, mostly intact. One seemed to have suffered almost no damage. The other was partially stove in, but since the meat was salted already, no one imagined the salt water would hurt it much. As to fresh water, that was happily of no immediate concern. It had been pouring down rain all night, and it was still. The men had only to hold their helmets up to rinse out the salt water, then hold them up again to get their fill of fresh.

The two casks of meat were broken open and a bit of food distributed to all hands. Thorgrim oversaw the operation, and he was parsimonious with the portions. He had no idea how long it would have to last. The storm might blow for another day or more—he doubted longer than that—but once it passed he would have little idea of where they were, or how long it would take them to reach land again. If, indeed, they were ever able to reach land again.

The eating was not too pleasant. Salt pork was meant to be boiled at some length to make it edible, and there was no chance of doing that on board a ship heaving in the seas and drenched with rain. So they gnawed at the salty, leathery meat and, hungry as they were, relished it.

And then, with their meal, their one meal of the day, finished and the remainder packed away, there was nothing more to do. Thorgrim sent Starri aloft to see what he could see. When he came down he reported seeing four of the other ships, all within a mile or so, all seemingly riding to sea anchors like *Sea Hammer*. Other than that it was just water, rolling in great, breaking waves as far as the eye could see. Which was not far, with the clouds and the driving rain.

"All right…" Thorgrim said. He scanned the sky but there was no hint at all of where the sun might be, and thus he had no idea of which direction they were being blown. South and east, he thought, but that was only a guess.

"Godi," he said next. "Get some men and round up all the barrels and such that you can find that can still hold any water. Rinse them out with rain water, then set up some sort of funnels with the cloth here to fill them as full as they can get. Try to keep the spray out of them."

Godi nodded. He and the others would see the sense in that. If the rain stopped, they would have no fresh water at all. Worse, with the spray and the occasional boarding seas they were forever getting mouthfuls of salt water, and that would quickly drive them mad with thirst if they had no relief.

Next Thorgrim set those men not helping Godi to rigging the disparate bits of cloth over the lowered yard, making something like a proper tent that might shelter them all. There would be no relief from the misery, but they could at least mitigate it some. It would make things more bearable, and, just as important in Thorgrim's mind, it gave the men something to do, some work that would improve their situation. The ship was snugged down and riding well to her sea anchor, there was nothing more that needed doing for her, save for bailing every once in a while. But with the chance of a watery death so close at hand, it would never do to let the men loll about and brood on their fate.

It took most of the day for the men to do as Thorgrim ordered, and by the time they were done they had collected a decent amount of water, covered the broken barrels to keep the spray out, rigged a shelter and pretty well exhausted themselves just moving around the rolling, pitching vessel. The rain had begun to taper off as the day wore on, which told Thorgrim it was a good job they had done what they had. The men found places to collapse on the deck, under the tent and jammed up against the ship's sides, or against the sea chests, lashed in place, where they could remain mostly secure.

Night settled down once more, and while the rain eventually stopped completely, the seas continued on as large as they had been, with *Sea Hammer* going up and down as each waved passed under. They were used to that motion now. It seemed as if they had been moving that way for so long that none of them could recall what it felt like to stand on solid, unmoving ground.

Thorgrim set a night watch, a man at every quarter, bow, stern, larboard and starboard. He organized their relief through the night, then he staggered aft and once again lay down in the very stern with Failend pressed up against him. Her seasickness had passed, but like everyone aboard, she was hungry and exhausted and happy to sleep, if for no other reason than to make the time pass more easily.

And they did sleep, right through the night, and once again Thorgrim woke in the pre-dawn hours. The cloth was over them for warmth, but since the rain had stopped they did not cover their heads, and when Thorgrim opened his eyes he could see stars above him. For a moment, still stupid with sleep, he looked at them with puzzlement. And then he realized what they were, and at the same time realized that the ship's movement had lessoned considerably.

The violent pitching was now more of a rocking sensation, the ship rising and falling with a long, slow motion.

We'll be able to haul that sea anchor in, he thought. From where he was, huddled under a cloth in the stern, he could not tell how much wind was blowing. Some, he was sure, but it did not seem as powerful as before.

He climbed carefully out from under the cloth, trying not to wake Failend, and moved along the deck. The lookouts were in place, he was happy to see, since that meant he would not have to pour his wrath down on anyone for their lack of vigilance. He stood leaning against the edge of the tent amidships and looked out toward what he thought was the east.

And he was right. Not long after he had taken his post he could see a discernable lightening along the horizon, and soon he could tell that he was not looking at a blanket of cloud anymore, but at clear skies overhead.

One by one the men emerged from under the tent and joined Thorgrim in looking off to the east. They were silent as the horizon went from gray to orange and yellow and then the edge of the sun emerged from the water, threw its blessed light over the sea, and every man aboard felt an unalloyed sense of relief.

Save for Thorgrim. His relief was tempered by the need to make some decisions. As long as the storm was raging and the ship as secured as she could be, there was not much that needed his attention, because there was not much he could do. But now, once more, their fate was in their hands, not the gods', and that meant he had to think of what came next.

Harald stepped up beside him. "The seas are quieter now. We've sailed in worse. Shall I haul the sea anchor in?"

"Not yet," Thorgrim said. The drag from the sea anchor was still giving the ship a more comfortable motion. No reason to change that just then.

"We'll have breakfast first," he said. "Get some hands and fish out some of the ballast stones from the bilge and make a fire ring. The ship's steady enough for that, if you're careful. There should be some dry wood in the hold, or mostly dry, that you can split up. Boil some of that salt beef and we'll have that. Then we'll see what's next."

A dozen men moved to follow Thorgrim's orders, and soon a fire ring was built and a fire kindled in the middle. Once the flames were high enough a tripod was set up with an iron kettle suspended above and tied to prevent it swinging too much. Warm food, Thorgrim knew, would do much to improve the men's strength and attitude. And the black smoke rolling up from the fire would serve as a signal. Thorgrim hoped it would be seen by any of his fleet that still lived and allow them to gather on that patch of sea and once again sail in company.

To where, he had no idea.

Food was served out and the fire seemed to be safe enough so Thorgrim had the men keep it going. They collected up broken bits of barrels that were well soaked with salt water and added those to the flames, and soon the black smoke was roiling up in a column that would be seen for miles around. Then Thorgrim set the men to putting the ship to rights, throwing all the shattered detritus overboard, stowing and lashing the things that had come adrift.

The sun rose and the day grew warmer and the seas smaller and soon the men were smiling and commenting openly on how they could hardly believe they had lived through that storm.

Thorgrim could hardly believe it either. But he kept that thought to himself.

"Night Wolf!" Starri called down from the masthead. He had clambered up there a moment before Thorgrim was going to order him up. "I see *Blood Hawk* and *Oak Heart*, and *Fox*, I think. Another, far off, that I think is the one they call *Black Wing*. And another, but it's so far I'm not sure it's a ship at all!"

Thorgrim nodded. Four others, maybe five. If, after such a storm, they had lost only one ship, then it would surely mean the gods were looking out for them. Which might lead one to wonder why the gods had sent the storm in the first place. To test the worthiness of Thorgrim and his men? Probably. It was hard to imagine any other reason. But Thorgrim did not waste much time thinking about that.

"How about land?" Thorgrim called. "Is there any land to be seen?"

"Not a bit!" Starri called down. "Just water. The land might well have been swallowed up in the storm!"

Yes, it might, Thorgrim thought. He ran his eyes over the men, buoyant and smiling in the warmth of their narrow escape. He wondered if it had occurred to any of them that if they did not find land within a few days, a week at most, when the food and water were long gone, they would be longing for a lung-full of salt water and a quick death.

The sun had not yet reached its highest point for the day by the time the other ships converged with *Sea Hammer* on that spot of ocean. *Blood Hawk* had been commanded, and ably so, by Olaf Thordarson, the oldest man aboard. *Oak Heart*, with the stoic Asmund, came up under sail, as did *Dragon*, and *Fox*, commanded by Hardbein, and lastly Halldor's *Black Wing*. *Falcon*, smallest of the fleet, was the only ship unaccounted for.

The seas were still too big for the ships to tie up to one another, so after they had exchanged brief accounts of their survival at shouting distance, they moved off to keep enough room between them so that they were in no danger of colliding.

The sun passed its high point and the men's jubilant mood seemed to taper off a bit and Thorgrim guessed that they were starting to understand how dire their situation still was. And that meant he had to do something. They could not wait any longer for *Falcon* to appear, which she was unlikely to do anyway. They had to get underway.

"Godi! Get some men and get the sea anchor in. Harald! We're going to set sail, cast off the lashings and get the halyard ready for hoisting." That got the men moving. And if it did not visibly improve their outlook, it at least took their minds from their troubles, because they knew that doing anything less than what Thorgrim expected would make their lives much worse than hunger or thirst ever could.

Thorgrim shouted over to *Oak Heart*, the nearest of the other ships, and told Asmund they would be getting underway and that he should pass the word along. Soon the men of *Sea Hammer* had the sea anchor in, the gallows put back up, the oars stacked and the yard ready for hoisting.

Thorgrim stood up on the sheer strake, one hand on the after shroud, and looked out over the water. *So…* he thought. *Where will we sail?*

With the sun now visible he could finally tell one direction from another, which was a relief. The wind was out of the northwest, which he guessed it had been for the past three days. So they had been driven southeast. They could run with the wind astern. That would be the easiest point of sail. But his gut told him there was only ocean to be found in that direction. Ireland and Engla-land would most likely be to the north somewhere. Of course, they couldn't sail north, or northeast or northwest, because they could not sail that directly into the wind. So it had to be roughly east or west.

Which one?

Thorgrim hopped down from the sheer strake and stepped aft, mounted the afterdeck and unlashed the tiller. "Harald! Hoist the yard! Set the sail for a larboard tack! Close hauled as she'll go!" A larboard tack meant east, and Thorgrim shouted the order as if he knew exactly what he intended to do, but in truth it was no more than an even chance. At least east took them closer to Norway and home.

They hoisted the yard, nearly all hands laying into the halyard to heave the massive spar aloft. The starboard sheet was brought aft and made fast, the larboard tack drawn down to the *beitass* run out over the larboard side. The new-built sail, spread to the wind for the first time, flogged a few times and then filled. *Sea Hammer* heeled a bit to starboard and began to gather way.

Thorgrim could see smiles fore and aft. The ship was alive once more, driving under her own power. Not moving grudgingly under the thrust of the oars, or being blown mindlessly where the wind was pushing her, but going where they wanted her to go, under the power of her own sail, her clean, sharp bottom cutting through the seas.

One by one the other ships of the fleet hoisted their own sails, set them for a larboard tack, and fell in in *Sea Hammer's* wake, a line of deadly longships, a sight to put terror in the hearts of any town or monastery that might see them appearing over the horizon.

For all that day they stood on, the wind holding steady, their course straight and true. As night came on Thorgrim had a lantern lit and hoisted up aloft and the other captains did as well, so that the fleet could stay together during the dark hours. In other circumstances they might have lowered their sails and lay a'hull for the night, but Thorgrim did not think they had that luxury, nor did he think anyone was interested in floating motionless above countless fathoms of water, populated by unseen horrors below.

For all the dangers of the sea, the night passed uneventfully, and the dawn found all the ships still within sight of one another. Breakfast was served out, as parsimonious as the day before, and the men settled in where they could. The sail was drawing well, *Sea Hammer* cleaving along, the seas tumbling down her sides, and even Thorgrim could not think of any task to set the men to, so he let them rest.

Starri was aloft. He would have been in any case, but at first light Thorgrim instructed him to keep a bright lookout, that they did not have much time—a day or two—to find land before things would start falling apart fast. In his years of seafaring, Thorgrim had seen what serous thirst could drive a man to do, and it was not good.

All through the morning they plowed on in silence, right up until the moment that Starri began to yell and whoop from his perch high above the deck.

"What is it?" Thorgrim shouted. "What do you see?"

"There, Night Wolf, there!" Starri shouted. But he was not pointing at the horizon. Rather, he was pointing straight up toward the sky as if Odin were coming down from the clouds.

Thorgrim scowled. He wondered what new madness had overtaken the man. But he could see other men looking up as well, and smiling and nodding their heads. He turned to Failend, who stood beside him.

"What is it?" he asked in a low voice.

Failend was also smiling. "Birds," she said. "A flock of birds, land birds, and they're flying in the same direction we sail."

Land birds... That was enough to make Thorgrim smile, too.

They stood on, with a new sense of optimism, and it was not long after that Starri reported he could see land ahead now: low, dark, and indistinguishable, just as most land looks from the sea. And soon they could see the rough dark line from the deck as well. Thorgrim saw men looking aft at him, nodding their heads, speaking low among themselves.

They think I knew all along, Thorgrim thought. *They think I have some knowledge that no one else has.* And that was fine. He would not disabuse them of that.

This is how reputations are made, he thought. *Through bluster and wrong assumptions.*

The wind was not what it had been, but it was still strong enough to move the fleet. The seas had continued to settle down, and with each mile covered, the distant land rose up higher. It was not long before they could make out some of the finer details: brown and green fields, hills, columns of smoke rising from unseen fires.

"Night Wolf!" Starri shouted again. "There's a boat of some sort, a fishing boat or something, a couple of miles ahead. Oh, they're running like scared dogs!"

But there was no chance of the boat outrunning the longships in a good breeze on their favorite point of sail, and soon they were swooping up alongside the unhappy boat and hauling the sail up to the yard to stop dead in the water just to windward of it. The rest of the fleet did the same, seven longships coming to rest in a great circle around the unhappy boat.

It was indeed a fishing boat, Thorgrim could see that. It was a quarter of *Sea Hammer*'s size, with a pile of nets amidships, an open hold filled with still flapping fish, and four very frightened men on the deck.

"Drop your sail!" Thorgrim shouted and pointed and waved toward the sail and yard and the men nodded and did as he asked, though Thorgrim did not know if it was the words or the gestures they understood. Once the sail was lying in a heap on the fishing boat's deck, the four men once again looked pleadingly toward Thorgrim.

"What land is that?" Thorgrim asked, pointing toward the distant shore. The oldest of the fishermen, whose leathery face was partially obscured by a thick, white beard, replied, waving his hands in an animated way. The words sounded not unlike his native Norse—he though he caught the words "net" and "headland"—but he could not understand what the man was saying.

Am I deaf, or is he speaking some odd tongue? Thorgrim wondered. He turned to Failend, who was nearby.

"Failend, what's this old fool saying?"

Failend shrugged. "I don't know. It's not Irish, whatever he's speaking. Not Norse, though it sounds like it."

"Louis!" Thorgrim called to Louis the Frank, who was leaning on the sheer strake and watching the exchange, as indeed were all the men aboard the ship. Louis looked up at the sound of his name.

"What is this dumb bastard saying?" Thorgrim called.

"I don't know," Louis called back. "Not Irish, not Frankish. Not Norse, but you probably guessed that."

"It's the language of Engla-land," Gudrid said, pushing off the sheer strake and stepping closer to Thorgrim. "I know this language. My father had slaves from here. Their words are not too different from ours."

Thorgrim nodded. "Well, then, I guess we know where we are," he said. He looked down at the fishing boat, the frightened, pleading look on the fishermen's faces. Such a boat had to come from some town or village, one that had a safe place for ships to land. Nor were they likely to have sailed very far from that village. He doubted that the fishermen had intended to remain at sea overnight.

"Tell them to come aboard. We'll take their boat in tow. They'll guide us to the harbor at their village. If they do their job well they'll have a piece of silver. If they try to trick us, I will personally rip their hearts from their chests."

Gudrid leaned over the rail and spoke, and the expression on the men's faces suggested that Thorgrim's mix of promise and threat had sparked the desired motivation in them. Harald threw a rope down and one of the younger men tied it to a post in the bow, and then the four of them climbed aboard.

It was only a few moments later that *Sea Hammer* and the rest of the fleet were once more underway, with Thorgrim at the helm and Gudrid and the old fisherman beside him. *Sea Hammer* was slower now, towing the fat fishing boat astern, but now at least they knew where they were heading.

Thorgrim looked forward, past the stem. The figurehead, Thor with teeth bared and hair flying, had been set back in its place, and it looked as if the son of Odin himself was leading the charge toward this new land.

Engla-land...

Thorgrim shook his head and his lips turned up in a bit of a smile.

The gods will have their fun...

Chapter Thirty

Then dared I not against the Lord's word
bend or break, when I saw earth's
fields shake. All fiends
I could have felled, but I stood fast.

The Dream of the Rood

A high ridge of land lay to the west of Swanage. From there one had a view of the small fishing village below and the long sandy half-moon beach that curved off in a gentle arc to the northeast before terminating in the high cliffs at the far end. And it was there, at the point where the grassy meadows began their slow rolling tumble toward the sea, that Nothwulf and Leofric sat on their horses and watched.

It was midafternoon, and the men could feel the effects of twenty miles of hard riding from Wimborne. Fortunately, they had been ready to ride at the very moment that the messenger had arrived, ready to ride inland for Sherborne. Instead, they rode off in the opposite direction, southwest toward the sea, the men-at-arms trailing behind.

Evidence of the apocalyptic storm greeted them all along the way: downed trees and roofless cottages and low places flooded until they looked like lakes. Just from the road they counted a half dozen folks dead, some crushed under debris, some just crumpled in the grass, killed by the cold or the battering of the wind or some such thing. They did not stop to discover more.

The riders skirted the long, shallow bay south of Poole and rode through the town of Wareham, which had fared even worse than Wimborne in the storm. The air took on the pungent smell of the sea as they turned east and rode the last few miles to the high ground outside Swanage.

The riders in their glittering mail were not the only ones on the road. Dozens passed them as they made their way from Wareham to Swanage, mostly poor fishermen and their wives and children, hunched under the loads they carried, all that they could save from the heathens who had come to their shores.

As if the Northmen had come to steal what these poor sods have, Nothwulf thought as his horse parted the stream of people, who stepped off the road to let them pass and made a gesture of respect to their betters.

At first Leofric stopped the people who were fleeing to ask them what they had witnessed. They all said pretty much the same thing. Early that morning they had gathered to take their fishing boats to sea, those few boats that had not been blown away or battered to jetsam on the beach. Then, one of the sharp-eyed young men had seen the sails on the horizon to the southwest. They feared those strange vessels, but they were also desperate to cast their nets after so many days of being pinned in their houses, and so the fleet put to sea.

But not for long. Half a mile from shore and it was clear the ships, seven at least, were making for Swanage, or somewhere near enough. That did not necessarily mean they were Northmen—they might have been king's ships, or even merchantmen. Just a few days before the storm other ships had been spotted off to sea, but they had sailed past and made no trouble for the village.

Still, it was most likely that they were raiders, and no one much cared to wait around to see. They had returned to shore, and once they could make out the rows of shields and the terrifying figureheads of the Norse longships, they had gathered what they could carry and fled, as directly away from the sea as they could go.

Nothwulf and Leofric listened to half a dozen variations of this story until it was clear that they would get nothing of any use from any of these people so they stopped asking. After that they just greeted the humble bows with unenthusiastic waves as they passed by. It was not until they reached the hilltop, with the town and the beach spread out before them, that they stopped and assessed the situation for themselves.

"Seven of the bastards," Leofric observed. "Four at least are tolerably big."

Nothwulf grunted. The ships were pulled up on the beach, a mile or so from where the two men watched from the saddle. The rest of the men-at-arms had been made to keep back, out of sight from the town. No need to announce their arrival until they knew what they were up against.

"Seven. That's what I count, too," Nothwulf said. The longships were not the only vessels on the beach. There was a smattering of fishing boats, the largest less than half the length of the smallest of the Northmen's ships. There were also fishing boats half-sunk in the shallow water, and others that seemed no more than piles of sea wrack heaved up on the sand by the massive seas that had recently pounded the shore.

"Seven ships…that could well mean three or four hundred warriors," Leofric said next. Nothwulf grunted again.

They could not tell from that distance how many of the whores' sons were there. They could see a few men milling around the ships or building fires on the beach, but most of them were lost from sight, no doubt ransacking the town below. Every now and then a few shield-bearing men could be seen moving among the thatched houses.

"I'm not sure what they'll find to plunder in Swanage," Nothwulf said. "Dried fish, I suppose. Spoiled ale. I would have thought the Abbotsbury Abbey or the priory at Christchurch would have been of more interest to them."

"They may get there yet," Leofric said. "I wonder where they've come from. I've heard no tales of Northmen raiding around here. But they must have been nearby. They certainly did not cross the sea in the storm we just witnessed."

"No," Nothwulf agreed. He did not know much about ships and the sea, but he was pretty certain that no vessel could have lived through the storm that had so battered Dorsetshire.

He did, however, know about fighting Northmen, as did Leofric. Northmen were a plague that grew more acute every year. Two generations before, the reeve of the King of Wessex and his men were killed by Northmen not twenty miles from that place, the first men in all Angel-cynn to die at Northmen's hands. Since then they had come again and again. Great armies of the bastards were said to be making themselves at home in the eastern parts of the land. Not five years earlier both Nothwulf and Leofric had joined the armies of King Æthelwulf in defeating the heathens near London.

The two men knew about fighting Northmen. They knew that Northmen could be defeated. And they knew it was no easy task.

"Well, if there's four hundred warriors…even if there's half that number…we're in no position to fight them," Leofric said. "Not until we call up the fyrd."

They had a little more than a hundred men-at-arms with them, good fighting men, but not nearly enough. They would have to mobilize the fyrd, the full-time farmers and tradesmen, part-time soldiers, who would assemble when needed for military action. They were no match for the Northmen's fighting prowess, but what they lacked in skill they could more than make up for in numbers. But that would take some time.

"Yes…" Nothwulf said, though his thoughts were off in another direction. "This is, you know, a great threat to the shire. All of Dorset could be overrun by these bastards."

"Yes," Leofric said, but hesitantly. "By four hundred warriors?"

"Well, not four hundred, but who knows how many more there might be? I'm only saying that this should not all fall to you, even if Swanage is within your holdings. We were on our way to Sherborne. I think we had better go there now, alert King Æthelwulf to this threat."

"And find out if this little tart Cynewise has the mettle to stand up to them?" Leofric said. "To command men in the defense of the shire?"

"Exactly. To see what she's made of, with the king right there."

Leofric nodded. "I see," he said, and it was clear that he did.

When the great storm had finally blown itself out, Cynewise and King Æthelwulf made a tour of Sherborne and the surrounding countryside. They mounted their horses, fitted out with the finest tack, while they themselves wore cloaks of deep scarlet and lined with fur. The king's tunic was edged with fine embroidery and Cynewise's gown was a silk of deep blue, like the sea, far off shore. Behind them streamed a retinue of servants and men-at-arms a hundred strong, each fitted out to match the king or the *de facto* ealdorman, depending on the household to which they belonged.

Oswin, the shire reeve, rode a few paces behind Cynewise and the king. It would fall to him to actually oversee the work that would go into rebuilding the town and the farms around, but he knew better than to speak unless spoken to by Cynewise or the king.

They spent the better part of the day making their inspection, stopping only for dinner, which had been set up in a wide field on trestle tables brought from the ealdorman's home in Sherborne and laden with food and wine from the kitchen there. It was a feast to feed the great crowd who accompanied the king, and the thought of how much it would all cost was enough to ruin Cynewise's appetite.

By late in the afternoon they were back at the ealdorman's hall, and they retired, exhausted, after a more modest supper.

Cynewise woke the next morning to the sounds of the household coming to life, but it was more than the usual bustle, and for a moment, in her half-awake state, she could not recall why. Then she did. The king and his retinue were leaving. With the destruction that the storm had brought to all of Wessex, Æthelwulf had decided to move quickly through the rest of his tour, assessing the damage as he did, calculating what would be needed to set it to rights, and then return to Winchester.

*Blessed, blessed storm…*Cynewise thought, still lying in the wide, soft bed in her sleeping chamber. Anything to get the old man out of Sherborne.

Not that the king's visit had gone badly, not at all. Æthelwulf had been pleased with Cynewise's devotion and loyalty to him even before his arrival. The cart train of gifts she had appropriated from Nothwulf and sent on to the king had helped in that regard, as had Æthelwulf's long friendship with her father.

There had been little talk of her brother-in-law, and no suggestion that Æthelwulf desired that Nothwulf should be installed as ealdorman. The king had often embraced her in what he imagined was a fatherly way, and Cynewise had endured his wandering hands. Things had gone pretty much as Cynewise had hoped, and now she wanted the king gone before anything might occur to muddy those clear waters.

Cynewise would call the *witan* together once the royal procession had moved on. The witan, a council comprised of the most important thegns as well as Bishop Ealhstan, was normally assembled to advise the king. But these times were not normal, and getting the witan's seal would give her the final mark of legitimacy.

She had ample support among the thegns, she guessed. King Æthelwulf was not the only one to whom she had given gifts and promises. Soon, soon, her place as ealdorman of Dorset would be carved in stone.

She sat up and called for Aelfwyn, who had just recently returned from Blandford, the place to which Nothwulf had carried her off. She had escaped in the confusion of the hearth-guard riding off in pursuit of phantom raiders. Aelfwyn had been vague with the details of how she had arranged for transport back to Sherborne, but Cynewise could well imagine. Aelfwyn was always adept at using the gifts and charms that God had given her.

Aelfwyn hurried in, made a curtsey and said, "Ma'am?" She had looked haggard and beaten upon her return, but she was quickly returning to her old self, bold and confident.

"I'm ready to dress," Cynewise said, tossing off the covers.

The process of dressing and getting her hair in order took most of the morning, despite the labor of Aelfwyn and two other girls. The delays were due mostly to Cynewise's foot-dragging, and that was a result of her wanting to avoid Æthelwulf for as long as she could, having grown quite weary of the old king.

When they were done at last Cynewise left the bedchamber and stepped out into the courtyard. It was all a'bustle there, with servants racing back and forth and the stable hands and the cooks and bakers all hard at work, making ready for the king and his people to get underway once more. Cynewise smiled. She was glad to see all this activity, all directed at sending Æthelwulf on his way.

The wagons that carried the king's necessities, all bright painted and tricked out with gilding, were crowded into the courtyard, the horses that pulled them standing patiently in their traces. The servants loading the wagon beds formed a stream of men moving back and forth, like ants at a honeycomb dropped on the ground. Cynewise nodded and continued to smile.

She looked toward the main gate, now open wide to make it as easy as possible for Æthelwulf and his train to leave, when she saw Oswin come in from the street beyond, moving fast, his face grim, his cloak flapping out behind him.

Oh, now what in all hell is this? she wondered. Oswin did not slow, did not veer off, just marched straight across the courtyard to where she stood. He stopped a few feet in front of her and made a half-hearted gesture of supplication.

"Yes?" Cynewise said.

"It's Nothwulf, ma'am," he said, *sotto voce*. "And Leofric. They're just a mile outside of the town and riding this way."

"Sneaking in? Trying to slip into Sherborne?"

"No, ma'am, not at all. They have banners and they're wearing their best clothes and mail. They have their hearth-guard with them. Near a hundred strong, as my men tell it."

Cynewise frowned, but at the same time she saw how clever this was. If either of them, Nothwulf in particular, had tried to sneak in, he could have been taken quietly. But by making such a show of their arrival there was nothing that Cynewise could do, unless she was ready to outright accuse Nothwulf of his brother's murder and arrest him in public, which she was not.

"There's good news as well, Lady Cynewise," Oswin said, still speaking low enough that no one else could hear. "I have word from Christchurch Priory. You father's ships arrived a few days before the storm. The men are encamped in the priory and no one the wiser. The storm delayed the messenger or I would have known days ago."

"How many?" Cynewise asked.

"Near two hundred. Ceorle's best fighting men. But I'm afraid the ships put to sea after setting the men ashore, and they might have been caught in the storm."

Cynewise waved this information away. "The ships are no matter," she said. "It matters only that my army is here. And that we see Æthelwulf and his train gone before Nothwulf and Leofric arrive. You must find some way to delay them, stop them somehow…"

That was as far as she got with that notion. A rider came in through the open gate, his horse moving at a trot, and he reined to a stop with a flourish and a whirling of a scarlet cloak.

*Bryning, son of a bitch…*Cynewise thought as she recognized the man. She turned back toward Oswin, her eyes full of fury and accusation.

Oswin shrugged. "He came in from a different way, I can assure you, ma'am. My men are watching Nothwulf's column. Clever bastard." The last he muttered under his breath, as if speaking to himself.

"My Lady Cynewise!" Bryning shouted, bowing in his saddle, his voice as deferential as any might ask, and loud enough to be heard by all of the household. "My Lords Nothwulf and Leofric are approaching the town and would wish to speak with you, and with his highness King Æthelwulf, if he is still in residence!"

And that was that. There was no getting out of it now. Æthelwulf had certainly heard those words, as had every man in his party. Even if she thought she could get away with arresting him, he and Leofric had one hundred men under arms, while her own hearth-guard would be useless against them. When Herelaf had failed to apprehend Nothwulf earlier she had ordered him stripped of his rank, flogged and cast out into the streets. But she did not think that example had been enough to instill the fear she required.

Cynewise was about to respond when the king himself stepped out of the long hall's big door and crossed over to where Cynewise and Oswin stood. "What do I hear?" he said. "Nothwulf is arriving? And Leofric. Good, good. I was hoping to see the both of them before I left. Never understood why they weren't here, the king's tour and all."

"Of course, my lord," Cynewise said. "I can't imagine why they are only now arriving."

And soon they did arrive, the two men riding through the big gates, followed by an impressive display of mounted soldiers, banners flying, armor jingling. Mostly Leofric's men, which was no surprise to Cynewise, since she had seen to it that Nothwulf had little left to make a big show. They dismounted, made their homage to the king, made their duty to her, their rage barely held in check. Then Nothwulf said, "We bring news, your highness, grave news, and perhaps we had better speak in private."

They left the courtyard and crossed into the long hall, Cynewise taking care to lead the way. This was, she realized, the most dangerous moment yet in her ascension to ealdorman. She climbed the dais and sat in the second largest of the seats there, leaving the most impressive for Æthelwulf. Leofric and Nothwulf pulled seats around so they were facing her and the king.

"Now, pray, tell me…" Cynewise began, but Æthelwulf cut her off.

"Nothwulf! Leofric! Good to see you both again. I had wondered where you were, couldn't understand why you were not here for my visit."

"We came as soon as we could, of course," Nothwulf said. "Nothing would keep us away. Save for the most pressing of your kingdom's business."

"Speaking of which," Æthelwulf said, "I was surprised to find you had not stepped in as ealdorman after your brother's shocking murder. But it seems as if you and Cynewise have managed things between yourselves."

"We are still working things out, my lord," Nothwulf said dryly. "But, pray, let me give you the news we bring." He paused a beat to let the words sink in. "It's the Northmen, lord. They've come ashore in Swanage. Seven ships."

"Seven ships might be as many as four hundred warriors," Leofric said.

"Bah!" Æthelwulf snorted. "I've fought more than that and beat them well."

"*Might* be four hundred warriors?" Cynewise said. "Did you not remain there long enough to be sure?" What she meant to imply was that the men had been backward in their courage, fleeing from the Northmen directly, and judging from the expression on their faces that suggestion was not lost on them. But it was apparently lost on Æthelwulf, who made no comment, though Cynewise had spoken the words for the king's benefit.

"By the time we arrived, the Northmen had overrun the town," Leofric explained with elaborate patience, and Cynewise could see he was purposefully speaking to her as if speaking to a child. "They were mostly hidden in the homes, but it was clear they were too many for my hearth-guard and my lord Nothwulf's to fight. We left a guard in place, and messengers to bring word of any movement, and then we rode here."

Left a guard in place? Cynewise thought. *Did you? Did you really think to do that?* But she did not put voice to these thoughts.

"Why should they land at Swanage?" Cynewise said instead. "There's nothing of worth there."

"Sister," Nothwulf said in his most patronizing tone, "you're new to our shire, I understand that. But Swanage, small as it is, has a good harbor, and it's a short way to Christchurch Priory or

Abbotsbury Abbey or even the churches at Wareham or Windborne Minster. Lord Leofric's holds are no poor wastelands."

Cynewise thought to ask why the damned Northmen didn't just go to Christchurch Priory straight off, but she held her tongue. She was losing control of the moment and she knew it.

"Well," she said, clapping her hands down on her thighs in a gesture of having rendered a final decision. "I'm sorry you chose to bring your fighting men here for a parade rather than leave them watching the Northmen, but there's nothing for it now. You must return to Swanage and keep an eye on the heathens there and make an attack if it seems at all likely to succeed. I will call up the fyrd and get them marching your way as soon as can be done. By tomorrow morning at latest."

Then, by way of reminding them that she was not without influence or the backing of powerful men, she added, "I'll send word to my father, as well. He has a strong hearth-guard, twice what was kept here in Sherborne, and I know the fyrd in Devonshire can be ready to march in precious little time. We'll find ample support there."

"Ha!" Æthelwulf shouted and stood up quickly. "There, you see, the young vixen has the situation well in hand!"

"Thank you, my lord," Cynewise said. "I'm grateful for your words." And she was, in a way that Æthelwulf himself did not understand, and that Leofric and Nothwulf most certainly did.

Chapter Thirty-One

*And since, by them on the fathomless sea-ways
sailor-folk are never molested.*

Beowulf

The English fisherman whom Thorgrim had conscripted was named Sweartling. At least that was what Gudrid told him. Thorgrim had not asked, and he really didn't care, as long as the man did as he was told. And it seemed he had.

Having conscripted the fishermen and his crew, Thorgrim's fleet got underway once again, sailing as close to the wind as they could. Thorgrim watched Sweartling's eyes moving from the edge of the sail to the distant shore to *Sea Hammer*'s wake astern, judging how they were making good their course, like any man would who was accustomed to ships and the sea. His three companions, men much younger than him, were huddled on the lee side, trying to be as inconspicuous as they could. Thorgrim wondered if they were the fisherman's sons. Probably. If so, they could be used to extract further cooperation, if needed.

But in the end it was not needed. Sweartling pointed to a spot just forward of the larboard beam, some point along a shoreline that appeared to Thorgrim to be no more than an unbroken dark line. He spoke and Gudrid translated.

"Sweartling says his village is that way, a place called Swanage, just to the south of that high spot there. Good beach for landing."

Thorgrim nodded and his eyes also moved from the edge of the sail to the distant shore to the ship's wake, and without conscious thought he calculated leeway and angles of sail, the effects of course and speed.

"We'll come about, get as close as we can on the next tack, then we'll take to the oars," he said.

The miles moved under their keel and Sweartling and his sons visibly relaxed, and when they were offered a meal of bread and dried fish they accepted with nods of thanks. Sweartling again pointed toward the spot of shore where he claimed his village was situated, and now Thorgrim could see high cliffs and what looked to be a long strip of beach and he guessed that even if there was no village there it would still make for a decent place to land. And that was something they needed very much. Their food and water would soon be exhausted, and the men already were.

Once they had made as much distance as they could on the starboard tack Thorgrim ordered the sail in and the oars out. The men did as they were told, though they put more effort into grumbling than into the actual rowing. Astern, the other six vessels did the same, following behind *Sea Hammer* like a long line of ducklings bringing terror and destruction to the shores of Engla-land.

From half a mile out even Thorgrim could see the village, a smattering of small huts, thatched roofs, thin columns of smoke rising here and there. The houses were square, not round, like the Irish fashion, and not encircled by earthen walls, as all the homes in Ireland seemed to be. The beach was very long and half-moon shaped and he could see some boats pulled up there, and more farther up the sand, where, he guessed, they had been deposited by the storm.

As they closed with the beach Thorgrim ordered those men not rowing to don whatever armor they had and to take up their shields if they had not been washed away in the two days of beating the ships had endured. Failend appeared with Iron-tooth in hand. She had bundled the weapon in tarred cloth and it had made it through the storm without seeing a drop of seawater. Now she carefully unwrapped it and handed it to Thorgrim. Thorgrim thanked her, buckled the belt around his waist.

The Englishman was talking again, and Thorgrim turned to Gudrid.

"He says he doesn't think there'll be anyone left in the village," Gudrid said. "He says they would have seen our ships a long way off and fled. He says he's sorry but they probably took anything of value with them."

Thorgrim could not help but smile. *What could they possibly have of value?* he wondered. But that did not matter. They were not there for plunder. No one went to a pathetic fishing village for plunder. They needed food, water, ale, a place to rest and set their battered ships to rights. That much he reckoned he would find.

They closed the last fifty feet and Thorgrim ordered oars in, and *Sea Hammer* ground up on the sand. Thorgrim made his way amidships and jumped over the side, his feet landing in knee-high water. He walked up the sloping beach and heard the sound of others jumping down behind him. Finally, well clear of the surf, he stopped, took a deep breath, and nearly fell on his face.

The ground under him was swooping and rolling and he had to actually take a wider stance to remain upright. He had experienced this before, this sensation that the solid earth was rolling like a ship at sea. But he had never experienced it to that degree, because he had never been in such violent seas for so long as they had been since leaving Ireland astern.

Behind him he heard cries of surprise and laughter as the rest of the men experienced that odd sensation. Failend came up beside him and clung to his arm.

"Thorgrim, what's happening?" she asked with a touch of panic in her voice. "Why is the ground moving like the ship?"

Thorgrim smiled. "It's not. It just feels it. This will happen, after you've sailed for some time in big seas."

"Great," Failend said. "I just got done puking on the ship, and now I'm going to puke on dry land."

Thorgrim was about to assure her she would be fine when he heard Starri Deathless whooping as he stepped up beside them. "Night Wolf! We had better go back to sea! The ship moves less than the ground does!"

Thorgrim smiled and nodded, but as his equilibrium returned, his mind turned toward the nearby village. He could see no movement there, no sign of life. He guessed Sweartling had been right about the people fleeing, and that was no great surprise.

More and more of his men were swarming up onto the beach, and Thorgrim heard another ship grinding into the sand. He turned and looked behind him. *Blood Hawk* had come ashore, her men leaping over the side into the surf, and the rest were closing in fast.

The men gathered around him were holding shields and spears and swords, wearing mail and helmets, but not one of them looked to be in fighting spirit. To a man they were grinning and looking around with the wonder of men who not long before thought they would never set foot on land again.

"Welcome to Engla-land!" Thorgrim shouted and that was met with cheers and swords and spears banging on shields. They were happy to be there. They would have been happy to be anywhere that had dry earth and food and water.

"Come along, follow me," Thorgrim said next and he and his men swept forward, off toward the small village. They approached with caution, but not an excess of caution. There still seemed to be no one there, and he doubted that in the few hours since their sails had appeared over the horizon any local lord could have summoned a force sufficient to match his warriors.

Starri was walking beside him, smiling and looking around as if he was witnessing something astounding. Even he did not seem to be anticipating a fight, which was good. Thorgrim doubted there would be any fighting.

"Starri," he said. "This village will be too dull for you, by half. Why don't you take a run up to the top of that hill and see what's there?" He nodded toward the sloping, grassy hill that looked down on the village of Swanage.

"I'll do that!" Starri said, eager for something with more promise than a deserted village.

"Better if no one sees you. No Englishmen, I mean. And keep hidden. No fighting, no matter who you see."

"Oh, Night Wolf," Starri said. "You know how sensible I am. How can you doubt me?"

Thorgrim smiled. He did know how sensible Starri was. That was why he warned him not to do anything foolish. But he said, "I would never doubt you."

And in truth, manic as Starri might be, he rarely made a hash of such scouting missions, and Thorgrim knew of no man who was better at that work.

Starri ran off to the west and Thorgrim and the others continued their slow advance. They were a dozen paces from the edge of the village when Thorgrim called for a halt. He could see the potential for trouble here, and not from the English. The English were the least of his worries now.

He turned and addressed the men behind. "We're all hungry and all thirsty. Whatever you find in the houses here, you collect it up and bring it down to the ships. We'll see everything is handed out fair."

There were grunts of acknowledgement and the men surged forward, swarming through the narrow, muddy streets between the homes. There they found nets strung up to dry and racks of split fish, some of admirable size. There were sundry barrels and heaps of kitchen scraps and a few sorry-looking gardens.

Thorgrim and Harald pushed into the nearest of the houses. It was small, maybe fifteen feet on each wall, built of weathered boards and thatch for a roof. The floor was dirt with a fire pit in the middle and the remains of a fire still smoldering there. An iron pot hung on a tripod over the fire.

Harald stepped quickly across the room and looked down into the pot. He snatched up the ladle that was sitting on the hearthstones and plunged it in.

"Ah," Thorgrim said, before Harald could eat. "All that goes down to the ship."

Harald put the ladle down and even in the dim light Thorgrim could see he was flushing red. "I…" he began. "I was just…"

"Of course you were," Thorgrim said. Harald ate more than any two men Thorgrim knew. He was sure the boy felt that he was going to die of hunger at any moment.

Thorgrim moved off to the side of the small house. There was a pallet of straw and a few blankets tossed on top. He nudged them with his toe, lifted the blankets, but there was nothing of interest there, or anywhere else in the house that he could see.

He stepped out into the sunlight, blinking after the gloom of the little hovel. Men were moving in and out of the houses, examining whatever detritus they could find in the streets. Some were pulling thatch from the roofs to see if anything of value had been hidden there, but they soon gave it up.

"Very well," Thorgrim said to the rest. "Let's collect up all the food and drink we can find and get back to the ships. I doubt there's anything else here worth having."

The next few hours were taken up with carrying or dragging anything that could be eaten or drunk back to the place where the seven ships were drawn up on the beach. It was an impressive haul, but of course it was midsummer and the crops and the fishing would be at their most fruitful. The food, not surprisingly, was mostly fish, with some bread and carrots and such. There was ale as well, and it was not as awful as Thorgrim would have guessed. He ordered generous shares of food and drink for all the men, and they dug in eagerly.

Sweartling and his sons were standing off by *Sea Hammer*'s bow, looking unsure of what they should do. Thorgrim called Failend to him.

"Please, would you go in my chest and fetch four pieces of silver. Good pieces, but not too big. One bigger than the rest."

Failend nodded and hurried off. Soon she was back with the silver and she placed it in Thorgrim's palm. Thorgrim looked at it: four irregular chunks of precious metal, part of some ornamentation from some church in Ireland that had been plundered and unceremoniously hacked apart.

"Good," Thorgrim said. "Thank you."

He crossed over to the four men, calling for Gudrid as he did. He looked Sweartling in the eyes and the man held his gaze, satisfied, apparently, that Thorgrim would not capriciously end his life. Far from it, Thorgrim handed him the largest of the four bits of silver, and handed the smaller ones to the others.

Sweartling's eyes went wide, and Thorgrim guessed he had either forgotten the promise made or never believed Thorgrim would make good on it. "Tell him he did as I asked. He has his silver. He can go now, him and the others."

Gudrid translated. Sweartling nodded and spoke, the words sounding so familiar that Thorgrim thought he should have been able to understand, but he could not.

"He thanks you," Gudrid said, "and he asks could they spend the night here?"

Thorgrim frowned. He did not expect that. But then, Sweartling had helped them, and been paid, and that might not be looked upon favorably by his neighbors. Better to appear as if he was being held prisoner.

"Certainly," Thorgrim said. "And he can have food and drink, him and his men." The fisherman might still prove useful.

Darkness was setting in and a massive fire was lit on the beach by the time Starri returned.

"Well, we might have had some fun, but these English are worse than the Irish when it comes to running from a fight," he said to Thorgrim as he took up a cup of ale and a chunk of dried fish.

"How's that?" Thorgrim asked. He was tempted to point out that the Irish had fought them and won at Loch Garman, but he held his tongue. He knew that Starri would have some explanation as to why that was not really the case.

"No one there when I got to the top of the hill. But I could see where all the people had gone, who fled from the village. And I could see there had been horses there, many horses. More than twenty, judging from the hoof prints and the shit. So there were armed men there, but they decided not to fight, cowardly dogs."

Thorgrim nodded. Twenty, thirty, one hundred armed men, they still would have been greatly outnumbered by the crews of seven longships, even depleted as those crews were. It was hardly a surprise they had declined combat.

"But there was no one who you could see?" Thorgrim asked.

"No one," Starri said.

"Well, that won't be the case forever," Thorgrim said.

They slept the night on the beach, with sentries posted all around, but no one came to disturb their rest. They were up at dawn the following day, fires lit, pots with fish stew hanging from tripods. Dry land and a hot breakfast seemed like an extraordinary luxury.

That done, the men were sent off to attend to various tasks, foremost of which was getting the ships back into sailing condition. They had faired remarkably well riding to their sea anchors, but of course there was damage. Part of *Long Serpent*'s sail had blown out of its lashings and now needed to be mended. *Fox*'s larboard sheer strake had been smashed in and *Black Wing*'s steering board had suffered damage. And all of the ships were leaking, thanks to the violent twisting to which the seas had subjected them.

As the men went off to their work, Thorgrim called Gudrid to him and told him to fetch the Englishman, Sweartling. He called Harald and Godi to him, and Louis the Frank as well, though he was not sure why. Louis seemed to know things. He was from Frankia and might have a better sense of the lands around here.

When they had gathered, Thorgrim said to Gudrid, "Ask this fellow if he knows where in Engla-land we are."

Gudrid translated. "He says Swanage."

Thorgrim tried to hide his annoyance. "He's told us that. But where is Swanage? North? South?" Gudrid translated.

"He says it's in…Dorsetshire…I think was what he said."

Thorgrim sighed. He did not know how to get Sweartling to understand the question, though in truth he was reasonably certain that the man would not have an answer anyway. He looked over at Louis. "Do you have any ideas?" he asked.

Louis shrugged, as Thorgrim knew he would. "You Northmen are the ones who come across the seas to plunder innocent people. How did you do that? How did you come?"

"We follow the coast of Norway south, and when it starts to tend north again we cross the seas to Engla-land, or the land of the Picts, wherever we land. To get to Ireland we sail north around the land of the Picts and then west."

"I see," Louis said, and Thorgrim was sure that even to one who was no sailor the problem would be obvious. They had come ashore somewhere in Engla-land, but until they knew where, they would not know in which direction to sail.

"I've seen a few maps," Louis said next. "My father had some, and I looked at them as a boy. I recall Engla-land was shaped sort of like a triangle." He squatted down and drew a narrow triangle in the wet sand. Thorgrim and the others leaned forward to look, as if they could divine some truth from the marks. Louis drew another line to the right of his triangle. "Frankia is here," he said.

"And Ireland is here?" Thorgrim asked, pointing at a spot to the left of Louis's triangle.

"Yes, somewhere here, I think," Louis said and he drew a circle where Thorgrim had pointed.

"Hmm…" Thorgrim said, looking at the crude drawing. "Dubh-linn should be about here," he said, poking a hole on the Irish coast. "And Loch Garman here."

Louis nodded. "The monks at Glendalough, they had maps of Ireland. Good maps. I studied them. And you're right, that is where Dubh-linn and Loch Garman are found."

"So the wind was from the north, mostly, and it must have blown us this way…" Thorgrim drew a line from Loch Garmin south through the gap between Engla-land and Ireland.

"And then we sailed mostly east, once the storm had passed," Harald said. "So, did we get blown south of the corner of Engla-land, and wind up on the southern coast, or are we on the west coast?"

"The coast here runs north to south," Gudrid offered, "but that might not mean anything."

They discussed the matter a bit more. If Louis was right about the shape of Engla-land, then Harald was right that they had to be on either the west coast or the southern coast. Anything beyond that was guessing. As it was they were guessing quite a bit.

"Once the ships are ready for sea, we'll sail east," Thorgrim concluded. "Keep to the coast. Eventually we have to find someone who knows where we are."

"And sack some poor monastery, no doubt," Louis said.

"No," Thorgrim said. "We'll sack some rich monastery. It's what we heathens do."

The rest of the day was spent doing some of the other things that heathens did: repairing their ships, maintaining their weapons, stowing gear on board, eating and drinking ale. The sun went down on their second day at Swanage and they still had not seen anyone native to that land. All of Engla-land might have been wiped out by a plague for all they could tell.

The light from the fire fell over the sand and the faces of the men sitting staring into the flames and touched on the bows of the longships pulled up onto the beach. The talk and the singing and the laughter had begun to die off when Starri Deathless appeared in the light. He sat down next to Thorgrim and Thorgrim handed him a cup of ale, which he eagerly drank.

"Well?" Thorgrim said.

"We will not be lonely much longer," Starri said, wiping his mouth with his sleeve. Thorgrim did not press him. He knew Starri would get on with the tale in his own time.

"I went…oh…two, three miles from here?" Starri continued. "And I nearly ran headlong into the men-at-arms, the mounted ones. The same as had been here before, I would think. It was getting dark and they were settling in for the night, but at least a hundred men and horses."

Thorgrim frowned. Why would they leave and then return, unless they were returning with considerably more men? They had only to look down from any of the high points encircling the beach to see that there were seven ships there, and they would have to know that seven ships meant a lot more than one hundred men.

"They're expecting more," Thorgrim said at last. "These one hundred, they've come to keep an eye on us while more soldiers are on the way. They'll probably summon a bunch of farmers and give them shields and spears and call it an army, like the Irish do."

Starri nodded. "No doubt. But the men I saw, they were not farmers. They had mail and swords and good-looking mounts."

"How close did you get?" Thorgrim asked.

Starri shrugged. "I could have cut some throats, if I wanted to. But I was doing as you told me, Night Wolf. Like I always do."

Of course, Thorgrim thought.

Harald and Godi were sitting nearby and listening to Starri's words. "Do you think they'll attack in the dark?" Harald asked.

"No," Thorgrim said. "Not many would dare try such a thing. Bécc did, and it did not work out well for him."

"So at first light?" Godi asked.

"First light," Thorgrim said. "If they're waiting for more men, and those men arrive before dawn. If not, I suppose the warriors Starri saw will keep an eye on us until more men show up."

The others nodded and considered those words. "And what do we do?" Harald asked.

"We'll arrange for some surprise for them, our hosts," Thorgrim said. "We're guests in their country, after all."

Chapter Thirty-Two

He knows this who is forced to forgo his lord's
his friend's councils, to lack them for long:
oft sorrow and sleep, banded together,
come to bind the lone outcast...

The Wanderer

Nothwulf left Sherborne riding at the head of an impressive column of men: his hearth-guard and Leofric's and even some men from his late brother's household. They had taken the time to stop at Nothwulf's home to outfit his men with their best armor and weapons, things they had left behind in their hurry to get clear of the town. There were banners of the three households streaming at the end of long poles.

And for all that, Nothwulf still burned with humiliation.

Bitch, the bitch, the damned bitch, he kept thinking, over and over, and whenever he tried to force his thoughts onto a more constructive road, they kept returning to that path. Cynewise had completely outfoxed him. Leofric had hinted at his suspicions that the girl was not the fool she seemed to be, but Nothwulf had ignored the suggestion. And he had been wrong.

"What say you, Leofric?" Nothwulf said, breaking his silence at last. "The king, how do you think he sees this whole business?"

The men were riding side by side over the road that was still muddy from the days of drenching rain. After leaving Swanage and the Northmen the day before, they had covered most of the distance to Sherborne. They spent the night at a tavern along the way, and then made their impressive entry through the city gates that morning.

"Æthelwulf is getting old," Leofric said, "and as he does, his mind turns more to God and less on his kingdom. I honestly don't know if he quite understood the situation here, and if he did, I think he wants it all to be worked out with no bother to him."

"I see," Nothwulf said and fell silent as he considered that. He had been hoping that the king would set all this to rights, to put him, Nothwulf, in his proper place as ealdorman. But that had not happened, and now he felt like a weak, puny fool for hoping that someone else would solve his problems for him.

The column of riders was moving swiftly, alternating between a walking pace and a trot, keeping the horses moving as fast as they could for the many miles they had to cover. Cynewise had made it clear, in front of the king, that Nothwulf made a mistake coming to Sherborne and leaving the heathens in Swanage. Nothwulf had even felt compelled to lie about leaving men to keep an eye on the Northmen. He was still smarting from all that, and now he was very eager to get back before the Northmen could do any mischief and compound his error.

But for all Nothwulf's push, the poor roads, made worse by the recent storm, and the need to feed so many animals and men, meant he and Leofric had no chance of reaching Swanage in time to do much of anything but watch the Northmen and wait. Nor was there much they could do, anyway. Even with the increase in their force they did not have men enough to fight the heathens until the fyrd joined them.

The sun was moving toward the hills in the west when they finally passed through Wareham. They continued on until they reached the low, grassy hill where they had stopped before.

"We'll spend the night here," Nothwulf said, pointing toward the hill. "The ground should be as dry as we could hope, and it's far enough from the town that there's little chance of the heathens discovering us." The men climbed groaning from their saddles, stretching legs and arms, unbuckling helmets and plucking them from their heads.

Somewhere on the road behind them, moving much slower than the hearth-guard, were wagons with food and ale and cooking gear and tents and blankets. Nothwulf had been unwilling to move at the weary pace the wagons would maintain, so they left them behind, with strict orders that they were not to stop until they had reached the place where the riders intended to spend the night. It would be well past dark by the time they did.

Nothwulf and Leofric ate some bread and cheese from their saddlebags and drank some wine from skins and stretched their limbs as the men were doing. They were about two miles from the hill that overlooked Swanage and there was still an hour or so of daylight left and Nothwulf was restless.

"We should go see what the heathens are up to," he said to Leofric and Leofric just nodded. They finished their food, took a last gulp of wine, then mounted up again. They rode in silence to the place where they could look down on the fishing village, stopping just short of the ridge, dismounting and approaching on foot.

Nothwulf could feel his stomach twisting as he stepped up the grassy slope. What would he do if the heathens were gone?

If they had sailed off never to be seen on that coast again, then he could claim victory, suggest that it had been he who had driven them off. But what if they had left to sack some other town, or one of the monasteries nearby? He would be accused of negligence, or worse. Cowardice. He would never get the office of ealdorman. And that might be the least of his problems.

You'll never be ealdorman in any event, he thought. *That little tart has outfoxed you all along.*

They reached the crest of the hill. Swanage, such that it was, lay spread out below them, and further along the crescent beach, exactly where they had been before, were the seven heathen longships. Nothwulf felt himself relax, even to the point where he could appreciate the irony. The sight of Northmen generally did not make people relax.

"Haven't moved a pace," Leofric observed.

"No," Nothwulf said. "They seem settled in now." There was a big fire burning on the sand thirty feet from the water's edge, the flames standing out brilliant in the fading light of evening. They could see the Northmen, many Northmen, sitting in the sand around the fire or moving between it and the ships, or engaged in various other activities. And Nothwulf felt the first green shoots of an idea sprouting in his head.

"You know," he said, "the heathens may have twice our numbers, but they have no discipline. And they're likely to be drunk soon, and fast asleep. Maybe we shouldn't wait on the fyrd. Maybe we should consider attacking straight off."

Leofric made a grunting sound. "Now? Our men are dead tired. And I'm not sure drink does much to impair the Northmen's fighting skills. Just the opposite, I would think."

"No, not now. Of course I wouldn't ask our men to go into battle after riding so far today. But tomorrow, just at dawn. We make our way down to the village, hide there, and then at first light we attack while the bastards are still asleep. Attack on horseback, cut them down as they rise."

"Attack on horseback? You mean, our men remain mounted?"

"Yes," Nothwulf said. "I've seen it done, and it can be damned effective, you know. The Northmen come stumbling to arms and we ride them down, cut them down. It'd be a slaughter."

"Might be," Leofric said grudgingly.

"Here's the thing," Nothwulf said, his voice dropping, despite their being alone. "If Cynewise raises the fyrd and sends them to our aid, then she appears to be the one in command. Or if her father sends men to help, then we're completely lost. But if we defeat the heathens on our own, with the king here, then it should be clear to all who the rightful ealdorman is."

"Humph," Leofric said, and Nothwulf was amazed how the man could convey, in that one sound, both his skepticism and his understanding that Nothwulf was right. They watched for a few moments more, then trudged back to where their horses stood chomping on grass, and soon they were back with the others, still sprawled in the grass. The men-at-arms were too exhausted even to grumble about the supply wagons having not yet arrived.

It was entirely dark, and most of the mounted warriors were asleep on the ground, when the lanterns hanging from the wagons came bumping and swinging into view, spots of light far off down the road, like tiny, frenetic stars. The sleeping men stirred as the wagons came rumbling up at last, and eager hands dug for the food and ale they carried.

When the men were sated with food and drink, Nothwulf called them together and explained his plan. He told them that in the predawn they would make their way to Swanage and be ready to fall on the heathens as soon as there was light enough for battle. The men listened. They nodded. They did not offer any opinions one way or another, because the luxury of opinions was reserved for men far above their rank.

Long after the last of the hearth-guard had turned in, Nothwulf and Leofric sat by a small fire and enjoyed a glass of wine. It came from a small barrel Nothwulf had fetched from his home in Sherborne, and the quality was well above what most men in the field might enjoy. Nothwulf had been toying with a thought for most of the evening, examining it like some strange rock found on the beach, and now he wondered what Leofric might think.

"You know, Leofric," he said at last, approaching the topic carefully. "That whore's son Werheard murdered my brother, right there in the cathedral…"

"I recall," Leofric said. "Being as I was only a few feet away."

"Well, of course he didn't act alone," Nothwulf continued. "I mean, he did the deed by himself, but sure there must have been others in on the plot. Some scheme. Werheard had no call to kill Merewald, that I can discover. Nor do I think he would have had the wits or the courage to do so unless he was goaded by others."

"Yes, I think that's right."

"When he did the thing, he was shouting 'To me! To me!' as if he expected others to join in. And now there's talk that I was the one behind it, that I arranged for my brother's murder."

"There's that talk, true, among some," Leofric said.

"But I've been thinking…" Nothwulf said, looking into the flames, not wanting the catch Leofric's eye as he made his outrageous supposition. "It seems such a horrible thing, I'm almost loath to say it out loud…but it seems as if Cynewise has benefited mostly from this. And it makes me wonder if perhaps she had some hand in Merewald's murder."

Nothwulf looked up.. He expected to see a look of shock on Leofric's face, but instead he saw an expression of amazement and pity. Leofric opened his mouth to speak, then closed it, and his face settled into a more neutral look as he considered his words.

"Yes, Lord Nothwulf," he said at last. "I would think it possible that the Lady Cynewise had some hand in this."

Nothwulf felt himself flush with embarrassment as he realized what a fool he had been, and still was. "This is no surprise to you," he said, a statement, not a question. "You knew that Cynewise had a hand in my brother's murder. Am I the only one who did not know?"

"I didn't know," Leofric said. "I still don't know. But her father's a very powerful man. Ambitious as well. Enough that he's probably not content to just be ealdorman of Devonshire. If he could be lord of Dorset as well, at least by proxy, then that would please him very much."

Nothwulf thought of the silver goblets adorned with the crest of Cynewise's father, Ceorle, that stood in Bishop Ealhstan's sacristy. He thought of Aelfwyn and Oswin and his ring found among Werheard's things. And suddenly it was as if a fog had lifted to reveal a great vista he had not even realized was there. Everyone else did, just not him. And he felt like more of a fool than ever.

"Who else, do you think..." he began, not sure what to say. "Bishop Ealhstan? Is he..."

Leofric saved him from his stumbling questions. "I don't know. I don't know for certain this was anything more than one madman deciding your brother should die. Or if Cynewise or her father or anyone else had a hand in it. But with all that's happened, it certainly appears that this goes well beyond Werheard. That Werheard was the basest of pawns in this game."

For a long time the two men were silent, staring into the flames. Then Nothwulf asked the obvious question, a question he would have asked no man other than Leofric, because he trusted no other man as much.

"What do I do?"

For some time Leofric did not answer. Finally, he said, "You beat the heathens into the ground. And then you see what happens next."

Nothwulf slept fitfully that night, when he slept at all, and he was up and moving even before the night watch came to wake him as he had ordered done. It was not the pending battle that agitated his mind: Nothwulf had seen fights enough that he no longer suffered from an excess of nerves. It was every other aspect of his life, the complete overturning of everything he thought he understood.

He woke the captains with a nudge of his toe and they in turn began to wake their men, who stood and stretched and spit and scratched and reached for skins of wine. The predawn dark was filled with the soft sound of men preparing for battle, of mail pulled on over heads and swords scraping out of sheathes and back in again, of men cursing in muted tones over things they could not locate in the dark.

That did not go on very long, because the men under the command of Nothwulf and Leofric were professionals and experienced and they knew their business. Horses were saddled and bridles buckled in place. The men mounted and sat waiting, and when Nothwulf and Leofric were mounted as well they rode out, their pace no faster than a walk. There was time. No need to hurry yet.

When Nothwulf and Leofric came to the crest of the hill from which they had observed the village below and the beach beyond they stopped and the hundred or so mounted warriors behind them stopped as well. They looked down at the land and sea below them.

The moon was set, but there was light enough from the stars that they could just make out the high ground to the north and west, and the dark beach and even darker sea. There was a small point of light, the dying embers of the fire they had earlier seen the Northmen gathered around, but nothing besides that. And that was good. If they could not see the Northmen, then the Northmen could not see them.

"Good," Nothwulf said softly. "Let's go."

He nudged his horse's flanks and rode off to the right, toward a wide path that led to the village of Swanage below, Leofric still at his side, the rest behind. The path was steep for a bit, and Nothwulf rode with care, and then it began to level out as it reached the flat land on which the village had grown. Now Nothwulf could make out the looming shape of houses ahead, the smattering of pathetic huts that the fishermen called home. He stopped again.

"You may dismount," he said in a loud whisper. He swung his leg over the saddle and stepped down to the ground, and heard the others doing the same, the sound no louder than that of the wind in the brush.

Then it was quiet again. The hearth-guard knew what to do now. They would wait. It was something with which every fighting man had considerable experience, more experience than with fighting itself.

Nothwulf and Leofric handed their horses' reins to the servant who had been walking alongside them and moved cautiously down the narrow dirt street between the houses toward the beach. There was nothing to be seen, really, just dark shapes and darker emptiness beyond. There was nothing for them to do but wait as well.

It seemed to take an extraordinarily long time, but Nothwulf knew it would. Standing motionless in the dark, eyes and ears sharp for anything, he knew the minutes would drag by at an excruciating pace. And they did. His eyes adjusted fully to the dark, and still there was nothing to see. His ears reached through the night, but he could hear nothing but the lap of waves and the slight rustle of the breeze and occasionally a noise from the men behind, which made him grit his teeth in frustration.

Then the sky began to grow lighter.

Not quickly, not dramatically, but a slight lessoning of the dark. Nothwulf felt his waning attention sharpen once more, and he peered out toward the beach and listened to every little sound. He expected to hear some noise from the heathens at some point: someone stirring, or yelling in his sleep, or snoring, even. But there was nothing.

The dark continued to fade, and the sky to the east showed a definite hint of gray below the blackness and still there was no sound from the heathens, the longships still lost in the dark.

"Not so long now," Nothwulf whispered to Leofric, unable to keep silent a moment more.

"Not long," Leofric agreed. "A bit more and we should mount up."

"Yes," Nothwulf said. They would mount their horses and charge down the beach before the Northmen were awake, or just as they were rising. Hit them as they were stumbling up from sleep, kill them before they were even fully awake. Nothwulf felt the excitement and the bloodlust shooting through him.

The light continued to spread, and Nothwulf's excitement continued to build, but with it came the first inkling of fear and doubt. Something was not right. He did not know what, or whether it was no more than a feeling with no merit, but he sensed that something was off.

The night continued to lift, the shapes of the houses on either side growing more distinct, the difference between beach and sea becoming plainer. *Soon, soon...* Nothwulf thought. He heard Leofric stir beside him, heard him softly clear his throat. He turned to speak but Leofric spoke first.

"My eyes are old," he whispered, "but I have an ugly feeling something is amiss."

Nothwulf frowned. He did not know what to say. He could not dismiss the thought because he had had it himself. He turned back toward the beach.

The darkness had begun to lift in earnest now. He could see the dark water and the light colored sand, the ring of dunes surrounding the landward side of the beach. He could see the cliffs at the far end of the long stretch of sand. But he could not see the longships, because the longships were gone.

Chapter Thirty-Three

[V]engeful creatures, seated to banquet at bottom of sea;
but at break of day, by my brand sore hurt,
on the edge of ocean up they lay, put to sleep by the sword.

Beowulf

The North Star was still visible high above, but Thorgrim did not need it anymore. The dawn was breaking in the east and he could make out the dark line of land stretching from bow to stern down the larboard side, and the open sea to starboard.

He felt himself relax as the spreading light revealed the closest shore still more than a mile away. Rowing through the dark, along a foreign coast, depending on the local knowledge of men who did not even speak your language, was never an easy thing.

He turned to Gudrid and Sweartling, standing beside him as he stood at the tiller. "Well?" he asked. Gudrid turned to Sweartling and spoke.

"He says you've held your course well," Gudrid said. "He says the place they call Christchurch Priory is just off the larboard bow, there." He gestured toward some distant and indistinguishable spot ahead of them.

Thorgrim nodded and turned his attention to the shoreline beyond the bow. Two or three miles away, he guessed, but it was hard to be certain. The sun still had not come above the horizon and the land off to the north was no more than a low, black uneven line.

The decision to get underway had happened rather quickly. Thorgrim Night Wolf was not one to ponder long on such things, and he did not ponder long on this one. He had promised Starri a surprise for the men-at-arms gathering outside Swanage, though even as he said it he was not sure what that surprise would be. But he had some idea.

The fisherman, Sweartling, who had remained with them, had grown more talkative as he felt more assured of his safety, and more aware of the riches that the Northmen carried in their ships. When Thorgrim questioned him, through Gudrid, about the lands around, what was to be found there, where the wealth was secreted, Sweartling talked. He was hesitant at first, but then, as Thorgrim gave him another piece of silver and kept the ale flowing, the man became increasingly enthusiastic. He described the poor fishing villages and the distant town of Wimborne, where he had never been and had only heard of, and the wealthy priory just ten or twelve miles away over the water, across a wide bay.

That last one caught Thorgrim's attention.

Starri Deathless had returned from his scouting work soon after, informing Thorgrim of the mounted warriors massing against them, and that had settled for Thorgrim a question that he had pretty much settled already. They had taken everything worth taking from the village called Swanage, which wasn't much of anything. They had managed to put their ships to rights, at least enough that they could take to the sea with the shore close at hand. He did not feel any particular need to fight for their hold on a pathetic, deserted village and a beach on which they did not intend to stay.

On the other hand, if Sweartling was anything like correct—and he had been thus far—one of the Christ-men's churches was just a few hours' pull at the oars away. Thorgrim had raided churches in Engla-land in his younger days, and had seen plenty of the churches in Ireland since, and so he had every reason to believe this one would be as plump with gold and silver as Sweartling suggested. It was time to go.

They waited until the night was well on, and the moon set over the horizon, before they began to push the longships into the water as quietly as they could. Thorgrim was certain the English would be watching from the village or the hills, if not all of them then a sentry at least. He did not want their departure to be seen. He did not want the countryside to be alerted to the wolves in the sheepfold.

He waited for the cry of warning to come from the dark, the burst of men-at-arms charging over the sand to stop them. But he heard nothing. The ships were floating, the oars run out the oar ports, and still there was no sound to be heard.

Sea Hammer took the lead, with a lantern hung from the masthead once they were well clear of the beach, and the rest fell in astern. They rowed easy. Sweartling, a fisherman quite familiar with those waters, directed their course by the North Star, and assured Thorgrim that there was no danger for miles ahead. But Thorgrim did not care to trust anyone other than himself, and they were in no great hurry, so they moved with caution, like men feeling their way through the dark woods.

But Sweartling was right, apparently, and the first light showed Thorgrim that there was still plenty of water around them. Now he had only to hope the fisherman was right about the Christ-church as well.

They pulled on and Thorgrim ordered food and drink served out and the men at the oars relieved. He could still barely make out the land ahead, and that meant anyone on the land would not see the longships at all, and that was good. They were stalking, moving in with stealth and caution. The less warning the Christ men had, the less opportunity they would have to hide their wealth, or carry it off.

Harald was at the aftermost oar, setting the rhythm of the stroke for the rest, making an easy pull of it, but now it was time to pick it up.

"Harald," Thorgrim said, his voice only as loud as it had to be. Sound, he knew, traveled easily over water. "Let's pick up the pace now. Land's in sight."

Harald nodded and with the next stroke he leaned forward a little quicker, pulled back with a bit more gusto, and the men ahead of him did as well. Thorgrim felt *Sea Hammer*'s speed build and heard the change in the note of the water running down the side. With the next stroke, Harald increased the speed again.

Thorgrim leaned over the side and looked astern. The ships in his wake were barely visible, but he could see them well enough to see he was leaving them astern. He was not worried about that. Soon they would realize that *Sea Hammer* was making more speed and they would row even harder to catch up. No ship in a fleet wanted to suffer the humiliation of being left behind.

The land was getting close, almost uncomfortably close, by the time the sun showed itself above the horizon and spread its light over the water, revealing what had been only shadows just moments before: a long, sandy beach backed by high cliffs, almost white, and topped with green. It looked as if some grassy hill had been hacked in two by a massive sword, and the seaward side carted off. There was no village or church that Thorgrim could see.

"Gudrid," Thorgrim growled. "Ask our friend if we're making the right landfall here."

They went back and forth a few moments, Gudrid and Sweartling, and then Gudrid said, "The church isn't on the shore. Just past the headland there's a narrow mouth to a harbor, and the village and the church are across that harbor and up a river."

"Up a river? How far?" Thorgrim felt himself getting angry.

Gudrid posed the question, then said, "Sweartling says not far. Two, three miles from here. He says you could not get into the harbor in the dark."

You had better be right, you sorry English bastard, Thorgrim thought but he said nothing. He looked back at the horizon. The sun had still not broken clear.

Two or three miles… That would not take long, and they would be hidden by the cliffs until the last moment. Hopefully there was no one watching from the high ground.

They continued on, with Thorgrim steering to hug the shore on Sweartling's assurance that there was water deep enough for the longships. Astern of them, the other six ships kept pace.

"Starri," Thorgrim said and Starri, who was sitting just forward of the afterdeck, jumped to his feet as if Thorgrim had spoken with some urgency, which he had not. Starri was getting keyed up for a fight. Thorgrim recognized the signs.

"Up to the masthead with you, Starri," Thorgrim said. "There'll be sandbars and such, I'll warrant."

Starri nodded, moved up the ship's centerline to the aftermost shroud and pulled himself aloft on the thick, tarred rope as easily as he had stood up a moment before.

The mouth of the harbor was just as Sweartling had said, sandy shallows framing an entrance cut by the water that ran through with the change of the tides. Thorgrim could see gulls swirling around in the air and he could smell the scent of the land mixed with the tangy smell of salt water. He judged it was mid-tide, but whether the tide was rising or falling he could not yet tell.

Gudrid stepped up. "Sweartling says the sandbars are tricky here. He says to keep rowing this direction, then turn for the shore and run straight in."

Before Thorgrim could reply, Starri called down from aloft, "Night Wolf! Don't run into the channel now, or you'll be aground for sure! Straight on a bit, then go in through the cut!"

"Thank you, Starri!" Thorgrim cried. And they did just that, rowing straight ahead and then putting the tiller over just as Sweartling and Starri both said it was time. *Sea Hammer* turned ninety degrees with her bow heading west, straight for the narrow cut in the long sandy beach. Thorgrim could feel the speed build as they approached and he knew the tide was rising and it would suck them right through if all went well, or pin them on the sand if it did not.

He looked over at Sweartling, who was leaning against the side of the ship and staring intently forward. He was not as sanguine now in the company of the wild Northmen as he had been. He did not know how Thorgrim would react if he put the longship up on the sand. Even Thorgrim did not know how he would react, but he did not think it would be pleasant for anyone, Sweartling in particular.

The beach was close at hand, just off the bows, and Thorgrim could see the shallow, sandy bars from the tiller where he stood. The current had them now, and the men at the oars were doing little more than keeping the ship straight, but that was at least as important as keeping her moving.

Sea Hammer shot through the gap and a wide, flat harbor opened up before them, quiet and peaceful in the calm of the early morning. The sun had not risen above the cliffs to the south of them and part of the harbor still lay in shadow.

"Starri!" Thorgrim called, loath as he was to shout. "Anything moving? Any boats?"

There was a pause, and then Starri called back, "Nothing, Night Wolf! I guess these English are all lay-abeds!"

Thorgrim smiled. He had never known a fisherman anywhere who was a lay-abed and he imagined they were just now loading nets aboard their boats and pushing them off into the water. It would not be long before they spotted the longships making their silent approach. They would spin around and pull like mad for the shore and spread the word that death was coming.

"Harald, faster now," Thorgrim said. They had to cover as much ground as they could before surprise was lost.

Harald nodded and leaned back quicker yet, giving a powerful stroke, and the others followed suit. Thorgrim looked astern. *Blood Hawk*, *Oak Heart* and *Fox* had come through the harbor entrance and *Dragon* and *Long Serpent* and *Black Wing* were coming behind.

Thorgrim looked forward, past the tall stem that held the figurehead aloft. He could see thin columns of smoke in the distance, the sign of some sort of village waking up.

"I can see some houses now! And the Christ-temple," Starri called.

"Good, Starri!" Thorgrim replied. "I think you can come down now!" Thorgrim was no longer concerned about Sweartling. The man had proved that he knew the navigation of those waters, and that he would not betray the Northmen, either from fear or greed or both.

Thorgrim steered *Sea Hammer* across the open water of the wide bay. It reminded him of Loch Garman. These shallow, sandy bays, surrounded by low marshy land, seemed common in Ireland and Engla-land, though they were all but unheard of in Thorgrim's native Norway.

They pulled for the distant shore, Sweartling making small corrections in the course to skirt the shallow banks on either side. The shore was a mix of sand and patchy grass and stands of scrubby trees, and the gulls whirled and dove in the morning light. Soon the wide bay began to narrow as *Sea Hammer* moved into the mouth of the river that Sweartling had told them about.

Starri had come down from aloft, but now he was halfway up the stem in the bow, like a second figurehead, looking forward. "There it is, Night Wolf!" he called back. "I see the church! Oh, and boats! There are fishing boats on the water." He paused then gave a bark of a laugh. "Ha! The whores' whelps are rowing now! I guess they've seen us!"

Thorgrim nodded. There was nothing for him to say. Every man not pulling an oar had already donned what armor he had, taken up their weapons and their shields. Now they were standing ready to go over the side as soon as *Sea Hammer* was in water shallow enough to do so.

He could see Failend up near the bow. She had her mail shirt on and her seax at her side and her bow—the thing that made her deadly indeed—held loosely in her left hand. Louis De Roumois stood beside her, leaning on the sheer strake.

Christians, Thorgrim thought. *They are both Christ worshipers.* He wondered what they thought about all this.

He reached down and snatched Iron-tooth from where it lay wrapped in furs and belted the weapon around his waist. He was already wearing his mail shirt. As for a helmet, he had long ago stopped caring enough about whether he lived or died in battle to bother with the inconvenience of wearing one.

He leaned over the side as far as he could and looked toward the shore. They were close enough that he could see the muddy bank where the fishing boats had run up. He could even see a handful of men—the crews of those boats, he imagined—running for their lives toward the Christ temple.

The monastery…they'll be warned soon enough, Thorgrim thought. It would have been nice to catch the people there still in their beds, but that was not likely to happen now. Not that it mattered very much. Even the most alert and well-armed Christ priest would not be much of an obstacle in their effort to sack the place.

Two more hard stokes of the oars and the shore was closing fast. Thorgrim was beginning to wonder how close to the beach they would get when he felt the soft jerk of the ship running up into the mud and the forward momentum coming to a stop. He did not have to pass the word to ship the oars. The men had been waiting for this moment and they eagerly pulled the long sweeps inboard and deposited them on the deck as they leapt to their feet and grabbed up weapons and shields.

Thorgrim released the tiller and moved forward, moving quickly but not too quickly. There was no call to run, and doing so would only encourage chaos. The men stood aside, making way for him. No one even thought to go over the side before he did.

A little forward of midships Thorgrim looked down and guessed that there was no more than a few feet of water there, though in the muddy bay it was hard to tell. He stepped up on the sheer strake and vaulted over and was relieved to find the water no higher than his waist. Sinking out of sight would have been too humiliating by half.

He pushed his way ashore and heard the others coming behind, men leaping over the side with such eagerness it sounded like a torrential rain, or a waterfall. The mud sucked at Thorgrim's soft shoes and the water fell away as he trudged up the bank and stopped well clear of the water's edge. The men behind him knew to be as quiet as they could. No one spoke, and their splashing made hardly a sound.

Thorgrim paused and listened. He could hear birds in the tall grass and the reeds rustling in the breeze. He could hear what might have been shouting, or might have been his ears playing tricks, he could not tell. What he did not hear, not yet, was the sound of panicked alarm. The fishermen had not yet alerted the monastery, or perhaps they were racing for the far hills and not bothering with the monastery at all.

"You men, form up in a swine array. Godi and Harald take the point. We'll be ready if anyone comes, and if not, we'll move when the others get ashore."

The men had been waiting for orders and those words sent them into a flurry, putting themselves in a swine array, a loose angled formation like a flock of geese in flight, with Godi and Harald at the apex. It was a formation generally used to break a shield wall, and it was very effective when employed by men of courage, strength and ability.

Thorgrim turned and looked out over the bay. *Blood Hawk* was just that moment running onto the mud and *Oak Heart* was only a ship-length behind. The others were in a staggered line astern, but they, too, were only moments from reaching the shore.

One by one the longships eased to a stop in the mud, and as they did their crews swarmed over the side, a crowd of Northmen with bright-painted shields and helmets and mail gleaming as much as it could after the neglect it had lately suffered. Some wore leather armor and under that the armor they wore tunics in an array of colors. They hurried ashore and formed up in loose lines and waited. At their heads stood their captains: Jorund, Asmund, Halldor, and Hardbein.

"Very well, you men!" Thorgrim shouted because he had to, loud enough for all to hear. "We secure the place first, worry about plunder after. Round up anyone you find and drive them into the Christ-temple, it'll be the biggest building. Don't kill anyone you don't have to kill. Everyone there, men, women, children, are worth more to us alive than dead!"

He wondered why he had added that admonishment about pointless killing. It was true, certainly, about the value of prisoners, but he had never felt compelled to say such a thing before. Was it for Failend? Was he becoming shy about killing Christ-worshipers? Or was he just getting soft-headed in his old age. He did not know, and did not care to think about it just then.

He turned and pushed through the crowd of men until he was standing a few paces in front of Harald and Godi. He lifted Iron-tooth above his head and marched off, down the well-worn path that led to a small village clustered around the walls of the monastery beyond.

The monastery itself was an impressive place, a great stone temple rising up amidst a cluster of small buildings, all half hidden behind a wall six feet high or so. And it was not a wall of earth or palisades, as was generally the case, at least in Ireland, but one built of stone, an impressive bit of work.

Bigger than Glendalough, Thorgrim thought. *Not quite as big as Ferns.* Then he thought, *I've come to know more about these Christ temples than any man who worships the true gods should.*

The sound of sharp ringing, sudden and insistent, pulled him from those thoughts. It startled him, and for a moment he did not know what he was hearing. And then he did. It was the bells from the Christ temple, sounding their alarm. Word had reached the people there that the heathens were ashore. The surprise was over.

Thorgrim moved faster, his pace close to a jog. They reached the cluster of houses and pushed down the dirt road separating them. The village was deserted, of course. If the people were smart they would have run for the hills. If not they likely fled to the monastery, which would put them right in the path of the greatest danger.

It did not take long to make their way through the houses and workshops and then there was only the stone wall surrounding the monastery in front to them. Thorgrim could see where a wide, hard-packed dirt road stretched off to the west, and he guessed that led to the monastery's main gate. He turned and jogged off in that direction.

Thorgrim reached the near corner and rounded it and there, as he guessed, was the tall wooden gate, one hundred feet away. He closed the distance quickly, then stopped. They could climb the gate, but that would make it easier for any defenders on the far side to kill them piecemeal as they did. Better to open the gates and lead the attack as a solid line of men.

"Starri!" Thorgrim called. "Go over the wall and…"

That was as far as he got. Starri ran past him and charged for the gate and Thorgrim doubted he had even heard the words. He was going over that wall regardless of what he was told.

Starri was stripped to the waist, as he generally was going into battle, and his two battle axes were tucked in his belt as he flung himself at the gate and his hands and toes caught what holds they could and he scrambled up.

Good, Thorgrim thought. Starri would be enough to occupy anyone trying to defend the gate while other, more rational men, opened it up.

"A few more, up and over and open the gate!" Thorgrim shouted. Godi and Harald raced ahead, as did Gudrid and a few others. Godi stopped and leaned against the wooden wall and linked his fingers and Harald put his foot in Godi's hands. Effortlessly, Godi lifted Harald up until the boy's hand could reach the top of the gate. Harald hoisted himself up and vaulted over, disappearing on the far side as Vali went next, and one of Jorund's men behind him.

Failend was last. Thorgrim had not even noticed her going forward, but now she put her foot in Godi's hands and he lifted her aloft and, small as she was, she looked smaller still held in Godi's massive hands. Godi seemed surprised as how light she was and he nearly tossed her right over the gate, but Failend caught herself and pulled herself up.

But she did not go over. Instead she stood on the top of the gate, balanced there, then took a half dozen steps to the top of the wall. She stood there and drew an arrow from her quiver and knocked it and shot, the motion smooth and seamless and lovely, and Thorgrim did not doubt that some unseen defender on the other side of the gate was now writhing on the ground with an arrow jutting from some part of his body.

Right in front he heard a creak, a loud groan, and the massive oak gate began to swing open, revealing the scene behind. Harald and Vali were pushing one of the doors, Gudrid and Jorund's man the other, and behind them Starri Deathless was whirling his axes and screaming and shifting side to side, engaging five men at once, leaping easily over the three who already lay dead at his feet.

The men who were fighting Starri, however, were not the only ones on that open ground in front of the church. There were more, many more, behind. Big men, bearded men, racing without hesitation toward the now-open gate.

"Onward! Onward!" Thorgrim shouted. He raised Iron-tooth and raced forward and the men behind him raised a great cheer, like a physical thing, as they followed him through the gates.

They rolled over the men whom Starri was fighting, cutting them down as they went, charged forward to meet the men behind, coming at them. They were not the men that Thorgrim had expected to see.

A hundred at least, probably more. Most carried shields and most seemed to have swords, warriors' weapons, and not the spears Thorgrim would expect to see wielded by farmers conscripted to fight. Some wore mail shirts and some wore helmets and they all wore tunics and leggings and not the long, brown robes of Christ priests. They were not fleeing from the screaming heathens as priests would have done, but rather charging at them, weapons ready for battle, meeting the heathens yell for yell.

They were warriors, and all Thorgrim could think was, *Where by the gods did these sons of whores come from?*

Chapter Thirty-Four

Within 'twas full of wire-gold and jewels; a jealous warden,
warrior trusty, the treasures held, lurked in his lair. Not light the task
of entrance for any of earth-born men!

Beowulf

Thorgrim expected the warriors in the monastery to be swept away by the fierceness and suddenness of the Northmen's attack, but they were not, and he was impressed. Instead they stopped in the headlong rush and tightened their line into something like a shieldwall and stood braced for the punch of men.

The Northmen had lost what little cohesion they had, and Thorgrim cursed himself for his stupidity in letting that happen. He had not expected a fight. The Christ priests did not fight back, and he had never seen warriors in a monastery. But then, it had been two decades since he had last plundered a monastery in Engla-land.

There is always an enemy, always an enemy, Thorgrim reminded himself. It was the stupidest of mistakes to assume there would be no one to fight back. It could be the last mistake.

He reached the line that the English men-at-arms had formed. A spear thrust out at him from somewhere behind the shields and he batted it aside with his sword and thrust back, Iron-tooth meeting only the metal boss of an English shield. More of his men appeared on either side and without a word they overlapped shields and pushed forward, slamming into the Englishmen with no effect save for the clash of shields and the roar of angry men.

Thorgrim could see them better now, the men in the shield wall against which they were pushing. He saw wild and unbound hair, he saw bare feet and men without leggings and some without tunics. He caught a glimpse of a warrior who had pulled his mail shirt over his bare flesh.

We did surprise you, you bastards, Thorgrim thought as he thrust and hacked at the men in front. It was clear to him that these men defending the monastery had not been ready for them, had not been waiting to defend the place. They had been asleep when the bells had started to toll, they had leapt from their beds or wherever they were sleeping, grabbed up what they could and raced to the fight. They might well be suffering the effects of too much drink the night before.

But for all that, they were trained men, experienced men. It did not take long to realize that. They stood with courage and discipline and pushed back against the Northmen, who greatly outnumbered them, who would soon run them over.

*Or not...*Thorgrim thought. He had made the mistake once already of thinking there was no surprise waiting for them, and it might have been fatal. He would not do that again.

He pushed hard against the shield ahead of him, slashing down again and again with Iron-tooth, forcing the men he faced to shy behind their shields to avoid the blows. Then, as the English braced for another stroke, he stepped back quick, stepped out of the shield wall and saw the men who had been on either side of him close the gap.

Thorgrim did not like that, stepping back from the fighting, did not like it at all, but he knew that sometimes a leader had to do just that. His men could stand up to the English shield wall, beat it most likely, but not if the English had some surprise assault they were ready to launch.

He moved back far enough that he could see most of the line of fighting men. The English were certainly outnumbered, that was clear, unless they had more men in hiding. Let these hundred or so get the raiders' attention, and then hit them from another angle. It was what Bécc and done to him at Loch Garman, and he would not forget it.

Thorgrim searched the far reaches of the monastery as best he could. He looked at the narrow places between buildings, and along the walls of the great stone church that took up the bulk of the space, but he could see no one, no mass of men waiting for their moment to launch an attack.

*Maybe this is it…*Thorgrim thought. There might not be any surprise waiting. This might be all the warriors there were. If the English men-at-arms had expected an imminent attack from the sea they would not have been caught unprepared. And if they were unprepared, they probably had not had time to organize a surprise attack.

Whatever reason these English warriors are here, it isn't to fight us, Thorgrim thought next. *Do they belong to the monastery? Do Christ priests have warriors?*

He raced off to his left. The shieldwall his men had formed was two and three men deep, a long line of shouting men, axes and swords rising and falling, and every once in a while a man staggering back from the line, blood streaming from a wounded head or arm, or spreading in a dark patch through the rent fabric of his tunic.

"Spread out!" Thorgrim shouted to the men crowded there. "Shift to your left, shift to your left!" If they could extend their shieldwall farther than the English could, then they could wrap around the enemy's line, start to squeeze in from two sides.

The men heard him and they moved, shifting off to the left, extending the line. Thorgrim saw the English warriors shift as well, to keep in front of the Northmen, but they did not have the numbers and their line grew thinner, the shields farther apart as they moved. Thorgrim knew they could not spread out much more or they would collapse like a wall of reeds.

And then a space opened up, just for a heartbeat, but long enough and wide enough for Thorgrim to get a look at the Christ temple beyond, and this time he did see something. Not warriors ready to join the fight, but something just as bad.

He turned back to the shieldwall, where the men in back were jostling to get into the fight. He grabbed a man by the shoulder and pulled him back. It was Ulf, from his own ship, and Armod beside him.

"Come with me!" Thorgrim shouted. He grabbed another man. That one he did not know, one of those who joined at Loch Garman. "With me!" Thorgrim shouted and the man nodded and Thorgrim grabbed two more as well. He waved Iron-tooth overhead and charged off. He saw Failend standing off to the side, an arrow knocked in her bowstring, looking for a target, and he waved to her to follow.

They charged off to the left, flanking the two fighting shield walls, running clear of the fight, unnoticed, moving at an angle toward the stone wall and the big Christ temple. Once they were clear of the others Thorgrim got a better look at what he had seen: a wagon standing by the big doors at the front of the church, a horse in its traces, a stream of brown-cloaked priests emptying the place of anything the heathens might want to steal.

Thorgrim and his band were halfway across the open ground when the priests saw them coming. One was standing at the back of the wagon, his arms full, and Thorgrim could see the glint of silver over the brown cloth of his sleeves. The man turned and looked right at Thorgrim and his mouth fell open and despite being a foot from the wagon he dropped his burden to the ground, turned and fled, his feet kicking the back of his long robe in an almost comical way.

The others did the same, dropping whatever they had in their arms, turning and running, some back into the church, but most off to the far side, as directly away from the Northmen as they could.

Save for one man. That one turned and threw his armload into the back of the wagon and raced for the seat in front. He practically leapt up in place, snatching up the reins as he did. He snapped the leather cords and yelled. The horse gave a surprised whinny, jumped a little, then started to run.

Thorgrim could feel his breath coming fast, could feel his legs starting to tire. He wanted to tell the others to go on ahead, to stop the wagon, but he could not gasp out words, so instead he pointed and nodded and hoped it would be enough.

And it was. Armod, young and quick, raced off past him, running as fast as he could, his legs reaching out in long, deer-like strides. The priest driving the wagon turned and looked back, then snapped the reins again as he saw Armod closing the distance. The horse ran fast but, incredibly, Armod ran faster still. The gap between Armod and the wagon was closing, and the gap between Armod and Thorgrim was opening up fast.

Failend stepped up beside Thorgrim, an arrow on her bowstring. She raised the bow and drew back, just as Armod reached out and grabbed the back of the wagon and vaulted onto the bed. He staggered as the driver swerved in hope of knocking him off, which he nearly did, but Armod grabbed the wagon's side as he fell and regained his balance.

Failend lowered the bow. "I have no shot," she said.

Thorgrim smiled. She could have put her arrow right between the man's shoulders, he was sure of it. She had shown considerable skill and little hesitation in dropping any of the many enemies they had encountered, but she was not willing to kill a priest.

As Armod worked his way forward, horse and wagon raced off with surprising and alarming speed, rocking violently. Armod moved cautiously, one hand on the wagon's side to steady his precarious footing. The wagon was nearly at the edge of the church and lost from sight when he reached out and grabbed the priest by the shoulder.

The priest kept the reins in one hand as he reached back to fight Armod off with the other, but with his attention divided he was no match for the Northman. Armod grabbed up handfuls of the priest's robe and yanked him up and threw him sideways. The priest flew from the wagon seat and hit the ground and rolled, a disorganized tumble of brown cloth and bearded face.

The wagon disappeared around the corner of the church as the priest pulled himself to his knees and faced the rest of the Northmen coming at him. Ulf reached him first, drawing his sword and raising over his head as he closed the last few feet, and Thorgrim had just enough breath to shout, "No!"

Ulf stopped and turned, sword still raised, as Thorgrim came stumbling up. "Worth more alive," Thorgrim managed to gasp and Ulf nodded and sheathed his sword, happy with that explanation. But Thorgrim knew it was not the real reason he had spared the man. This priest had been brave while the others had fled. Thorgrim respected that. He could not bear to see the man cut down, no weapon in his hand, just because he had been the only one with courage.

Before Thorgrim could say another thing the wagon reappeared around the corner of the church, now moving at a reasonable speed, the horse panting but calm, Armod holding the reins. He pulled to a stop and Thorgrim looked down into the wagon bed. Silver candlesticks and silver and gold chalices, silver plates and bowls and incensors, and some of those odd, bejeweled boxes in which the Christians kept the withered body parts of their dead leaders. In all a fortune that had nearly slipped away.

The shouting behind had not died off, if anything it had grown louder. Thorgrim looked back toward the fight, shieldwall against shieldwall. The English, outnumbered as they were, were fighting like demons, not yielding a foot, countering the Northmen blow for blow. But they were paying a price for that bold stance. Thorgrim could see dead men at their feet, the bleeding bodies of their comrades on which the living were stepping as they held the raiders back. And though he could not see from there, he had no doubt that many of his own men were wounded and dead, and in that chaotic fighting more would fall.

"Come along, back to it," Thorgrim said. They had managed to get behind the English line, and now they had a chance to hit the enemy in the back, in a way the English would not see coming. Thorgrim was only sorry there were so few of them, just him and Armod and Ulf and a few others. Even a dozen more could have done real damage.

And then he looked back at the wagon.

"Everyone in!" he shouted, leaping up onto the seat beside Armod, who seemed to have a knack for driving the thing. Ulf and Failend and the rest swarmed up into the bed and Thorgrim pointed at the fighting men. "There, Armod! Right into the English shield wall, roll them right up!"

Armod nodded and snapped the reins and snapped them again and once more the skittish horse leapt ahead. Thorgrim braced himself. He heard a shout from behind and turned to see one of the men, the one whose name he did not know, tumble from the bed and lay sprawled on the ground. But like a sailor overboard in a storm, there was no going back for him.

They were less than a hundred yards from the fighting, and the horse covered the distance fast. Thorgrim saw movement behind him, and then he saw Failend, standing and leaning against the wagon side. She had an arrow on her bowstring and as she braced against the movement of the wagon she drew back and let fly, then snatched another arrow as she did.

Thorgrim looked ahead again. He had no doubt that Failend's arrow had taken one of the English down, but in the growing pile of bodies he could not tell which one. They had halved the distance to the line and Thorgrim could see that Armod understood what he wanted—not to drive straight into the English, but to hit them at an angle, to run right up the length of their shieldwall.

"Good!" he shouted. "At them!" He looked back over his shoulder. "Stand ready!" He recalled that Harald had done something very much like this, during the fight at Glendalough. It had worked very well then, and Thorgrim hoped it would again.

They were twenty-five yards away when the closest of the English warriors saw them coming, then more men looking up with surprise on their faces. Thorgrim could see them backing away and in a few instances, their attention diverted, they were struck down by the swords and spears from the Northmen's shieldwall against which they were pressed.

Armod shouted and flicked the reins and the horse, which seemed to be once again in a full-on panic, ran harder still. Those men in the animal's path could see that they would be run down by the crazed beast and the wagon it was pulling behind if they stayed where they were. They were blocked by the Northmen in one direction so they took the only course left to them: they turned and fled in the other.

One by one, and then nearly all at once, the English broke and ran, not in any coordinated way but in a mad frenzy, fleeing the wagon and the Northmen who were close to overwhelming them. They flung shields aside as they stumbled and pushed their way clear of the wagon, and as the wagon passed, the Northmen took off in pursuit.

The English were in full flight, and most kept running, though some stopped to face their enemy rather than take a sword or spear in the back. Thorgrim saw his men slamming the English with the fronts of their shields, sending them sprawling, or hitting them on the side of the head with the flats of their swords and axes and knocking them to the ground. He did not see his warriors cutting or killing men who were fleeing or giving up. He had reminded them of the value of hostages and slaves and his men had taken that to heart.

The wagon reached the end of the ground where the English had stood. Armod pulled on the reins and the horse kicked and bucked and thrashed its head, but it slowed enough for Thorgrim and the others to jump off.

Thorgrim hit the ground, stumbled, then stood and looked out over the open ground and the fighting men there. There was no battle any more, just dozens of smaller fights. He searched for the place where he might most effectively join in, but there was nowhere that he could see.

Most of the fighting had stopped, with the English either dead or knocked out cold or kneeling with arms raised and faces that looked as if they expected to be killed then and there. Thorgrim walked around to the back end of the wagon. Three men were struggling to hold Starri back as the berserker screamed and thrashed, which, to Thorgrim, had come to mark the end of any fight.

"Get their weapons! Make them lie face down!" Thorgrim shouted. His mind was working through the myriad things to which he had to attend. In battle there was no time for such worry or consideration. A man's thoughts were blown out like a candle in a breeze and he moved and reacted with pure, mindless drive. It was a beautiful thing. But then the fighting ended and the world reasserted itself, and victory meant many, many decisions to make.

The Northmen were shoving the kneeling, terrified English warriors to the ground and Thorgrim had no doubt that each of them lying face down was braced for a sword through the back.

Would their God welcome a man who was killed with no weapon in his hand? Killed having surrendered? Thorgrim wondered. He was not sure about that. He would have to ask Failend. He was curious.

"Jorund!" Thorgrim shouted. Jorund was about thirty feet away. He had just shoved a prisoner to the ground and he stood with his back to Thorgrim. "Jorund!"

Jorund turned and looked over. There was a big gap in the front of his shield where a section of the wood had been hacked away. Half his face was covered in blood from a slash high up on his cheek. The two long braids in his beard were stuck to the blood that coated his mail shirt.

"Yes, Thorgrim?" he shouted.

"Get the men from your crew, and any more you might need, and sweep through this place. Take any prisoners you find and see them secured. Don't kill them if you don't have to. Make sure none of these Christ priests make off with any of our silver or gold."

"Right!" Jorund said, nodding.

"Are there any of your men who are good with the wounded?" Thorgrim asked next. "Who know about healing?"

"Some," Jorund said.

"Good," Thorgrim said. "Tell those to look to the wounded. Take the rest of your men with you."

Jorund nodded again and began to shout out orders, calling for the men of *Long Serpent* and *Black Wing* to rally to him. Thorgrim would have preferred to set Godi or Harald to this task—there was too much mischief that men could get into when securing prisoners and plunder. But it was important to show Jorund that he was trusted, and just as important to put Jorund and his men to the test, to see if that trust was warranted.

Jorund was just leading his men off when Harald came over from across the ground. He, too, had a great deal of blood on his mail and his face and his leggings.

"Are you hurt?" Thorgrim asked.

Harald looked surprised, then looked down at himself, at the blood that was splattered all over him. "No," he said, as if he did not understand the question. Behind them, Starri had stopped fighting and now, as the berserker state left him and he found himself still alive, still trapped in the drudgery of Midgard, he was weeping loudly, as was his custom.

"Good fight, good victory, Father," Harald said. "The gods are still smiling on you."

"Perhaps," Thorgrim said. What the gods felt was not at all clear to him. They had not favored him in his fight with Bécc, but then again they had blown him free of Ireland at last. It seemed impossible for a man such as himself to know what the gods were about.

Nor did Thorgrim have a moment to ponder it. "Anyway," he said, "things have turned about. You used to try to imitate me, and now I'm imitating you."

Harald looked even more puzzled. "How so?"

"The wagon," Thorgrim said. "What I did, running it into the enemy. You did just that thing once, back at Glendalough."

Harald frowned and looked off into the distance, as if trying to peer back though a great expanse of time, which Thorgrim found amusing, given Harald's mere seventeen years on earth. "Oh, yes, I suppose I did!" Harald said, remembering at last.

Thorgrim nodded. He could understand Harald's forgetting. It had been a busy time, these last few years. Thorgrim himself felt certain he did not remember half of it.

He looked around him. A dozen men were tending the wounded, some kneeling and examining groaning and bleeding men, some tearing up strips of cloth taken from the dead to bind the wounds of the still living. There were shields and spears and axes and swords and helmets scattered around the trampled earth. Above them all, the sky was blue, the sun was shining, the weather not at all in keeping with the suffering on the ground.

How many did we lose? Thorgrim wondered. It did not seem too many, not in proportion to the plunder they found, the hostages they had taken. Jorund and his people had sworn their oath to Thorgrim because they thought they were joining with a lucky man. So far he had given them no reason the keep thinking that. Until now.

He turned and looked in the other direction. His men had finished stripping the prisoners of their weapons and mail. The gear they had liberated was now heaped in a big pile and the English soldiers, wearing just tunics and leggings, and some not even that, remained face down on the ground.

"Gudrid!" Thorgrim called and Gudrid jogged over to where he stood. "You're the only one among us who can speak the language they speak here, as far as I know. Harald, it looks like you lose your job as translator."

"Thank the gods," Harald said.

"For now," Thorgrim said. "If we don't get clear of Engla-land soon, you'll meet some pretty thing who'll steal your heart, and next you'll be speaking this language, too, just to get under her skirts." Harald blushed and Thorgrim turned to Gudrid. "My son has a gift for languages, but the motivation has to come through his leggings."

Gudrid smiled and Harald blushed harder.

Thorgrim looked out over the field of battle. "We'll put these men, these prisoners, in the temple there, best way to keep them out of mischief. Tell them to get on their feet."

Gudrid nodded and rendered Thorgrim's orders in English, loud and direct. The prisoners stood, warily, eyes wide, still expecting to be cut down at any second. Or at least that was how they looked.

"Tell them if any of them try to fight, they'll die. If they don't fight, then they can live."

Gudrid translated, but the prisoners did not look any less concerned, and Thorgrim hoped that Gudrid had as good a command of the language as he claimed. He called out to his own men to make a circle around the prisoners, weapons ready, though he did not think the English would put up a fight. They were without their weapons and armor. He had given them the hope of living if they did not fight, and they had to know they would certainly die if they did.

Once more he wondered if their god looked favorably on men who died fighting. That would be a good thing to know. It could have a big influence on how a man might act as a prisoner.

Must ask Failend about that, he thought again.

With the English on their feet, those still able to stand, Thorgrim told Gudrid to order them into the temple. At first they seemed to not understand the words, but when Gudrid pointed and shoved one of the men in that direction, the others caught his meaning. Slowly and sullenly they began to shuffle off, herded along by the circle of Northmen.

The church was dark and cool and voluminous inside. Thorgrim came in behind the prisoners and their guards. He told Gudrid to tell the English to sit on the floor. Gudrid yelled, pointed, and the prisoners obeyed, still slow and sullen.

It was not long after that Jorund returned. He had a bag over his shoulder, filled to bulging, odd shapes visible where the cloth was stretched tight. He stepped over to Thorgrim and dropped the bag on the stone floor. Thorgrim could see the dull gleam of silver. More chalices and plates and such. He grunted at the sight.

"Caught one of the dogs hiding in the stable with this," Jorund explained. "Trying to make off with our plunder."

"The dogs," Thorgrim agreed and he started to ask about prisoners when the first of what turned out to be two dozen priests in brown robes were herded through the door. Behind them came a score of men, women and children. The men appeared to be smiths and stable hands and bakers and tanners and others of various trades, the women their wives, stout and strong and worn down from years of labor and bearing children. These were the people who did not follow the Christ God as the priests did, but who did the actual work of the monastery. Soon they, too, were sitting on the ground. They looked to be waiting for something, and not expecting it to be good.

Jorund remained at Thorgrim's side, and Godi and Harald and Halldor and Hardbein joined them. They would be looking to him for decisions.

"Well, Thorgrim?" Jorund asked. "What now?"

It was something Thorgrim had been considering, and he gave the only answer he had been able to come up with.

"I think we had better find some breakfast," he said.

Chapter Thirty-Five

It was there that the Lord opened up my awareness of my lack of faith.
Even though it came about late, I recognized my failings.
So I turned with all my heart to the Lord my God.

St. Patrick's *Confessio*

Father Finnian arrived at the monastery at Ferns just in time to help Brother Bécc mac Carthach to his final reward. The peripatetic priest had been traveling south along the coast, attending to the business of the Abbot of Glendalough, and to other business of which the abbot was not aware. He had arrived at Beggerin and found, to his surprise, that the monastery was all but deserted.

All, but not completely. A few of the local sheep herders were there, tending their flocks in the fields surrounding the monastery, unwilling to leave their charges until the threat to their own lives was clear and immediate. Finnian blessed them. He told them that they cared for their flocks with the same love and dedication with which Christ cared for them. He asked them where everyone had gone.

The shepherds told him of the heathens' attack, of the Irish men-at-arms under the command of a monk from Ferns, of the fighting on the beach. The more they talked, the more Finnian realized that they were repeating things that they had only heard, second or third hand. But from the evidence before his eyes he could see that their tale was not too far wrong.

He was ready to move on to Ferns when two extraordinary things happened nearly at once.

The first was a battle on some beach at the far side of the bay of Loch Garman. Finnian went down to the water's edge and stared out to the west. He was no stranger to that area, and he was fairly certain

316

that there was nothing of note on the other side of the bay, and yet the sound of fighting came clearly over the water.

Finnian squinted and stared at the far shore, three miles away. He could not tell for certain what he was seeing, but he thought he saw movement, dark points moving on the lighter colored earth, men maneuvering on a beach. It made sense, considering the sounds that were coming to him, faint but distinct. The ping of steel on steel heard from far off, the muted, barely discernable sound of shouting. But the sky was covered by a dark overcast, and between that and the distance, he could not tell anything for certain.

Not long after that, the second phenomena made its appearance: a storm the likes of which Finnian had never seen. It started with the wind, which built quickly from a stiff breeze into something unearthly. It tore out of the north, howling in his ears, ripping the normally still water of the bay into a steep chop topped with whitecaps that looked gray in the dull light. After that came the rain, driving nearly sideways, stinging like the lash of a whip. Finnian knew that he should make his way back to the deserted monastery and find some shelter, and suggest to the handful of shepherds that they do the same. But he could not tear himself from the beach.

He did at last, fighting his way back to the walls of Beggerin where he found the sheep herders had driven their flocks into a few of the larger buildings. But not the church, he was happy to find.

For three days Finnian sheltered himself in the church. He spent most of his time prostrate before the altar. He thought it quite possible that this was the end of time, and if so, that was the position he intended to be in when the Lord returned.

But it was not the end of time, and on the fourth day he was able to leave the monastery, walking over sodden roads and fields north toward Ferns. The destruction was everywhere—trees blown flat, cottages with not a shred of a roof left, sheep and cows wandering lost across the countryside—but Finnian feared that the battle he had witnessed, the men fighting on the beach, had left destruction far worse.

He arrived at Ferns at last, and was ushered in to see Abbot Columb, who met him with a mixture of pleasure and wariness, which was how abbots tended to greet him. Finnian told Columb about the battle at Loch Garman, and Columb told him what he knew of it, pieced together from the tales of various participants. He told Finnian that Brother Bécc's leg had been shattered.

"Brother Bécc?" Finnian said, crossing himself. He knew Bécc well, knew his qualities, his skill as a fighting man, the depth of his devotion to God. It did not surprise him that Bécc had been in the middle of this. As much as Bécc loved the Lord, he hated the heathens even more. "Will he recover from this? Will he walk again?"

"He won't walk," the abbot said, "I don't think he'll even live through the night. The leg was ruined so one of the brothers who has some knowledge of surgery, he took it off, but Bécc does not seem much improved."

"Has he made his confession?" Finnian asked. "Has he had the final sacraments?"

"He's been anointed," Columb said. "But he has not made his confession, or received the Eucharist. He will not speak. Not to me, or anyone who has spoken to him."

Finnian frowned. "Let me try, please, abbot," he said.

The abbot sighed. "You may as well," he said. "Bécc, I think, is in great pain, and his leg is but a part of it. A small part."

The abbot led Finnian to the cell where Bécc lay on a rough wooden bed, a priest sitting by his side, bent over and murmuring in prayer.

"Father Niall, leave us please," Abbot Columb said. The priest looked up and Finnian could see he had been crying. He nodded, stood and hurried out.

Finnian looked down at Brother Bécc. Finnian had known Bécc for many years and he knew he had never been a pretty man. The horrible wound he had suffered from the Northman's sword, which had taken off half his face, had made his condition much worse.

Incredibly, he looked even worse now, lying on his deathbed, ashen and bathed in sweat, the scar tissue that made up half his face taut and hard-looking. What teeth he still had were clenched. But when he rolled his head and looked up at Finnian there was a flash of recognition on the man's ruined face, and Finnian was glad to see it.

He pulled the stool that Father Niall had been using closer to the bed and sat down, leaning close to Bécc. "Brother, it's me, Father Finnian. Do you hear me?" he said. He was not sure Bécc actually recognized him, or was aware of what was going on around him.

But Bécc nodded his head. "Yes, Father, bless you…" he said, his voice horse and no louder than a whisper.

Behind him, Finnian heard the abbot clear his throat. "I'll leave you two," he said and Finnian heard him turn and move toward the door. He leaned closer still.

"Listen, Brother, the end is near," Finnian said. "You know it is. Let me hear your confession and receive the Lord before you pass."

Bécc shook his head, so weakly that Finnian was not certain at first that that was what he was doing. "No, Father," he said. "My sins are too great…the Lord cannot forgive me."

"Don't presume to know what the Lord will and will not do," Finnian said, but gently. "There is your first sin, your pride. It's the first sin of most men. Men like you, most especially."

Bécc looked at Finnian and for a moment he did not respond. Then he shook his head again.

For a moment the two men looked at one another and said nothing. Then Bécc began to cough, and he coughed for some time, heaving and spitting up blood, his face twisted with the agony of it.

Finnian waited. When Bécc had settled back down he said, "Very well. Forget God. Tell *me* your sins."

Bécc looked at him once again. Again he said nothing.

"We have known each other a long time, Bécc mac Carthach," he said. "And I have seen many sins though the years, those of other men and mine as well. You will not surprise me. And you will not lose my love."

For a long moment Bécc continued in silence. And then he spoke, and his voice was weaker than it had been before the last bout of coughing. "Very well, Father. I'll speak. You're right about pride, of course…" Bécc paused and collected his thoughts and his last bits of strength. "And I am the most prideful of men. Which is why I thought that I knew better than God himself.…"

Bécc continued to speak. The words built in momentum as he told Finnian the tale of his decision to betray the Northmen, of his desire to kill them all, how prideful and blind he had become. Of the ghastly sins, the deception, the murder he had committed in that passionate and consuming rage. And Finnian listened and he did not interrupt. He could hear the pure contrition in the man's voice, the agony he suffered over what he had done. Bécc's tale did not surprise him, and it did not shock him, though it was the most surprising and shocking thing he had heard in many years.

As Bécc talked, his voice sounded clearer and the tension in his face seemed to relax a bit and he did not cough. And then he finished and he laid his head back, and Finnian could see the man's exhaustion. It had a finality about it.

"And it was all for naught," Bécc said. "All my sins, and yet the heathens sailed away."

"No, Brother, no," Finnian said. "I was on the beach at Beggerin. I watched the heathens sail. The Lord drove them from the harbor, swept them out to sea. They could not have lived in such a storm. God himself finished the work you started."

Bécc's head rolled over and he looked up at Finnian. "Truly?"

"I swear on my hope of heaven, I saw the heathens swept out to sea," Finnian said in a tone that conveyed the truth of his words. He saw what he thought was a trace of a smile on Bécc's tortured face. And he could see the peace as well. He reached over and made the sign of the cross on Bécc's forehead.

"The Lord forgives you your sins," he said softly. He reached down and picked up the small silver dish that Father Niall had left. A few crusts of the Holy Eucharist lay in the bottom. Finnian lifted one and placed it gently in Bécc's mouth, and he was relieved to see Bécc slowly chew and swallow. And then he closed his eyes.

The door opened behind him and he heard soft steps on the stone floor. He looked up. Father Niall was there. His eyes were red and the trails of his tears were visible on his cheeks.

"How…" he began, and then stopped.

"He's gone," Father Finnian said. "He was a hard man, but now he rests in the arms of God."

The sun rose and revealed more and more of the beach at Swanage. As Nothwulf and Leofric and the men-at-arms with them rode out over the sand they could see the blackened and still smoldering pits where the fires had been, a scattering of animal bones with the meat gnawed off, a couple of shields too shattered to be of any use. They could still see the V-shaped gouges in the sand where the bows of the longships had been pulled ashore.

They stared out to sea, slowly running their eyes from the north to the south, scanning every bit of ocean that was visible to them. There were no ships to be seen.

Nothwulf swiveled around in his saddle. "Bryning," he snapped at the man behind him. "Take a couple of men and get up on those cliffs." He pointed toward the high, jagged cliffs at the north end of the beach. "Look for those damned ships, see where they've gone."

Bryning nodded, called for a few men and rode off. They rode fast. Bryning knew better than to dawdle just then.

"So," Nothwulf said, turning back to Leofric. He could feel that panic rising. Much as he felt he should be in command of this situation, he was in the wilderness. "What do we do now?"

"We don't go back to Sherborne, not empty-handed," Leofric said. "That much is certain. If the king's still there then Cynewise will make a great show of her disappointment in our failure."

Nothwulf nodded. Leofric was kind to refer to it as *their* failure, but in truth he, Nothwulf, would bear the entire load. "So…?"

"So we hope that Bryning can see those damned ships and tell where they're bound. If they're heading to sea we return and declare our victory. If they're going to sack some poor town or monastery…Christchurch, perhaps…then we wait for the fyrd to arrive and then we attack. In any event we do not go back to Sherborne until we have a good tale to tell."

"There's no other choice," Nothwulf agreed. He understood that Leofric had ulterior motives for giving this advice. This was his land, Swanage and Christchurch were his holdings. He was both obligated and motivated to defend them, and having the help of the shire's fyrd and Nothwulf's men would be a great advantage.

But that was all right, because once again their interests aligned.

There was little point in remaining on the beach, so Nothwulf and Leofric led the mounted soldiers back up the path to the camp above. They had their breakfast and soon after Bryning returned and told them that he had been able to see nothing of the longships from the high cliffs to the north.

"What do you think, Leofric?" Nothwulf asked. "Do we dare hope the heathens have sailed off?"

"We can hope," Leofric said, "but we'd better be damned certain of it before we start telling them so in Sherborne. You will not want to tell the king you've driven them off only for him to find you're wrong."

Nothwulf agreed with that. He and Leofric picked their smartest and most reliable men and sent them out in every direction, to Wareham and Poole and Christchurch Priory and Metcombe Regis. They were charged with finding out where the damned heathens had gone.

Neither Nothwulf nor Leofric expected an answer for a few days at least, but that did not make the waiting any less intolerable. Happily the men of the fyrd began to arrive soon after the scouts had left, and the logistical nightmare that they represented helped take the men's minds from their other concerns.

The fyrd arrived in tens and twenties, reluctant and wary men who just days before had been tending their farms and now were trudging to the coast through lands they had never seen, carrying shields and spears. Some came with their own food and ale, but most did not, and that meant that Nothwulf and Leofric had to send others to gather what they could from the countryside, and dole out their own silver to get it.

By the time the scouts began to return, the army under Nothwulf's command had swollen to more than three hundred men, enough to overwhelm the heathens with numbers, even if they lacked the Northmen's prowess in battle.

But they still had nowhere to go, because the scouts who returned from Wareham and Poole and other points west had nothing to report. No heathens, no sign of heathens, not even a rumor of the bastards.

So Nothwulf sat in camp and waited and watched his silver disburse around the countryside as he bought more and more food and ale. He considered his options, what he might do if the heathens were never found, what he might say to King Æthelwulf to make it clear to the old man that he, and not that simpering pretender Cynewise, should sit in the chair of the ealdorman of Dorset. And he worried until his stomach ached.

Then, three days after they had found the beach empty, riders returned from the east, from Christchurch Priory. And they had a different tale to tell, exactly the one Nothwulf so wished to hear.

"Bryning! Get these whore's sons on their feet! Break the camp, get ready to march!" Nothwulf shouted. It was just a moment or two after the scout had finished telling of the people he had met fleeing from Christchurch, the longships he had seen from a distance pulled up on the beach. The heathens had been discovered, and now Nothwulf had men enough under his command to crush them and march his prisoners back to the king.

It did not take long to get the army on the move, though it was longer than Nothwulf would have liked. The fyrd was stretched out in a long line on the road, with part of the mounted warriors leading the way and some coming up behind. Nothwulf, with Leofric at his side, took the lead as they moved out, a slow-moving, grim parade marching through the fine summer day.

Nothwulf was jubilant, his spirit singing. He had been in battle often enough and he liked it, which was one of the many things that marked him as a leader where his brother had not been. And Cynewise certainly was not.

"What say you, Leofric?" he said. "A few days we should have this taken care of, the situation in hand."

"Should do," Leofric said in a tone so lacking in enthusiasm that Nothwulf looked over with concern.

"What is it? You're concerned?"

Leofric shrugged. "I have no reason to be concerned," he said. "We know where the heathens are, and we have reason to believe we're more powerful than them. It's just that…"

"Yes?"

"Nothing has been as it seems," Leofric said. "The devil is in this business. There are people arrayed against us, and we don't even know who they are. Cynewise, sure, but who are the others? Are there others? It's just a bad business, and I'm thinking this campaign will not be the simple matter that it seems."

"I see," Nothwulf said, though he was not sure he did. It seemed simple enough to him. The heathens were at Christchurch Priory and he and his army were marching to fight them and kill them. Simple. But Leofric was right as well. There were forces of which Nothwulf was not aware, plots unfolding that he had not seen before.

Who else, what else, might be part of this whole affair? What unexpected thing might happen next to render his situation even more desperate? Nothwulf felt his buoyant mood wilt like a cut flower under the summer's sun.

Epilogue

Hail, thou who hast spoken! Hail, thou that knowest!
Hail, ye that have hearkened! Use, thou who hast learned!

The Song of Spells

The fighting done, the surviving enemies secured, plunder gathered, the Northmen stayed at Christchurch Priory for breakfast. And then they stayed for dinner and for supper and then they bedded down for the night, with sentries posted along the low stone wall and guards surrounding the prisoners in the church.

But no one came to disturb their rest, and the prisoners did not make any attempt to leave their confines. So the following morning they had breakfast once again.

They ate outside in the open ground that had been their battlefield and was still marked with dark patches of blood, soaked into the earth. They pulled chairs and benches and tables out of the many buildings scattered around the monastic grounds. They ate outside because it was warm and the sun was shining and a soft breeze was blowing and it felt good.

"Been here in Engla-land…what? Five days?" Godi said. "And we haven't seen a drop of rain since the storm that brought us here."

"It's not Ireland, that I can tell you," Gudrid said. "Another week of this and we might finally dry out."

Thorgrim nodded and said nothing. But it had occurred to him that, so far, Engla-land seemed to have much to offer. The monastery was stuffed with food and ale and the plunder had been very good. There were no women, save for the largely unappealing wives of the tradesmen, but other than that, this place seemed all but ideal.

Breakfast certainly was excellent: fresh bread and fresh meat and cheese and decent ale. The Northmen ate their fill and then saw to it that the prisoners ate as well, if not as heartily. That done, it was time to attend to the dead.

With Gudrid translating, Thorgrim ordered the tradesmen who were being held prisoner, along with a dozen of the English soldiers, to lend a hand. They were marched under guard from the dim interior of the church, blinking in the sunlight and shielding their eyes. In the aftermath of the battle, the dead had been moved off to the side of the open ground and covered with whatever cloth could be found. Now men were sent for wagons, and when they returned the cloth was pulled aside to reveal the bloated, gray corpses underneath.

The prisoners were set to work stacking the dead in the wagons, English in one wagon, Northmen in the other. Only eleven Northmen, Thorgrim was glad to see. But among them was Olaf Thordarson, a good man, one of the few left who had sailed with them from Norway under Ornolf the Restless. They had been shoulder to shoulder in the shieldwall many times, and Thorgrim was sorry indeed to lose him.

You are feasting with Odin now, Thorgrim thought, *and you'll be there to welcome me to the corpse hall.*

With the dead loaded, Thorgrim called to Failend and Louis de Roumois. "For these English to bury their dead proper, what do they need?" he asked.

"A few of the priests in the church," Louis said. "They'll need a book of scripture, but there are some there, I saw. The covers are ripped off, as you heathens do, but the books are there."

Thorgrim nodded. Louis used the Irish word to refer to the bundle of papers so beloved by the Christians. There was no word in the Northmen's language that meant exactly that, but Thorgrim knew what he meant.

"They'll need holy water, too," Failend said.

"Holy water? Where do they get that?"

"They can turn any water into holy water. They bless it."

"Bless it? They use some magic to change the water into something else?" Thorgrim asked. He found the idea that the Christ priests had that sort of power unsettling.

"Not magic," Failend said. "They…just bless it."

"Is it still water after they do this?" Thorgrim asked.

"Yes...no... It's Holy Water. Something different," Failend said.

Thorgrim nodded. It was clear this blessing was some sort of Christian magic, though Failend said it was not. It made no sense to Thorgrim, but little of what the Christians believed did, so he let it go.

"All right," he said. "I want you two to take a dozen of our men and go with the Christians to bury their dead. Let them get priests and this magic water and whatever else they need. Shovels and men to dig. You see they don't get up to any mischief."

Failend and Louis nodded. Thorgrim suspected they were relieved to not have to take part in the Northmen's heathen ceremony.

The wagon bearing the dead Christians rolled off toward the graveyard outside the monastery walls, and soon after the wagon with the Northmen followed, turning away from the cemetery and toward the edge of the water where the longships were hauled up and anchored on shore. There the Northmen, living and unwounded, pulled out shovels and set to work digging graves deep enough that the bodies of their fellows could rest undisturbed.

When the graves were dug, the dead men were laid carefully at the bottoms, swords and seaxes and spears by their sides, shields across their chests. Two cows, liberated from a nearby field, were sacrificed on the edge of the graves. The blood that flowed from their slit throats was collected up in wide bowls held by the dead men's comrades.

Thorgrim held a small oak sapling, leafed out in its summer foliage, and he dipped the leaves in the bowls of blood and sprinkled the blood liberally on the dead men in their graves while he called on the gods and the Valkyrie to see them borne swiftly away to Valhalla. And then they covered the men with English soil and returned to the monastery to feast and think on the men who now joined generations of warriors at Odin's eternal feast.

They remained the rest of that day, behind the walls of the monastery, eating and drinking ale and wine and enjoying their idleness. There seemed to be no armies gathering to retake the place from the heathen marauders, so they stayed another night as well. Sentries were posted and still they had nothing to report.

But Thorgrim had been around far too long, and knew far too much about luck, to think it could go on much longer. And he knew that nothing would make a man's luck end quicker than his counting on it to remain. So he called Starri and a half dozen other men, and asked Jorund to pick some of his men who would be good at scouting and he sent them out on horseback in various directions to see if there were any armies on the move, any threat they would have to counter soon. And then he went to bed.

This cannot go on, Thorgrim mused. It was dawn the following morning and he was lying under a blanket in a bed in a house that must have belonged to one of the chief priests, because it was big and had rugs on the floor and tapestries on the wall and a long oak table and chairs. For all his wealth, Thorgrim had never enjoyed an excess of luxury, but he was enjoying this now. Beside him, Failend breathed softly in her sleep. They had made love the night before, something they had not done in some time, and that only added to his sense of peaceful comfort.

No, this cannot go on, he thought again. Regardless of what the scouts discovered, they could not remain there much longer. He had no idea of how remote this Christchurch was, but he doubted it was so far from anything else that their presence would go unnoticed for long. He had personally seen many people fleeing before them as they came ashore, and they would have carried word of the coming of the heathen raiders.

Sweartling had not been much help in telling them what towns if any were close by, since he apparently did not know either, though he believed that the ealdorman's home at Wimborne was not so far away.

Ealdorman…Thorgrim thought. That was a word strange to him. It had taken Sweartling and Gudrid some time, back and forth, to come to an understanding of what it meant. It was, apparently, the English word for a jarl, or as close as the English came to such a thing. It was a man of high rank, in any event. A man who would have warriors under his command.

Once they had eaten their breakfast Thorgrim called his chief men together for a council of war. Jorund joined them, as did the captains of the other ships and Godi and Harald. He asked Louis de Roumois as well, thinking Louis, as a Frank, might know more about

Engla-land than the Northmen did. Starri for once did not join them, being still out on his scouting mission.

"There are some choices for us to make," Thorgrim said as the men settled in a circle of chairs and benches. They were outside still, enjoying the sun and the warmth. "And those choices are about when we leave here, and what we do with the prisoners."

The others nodded. No one spoke.

"With the prisoners, there are three things we can do. We can take them to the slave market, in Frisia, I suppose. We can hold them as hostages and see if any will pay for them. Or we can sail today and leave them here."

The others nodded again and looked from one to the other. Jorund spoke first.

"Leaving them here is like throwing silver into the ocean," he said. "They're worth a lot. As slaves they're worth a lot."

That was true. After silver and gold, slaves were the most valuable plunder of all. And slaves were more abundant and easier to come by than silver and gold.

Asmund, commander of *Oak Heart*, spoke next. "Slaves are of great worth, but they're a great problem as well. We'll have to feed them all, and give them water for the voyage. And we don't know how many day's sail we are from Frisia."

This time Thorgrim nodded. Asmund's thoughts were his own. In his mind, the great difficulty and expense of transporting so many men to the slave markets outweighed any profit that might be had from them. Even more so considering, as Asmund said, they did not even know where they were, or how far they were from Frisia.

But Jorund was correct as well. They could not just leave them behind.

"Louis," Thorgrim said and Louis looked up, surprised, having apparently not thought his advice would be sought. "Will the English pay a ransom for these men?"

Louis shrugged. "They'll pay some, I would think," he said. "This priory, it looks to be an important place." He looked around, gestured at the big church and the extensive grounds with their dense cluster of buildings. "The lives of the priests and the abbot will be worth something to someone. And the men-at-arms, too. They're in someone's service, and he's likely to pay to get them back."

"You think these men are oath-sworn to someone else?" Thorgrim asked. "They don't belong to the monastery?"

"Monasteries do not usually have men-at-arms in their service," Louis explained.

Thorgrim frowned. He thought about Bécc and the warriors under his command. He had assumed those men were part of the monastery at Ferns, but maybe not. He would have to ask Louis about that, at some other time.

"Why would anyone pay for the hostages," Halldor asked, "when they can just as well attack this place as we did and try to free them? And rid Engla-land of us as well? Sure the local jarl can raise an army against us."

Thorgrim waited to see if anyone else had an answer, but no one did, so he provided the best one he could. "The jarls around here won't know how many we are, but they'll see seven ships and know we're a strong force. And we are. Besides, we have hostages. I think they'll lose interest in attacking us if we start cutting priests' throats and tossing them over the wall. Isn't that right, Louis?"

Louis looked at Thorgrim for a moment. He did not care to answer that. But finally, grudgingly, he said, "Yes, I suspect that's right."

And so it was decided. They would load the ships with stores and the plunder they had taken. They would make ready to leave at any moment. And then they would wait to see who came to them, and what they had to offer.

They did not wait long. First back was Starri Deathless and the two men with him. They had ridden east along the coast and they had found nothing but a few more small, inconsequential villages. Then a short time later, one of Jorund's men, a wiry fellow named Ofeig, returned from scouting west. He and the two men with him were red-faced from hard riding, and their horses' flanks were slick with sweat.

"There's an army marching toward us. They're still ten miles away, I would think," Ofeig reported to the assembly of chief men. "Some men on horseback, some with mail. Most on foot. Spears, no mail. Shields. Maybe two hundred or more."

The men nodded slowly as they listened. They each understood the implications of this report. The men on horseback would be trained fighting men. Those on foot were something else, likely farmers or tradesmen or such, called up to help fight off this new threat. Not real warriors. But in big numbers they were a genuine threat, a lesson Bécc had reinforced.

"I suppose these men, the ones marching here, are the men we'll wish to speak with," Thorgrim said. "They may be the ones to pay a ransom for the hostages." And so they waited. But it was not the men-at-arms who came there first.

It was a single man, or more correctly a single man with four guards riding behind. He was a good ways off when the sentry on top of the wall reported him approaching. Thorgrim climbed up to see for himself, and watched as the riders came closer. One of the men on horseback held a pole with a white cloth tied to it, and Thorgrim guessed that it was a sign that they wished to speak.

"Open the gate," Thorgrim said.

The five riders rode through and the gate was closed behind them, but they did not seem bothered by that. The man leading the others slipped down from his horse and stood waiting for someone to approach. And Thorgrim did, with Jorund and Gudrid on either side.

The man spoke, looking directly at Thorgrim, and the two men held one another's eyes. He was about Thorgrim's height but a bit stockier, with light brown hair, the color of beach sand, and a neatly cropped beard. He wore mail and a cloak and his clothes and shoes were good. Not the fine clothing of a very wealthy man, but that of a prosperous man. An important man. He wore a sword and he carried himself with surety.

When the man was done speaking, Gudrid said, "He says his name is Oswin and he is the…shire reeve…" Gudrid stumbled a bit on the unfamiliar term. "I understand that means he has some authority around here. He says he was sent by his ealdorman, his jarl, to see what our business is here, what we want."

"Tell him we have what we want," Thorgrim said. "Gold, silver, many slaves for the markets in Frisia."

Gudrid translated. Oswin nodded. His expression did not change. Then he spoke.

"He asks if some of the slaves are men-at-arms," Gudrid said. "If you would be willing to take a ransom for them."

Thorgrim smiled. "He'll pay ransom for the men-at-arms, but not the priests?"

Gudrid and the man exchanged words. "He says he will pay for the priests as well," Gudrid said, though it was clear that to this Oswin the priests were an afterthought.

"Ask him if his plan is for me to keep talking long enough for his other army to get here, the one marching from the west."

Gudrid translated, and for the first time Thorgrim saw a flicker of surprise on Oswin's face. Then he replied.

"He says that is not his army. It's an enemy, a powerful enemy," Gudrid said. "An enemy of both of us."

An enemy of both of us? Thorgrim thought. *When did you and I become allies?*

"Oswin says they will drive us from this place," Gudrid continued. "He also says that we can fight them, and the men-at-arms we hold as prisoners can join us, and then we'll defeat this army and then there will be plunder much beyond what was here. He says there's not much time."

Thorgrim smiled again. He could not help himself. As a young man he had gone a'viking on the east coast of Engla-land. They had stormed ashore, plundered, taken slaves and silver and food and ale and had disappeared over the horizon. Quick. Clean.

Now it seemed that he could not set foot on shore without getting tangled up in some local mess. He had longed to leave Ireland behind, with its spider webs of intrigue and betrayal and wars between one pathetic kingdom and the next. He had finally got free of that place, and yet the intrigue and betrayal seemed to have followed him across the sea.

Will this ever end? he asked himself. Had the Northmen been coming to those shores in such numbers, and for so long, that they were now part of this world of Ireland and Engla-land?

So it seemed, and it did not seem likely to end anytime soon. Like Loki, chained to the rocks, a snake's poison dripping on his head until the end of time, he would be forced to play these games of men, all in the vain hope that he would someday be allowed to reach his home.

The gods will have their fun...

Would you like a heads-up about new titles in The Norsemen Saga, as well as preview sample chapters and other good stuff cheap (actually free)?

Visit our web site to sign up for our (occasional) e-mail newsletter:

www.jameslnelson.com

Other Fiction by
James L. Nelson:

The Brethren of the Coast:
Piracy in Colonial America
The Guardship
The Blackbirder
The Pirate Round

The Revolution at Sea Saga:
Naval action of the American Revolution
By Force of Arms
The Maddest Idea
The Continental Risque
Lords of the Ocean
All the Brave Fellows

The Only Life that Mattered:
The Story of Ann Bonny, Mary Read and Calico Jack
Rackham

The Samual Bowater Novels:
Naval action of the American Civil War
Glory in the Name
Thieves of Mercy

Glossary

adze – a tool much like an ax but with the blade set at a right angle to the handle.

Ægir – Norse god of the sea. In Norse mythology he was also the host of great feasts for the gods.

Angel-cynn - (pronounced Angle-kin). Term used in the writing of Alfred the Great and the Old English Chronical to denote both the English people of Teutonic descent, namely the Angles, Saxons and Jutes, and the land they occupied. This seems to be the only term used to denote the country of England until the Danish conquest, after which the island was refered to as Engla land.

Asgard - the dwelling place of the Norse gods and goddesses, essentially the Norse heaven.

athwartships – at a right angle to the centerline of a vessel.

beitass - a wooden pole, or spar, secured to the side of a ship on the after end and leading forward to which the corner, or clew, of a sail could be secured.

berserkir - a Viking warrior able to work himself up into a frenzy of blood-lust before a battle. The berserkirs, near psychopathic killers in battle, were the fiercest of the Viking soldiers. The word berserkir comes from the Norse for "bear shirt" and is the origin of the modern English "berserk".

block – nautical term for a pulley.

boss - the round, iron centerpiece of a wooden shield. The boss formed and iron cup protruding from the front of the shield, providing a hollow in the back across which ran the hand grip.

bothach – Gaelic term for poor tenant farmers, serfs

brace - line used for hauling a **yard** side to side on a horizontal plane. Used to adjust the angle of the sail to the wind.

brat – a rectangular cloth worn in various configurations as an outer garment over a *leine*.

bride-price - money paid by the family of the groom to the family of the bride.

byrdingr - A smaller ocean-going cargo vessel used by the Norsemen for trade and transportation. Generally about 40 feet in length, the byrdingr was a smaller version of the more well-known *knarr*.

cable – a measure of approximately 600 feet.

clench nail – a type of nail that, after being driven through a board, has a type of washer called a rove placed over the end and is then bent over to secure it in place.

clew – one of the lower corners of a square sail, to which the **sheet** is attached.

ceorl – a commoner in early Medieval England, a peasant, but also a small-time landowner with right. Memebers of the ceorl class served in the **fyrd**.

curach - a boat, unique to Ireland, made of a wood frame covered in hide. They ranged in size, the largest propelled by sail and capable of carrying several tons. The most common sea-going craft of mediaeval Ireland. **Curach** was the Gaelic word for boat which later became the word curragh.

dagmál – breakfast time

derbfine – In Irish law, a family of four generations, including a man, his sons, grandsons and great grandsons.

dragon ship - the largest of the Viking warships, upwards of 160 feet long and able to carry as many as 300 men. Dragon ships were the flagships of the fleet, the ships of kings.

dubh gall - Gaelic term for Vikings of Danish descent. It means Black Strangers, a reference to the mail armor they wore, made dark by the oil used to preserve it. *See **fin gall**.*

ell – a unit of length, a little more than a yard.

eyrir – Scandanavian unit of measurment, approximatly an ounce.

félag – a fellowship of men who owed each other a mutual obligation, such as multiple owners of a ship, or a band or warriors who had sworn allegiance to one another.

figurehead – ornamental carving on the bow of a ship.

fin gall - Gaelic term for Vikings of Norwegian descent. It means White Strangers. *See **dubh gall**.*

forestay – a rope running from the top of a ship's mast to the bow used to support the mast.

Frisia – a region in the northern part of the modern-day Netherlands.

Freya - Norse goddess of beauty and love, she was also associated with warriors, as many of the Norse deity were. Freya often led the **Valkyrie** to the battlefield.

fyrd – in Medieval England, a levy of commoners called up for military service when needed.

gallows – tall, T-shaped posts on the ship's centerline, forward of the mast, on which the oars and yard were stored when not in use.

gunnel – the upper edge of a ship's side.

hack silver – pieces of silver from larger units cut up for dsitribution.

halyard - a line by which a sail or a yard is raised.

Haustmánudur – early autumn. Literally, harvest-month.

Hel - in Norse mythology, the daughter of Loki and the ruler of the underworld where those who are not raised up to Valhalla are sent to suffer. The same name, Hel, is given to the realm over which she rules, the Norse hell.

hide – a unit of land considered sufficient to support a single family.

hird - an elite corps of Viking warriors hired and maintained by a king or powerful **jarl**. Unlike most Viking warrior groups, which would assemble and disperse at will, the hird was retained as a semi-permanent force which formed the core of a Viking army.

hirdsman - a warrior who is a member of the **hird**.

hólmganga – a formal, organized duel fought in a marked off area between two men.

jarl - title given to a man of high rank. A jarl might be an independent ruler or subordinate to a king. Jarl is the origin of the English word *earl*.

Jörmungandr – in Norse mythology, a vast sea serpent that surrounds the earth, grasping its own tail.

knarr - a Norse merchant vessel. Smaller, wider and more sturdy than the longship, knarrs were the workhorse of Norse trade, carrying cargo and settlers where ever the Norsemen traveled.

Laigin – Medieval name for the modern-day county of Leinster in the south east corner of Ireland.

league – a distance of three miles.

lee shore – land that is downwind of a ship, on which a ship in in danger of being driven.

leeward – down wind.

leech – either one of the two vertical edges of a square sail.

leine – a long, loose-fitting smock worn by men and women under other clothing. Similar to the shift of a later period.

levies - conscripted soldiers of 9th century warfare.

Loki - Norse god of fire and free spirits. Loki was mischievous and his tricks caused great trouble for the gods, for which he was punished.

longphort - literally, a ship fortress. A small, fortified port to protect shipping and serve as a center of commerce and a launching off point for raiding.

luchrupán – middle Irish word that became the modern-day Leprechaun.

luff – the shivering of a sail when its edge is pointed into the wind and the wind strikes it on both sides.

Midgard – one of nine worlds in Norse mythology, it is the earth, the world known and visible to humans.

Niflheim – the World of Fog. One of the nine worlds in Norse mythology, somewhat analogous to Hell, the afterlife for people who do not die honorable deaths.

Njord – Norse god of the sea and seafaring.

Odin - foremost of the Norse gods. Odin was the god of wisdom and war, protector of both chieftains and poets.

oénach –a major fair, often held on a feast day in an area bordered by two territories.

perch - a unit of measure equal to 16½ feet. The same as a rod.

Ragnarok - the mythical final battle when most humans and gods would be killed by the forces of evil and the earth destroyed, only to rise again, purified.

rath – Gaelic word for a **ringfort**. Many Irish place names still contain the word Rath.

rod – a unit of measure equal to 16½ feet. The same as a perch

rove – a square washer used to fasten the planks of a longship. A nail is driven through the plank and the hole in the washer and then bent over.

ringfort - common Irish homestead, consisting of houses protected by circular earthwork and palisade walls.

rí túaithe – Gaelic term for a minor king, who would owe allegiance to nobles higher in rank.

rí tuath – a minor king who is lord over several **rí túaithe.**

rí ruirech –a supreme or provincial king, to whom the **rí tuath** owe allegiance.

sceattas – small, thick silver coins minted in England and Frisia in the early Middle Ages.

seax – any of a variety of edged weapons longer than a knife but shorter and lighter than a typical sword.

sheer strake – the uppermost plank, or strake, of a boat or ship's hull. On a Viking ship the sheer strake would form the upper edge of the ship's hull.

sheet – a rope that controls a sail. In the case of a square sail the sheets pull the **clews** down to hold the sail so the wind can fill it.

shieldwall - a defensive wall formed by soldiers standing in line with shields overlapping.

shire reeve – a magistrate who served a king or ealdorman and carried out various official functions within his district. One of the highest ranking officials, under whom other, more monor reeves served. The term shire reeve is the basis of the modern-day *sherriff.*

shroud – a heavy rope streching from the top of the mast to the ship's side that prevents the mast from falling sideways.

skald - a Viking-era poet, generally one attached to a royal court. The skalds wrote a very stylized type of verse particular to the medieval Scandinavians. Poetry was an important part of Viking culture and the ability to write it a highly-regarded skill.

sling - the center portion of the **yard.**

spar – generic term used for any of the masts or yards that are part of a ship's rig.

stem – the curved timber that forms the bow of the ship. On Viking ships the stem extended well above the upper edge of the ship and the figurehead was mounted there.

strake – one of the wooden planks that make up the hull of a ship. The construction technique, used by the Norsemen, in which one strake overlaps the one below it is called *lapstrake construction.*

swine array - a viking battle formation consisting of a wedge-shaped arrangement of men used to attack a shield wall or other defensive position.

tánaise ríg – Gaelic term for heir apparent, the man assumed to be next in line for a kingship.

thegn – a minor noble or a land-holder above the peasant class who also served the king in a military capacity.

thing - a communal assembly

Thor - Norse god of storms and wind, but also the protector of humans and the other gods. Thor's chosen weapon was a hammer. Hammer amulets were popular with Norsemen in the same way that crosses are popular with Christians.

thrall - Norse term for a slave. Origin of the English word "enthrall".

thwart - a rower's seat in a boat. From the old Norse term meaning "across".

tuath – a minor kingdom in medieval Ireland that consisted of several **túaithe**.

túaithe – a further subdivision of a kindom, ruled by a **rí túaithe**

Ulfberht – a particular make of sword crafted in the Germanic countries and inscribed with the name Ulfberht or some varient. Though it is not clear who Ulfberht was, the swords that bore his name were of the highest quality and much prized.

unstep – to take a mast down. To put a mast in place is to step the mast.

Valhalla - a great hall in **Asgard** where slain warriors would go to feast, drink and fight until the coming of **Ragnarok**.

Valkyrie - female spirits of Norse mythology who gathered the spirits of the dead from the battle field and escorted them to **Valhalla**. They were the Choosers of the Slain, and though later romantically portrayed as Odin's warrior handmaidens, they were originally viewed more demonically, as spirits who devoured the corpses of the dead.

vantnale – a wooden lever attached to the lower end of a shroud and used to make the shroud fast and to tension it.

varonn – spring time. Literally "spring work" in Old Norse.

Vik - An area of Norway south of modern-day Oslo. The name is possibly the origin of the term *Viking.*

wattle and daub - common medieval technique for building walls. Small sticks were woven through larger uprights to form the wattle, and the structure was plastered with mud or plaster, the daub.

weather – closest to the direction from which the wind is blowing, when used to indicate the position of something relative to the wind.

wergild - the fine imposed for taking a man's life. The amount of the wergild was dependant on the victim's social standing.

witan — a council of the greater nobles and bishops of a region, generally assembled to advise the king.

yard - a long, tapered timber from which a sail was suspended. When a Viking ship was not under sail, the yard was turned lengthwise and lowered to near the deck with the sail lashed to it.

Acknowledgements

It has been an honor and a delight for me to see how well the Norsemen Saga has been received. The books have allowed me to immerse myself in all things Viking, which has been a wonderful journey. And I will be the first to say that the series' success has been the result of a lot of hard work by a number of very talented people. As ever, I have the team to thank: Steve Cromwell for his eye-catching covers and (with many past books, if not this one) Alistair Corbett for his photography. Alicia Street at iProofread and More has once again saved me from numerous embarrassments, and Chris Boyle has again brought his cartographic skills to bear. Nat Sobel, Judith Weber and all the folks at Sobel Weber Associates, Inc. have continued their efforts to bring the series to an international audience.

And of course, my first mate, my beloved, Lisa.

I often get e-mails from readers asking how long I will continue the series. My answer as of now is, as long as the books meet with the sort of enthusiasm they are currently finding, I'll keep writing them. And so for that, I must thank the folks to whom I have reason to be most grateful – the readers who continue to follow the adventures of Thorgrim and company. Thank you.

10941616R00203

Printed in Great Britain
by Amazon